Praise f

of Ba

Summer a

"A seaside cottage with a mysterious past and a woman looking to unearth secrets of her own.... Barbara Davis envelopes her readers so thoroughly into life on Florida's Gulf Coast that you'll find yourself reaching down to brush sand off your toes and licking margarita salt off your lips."
—Erica Marks, author of *It Comes in Waves*

"I can't resist a story with a journal at its heart, and the journal in *Summer at Hideaway Key* is powerful, emotional, and illuminating."
—Diane Chamberlain, *USA Today* bestselling author of *The Silent Sister*

"Artfully weaving past family secrets into a beautifully told story of sibling rivalry, self-sacrifice, and self-discovery, Barbara Davis has created another powerful page-turner."
—Barbara Claypole White, award-winning author of *The Perfect Son*

The Wishing Tide

"Everything I love in a novel... an old inn and a deeply felt and explored love story with a smart, relatable heroine and a handsome hero with a mysterious past... elegant and haunting proof that secrets buried in the heart will always rise to the surface."
—Erika Marks

continued...

Written by today's freshest new talents and selected by New American Library, NAL Accent novels touch on subjects close to a woman's heart, from friendship to family to finding our place in the world. The Conversation Guides included in each book are intended to enrich the individual reading experience, as well as encourage us to explore these topics together—because books, and life, are meant for sharing.

Visit us online at penguin.com.

"With some books, it is difficult to pick just 'one thing' to highlight. *The Wishing Tide* by Barbara Davis is one of those books." —*USA Today*

"A captivating read about fighting for the life you want and daring to believe that happily ever after can exist outside of fairy tales . . . this lyrical novel will haunt you from the first page to the last."

—Barbara Claypole White

"Filled with wonderful descriptions of North Carolina's Outer Banks, *The Wishing Tide* is a book about love and loss and finding your way forward. I could not read it fast enough!"

—Anita Hughes, author of *Lake Como*

"One of the best stories out there, and Davis is genuinely proving herself to be one of the strongest new voices of epic romance."

—*RT Book Reviews* (4½ stars)

"Great reading any time of year! Finely crafted, Barbara Davis—oh, and this would also make a phenomenal movie!"

—Crystal Book Reviews

The Secrets She Carried

"Barbara Davis wowed me with her flawless blending of past and present in *The Secrets She Carried.* Her compassion for her characters made me care and her haunting tale kept the pages flying. A poignant, mysterious, and heartfelt story." —Diane Chamberlain

"I was swept into Adele's heartbreaking life and her devotion to those she loved." —Susan Crandall, author of *Whistling Past the Graveyard*

"I read Barbara Davis's debut novel, *The Secrets She Carried,* deep into the night—one minute rushing to discover how the mysteries resolved, the next slowing. . . . Adele Laveau's haunting voice and Leslie Nicholl's journey toward understanding lingered long after I read the final page of this engrossing tale."

—Julie Kibler, author of *Calling Me Home*

"*The Secrets She Carried* is a beautifully crafted page-turner with many twists but a simple theme: No matter how far you run, you can't escape your past. Part contemporary women's fiction, part historical novel, the plot moves seamlessly back and forth in time to unlock family secrets that bind four generations of women. Add a mysterious death, love that defies the grave, and the legacy of redemption, and this novel has it all."

—Barbara Claypole White

"This beautifully written novel tells a tale of epic romance, one that lasts through the decades and centuries. All centered on a plantation home in small-town North Carolina, love stories unfold as the novel progresses through both past and present, and hidden secrets, once thought long buried, slowly reveal themselves. It's a beautiful story, and Davis does an amazing job telling it." —*RT Book Reviews*

"Davis's writing is heartfelt and effective." —*Kirkus Reviews*

"Davis has a gift for developing flawed characters and their emotionally wrenching dilemmas. The small-town setting, full of gossip and prejudice in the Depression years, feels realistic . . . a very satisfying tale."

—Historical Novel Society

OTHER BOOKS BY BARBARA DAVIS

The Secrets She Carried

The Wishing Tide

SUMMER AT HIDEAWAY KEY

BARBARA DAVIS

NAL ACCENT
Published by New American Library,
an imprint of Penguin Random House LLC
375 Hudson Street, New York, New York 10014

This book is an original publication of New American Library.

First Printing, August 2015

LIBRARY OF CONGRESS CATALOGING-IN-PUBLICATION DATA:

Davis, Barbara, 1961–
Summer at Hideaway Key / Barbara Davis.
pages cm
ISBN 978-0-451-47458-2 (softcover)
1. Vacation homes—Fiction. 2. Family secrets—Fiction. 3. Domestic fiction. I. Title.
PS3604.A95554S86 2015
813'.6—dc23 2015011033

Printed in the United States of America
10 9 8 7 6 5 4 3 2 1

Set in Carre Noir Std.
Designed by Alissa Theodor

PUBLISHER'S NOTE
This is a work of fiction. Names, characters, places, and incidents either are the product of the author's imagination or are used fictitiously, and any resemblance to actual persons, living or dead, business establishments, events, or locales is entirely coincidental.

Penguin
Random
House

To the survivors, who believe cancer is a word, not a sentence—and to those who held their hands along the way

ACKNOWLEDGMENTS

Some books seem to write themselves, while others come into the world kicking and screaming—thrashing, gut-wrenching, bloody. But the one thing I know for sure is that no book makes it onto the shelf without a team of midwives, that dedicated circle of family, friends, lovers, and professionals without whom our work might never come into the world. And so, without further ado . . .

To my critique partners, Lisa Cameron Rosen, Matt King, Doug Simpson, and Mitch Richmond, who read, suggested, reread, and suggested some more, you have my undying gratitude for your wit, honesty, generosity, keen eyes, and irreplaceable friendship.

To Tom, the absolute love of my life, and my wonderful mother, Pat, who have acted as my cheerleaders, as well as my personal crisis hotline during the writing of this book. I honestly don't know how I would have made it though this one without the two of you holding my hand.

To Nalini Akolekar, of Spencerhill Associates, the smartest, coolest, most supportive literary agent in the world, who has been with me since day one, thank you for believing in me and for always standing in my corner. You were truly the answer to a prayer.

To Sandra Harding, editor extraordinaire, and the entire team of amazing professionals at Penguin/NAL, thanks for making my job such a pleasure, and for making me look good. True pros all.

To Lauren Rochelle, mixologist at Disney World's Narcoossee's restaurant, for creating the scrumptious recipe for Salty's infamous Pink Flip-Flops. (Recipe included at the end of the book!)

And finally, to my readers, so many of whom I have come to think of as friends, you have my eternal thanks for enriching my experience as a writer, for your kind support, for your invaluable feedback, and for your treasured words of encouragement. You are never far from my heart as I write.

SUMMER AT HIDEAWAY KEY

PROLOGUE

June 21, 1953
Mims, Tennessee

Something was wrong. Bad wrong.

A rooster tail of scorched yellow earth kicked up as the pickup rounded the corner onto Vernon Dairy Road. I cut my eyes sideways at Mama, rigid behind the wheel, but bit my bottom lip to keep silent. I didn't like the look on her face, like she'd just been told the Rapture was coming and she'd been caught off guard. But mostly, she looked tired. Beneath the streaky traces of last night's powder, her face was pale and strained, her eyes puffy and red, though whether that was to do with tears or drink, I couldn't say.

Both, probably.

Beside me, Caroline was mute, huddled against the passenger-side armrest, her beloved rag doll, Chessie, clutched to her chest, wide green eyes fixed on some invisible point beyond the cracked windshield. Her hair was snarled from sleep, a coppery halo around her pale young face. We'd barely gotten breakfast down—milk and hunks of leftover corn bread—before Mama shooed us from the table and out of the house.

I thought of the battered suitcase bumping around in the back of the truck, then tried not to think about it. I didn't want to remem-

ber the way Mama's eyes slid away from mine when I spotted it, or how the sleeve of my sister's blue dress had spilled out from one corner. There was something ominous about that sleeve, something ominous, too, in the way Mama had pressed that old hand-me-down doll into Caroline's hands as she herded us out the door and across the front yard, past the empty plastic swimming pool and the old tire swing Daddy put up the summer he went away for the last time.

Mama was quiet behind the wheel, her eyes hard on the road as it ground away beneath the tires, as if she'd made up her mind about something and there was no going back. In her rumpled hat and too-tight dress she looked as threadbare as Caroline's old rag doll, like her stuffing might come loose any minute. Desperation. The word popped into my head without having to reach for it. It was written all over her face, coming off her like last night's bourbon.

We'd been driving almost two hours, and I still hadn't scraped up the nerve to ask where we were going. Maybe because I knew I wouldn't like the answer. Or maybe because I couldn't think over the words echoing in my head. Something's wrong. Something's wrong. *Not the regular kind of wrong, like when Daddy would disappear for weeks at a time, or Mama would lose another job because she didn't have money to put gas in the truck, but the really bad kind of wrong, like when Sheriff Cady had come to the door to say that Daddy wouldn't be coming back ever. Today felt like that kind of wrong—the kind that changed things forever.*

A fresh cloud of dust churned up from the road, boiling into the open windows, coating the dashboard with another layer of grit. We were passing an empty field of sun-bleached scrub, an ugly stretch of nothing that made me want to leap from the moving truck and run all the way home. Turn around! *I wanted to yell at Mama.* Turn around and let's go home. *But I didn't. There were tears in her eyes now, and I couldn't bear the sight of Mama's tears.*

The road narrowed to a single lane as we passed under a peeling wood sign. I had to squint to make out the letters: Mt. Zion Missionary Poor Farm.

Poor farm?

I shot Caroline a panicked look, but she just kept on staring straight ahead, her green eyes fixed on the narrow swath of dirt road. Either she hadn't seen the sign, or she didn't know what it meant. But I knew.

I knew money was tight, and had been for a while. We hadn't had milk in weeks, and more nights than not, dinner was nothing but corn bread and collards. But we'd been through rough patches before and Mama always found a way. Sometimes, when she was between jobs, she would bring a man home from the Orchid Lounge. Sometimes he would even stay a few weeks. But there hadn't been any men for a while—or any jobs, either.

Up ahead, a big white farmhouse shimmered into view against the hot blue sky. Beyond the house was a small whitewashed chapel, and beyond that was a scatter of smaller houses and outbuildings, all crisscrossed with a maze of split-rail fences. A handful of men milled about in overalls and dirty boots. A few looked up with dull eyes as the truck rattled up the circular drive and stopped in front of the house.

I sat stock-still while Mama climbed down out of the truck, then went around to drag the old suitcase out of the back. If I didn't move, if I didn't get out of the truck, maybe it would all go away. Or maybe if I said a prayer. But there was no time for prayers. Mama was coming around to the passenger side and opening the door. Caroline tumbled out obediently, Chessie dangling limply from the crook of her arm. I had no choice but to scoot across the sticky seat and follow my sister.

Mama pointed to the suitcase and then to Caroline, charging me with the care of both while she went inside to see to things. I thought I caught a whiff of bourbon on her breath. Last night's, I remember hoping, though I didn't think so. I watched as Mama mounted the porch steps and disappeared through the screen door with a soft slap. I couldn't say for sure what things she was going to see to, but I had a pretty good idea.

Poor farms were for people who couldn't feed themselves or their families, a place where grown-ups and children earned the food in their bellies and the roof over their heads by working in the fields. I had heard of such places, and what folks said about the people who went to them—people willing to take a handout because they were too lazy or too dull-witted to find real work.

We would be those people now.

I eyed the old suitcase with a sick feeling, wondering how Mama had managed to pack three people's clothes into one small case. The thought filled my head with a low, dull buzz, like a swarm of irate bees, though I couldn't put my finger on why the thought kept nagging at me. It wasn't until I heard the screen door slap again, and looked up into those guilty green eyes—eyes just like mine—that I realized Mama had left the truck running.

ONE

June 5, 1995
Manhattan

Lily barely registered the sound of her own name being spoken, jumbled together with a lot of legalese. The lawyer was doing his thing, parceling out her father's worldly goods like door prizes at an Amway rally—stocks, bonds, corporate holdings. She didn't care. Not about those things.

She should have been there when he died. Instead she had lingered in Paris, working out the details of her next strategic career move—a move that would land her at one of the hottest design houses in Milan. It didn't help that her mother had waited until the last possible moment to inform her that her father was seriously ill. Finalizing the details had taken only a day, but the delay had cost her dearly. She'd been so busy trying to make her father proud that she'd missed the chance to say good-bye.

And now, twenty-four hours after landing at JFK, she was sitting in Stephen Singer's Manhattan office, listening to the terms of Roland St. Claire's last will and testament. Except she wasn't really listening. Her mother was, though, with her signature blend of disappointment and disapproval stamped all over her perfectly powdered face. When it came to money and getting her due, Caroline St. Claire didn't miss a trick.

She had certainly dressed for the occasion, Lily noted frostily—black Norma Kamali with gold buttons and a skirt just short enough to show off surprisingly good legs.

Widow couture?

Perhaps there was something to that. Perhaps her mother had inadvertently stumbled onto the signature niche that had been stubbornly eluding Lily all these years, despite fashion degrees from both Parsons and IFA, and nearly ten years at various Paris design houses.

"Miss St. Claire?"

Lily blinked, vaguely aware, as she stared at the sheaf of papers being pushed across the desk, that a response of some kind was expected. "I'm sorry, what?"

Stephen Singer smiled, tapping the stack of pages with the flats of his fingers the way one might pat a puppy or child on the head. "I was saying we've come to the portion of your father's will that concerns you."

"Oh yes. Thank you."

She really didn't understand why they needed to sit through this. Her father's holdings, liquid or otherwise, were hardly a secret, at least not to anyone who read the *Wall Street Journal* or *Fortune* magazine. Nor was it likely she or her mother would ever starve. They were grieving—or at least she was—wearing black and sipping bad coffee while they pored over the man's portfolio, carving up things he'd spent his life building. She just wanted it over.

Lily picked up the papers and placed them in her lap, not bothering to follow along as Mr. Singer started to read. It was mostly about her trust fund—dollar amounts, dates of scheduled payouts. None of it interested her. She was staring out the window, at the smoggy stretch of Manhattan skyline, when a sharp intake of breath got her attention. Snapping her head around, she was surprised to see that the color had all but drained from her mother's cheeks.

"That isn't possible," Caroline replied emphatically to whatever her father's attorney had just said. "Roland hasn't owned that property for years."

Singer cleared his throat, adjusting himself uneasily in his high-backed leather chair. "Mrs. St. Claire, you might not be aware that your husband reacquired the property last year. Your sister—that is, Ms. Boyle—bequeathed it to him upon her death. And now Roland has bequeathed it to your daughter."

Lily blinked at Singer, then turned to her mother. "What property?"

Caroline stared back as if she hadn't heard the question. Beneath all the carefully applied makeup, her face had suddenly gone the color of ash.

"Mother?"

Singer jumped in to fill the void when it became obvious that Caroline wouldn't answer. "The property in question is Sand Pearl Cottage."

Lily ran the name around in her head but came up empty. "I've never heard of it."

He shot Caroline a pointed look before going on. "No, I don't suppose you would have. It's down on the Gulf Coast of Florida, on a little spit of beach called Hideaway Key. It used to belong to your mother's sister." He paused briefly when Caroline opened her mouth to interrupt, sending her a quelling look. "As I was saying, your aunt Lily-Mae owned the cottage for years, and then left it to your father. Now he's passed it on to you."

All of a sudden, Singer had her full attention. Lily-Mae Boyle had left her a cottage? "Why me? I've never laid eyes on the woman."

Singer's lips thinned. "Yes, well . . . perhaps that's why."

Lily tried to wrap her head around what she was being told, but she wasn't having much luck. For as long as she could remember, the name Lily-Mae Boyle had been forbidden in their home, an edict Lily-Mae's death, one year ago, had done nothing to change. And yet she had remained a part of their lives, a shadowy but palpable presence in the St. Claire household. It irked her that despite her thirty-year fascination with the exiled Lily-Mae, she still didn't understand the long-standing feud between her mother and her aunt. She only knew the sisters had sparred briefly for her father's affections, and that her mother had emerged the victor.

"I won't allow it." Caroline's voice crackled in the silence. "It's a mistake. My daughter will not have anything to do with that... that... place."

"Caroline." Singer drew the name out on a sigh, as if addressing a headstrong child. "Do I need to remind you that your daughter is well beyond the age of twenty-one? In fact, if memory serves, and you can trust me when I tell you it does, Lily will be thirty-six on her next birthday, which means you have absolutely no say—in this or in anything else she might choose to do. Roland was very clear about her having the cottage. Period. Now, with your permission, I'd like to move on to the final paperwork."

Caroline's chin came up a notch, as it always did when she didn't get her way, but she said nothing more.

As Lily navigated the snarl of downtown traffic, she could barely recall the rest of the meeting, except that it had all been rather surreal. She had signed where she was told to sign, initialed where she was told to initial, and then dutifully accepted the paperwork Singer handed her as she left his office, including the key to a beach house that until two hours ago she hadn't known existed.

She was leaving for Milan in a few weeks. What was she supposed to do with a beach house? Although, at the moment, she had to admit the prospect of hiding out for a few weeks at a seaside cottage had its appeal. Just the thought of returning to her parents' Gramercy town house made her squirm, especially now that her father was gone. Unfortunately, short of checking into a hotel, she had nowhere else to go. It hadn't made sense to hang on to her loft when she left for Paris. And she'd been right. In nine years she'd been home less than a dozen times, usually for Christmas, or her father's birthday. Now, she would have happily paid rent on an empty flat if it meant having a place to escape her mother's present mood, or for that matter, most of her moods.

Lily stole a sidelong glance at Caroline, sitting sullen and white-faced in the passenger seat. She refused to talk about her outburst in Singer's office, or to explain her reaction when the cottage became part of the conversation. Fine. Let her pout, or fume, or whatever *this* was. At the moment, Lily was too jet-lagged to launch into a proper cross-examination, but that didn't mean she wasn't going to get to the bottom of whatever was going on—because something was definitely going on.

She swallowed a groan as she stepped into the elaborate foyer and kicked off her shoes. It was full of flowers, sickly sweet blooms that kept arriving every day as news of her father's death rippled through the world of international finance. Roses, lilies, gardenias—their cloying scent made her stomach turn. And the sight of them broke her heart. Stacks of sympathy cards crowded the foyer table, condolences from friends and colleagues all over the world. Most would have gone unopened had she not come home. Her mother couldn't be bothered.

It was true that her parents hadn't been close; they'd never pretended otherwise, even for her sake. But there was such a thing as decency, as respectful grieving for a husband of thirty-plus years. So far, her mother hadn't shown any.

Caroline pushed past her, making a beeline for the bar. Lily checked her watch; a little past noon, so technically a martini wasn't a complete no-no, but she couldn't help wondering when her mother had started drinking so early. She'd never been an easy woman to read, her emotions wrapped so tightly that Lily sometimes wondered if she had any at all. But then, maybe her husband's death was affecting her more than she cared to let on. On impulse, Lily crossed the living room, laying a hand on Caroline's arm.

"Mother . . ."

Before she could form her next words, Caroline pivoted to face her. "You will not keep that cottage—do you hear me? Your father had no business leaving it to you."

Lily dropped her hand and stood studying her mother with something like fascination. Her cheeks were a mottled crimson, and she was actually trembling. "All right, Mother. What's this about? All this anger, and . . . I don't know what. You obviously have some sort of problem with Daddy leaving me this cottage, so what is it?"

"He had no right."

"No right to what? Have a place of his own?"

"Not that place—no."

"So this is about Lily-Mae? Because the cottage used to belong to her, and Daddy accepted it without your permission?"

Caroline faltered as she filled a martini glass, sloshing Tanqueray onto the marble bar top. She ignored the mess, lifting the half-full glass and draining it in one long swallow. "You know you're not to use that name in my house. Not today. Not ever."

Lily felt her patience starting to fray. "Honestly, Mother, the woman is dead—your sister is *dead*—and so is Daddy. And you still can't let go of this ridiculous feud. Why? Please tell me you're not still nursing a grudge against a dead woman because a million years ago she had eyes for my father. He married you. And *she* never married at all, which means we're all the family she had. Why wouldn't she leave the cottage to Daddy? She knew you'd never accept it."

Caroline glared at her like a truculent child. "No, I wouldn't have. And you're not accepting it, either."

"That's ridiculous, and you know it! Your feud with Lily-Mae has nothing to do with me. How could it? I never met the woman. But maybe Mr. Singer was right. Maybe that *is* why Daddy left me the cottage. Because he thought I should at least know something about the woman I was named for. God knows, I've never learned anything about her from you."

Caroline turned back to her pitcher of martinis, the thin glass rod tinkling as she stirred. "No, you haven't. And there's no point now. She's dead, and it's over."

"What's over?" Lily demanded, frustration finally boiling over. "What happened to make you hate her so? To make you *still* hate her? Are you jealous? Is that it? She was famous, and you weren't? Is that what all this has been about?"

"That's enough!"

"No, it really isn't. I want to understand, and have since the day I found that magazine clipping of Lily-Mae in your dresser. Do you remember that? I was snooping around, and there it was, at the bottom of one of the drawers. You walked in and I held it up. When you saw what it was you snatched it out of my hand, and then you slapped me. Six years old, and you slapped me in the face. You'd never laid a hand on me until then, and never have since."

"I was trying to teach you about going through people's things," Caroline said stiffly, but she had gone a little pale, her free hand fluttering anxiously at her throat. "It's what parents do."

"No, you just pretended it was about the snooping. Even then, I knew there was something else going on, something you were hiding. I've never forgotten that day, or stopped wondering what it was you weren't telling. I'm wondering about it right now, quite a lot, in fact. So why not just tell me the truth? Is this about Daddy? Because all those years ago he and Lily-Mae went out a couple of times? Because, honestly, Mother, it feels like more than that—a lot more."

Caroline picked up her freshened glass and moved to the window, gazing out at the hazy city skyline. When she finally turned back, her eyes held a note of pleading. "Isn't it enough that I'm asking you to leave this be, Lily? Can you not be loyal to me just this once?"

Lily caught the faint Tennessee drawl that sometimes crept into her mother's speech when she was upset. But it was the word *loyal* that jumped out at her now, better suited to wars and territorial disputes than conversations between mother and daughter. But then, the word *war* wasn't completely off the mark when describing their relationship over the years, the cool, careful distances, tensions that never quite erupted into full-scale conflict. A cold war. And now, for reasons she couldn't fathom, at a time when they should be bonding over the death of her father, it seemed the hostilities had resumed.

"Just this once?" Lily repeated softly, still absorbing the sting of the words. "You're saying I've been disloyal to you in the past? That I've *always* been disloyal?"

Caroline's face didn't soften. "I'm saying you've always taken your father's side in everything, and now you're doing it again. You know how I feel—how I've always felt—and still, you keep prying. If you care about my feelings you'll drop this obsession of yours, and get rid of that horrible place."

"Why horrible? You keep saying that, but you won't say why."

"The *why* isn't important, Lily."

"Of course it's important. Look, I'm trying to understand all this. I really am. But you're not helping. Mr. Singer said Daddy had reacquired the property, which makes it sound like it was his to begin with, and that Lily-Mae was just giving it back. Is that what all this loyalty talk is about? You think Daddy should have said no to the cottage? Or is it because he accepted it without telling you? Because I can totally see him not sharing that information. I mean . . . look at you. This is *not* normal behavior."

Caroline was trembling in earnest now, her fingers white around the stem of her glass. "Your father was a fool. He couldn't help . . ."

"What?" Lily shot back. "Being decent? It was obviously more than *you* were willing to do. Maybe my getting the cottage was what Lily-Mae had in mind when she left it to Daddy. Did you ever think of that? That maybe she just wanted to leave me something?"

"She never cared about you. She never cared about anyone but herself."

"And Daddy," Lily said softly. "That's what this is really about, isn't it?"

Caroline took a step back, as if the words had touched her physically. "She always won. Whatever she wanted, she got. But not your father. Your father belonged to me. And now she's dead—done with things that don't belong to her."

Lily heaved a sigh. "I don't know what that means, Mother."

"It means the less you have to do with that woman—and that place—the better for all concerned. The job in Milan is what you should be thinking about, Lily, your career. Not wasting your time worrying about a dead woman you never met."

Lily blinked at Caroline, not bothering to hide her surprise. "Suddenly you're interested in my career? When you've barely bothered to keep up with where I've been the past nine years? Pardon me if I'm just a little bit skeptical. I also find it odd that you can't wait to send me packing. Most mothers would want their daughter with them after losing their husbands, but not you. You can't wait to send me off to Milan. Why is that?"

Caroline's gaze narrowed, the whites of her eyes flashing as she waved a finger under Lily's nose. "I will not stand here and be questioned in my own home, not about that woman, and not by you."

Lily simply stared at her. Something about that finger, about the way her mother stood there glaring, as if her word were absolute, sent some tiny wheel or gear clicking into place. She was finished arguing, finished asking questions.

"Don't worry, Mother. You won't have to. I'm leaving. But before

I do, let me remind you that *that woman*, as you insist on calling her, was your sister. And that *place* you talk about with such contempt was a gift from my father—my *dead* father—and it's the last thing he's ever going to give me. So I'd appreciate it if you'd at least pretend to respect Daddy's wishes. Now, if we're finished here, I'll go and pack."

Caroline's eyes had lost some of their fire. "You're leaving for Milan? Now?"

"No. I'm leaving for Florida. I'm going to see what all the fuss is about."

TWO

1995
Hideaway Key, Florida

Lily lowered all four windows, savoring the gush of sticky, salty air that poured in as she blew past the shell-shaped sign welcoming her to Hideaway Key. For a moment she felt an absurd urge to turn on the radio and find a Jimmy Buffett tune—or maybe the Beach Boys. Her father had been crazy about the Beach Boys.

She couldn't help smiling as she recalled the Saturday afternoon he had dragged out his album collection and cranked up the old stereo, how he had lifted her into his arms and slow danced with her in the living room, crooning the words to "Don't Worry Baby" softly against her cheek.

The memory brought a sudden sting of tears. She hadn't thought of that day in years, but was glad she'd recalled it now. She would like to think he was happy once, that he had at least a few good memories to sustain him through less happy times, but she wasn't sure. As far back as she could remember he had stressed the importance of finding her right place in the world, of listening to her heart and following her own North Star. There had always been something faintly intense about those lectures, as if drawn from a deep well of unhappy experience.

Lily pushed the thought away as she cruised past ice-cream parlors and hot dog stands, surfside bars and beachwear shops. There were a handful of motels, too, flat-roofed mom-and-pops with names like the Surf Rider and the Sea Grape Inn. Sadly, none of them were advertising vacancies. It was starting to look as if she would have to head out of town to find a bed for the night. But first, she wanted to find the cottage while it was still light and give it a quick once-over.

Sand Pearl Cottage.

She liked the name. It was charming, like something from a fairy tale. And it was hers. Over the past two days, what had begun as an impulse was starting to feel like a much-needed reprieve, a bit of breathing room before she headed to Milan at the end of the month. Or maybe she just wanted somewhere to hide, a place to lick her wounds and sift through her emotions. Grief over the loss of her father and mentor. Resentment of her mother's petty dramas. Guilt for the way she had ended her relationship with Luc.

And beneath it all, a restlessness that never seemed to leave her, the sense that there was something more she was meant to do, something just beyond her grasp that would finally feel right—her elusive North Star, perhaps. Or maybe it was only a fancy, felt more keenly now that her father was gone.

The first three emotions she understood. It was the last that baffled her. Since her first conversation with Dario Enzi, her contact at Izzani, she'd been trying to convince herself that she was excited about going to Milan. She wasn't, though. It was just what she did, what she had always done, because her work was who she was, a way of proving to the world that she was more than just Roland St. Claire's little girl. So, here she was, twelve hundred miles from home with three weeks to figure it all out, and not the slightest idea where she was going to sleep.

The cottage wasn't likely to be an option after sitting vacant for more than a year. She'd need to find a motel, and soon. After two days behind the wheel, she didn't care what the place looked like as long as it had a bed and a shower. She'd find someplace to grab a quick dinner, ask a local for directions to the cottage, give the place a once-over, and then find somewhere to crash. As for what came next, she had no idea. Until she'd gotten a good night's sleep she refused to make anything resembling a plan.

Dinner turned out to be an omelet and coffee at Sonny's Omelet Barn, a bustling greasy spoon on the outskirts of town. Janice, her waitress, recommended two motels in Arcadia Beach, the next town south, then scratched out a rough map to the cottage on the back of a paper place mat.

It took three U-turns, but Lily finally managed to locate Vista Drive, a narrow, winding lane lined with trees that looked as if they'd been transplanted from a jungle. As instructed, she followed the lane to the end, surprised when it opened up onto a broad cul-de-sac. Unfortunately, there wasn't a house in sight.

Lily checked the makeshift map again, assuming she'd missed a turn, but Janice's directions clearly said to go to the end of Vista Drive. She was about to turn around when she noticed a set of mailboxes neatly camouflaged by an unwieldy gardenia bush, and just beyond, what appeared to be a pair of driveways branching off toward opposite sides of the cul-de-sac. After consulting the place mat one more time, she took the right-hand drive, leaning forward over the wheel to peer through the thickening canopy of foliage.

The tires crunched noisily as she came to a stop at the end of the crushed-shell drive. She cut the engine, fished the cottage key from her purse, then stepped out onto the drive. It was the stillness she noticed first, not silence exactly, since there were birds trilling somewhere up in the trees, and the papery rustle of palm fronds overhead, but a sense of calm she hadn't felt in years—or ever, really. And there was something else, too, beneath the quiet: a low, hypnotic thrum, like a pulse.

It took a moment to identify the sound, and to realize it was coming from behind the trees. The sea. Searching for an alley or a walkway of some kind, she finally located a narrow slate path and ducked into the shadowy overgrowth, homing in on the sound until she broke from the hedges and out into a small clearing.

There was a moment of confusion as she stood there, trying to reconcile the quaint cottage of her imagination with what actually stood before her—a decaying bungalow with drooping shutters, weed-choked window boxes, and a sadly sagging front porch. Maybe there had been some kind of mix-up. Maybe she had copied the address down wrong. But no, the peeling sign swinging over the porch clearly read SAND PEARL COTTAGE.

Lily had no idea how long she stood there before she finally ventured up onto the front porch. She sighed as she surveyed further signs of neglect: flaking paint, windows rimed with salt and grit, and the desiccated remains of a pair of geraniums on either side of the front door. It wasn't grand, and clearly never had been, but it had been charming once, before it had been allowed to go to ruin.

Narrowly missing a rather formidable spiderweb, she reached for the screen door. The hinges moaned as she pulled it back, like something out of a slasher film. Lily thought vaguely of squatters and vagrants, and about the wisdom of entering the cottage alone, then shrugged off her concerns. This was the Gulf Coast of Florida, not Washington Heights. Places with names like Hideaway Key didn't spawn vagrants and crackheads—did they? It was the spiderweb that finally convinced her, its size and location suggesting longevity. If anyone had gone in through the front door, they hadn't done it recently.

Breath held, she slid the key home, surprised when it turned with little resistance. Inside, the air was stale, thick with disuse and the faint pong of mildew, the way she'd expect an old attic to smell. She hovered in the doorway a moment, waiting for her eyes to adjust to the gloom, then wondered if the power might still be on. Unlikely, after more than a year. Still, she found herself groping for a wall switch.

She was surprised when the frosted globe overhead actually flared to life, but even more astonished when she glanced around the small living room. She hadn't given much thought as to whether the cottage would be furnished, but she certainly hadn't expected to find it crammed floor to ceiling with boxes. The sight almost made her dizzy: cartons of every shape and size, some sealed, some not, stacked side by side, one on top of another, so that they formed a kind of cardboard maze.

But it wasn't only the boxes that left Lily fighting a wave of claustrophobia. It was the clutter, a hodgepodge of chairs, tables, lamps, and knickknacks jammed into every square inch of the already tiny room; Lily-Mae's things, by the look of them, still here more than a year after her death.

Had no one wanted them?

It was entirely possible. Her aunt had never married, one of the few facts Caroline had ever volunteered, clearly relishing her sister's loveless, childless lot in life. It felt odd standing here now, among her things. She knew so little about the woman, almost nothing in fact, except that she'd been a bit famous once—a spokesmodel for some beauty cream or other—and had briefly caused quite a stir. It was all she knew, and even that she'd had to discover on her own, since her mother flew into a rage anytime Lily-Mae's name was mentioned in her hearing.

Her mother's long-standing hatred still baffled her. But then, so much about Caroline St. Claire baffled her. Like why she refused to talk about her childhood, why there were no photographs of her as a girl, no yearbooks, or scrapbooks, or memorabilia of any kind—as if she refused to acknowledge any life at all before marrying Roland. And now there was Sand Pearl Cottage, this place her mother abhorred and begrudged her. Why?

Lily stepped into the maze with a kind of morbid fascination, sidling carefully until she finally reached the opposite side of the room. The furniture, what she could see of it, was of good quality, but felt strangely formal for a seaside cottage, as if the contents of an entire Manhattan penthouse had been crammed into this tiny bungalow.

There was a matching chair and settee in off-white brocade, a mahogany table with gracefully curved legs, and a beautiful writing desk finished in glossy black enamel. Lily switched on a small brass banker's lamp and surveyed the items on the blotter—several good pens, a brass caddy stocked with tissue-thin sheets of pale blue stationery, a glass paperweight with some sort of scarab suspended inside. If she'd been hoping to find evidence of her aunt's sordid past here, she was clearly wasting her time.

It was nearing full dark, Lily saw, as she turned to peer out the sliding glass doors, only the faintest blush of peach lingering along the crease between sea and sky. She fumbled a bit before locating the latch, but finally the door slid back, letting in a rush of sea sounds and salt-tanged air. She couldn't see much as she stepped out onto the deck. There were a pair of white plastic chairs, and a narrow set of steps leading down to the beach, not that she had any intention of using them in the dark. Instead, she folded her arms close to her body and held very still.

The breeze played havoc with her hair, whipping at the ends of her ponytail, teasing strands free to tickle the nape of her neck. On impulse, she tugged her scrunchie free, letting the wind have its way. The humidity would play hell with it, but she didn't care. She closed her eyes and simply held still, reveling in the briny air and the achingly sweet music of the sea.

She couldn't say how long she stood there before finally drifting back to reality, but the glow on the horizon had faded, leaving the sky an inky shade of indigo. She was struck by the darkness, by the absoluteness of it, as if someone had snuffed out the world with a heavy blanket. In New York—or in Paris, for that matter—it was never completely dark. There was always light, always people going places and doing things.

She'd found it exhilarating once, back when she was fresh out of school and ready to take the world by storm. But life had a way of tarnishing dreams. It didn't care about your résumé, your trust fund, or your last name. It brought you back to reality with a bump—sometimes more than one. And it could land you in some pretty unexpected places, though there were certainly worse places to languish than a cottage by the sea.

She might have lingered out in the dark if she hadn't been so exhausted, but there was still the matter of sleeping arrangements to be dealt with. Stepping back inside, she was struck once more by the sheer number of boxes in the tiny living room. What was it all, and what was it doing here? Were the rest of the rooms like this? The thought made her head spin. What if this barely controlled chaos was just the tip of the iceberg? She glanced at her watch. It was already heading for nine, but the full tour wouldn't take long. There were only a handful of rooms, and she'd at least know what she was dealing with.

There was a small sunporch off the living room. Just as she had feared, the small space was chock-full of cartons, stacked in corners, piled on chairs, and spilling out into the narrow hallway. She fared no better in the small bedroom facing the driveway, a guest room presumably, furnished with a pair of Bahama beds, a small table, and a lamp, and dizzily stacked with more boxes. Sighing, she turned away. Other than the kitchen and breakfast nook, both of which appeared to have escaped the clutter, there was only one room left, a slightly larger bedroom situated at the back of the cottage, with a pair of glass sliders that opened onto the deck.

Lily peered in from the doorway but couldn't make out much with just the glow from the overhead hall light. Groping blindly, and somewhat noisily, she finally managed to locate a lamp and flip the switch, then groaned audibly as she took in her surroundings. No boxes, at least, but so much . . . stuff. Then it hit her—these were Lily-Mae's things, her *personal* things, all precisely as they had been the day she died.

All her life, Lily had longed to know more about her aunt. Now, inexplicably, she found herself standing in the woman's bedroom. It was a vaguely unsettling sensation, as if she had stepped into someone else's shoes—and someone else's life.

The thought was like a breath on the back of her neck, chilly and warm at the same time. She hadn't given much thought to what she might find when she arrived, but even if she had she would never have imagined Lily-Mae's things would still be here. And what things they were. Everywhere she looked there seemed to be some new piece of treasure: leather-bound books, exquisite porcelains, bits of silver and fine-cut crystal, all displayed like museum pieces about the room.

All except one, that is.

Lily stepped to the bow-front bureau, eyeing the simple jar of seashells placed carefully at its center. She ran a thoughtful finger around the rim, thick and bubbly with just a hint of green in the glass. It felt wrong somehow. In any other beach house a jar of shells would be standard décor, part of the natural seaside ambiance. But her aunt's tastes had clearly run toward the formal, leaving Lily to wonder why such a simple thing had been singled out for what felt like a place of honor.

One more question without an answer.

It was ironic. All her life she'd been denied Lily-Mae's story, denied the chance to know who she was and what she had done that was so very wrong. Now, through no effort of her own, she found herself smack-dab in the middle of that story, apparently tasked with sifting through the remnants.

She had her father to thank for that—or to blame for it. Had he known all of this was here when he arranged to leave her the cottage, or was it all merely chance? Perhaps he'd meant to have the place cleared out but never got around to it. His death *had* been sudden, and it would explain all the boxes. There was no way to know. And it didn't really matter. Whatever the reason, it was hers to handle now.

But when, and how? She was supposed to be in Milan by the end of the month. There simply wasn't time to deal with all this—whatever it was. In fact, just thinking about it made her head hurt. A hotel. A shower. A bed. She needed all three before she could begin thinking about logistics.

Exhausted, and dangerously close to tears, Lily reached for the lamp, preparing to switch it off when she spotted the book on the nightstand. *Wuthering Heights* had always been a favorite of hers. Apparently it had been one of Lily-Mae's as well. The book had been read often, its dark leather spine worn shiny-smooth, its pages well thumbed. And it appeared there was a passage marked, a scrap of paper peeking from between the pages—perhaps where Lily-Mae had left off reading?

Curious, Lily eased down onto the bed and slid the copy of *Wuthering Heights* into her lap, turning to the casually marked page. She was expecting to find a bookmark. Instead, she found a sheet of pale blue stationery folded between pages 264 and 265. She spread the sheet flat, running a finger along the center crease to smooth it, then sat staring at the lines of loopy, elegant script. Whatever it was, it was dated October 1994, approximately one month before her aunt's death.

A letter? A confession of some sort?

Lily couldn't help feeling a pang of guilt. It was silly, she knew.

Lily-Mae was dead and gone, and had been for more than a year. She just wasn't sure that gave her the right to peer into someone's private thoughts. Still, the lines beckoned.

October 2, 1994

I have been reading Wuthering Heights *again tonight—about Catherine Earnshaw and the poor end she made. I am like her, though, in many ways, and have begun to wonder about my own end, about the pain I have caused, and the pain I have endured. Perhaps they will balance. I don't know. Still, I have had my day in the sun, my brief but shining moment, as they say, and can cling now to that time, to what was sweet, and right, and good. I have much to mourn, but little to regret as my days wind down. We do what we must, after all, to guard our hearts—and the hearts of others. Such a fragile thing, the heart, so easily broken and robbed of its secrets. But strong, too, when it must be. Twice I have loved, and twice I have lost, the pain of it like dying. But now, at the end of things, I find I would not make different choices. I have loved with my whole heart, have tasted both sin and sorrow, and have made my peace—not only with what was, but with what could not be. It is our lot in this life, to love and to lose. We flail for a time, afraid of drowning in our grief, and then finally go quiet, content to simply drift when our horizons are lost and there is nothing left to swim to. Soon even my drifting will be over. I will not send this. I meant to when I began it, but find now that I cannot. There is too much truth in it for sharing, even with you—even now.*

Lily read over the poignant words a second time, and then a third. It was a letter, obviously, but a letter to whom? And for that matter, *by* whom? The date would seem to confirm her suspicions that Lily-Mae was the author, but without a greeting or signature, there was no way to be sure. It was moving, whoever had written it, the language dark and vaguely haunting. But it was the opening passage that resonated with Lily, the reference to poor Catherine Earnshaw, doomed to wander the moors for all eternity after a life of tragic mistakes, forever separated from her beloved Heathcliff.

It felt odd, though, somehow, unexpected. Perhaps because literary references didn't quite dovetail with her mother's lurid accounts of Lily-Mae, which tended to conjure images of a libertine who smoked cigars and sipped sugar-laced absinthe, swore like a sailor, and wore fishnets to church. Hardly the stuff of a Brontë heroine, or a Brontë reader, for that matter.

Lily stifled a yawn as she folded the tissue-thin sheet back along its crease and prepared to return it to the book. One thing was certain. She wasn't going to solve the mystery tonight. She'd read it again tomorrow, after a good night's sleep. Or maybe she'd read it just once more.

THREE

Lily squinted at her watch but gave up when her eyes refused to focus. She felt vaguely headachy as she propped herself up on one arm. Something was wrong. There was sunlight streaming into the room, great yellow puddles of it splashing across unfamiliar sheets. And she was still wearing yesterday's clothes.

It came back to her in a snatches. *Wuthering Heights.* Catherine Earnshaw. An unsent letter, read and reread into the wee hours. Words teased carefully apart, like a riddle that needed solving, until she'd finally collapsed into a fitful sleep, Lily-Mae's letter still in her hand, its words still running through her head.

She looked around for the letter, finally spotting it on the floor. Retrieving it, she folded it neatly and returned it to the pages of *Wuthering Heights.* There was no need to read it again. The words were already burned into her memory, and would be for a very long time. *Twice I have loved, and twice I have lost, the pain of it like dying . . . I . . . have tasted both sin and sorrow.* So much grief for one page—and one lifetime.

And far too many questions to be dealt with before she'd had at least one cup of coffee. Donning mental blinders, she ventured out into the parlor, pretending to ignore the chaos as she navigated a path to the sliding glass doors. Maybe some fresh air would help her get her bearings.

She frowned at the year's worth of salt and grime obscuring the large glass panes, wondering as she fumbled with the latch if there was enough Windex in the state of Florida to ever get them clean. The thought evaporated as she stepped outside, her breath caught suddenly in her throat.

The sheer expanse of bright blue water was unexpected somehow, like a gleaming gem in the late-morning sun, the blinding stretch of pearl-white sand unmarred by so much as a footprint. It was the emptiness that caught her off guard, the sensation that she was alone in the world. She didn't mind it. She was fine with alone. She *liked* alone. Perhaps a little more than was good for her.

Eyes closed, she tipped her face to the sky, reveling in the buttery warmth of the sun and the beguiling sensation that nothing mattered but here and now. But it wasn't true. Here and now wasn't real. Milan was real. Her father's death was real. The mess back inside the cottage was real. Only she didn't want to think about any of those things. For once in her life, she didn't want to *think* about anything, *do* anything, *be* anything.

Unfortunately, she had no idea how to *do* nothing. Strategic moves, ladder climbing—that's what she was good at. In the ten years since she finished school, she'd left four different design houses, each time for bigger and better opportunities—better titles, more prestigious labels. It was why she had accepted the Milan job. But then, only a fool would have turned it down. Anyone who knew anything about the fashion industry knew what being tapped by Izzani meant. It was a huge deal, the job every up-and-coming designer dreamed of, and it was hers.

So what was she doing here? She should be getting ready for Milan, not hiding out at some beach house, prowling through a dead woman's things—and a dead *stranger*, at that. Maybe her mother was right. Maybe she should be focusing on her career instead of Lily-Mae. If she was smart, she'd book the first flight she could get instead of waiting for the end of the month. There was nothing standing in her way, no ties left in Paris, nothing for her back in New York now that her father was gone, and certainly nothing keeping her here.

She could pay someone to clean the place out, put it on the market, and just drive away. She could pretend she'd never heard of Sand Pearl Cottage, never stood in Lily-Mae's bedroom, never read the unsent letter. Except she wasn't ready to do any of those things—at least not yet. She wasn't due in Milan for three weeks, which meant she had three weeks to rake through the mess and piece together the story of Lily-Mae Boyle.

But before she touched the first box she was going to need a shower, coffee, and some breakfast.

It was eleven o'clock on a Thursday, and Hideaway Key's historic downtown was already a hub of activity, its clever shops and trendy restaurants bustling with sunburned tourists and well-heeled locals. Lily strolled down De Soto Avenue's palm-lined sidewalks, stuffed to the gills after a late breakfast, taking it all in.

It was warm for a walk, but she didn't care. She was already in love with the tiny downtown, deliciously Art Deco, with its glass-block windows and smooth stucco curves—like something right off an old postcard. The shops catered mostly to tourists, everything from jewelry stores and art galleries to bakeries selling gourmet dog biscuits.

She was browsing the shopwindows, admiring colorful tropical-themed displays, when one shop in particular caught her eye, though whether the attraction had to with the smartly displayed window or the neon pink sign above the door, she couldn't say. Sassy Rack Boutique. Fun and original. On impulse, she stepped inside.

A gorgeous brunette with a pink and orange scarf tied around her head glanced up from behind the register. She wore a dress of coral silk that fluttered prettily around her tan limbs as she crossed the shop. Lily put her somewhere in her mid-fifties.

"Welcome to Sassy Rack!" the woman chimed with a drawl so syrupy it could only be real. "Looking for anything special?"

"Just browsing, actually. Your windows caught my attention. Whoever does them has a good eye. It's a really nice mix of colors and patterns."

"Thanks. That would be me." She stuck out a hand. "I'm Sheila. Sheila Beasley."

"I'm Lily. So, you're the owner?"

"I am. I'm also the stock clerk, the cashier, and the window washer." She rolled her eyes comically. "The joys of being self-employed. So, New York or New Jersey?"

"New York. Is it that obvious?"

Sheila smiled, a shimmer of peach gloss setting off perfect white teeth. "Not very. But it's kind of my thing, picking up on accents and guessing where folks are from. If there was a way to make money at it, I could give up the cashier job."

Lily laughed, liking Sheila Beasley already, for her easy smile and throaty chuckle, as well as her unique personal style.

"Hey, stay right there," Sheila said, holding up a finger. "I just got a shipment of dresses in this morning, and there's an orange silk wrap that would look great on you."

It was on the tip of Lily's tongue to say she wouldn't be needing any dresses while she was in Hideaway Key, but Sheila was gone before she could get the words out. In the meantime, she browsed the shoe display, eyeing a pair of strappy pink sandals she didn't need and would probably never wear.

She had just picked up the left shoe when she heard an odd rumble and turned to find a massive orange tabby strolling languidly in her direction. Smiling, she watched as the cat made a beeline for her legs, tail waving like a flag in the breeze. It wove a lazy figure eight around her ankles, then paused to gaze up at her with sleepy yellow eyes. Lily bent down and gave the orange head a scratch, noticing as she did that one of its ears was badly gnarled, one side of its face horribly scarred. He—assuming it *was* a he—was also missing an eye.

"Poor baby," she crooned as the cat scrubbed a cheek against her hand. "What happened to you?"

"I see you've met Galahad."

Lily stood, flicking orange hair from her fingers. "His name is Galahad?"

"Sure is." Sheila scooped the cat up into her arms. "As in Sir Galahad. Because he's as brave as a lion, poor thing."

"Poor thing is right. He's all scarred up."

Sheila pressed a noisy kiss on Galahad's head before setting him back down. "You should have seen him when he showed up in the alley behind the store. He was a wreck. Skin and bone, with oozing sores all over him. It was a good month before he'd let me get close. Then another week before I could coax him to eat. After that, I couldn't have shaken him if I wanted to. He must've known I have a tender spot for scarred things."

Scarred things?

The remark caught Lily off guard, but she decided to let it go. It wasn't exactly the kind of thing you questioned someone about, especially someone you'd only met ten minutes ago.

"I hung the orange silk in the first dressing room," Sheila told her, steering the conversation back to business. "I grabbed a couple of other things, too. I don't get many redheads in the shop, so I went a little crazy with colors. Try them on and let me know what you think. And if you need a different size, just holler."

Lily slipped into the dressing room and kicked off her shoes, then looked through the pieces Sheila had chosen. She was more than a little impressed. Every item was one she would have chosen for herself, the most flattering styles for her body shape, the ideal palette for her coloring. She had also known what sizes to pull, another hallmark of a pro. Pros knew body types: how to disguise nature's shortcomings and accentuate her gifts. It was what clothes were all about, after all, making a woman—or a man for that matter—feel good in the skin they were born with.

She was pulling on her third dress when Sheila tapped on the door. "Hey, sugar, I don't know what you've got on, but whatever it is, take it off and try on this suit." A tiny teal two-piece appeared above the door. "I just found it in a box in back, and I swear it's got your name on it."

Lily eyed the swimsuit with something like panic. "I *cannot* wear that."

"Why not? What do you usually wear?"

Lily poked her head up over the three-quarter door. "I don't."

Sheila quirked one dark brow. "Well, now, I'm guessing that makes you pretty popular back home."

Lily couldn't help giggling. "It would at that, but I meant I'm not really a beach person."

"Not a beach person?" Sheila clucked her tongue. "Honey, I don't know who your travel agent is, but you might want to get your money back. You just happen to be standing two blocks from the most gorgeous beaches in the state of Florida."

"I just meant—"

Sheila broke the tension with a toothy grin. "I'm just teasing. I know what you meant. Now, try the suit. It's going to work—wait and see."

Lily eyed the swimsuit warily. She was going to be here only a few weeks. She didn't *need* a swimsuit—and certainly not one that fit in the palm of her hand. But the color was wonderful, and the faux-leather fringe and turquoise beads were fun. Against her better judgment, she shimmied into the thing, then turned in a slow circle before the mirror.

It was an awful lot of skin—an awful lot of *very white* skin. Still, it was flattering. The teal set off her fair complexion and red hair, and the high-cut bottoms lengthened her legs. The top was a problem, though. She tugged at the triangular patches, hoping to stretch the coverage, but no matter how hard she tried the tiny halter seemed to reveal more than it concealed.

"Come on out and let me see," Sheila hollered through the door.

"Not on your life!"

"Doesn't it fit?"

Lily bit her lip as she took another look at the rear view. "It's cute, but it doesn't leave much to the imagination."

"Hang on." Lily heard the receding slap of sandals, followed by their reapproach. "Try this."

Lily slipped on the gauzy cover-up, then reassessed. "Better. But I'm still not coming out."

"Fine. As long as you're in there, here are a few more things to try."

Before it was over Lily left Sassy Rack with a swimsuit and cover-up, several skirts, two breezy little dresses, shorts, tops, flip-flops in a rainbow of colors—and a practical, if slightly ridiculous, straw hat. She had no idea where she'd ever wear any of it—certainly not Milan—but the shopping was fun, and it had helped take her mind off what was waiting for her back at the cottage. But now play-time was over. It was time to find the nearest market, stock up on staples, and then get to work on those boxes. Three weeks would be up before she knew it.

FOUR

Lily dropped her armload of shopping bags onto the bed with a sigh of relief, then shook the blood back into her fingertips. The groceries were still in the trunk, waiting to be brought in, but she had wanted to find the orange silk and hang it up first. If she didn't, the thing wouldn't be worth wearing.

It took a bit of rummaging, but she finally managed to locate the dress, loosely folded and wrapped in pink tissue. Shaking out the folds, she pressed the silk wrap to her body and sidled toward the mirror, swearing softly when her foot snagged on something and nearly sent her toppling. Dropping to one knee, she groped blindly beneath the bed until she came out with a long, flattish box. It had seen better days, its corners taped, its flaps battered and creased, as if they'd been opened and then refolded on themselves again and again. Her hands hovered briefly as she pondered what might be inside. Shoes, maybe, or winter clothes, packed away and forgotten.

She was about to pull back the first flap when she heard what sounded like the front door. Had she left it open? She couldn't remember, but with her arms full of bags it was certainly possible. Head cocked, she listened again but heard nothing. Then it came again, accompanied by a faint rustling and the unmistakable sound of footsteps. Easing from the bed, she tiptoed to the hall and peered around the corner, then took a sharp step backward—the natural reaction to finding a complete stranger standing in your living room with an armload of groceries.

Dark-lashed green eyes met hers, amused and free of threat. "Howdy, neighbor."

Lily blinked rapidly, still trying to process the man's presence.

"I was just on my way over," he added, clearly unaware of her distress. "I was coming to introduce myself when I saw your trunk open."

Lily eyed him with one hand on her hip, her adrenaline level gradually returning to normal. "Well?"

"Well, what?"

"Introduce yourself."

"Oh, right. I'm Dean. Dean Landry. I live next door."

"No one lives next door."

"Okay, not right next door, but about fifty yards to the south. Here, I'll show you, if you'll take these."

Wary, Lily took the grocery bags he held out, depositing them on the kitchen counter, before following him out the sliding glass doors.

"Here," he said, calling her to the end of the deck. "Come stand right here."

Lily followed his outstretched arm, squinting through a curtain of palms until she caught a glimpse of what he was pointing at. It was like something from a travel poster, twin stories painted the same clear blue as the sky, a pair of wraparound decks, and a roof that gleamed like a new dime in the afternoon sun. But even more impressive than the house was the trellised stone patio stretching down to the beach, along with a massive fireplace that looked to still be under construction.

Lily turned to him, not bothering to hide her surprise. "How on earth could I have missed a place like that?"

"Oh, you can't see it from the road, only from the beach. And here, apparently, if you stand on your toes."

"It's gorgeous, especially the patio."

Dean nodded his thanks. "One of these days I'll actually finish it."

"You did the stonework yourself?"

He puffed up a little, pride written plainly on his face. "I did all of it myself. Every nail and board, from the sand up."

Lily stole another quick glance. He was tan and tall, with a nicely chiseled face, definitely the type that belonged in a beach house, though in his crisp blue oxford and neatly creased khakis, he hardly looked like the hard hat type. Her eyes slid to his hands. No discernible calluses. No ring, either. Single? It was an awful lot of house for one guy. Or maybe he wasn't single, just a guy who didn't do rings. At any rate, it was none of her business.

She couldn't help wondering, as she turned to go back inside, what he thought about Lily-Mae's dingy little cottage squatting beside his dream house. Or maybe she was better off not knowing. She wasn't crazy about being the scourge of the neighborhood, even if that neighborhood consisted of only two houses.

He was still on her heels as she stepped into the kitchen, showing no signs of making an exit. Perhaps if she started unpacking the groceries he'd take the hint and leave. Not that she was eager to tackle whatever science projects might be incubating in the fridge, but the sooner she finished with the groceries, the sooner she could get back to the box in Lily-Mae's bedroom.

Unfortunately, he didn't seem to be taking the hint. She could feel his eyes following her about the kitchen, could sense him waiting for something. She glanced up from her bag of vegetables, one brow raised questioningly. "Yes?"

His bland smile was vaguely irritating. "It's your turn."

"My turn to what?"

"To introduce yourself."

"Oh." Lily flushed at her lack of manners. "Sorry. I'm Lily St. Claire."

"Good to meet you." He wandered away then, far too comfortable as he made a brief survey of the living room. "So," he said finally, hands resting easily on his hips. "Are you packing or unpacking?"

"I'm not doing either," she answered, fishing a head of romaine and two tomatoes from one of the bags. "This was all here when I showed up. It belongs . . . belonged . . . to my aunt."

Dean reappeared suddenly from the living room. "The woman who lived here was your aunt?"

"She was. I never knew her, though. She was sort of persona non grata. She and my mother didn't get along."

Dean's face hardened briefly, a fleeting grimace that quickly morphed into a kind of crooked half smile. "Aren't families wonderful?"

Lily narrowed her eyes. Something in his tone belied the smile, a tinge of bitterness that felt uncomfortable between strangers. Or maybe she'd only imagined it. Either way, she let it pass. If she engaged, he'd only stay, and she really wanted to get back to the box on Lily-Mae's bed.

He was watching her, waiting for her to say more. When she didn't, he picked up the thread of the conversation himself. "I think I heard something about her being famous once, didn't I? She was a model or something?"

Lily stifled a sigh. Apparently, he wasn't going anywhere. "She was. Or at least I've been told she was. I saw a picture of her once. She was beautiful."

"It runs in the family."

He was smiling now, one of those sharp white smiles that made you feel like you were about to be put on a spit and roasted for dinner. She really didn't have time for this. She had things to do, boxes to unpack.

"Look, I hate to run you off after you brought in my groceries and all, but as you can see, I've got tons to do here."

Dean followed her gaze to the boxes. "I'll say. So you really don't know what all this stuff is?"

"No. Like I said, it was here when I showed up."

He said nothing at first, his attention on arranging cans of clam chowder and minestrone into two neat rows on the kitchen counter. "This is an awful lot of soup," he said finally. "How long were you planning to stay?"

Lily eyed him keenly. Had she only imagined the too-casual tone? "I'll be leaving at the end of the month."

"So three weeks."

"Yes. I inherited the cottage, and need to figure out what to do with it before I leave for Milan."

"What's in Milan?"

"Work," she answered curtly, wondering why she was getting the third degree.

"Ah." He was smiling again, like the proverbial cat with the canary. "Might I make a suggestion, then?"

"A suggestion?"

"You said you need to decide what to do with the cottage. Why not sell it to me?"

It took a moment for the words to register. "But you have a house—a beautiful house—right next door. Why would you want another one?"

"I don't want another one. I want a bigger one."

Her eyes widened. "Bigger than the one next door?"

"I have a plan."

Somehow, she didn't have a hard time believing that. He seemed the type who had a plan for everything, smiling right along, and all the while the wheels were turning.

She eyed him coolly. "What kind of plan?"

"I want to knock it down."

Lily stared at him. He hadn't batted an eye when he said it. "Knock it . . . down?"

"I'm an architect," he said, as if that explained everything. "I was halfway through building the one next door when I got an idea for a new design, a bigger and better design. I want to knock them both down and start over. But I'll need both lots."

"But you just told me you built that house yourself. You haven't even finished the fireplace."

"And I won't have to if you sell me the cottage."

"I don't understand." And she really didn't. "How can you think of knocking something down that you built with your own two hands?"

"It's just a house."

The response stunned her, or maybe it was just the cavalier way he'd said it. "It wouldn't crush you to destroy a house you designed and built yourself?"

"Not if I'm building something better. And it would be. I've actually had my eye on this property for years. I tried to grab it when I bought the lot next door."

His answer surprised her. "You wanted to buy Sand Pearl Cottage?"

"Not the cottage, the property. But your aunt's attorney wouldn't even talk to me. Said she wasn't interested in selling. So I settled for the single lot. Then, halfway through the build, I heard she died. Sorry, not to be morbid, but I never knew your aunt, so I thought, *Here's my chance.* But when I called to inquire, I was told the property wasn't for sale, that it had reverted to a family member. And now here you are."

"My father," Lily said flatly.

"I'm sorry?"

"The family member it reverted to was my father. He died two weeks ago."

Dean closed his eyes, shook his head. "I'm sorry. I didn't realize... Damn it. Were you close?"

"Pretty close, yes."

"I didn't mean to sound callous, really. I forget how it is with some families."

Some families?

If possible, Lily found the remark even more bizarre than his intention to bulldoze his own house. Were there families in which death *didn't* elicit sadness? She tried not to think of her mother as she scooped up an armload of soup and carried it to the panty.

"So, where's home?" he asked, clearly trying to fill the sudden awkwardness.

Lily pondered the question as she stacked her soup cans onto the pantry shelves, particularly the way it had been phrased. Most people said *Where are you from?* or *Where do you live?* Those were easy questions, with neat, factual answers. But he hadn't asked her either of those, and she found herself groping for a response. Paris wasn't home. It was where she'd gone to school, where she'd worked for years, made friends, met Luc. But it had never felt like home. And what of New York? She'd given up her apartment, lost touch with her friends. With her father gone there was nothing there for her, either. The realization startled her.

"I was born in New York," she said finally. "But I've been living in Paris on and off for the last nine years. It's where I went to school. I've worked there pretty much ever since. And now I'm off to Milan."

"What do you do that takes you to all these exotic locales?"

"I'm a fashion designer."

"Ah, we're in related professions, then."

Lily cocked her head, curious and confused. "I design clothes. You design houses. How is that related?"

"We both design things people live in."

"That's a bit of a stretch, don't you think?"

"Not at all. Clothes and houses have a lot in common. They're both about image."

"And comfort," Lily added pointedly. "They should be about comfort, too. Not just image."

Dean nodded, conceding her point. "Comfort. Sure. Now—back to business. We were talking about you selling me this place."

"Were we? I don't remember that part."

He was annoying, but fascinating, too, with his odd mix of brashness and charm. The box-office smile didn't hurt, either. And yet there was something just a little too self-assured about him, like someone used to getting what he wanted.

"Okay, I was talking about it. But I believe you were about to say yes."

"Was I really?"

His smile dimmed, becoming more businesslike, polite with just a hint of condescension. "You're sitting on a very valuable piece of property, one that will net you a nice piece of change."

She was annoyed now, growing tired of his sales patter. "I don't need change, Mr. Landry."

"Everyone needs change, Ms. St. Claire. Even daughters with trust funds."

Lily felt her hackles rise. All this time, he'd been baiting her, never once letting on that he knew who she was—or rather, who her father was. He'd been waiting to use it, like an ambush.

"Is this how you generally conduct business, Mr. Landry? A charm offensive, followed by a wrecking ball?"

"I'm sorry," he said, as if genuinely surprised that he'd offended her. "I just assumed—and maybe I shouldn't have—that this place wouldn't exactly be your cup of tea. I thought—hoped, actually—that you'd be eager to dump it. I'm not looking for a bargain or anything. I'm willing to pay fair market value. For the land, that is. The cottage isn't of any value to me, obviously."

Lily shot him a too-sweet smile. "Oh, obviously."

"Was I wrong? Because if I was, and you're planning to stick around, I'd be happy to help you get the place in shape. It needs some TLC, and I'm guessing a ton of structural stuff—roof, deck, probably the electrical, some plumbing—but there's lots of potential, and I've been known to come in handy. I'm also a pretty fair tour guide if you're looking for someone to show you Hideaway Key's finer points."

He was flashing that smile again, all teeth and boy-next-door charm, and hoping to discourage her with a daunting list of repairs. The problem was, he was right on point. She wasn't going to be here long. It didn't make sense to hang on to the place if she was going to be half a world away. So why not make Dean Landry's day and name her price?

For starters, she had no idea what a fair price would be. But mostly, it had to do with the fact that she couldn't bear the thought of a bulldozer smashing something that had been a gift from her father. It also had to do with a little girl and a magazine clipping, with secrets, and feuds, and an unsent letter. Everyone had a story, and Lily-Mae's was here somewhere, in cardboard boxes and silver trinkets, even in the simple jar of shells displayed on her bureau. There would be plenty of time to decide the cottage's fate, but not before she knew a little something about the woman who had called it home.

"Mr. Landry—"

"Please, call me Dean."

"Dean—I really haven't decided what I'm going to do with the cottage, but at the moment you are wasting your time. I am not easily daunted, and I don't rush decisions. When and if I decide to sell I'll be sure to let you know."

Dean's smile never faltered. "I'll take that as my cue, then. If you change your mind I'll be next door." He turned away, stepping out onto the deck, apparently planning to take the back stairs. At the last minute, he stuck his head back in. "My offer still stands, by the way, about being your tour guide."

He saluted her then, with a smart click of his heels, and disappeared down the steps. It didn't dawn on her until he was gone that she'd forgotten to thank him for bringing in her groceries.

FIVE

Lily felt like a child on Christmas morning: curious, excited, and just a little afraid that she would end up disappointed. She wasn't sure what she expected the box to contain, but as she dragged back the flaps and stared at the jumbled contents she found herself more surprised than anything else.

They were a child's things, worthless to all but the one who had packed them away. One by one, she lifted them out—a handful of old lesson books bound together with twine, a small Bible in scuffed red calfskin, a rag doll missing one black button eye, a scarred leather picture frame that opened like a book.

It was the rag doll that captured her interest first. Its very presence told Lily it had been precious once, but there was something forlorn about its flaccid limbs and blank expression, faded after so many years into near nothingness. It had had a name once, lost now after so many years, had been carried everywhere, a beloved friend and confidant. Suddenly, the idea of tossing the poor thing back in the box seemed unthinkable. Instead, she propped the doll against the bedside lamp, neatly crossing its arms and legs.

Next, she picked up the frame. It felt fragile as she laid it open on her lap, the left side vacant, missing its small pane of glass, the right side still intact and in possession of its old black-and-white photo. Lily stared at the tiny family, faded with age and beginning to yellow, recognizing the youngest subjects instantly. Despite the obvious difference in ages—somewhere around six and ten—the girls looked uncannily alike, and far too much like Lily had as a child to be anyone but Caroline and Lily-Mae. Which meant the adults in the photo were her grandparents.

Lily ran a thumb over the glass. It was strange to think of them as real. Aside from the fact that they'd lived somewhere in Tennessee, Caroline had never spoken of her parents—not their names, or fates, or anything at all. Now, suddenly, she was staring at them. The woman was beautiful, but there was a melancholy quality in the large, deep-set eyes, a hint of discontent that reminded her eerily of Caroline. The man's face, too, seemed to tell a story, his expression rigid and resentful, as if he'd rather be anywhere in the world than where he was at that moment.

Working the photograph free, she scanned the back for names, a date—anything that might give her an idea when or where it had been taken. There was nothing. After replacing the photo, she folded the frame closed and set it aside, wondering what it said about the sisters, that one had held on to these things—childhood things, family things—while the other had spent decades trying to erase that part of her life.

She picked up the Bible next, a palm-size New Testament covered in coarse red leather. There was an inscription on the front page, so thin and badly slanted Lily had to squint to make it out.

To Lily-Mae Boyle.
Baptized June 14th, 1952.
May God bless and keep you.
Mama

Mama.

Lily sounded the word over and over in her head, letting the feelings it conjured wash over her. Warmth. Family. Love. Had her mother used the term as a child? It was hard to imagine—impossible, actually. From Lily's earliest memory, Caroline had insisted on the more formal *Mother.* Cool. Distant. Loveless.

Banishing the thought, Lily returned to the Bible, flipping idly through tissue-thin pages until she came across one that had been neatly folded down. Near the bottom, on the right-hand side of the page, a passage had been underlined.

Blessed be ye poor: for yours is the kingdom of God.

Had the underlining been the work of Lily-Mae, or her mama? There was no way to know, but the passage—the only one marked, as far as Lily could see—hinted at rather humble beginnings, circumstances that, if true, her mother had not only managed to conceal but had gone out of her way to reverse. It never occurred to her that Caroline St. Claire—polished to the point of hauteur—hadn't always traveled in the best circles, worn the finest clothes, and spent her summers abroad.

It was starting to occur to her now, though. In fact, it was starting to make a great deal of sense. Could all of it—the rancor, the arguments, the refusal to even mention her sister's name—boil down to selfishness and pride? A need to distance herself from a less-than-rosy childhood and a beautiful sister with a past? It boggled the mind, though perhaps not as much as it should have.

Aren't families wonderful?

Dean's words floated into her head. They had seemed harsh at the time, but at that moment Lily was inclined to agree with him. Glancing at her watch, she was surprised to find it nearly eleven o'clock. No wonder she was wrung out. Half her brain was still on Paris time; the other half was running on empty after having stayed up half the night dissecting Lily-Mae's unsent letter. And to top it all off, she'd skipped dinner.

Lily eyed the final item in the box with waning curiosity, weighing her need for food against her need for sleep. There was tomorrow, after all, and a bundle of grammar school notebooks wasn't likely to shed much light on a grown-up feud between sisters. Still, they had meant something to her aunt, or she wouldn't have bothered to keep them. Sighing, she reached for the stack and tugged the twine knot free, sending the notebooks tumbling onto the spread.

They were the old-fashioned kind, mottled black-and-white cover with a strip of black cloth tape running down the spine. On the nameplate of each, the name Lily-Mae Boyle appeared in loopy schoolgirl script. Lifting one from the pile, she turned to the first page, expecting lists of vocabulary words, or strings of math problems. Instead, she found herself looking at what appeared to be the carefully penned lines of a young girl's diary.

SIX

July 17, 1953
Mt. Zion Missionary Poor Farm

It's been a month now since Mama packed that suitcase and drove me and Caroline to Mt. Zion. I didn't let myself cry as I watched her drive away. She made me promise to be brave, and to look after Caroline. So that's what I was doing. I was being brave. Or at least pretending to be.

Mama's had her hands full lately, well, for a long time really, with Daddy being gone so much. It wasn't new, him going off. He'd stay gone for weeks at a time, sometimes even months. Then one day the sheriff came knocking on the door. He told Mama that Daddy'd gone and gotten himself shot for cheating at cards, and that he wouldn't be coming back. That's when everything went bad, when Mama got lonely and the bourbon took hold of her.

She used to be pretty—so pretty men's heads would turn when she passed them on the street. Then she took to drinking, staying out nights, getting up later and later. It was up to me to get Caroline out of bed, to get her fed and make sure she got herself to school. I didn't mind, but Caroline did. All of a sudden it was as if we weren't sisters anymore. She didn't get why I was always bossing her around and acting like her mama. She was too young to understand that her real mama couldn't be there for her.

And now we're here—and Mama's not.

She's gone off to find a new husband, someone to take care of us while she gets well. She promised to write, but it's been weeks and we haven't had a single letter. Maybe finding a husband's going to be harder than she thought. Lord knows she never had much luck at home, except for Daddy—not that she didn't try. She tried and tried and tried. I just wish she'd hurry. Mt. Zion isn't a nice place.

I worry a lot, mostly about my promise to look after Caroline. I don't think I'm doing a very good job. All she does is cry and tote that stupid doll around everywhere she goes. Chessie. It's a silly name for a doll, but that's what she calls it now. I don't know what she wants with the silly thing anyway. It's only got one eye, and its hair's all ratty. But then, it was already in bad shape when Mama made me give it over—and I'm pretty sure it wasn't new when she first gave it to me. One day I'll buy Caroline a new doll, a real one, with glass eyes and shiny hair, and then maybe she'll stop crying.

I don't blame her for being sad. I'm sad, too, though I try not to let her see. I miss home. I miss my books, and the room I shared with Caroline, the one with the window that looked out over that slimy old pond. Here, we're crammed into small wooden houses called dorms, ten beds to a room, with one bathroom to share—like Noah's Ark, only hotter, I expect, and without the rain.

It hasn't rained a lick since we got here. Everything's covered with a fine yellow grit. It blows in through the screens, gets in my bed and in my hair, until I swear I can taste it at the back of my throat. Sometimes I think I'll always taste it, no matter how far I ever get from this god-awful place. And one day I will get away.

When Mama comes.

The days are long and blistering hot, especially if you work in the laundry. That's where they put Caroline and me. It's where most of the young girls work. The older ones and the women go to the kitchen. We're up before the sun. I hear the crickets sometimes, still singing while I dress and wash my face. Then, the minute breakfast is over, we're up to our elbows in sheets, and towels, and uniforms from the prison over in Ransom. That's where we stay until supper. The boys and men work in the barns, or out in the fields. Everyone works here.

It's atonement, Brother Zell tells us from his pulpit on Sundays, for the sin of being poor. Harwood Zell is the superintendent of Mt. Zion. He says poverty's a disease that can only be cured by hard work and repentance, but that doesn't sound quite right to me. Mama never was one for church, but she made us go to Sunday school every week, and I don't recall them ever teaching us anything like that on Sunday mornings. In my Bible it says "blessed are the poor," but maybe Brother Zell skipped over that part.

I don't understand him saying we need to repent of being poor. I never met a living soul—here at Mt. Zion, or anywhere else—that didn't already repent of being poor. Not that it ever did them much good. It seems to me that poverty isn't a disease at all, but more like a defect a person's born with, like a harelip or a clubfoot. It marks you, so that for as long as you live folks'll know you're poor, and do their level best to keep you that way. That's what Daddy used to say anyway.

Sister Ruth is in charge of the women. That's Brother Zell's wife. She's thin as a broomstick, all elbows and shoulder blades, with a face like an old pickle. She doesn't like me. I can see it when she looks me up and down—like she just got a whiff of the chicken coop. I don't know what I ever did, or didn't do, to make her look at me like she does, but I can tell she's itching to bring me down a peg, so I'm careful not to give her a reason. I keep to myself and do my work, and Caroline's, too, if she falls behind, which she does most days. You get punished here if you don't get your work done.

At least there's plenty to eat—unless you get in trouble. Then they cut your rations. Or they send you to clean out the chicken coops, where the smell's so bad you retch the whole time. But there's one more punishment—the one no one wants—and that's getting sent to work in the slaughter barn. That's why most of us do what we're told.

There's no proper schooling, and no books, either—except for the Bible and the notebooks they give us to practice our sums and letters. We're not likely to make much of ourselves, they tell us, and so we don't really need more than that. I don't use my notebooks for sums, though. I use mine to scribble down things I want to get out of my head, like I've done since the day the sheriff came about Daddy. Not that I have much time, or much privacy. Lights go out at nine. But sometimes, when the moon is high, I can see enough to scribble a few lines—like now. I don't think I could bear this place without my notebooks. I think the misery of it might swallow me up.

I don't sleep much anymore. Instead, I lie awake, listening to the night sounds coming through the screens, wondering how they can sound so much like home when everything else is so different. And then, every night, comes the creak of Caroline's bedsprings, and I know she can't sleep, either. A minute later she's beside me, burrowing in like a tick, her face pressed into the crook of my neck, like she used to when she was a tiny thing. We drift off that way, my arm around her little body, hers around Chessie until she finally whimpers herself to sleep.

On Sundays there's church, and a half day off. That's when the families come to visit—those lucky enough to have families. That's the hardest day, Sunday. But it used to be the best day, when Mama would cook breakfast, and Caroline and I would play dress-up, or take a picnic down to the pond, back when she used to let me call her Bitsy.

It's not like that between us anymore. It started when I changed schools, and then the boys started coming around. It's even worse now that we're here. She pouts most of the time, always mumbling that this or that isn't fair. I can't fault her for it, but I'm scared sometimes that Mt. Zion will leave a bitter taste in her mouth, that it will end up tainting her somehow, if it hasn't already.

Poor thing. She's never really had anything of her own, nothing that wasn't some kind of charity. Her clothes, Chessie—even Mama—belonged to me first, and were all a little worse for wear by the time they got to her. Especially Mama. I had the best of her, while poor Bitsy wound up with the leftovers. I'm not sure she'll ever forgive me for that, or that she even knows she blames me for it. She does, though, and I don't know how to make it right.

February 4, 1954

Mt. Zion Missionary Poor Farm

I've started to think Mama's never coming back. It's only been eight months, but it feels like I've never lived anywhere else, like I was born here, and like maybe I'll die here. And people do die here.

Cindy Price died here.

Cindy was my friend, or as close to a friend as you can have in a place like Mt. Zion. She was a year older than me, and was here two years longer. She came with her mama, and a little brother named Zeke. She said her daddy went off looking for work and never came back. There's a lot of those stories here. At least she had her mama with her, not that it made much difference in the end. Cindy took sick just before Christmas, something down in her chest that made her bring up blood when she coughed.

They never did call a doctor. Brother Zell wouldn't allow it. But they prayed and prayed over her. Sister Ruth said if the Lord's will was for her to be healed, then she would be. If not, she'd meet her maker, and no doctor could change it, so why waste good money? It made me sick, all that talk about God's will. What had Cindy ever done to make God turn his back? And all the while she's coughing and wasting away in the infirmary. They let me see her twice, but that last time I don't think she even knew me. She'd gone a funny color and her breathing sounded like a rusty saw. I don't know if there's a God or not, but I knew as sure as I stood there that day, that if there was, he had already made up his mind about Cindy.

No one told me when it happened, or that they'd already put her in the ground. Only her mama and Zeke were allowed to go when they buried her, but I snuck out there later, when someone finally did tell me. There's a field out behind the slaughter barn. It's all scrub with no trees, just rows and rows of whitewashed wooden crosses with numbers instead of names. The names and numbers are written in a book that Sister Ruth keeps in her husband's office. I didn't know what number they gave Cindy, but I didn't need to. She was easy to find. I only had to look for the fresh mound of dirt.

I wish Mama would come.

I've been taken from the laundry and moved to the kitchen—away from Caroline. Sister Ruth tries to pretend it's an act of kindness, but I know better. I'm being punished for sneaking out to Cindy's grave. I begged and begged to let Caroline come with me to the kitchen, or for them to leave me where I was, but she wouldn't hear any of it. She got all red in the face, and called me an ungrateful bit of trash, then said maybe I'd like to take the matter up with Brother Zell. I could see by the way she was smiling at me, like she had pinned me in a corner, that she didn't think I'd go. I did, though, the very first chance I got.

It was the first time I'd been to his office. It smelled like stale cigarette smoke, and the fried pork chops he'd just had for lunch. The plate was still on his desk, a half-smoked cigarette crushed out in the cold gray gravy. For a moment, I couldn't look away from that plate, as if everything I needed to know about Harwood Zell was there somehow.

I'm still not sure what it was, maybe the lazy way he looked me up and down with that cigarette dangling from the corner of his mouth, like I was one of those pork chops he'd just eaten, but it made me want to run out of there, and keep right on running. I didn't, though, because of Caroline. Instead, I made myself look him in the eye.

He was dressed all in black—black trousers with a black shirt buttoned up tight against his Adam's apple. Even his suspenders were black. His straw-colored hair was slicked down hard, shiny with tonic, but one lock kept falling forward, like a little bit of himself that refused to be tamped down.

He sucked hard on his cigarette, looking up at me through the smoke with a half smile that made his eyes look piggy. "Sister Ruth says you've been a naughty girl, Lily-Mae. Is that true?"

It wasn't until then that I realized I'd never heard him speak, except from his pulpit on Sundays, when his voice would thunder down into the pews and scare us all to death. But his voice was different now, soft and steely—like a trap. The urge to run was there again, but my legs wouldn't move. I wanted to say I was fifteen, and that fifteen-year-old girls are too old to be called naughty. Instead, I kept my eyes on my shoes, and tried to explain.

"I made a promise, sir, having to do with my sister."

"A promise?"

"Yes, sir, to my mother, the day she brought us here."

"And what was this promise?"

"To look after my little sister until she came back for us. That's why I don't want to go to the kitchen. Because I'd be breaking my promise to look after Caroline."

Brother Zell folded his hands on the desk and looked me over some more, as if he was sizing me up for a new dress. It made me want to cross my arms over my chest, but I didn't. I just stood there, staring at that cigarette butt, drowning in its puddle of gravy.

"She's younger than you, you say?"

I nodded, though I was sure he already knew this. "She's almost thirteen."

"Thirteen. Well, now, that's not so young. I should think she'd be able to get along by herself."

"No, sir. The work is too hard." I had blurted it without thinking, and saw by the look on his face that I had better explain. "She hasn't been herself since we came to Mt. Zion. She misses our mama and wants to go home."

"And what about you, Lily-Mae? Don't you miss your mama?"

"Yes, sir, I do."

"And yet you manage to finish your work, and most of your sister's, too, from what I'm told."

I didn't know what to say to that. Obviously someone had seen me swapping my finished sheets for Caroline's dirty ones, and told Sister Ruth. My stomach knotted as I stood there, wondering what my punishment would be.

But Brother Zell didn't look angry. In fact he was smiling, the grease from his lunch glistening wetly on his lips and chin. "You know," he said, leaning forward to stub out his cigarette. "I've seen you around, in the mess, and at Sunday service, and I can see that deep down you're a good girl. If you've broken any rules it was only to keep your promise."

My legs went rubbery with relief. "I can stay in the laundry with Caroline?"

The greasy smile widened, as if he were about to share some great secret. "I think I know a better way to help you keep your promise, Lily-Mae."

There was something in his voice that kept me from saying

thank you, something that made me feel just a little bit skittish. I waited.

He reached for a pack of cigarettes and lit one, pulling hard on it. "I could see to it that Caroline was sent to the kitchen, where the work is easier. Would you like that?"

"She'd be with me?"

He didn't answer right away. Instead, he blew out a mouthful of smoke, and pointed to the chair across from his desk. I didn't want to sit, but I did as I was told. I could tell something bad was coming, and that maybe I had better be sitting when it did.

He stretched back in his chair and hooked a thumb into his belt. "Actually, I have something else in mind for you. Can you read and write, Lily-Mae?"

I stuck out my chin. "I want to go to the kitchen with Caroline. Or for the both of us to stay in the laundry."

Brother Zell pretended not to hear. He just kept on with that bland smile of his, that smile that all of a sudden didn't feel bland at all. "Are you good with numbers?"

"But you said—"

"I've been thinking lately that I could use a little help here in the office, someone to copy down my sermons, look after the ledgers, that sort of thing. I think you might do nicely."

"Can't Sister Ruth help you with those things?"

His eyes went hard and small, and for a moment I thought I saw the smile slip. "My wife has enough to do, Lily-Mae, looking after our girls, as well as her duties for Mt. Zion. I couldn't possibly ask her to help me here, too. That's why I need you to do me this favor." As he sat up and smashed out his cigarette he locked eyes with me. "And in return, I'd be willing to do you a favor. I'll help you keep your promise."

"How?"

"By seeing to it that you don't have to worry about Caroline. No one will bother her, or count how many potatoes she peels in a day. So long as you're working for me."

"I don't understand."

But somehow I did, and all at once I knew why Sister Ruth had always disliked me. Because she'd always known that someday her husband would ask me this favor, and because she knew there would be no way for me to say no when he did.

July 24, 1954
Mt. Zion Missionary Poor Farm

More than a year now, and still no word from Mama. No letters, either. Every day when the mail truck comes I hurry to the office, but there's never anything with my name on it, and I have to tell Caroline there was nothing again today. Her dislike has begun to harden now, into something deeper and more permanent. I see it in her eyes, in the narrowed looks she throws at me when she thinks I don't see. Because I can't fix this, and because no matter how badly I want to, I can't make Mama come back.

I try all sorts of things to lift her spirits. I make up songs and games, the kind that used to make her laugh. And I talk about the things we'll do when Mama comes and takes us away from here—or I used to, before she stopped believing them. I wonder if it's because she can hear in my voice that I've stopped believing them, too.

And there's something else now, between us. She doesn't say it, but she's mad at me for working in Brother Zell's office while she's stuck in the kitchen, shelling peas and scrubbing pots. She's jealous of the presents, too—the books and candy and hairpins—even though I've never kept a single one for myself. She's happy enough to take them, but they don't make her happy for long. Nothing does.

She thinks I've left her to fend for herself. She doesn't understand that I'm trying to protect her, or that I'd much rather be in the kitchen shelling peas or scrubbing pots than anywhere near Sister Ruth's husband.

It's not the work I mind. I answer the phone and take down his messages, file lots of papers and empty his ashtrays. And there are the ledgers to keep, two full sets, one red and one green, where I record all sorts of payments. Brother Zell's very particular about his ledgers, about them not getting mixed up, and making sure they're always added up properly. He's never said what they're for, or where all the payments come from, and I never ask. The less mind he pays me, the better.

It's not a very Christian thing to say, I know, especially with him being a man of the cloth and all, but I don't like him very much. Or maybe trust is a better word. I don't trust him. He watches me when he thinks I don't know it. And then, when I catch him, he smiles that sly smile of his, like a rat who knows where the cheese is hidden.

And if it isn't Brother Zell studying me, it's his wife. I can hardly turn around these days without finding those sharp gray eyes of hers on me, looking me over like I could use a good scrubbing. She's always hovering, turning up in places she knows I'll be. One night last week I left supper early to go back to the dorm. I was alone when she came in, sitting on the edge of my cot. I don't know if she was surprised to see me there or not, but something told me she knew good and well I'd be there, like maybe she'd followed me on purpose.

I was sewing a button onto one of Caroline's dresses. I didn't look up from my needle. I didn't want to meet her gaze. She has a way of making me feel like I should be apologizing for something. But I could feel her standing there, just watching. It was her way of letting me know there was nothing I, or anyone else, could ever hide from her. But I already knew that. Everyone knew that.

I'm just glad she didn't catch me with my notebook. I wouldn't like her reading the things I've written about her husband, like how he hides behind that big black Bible on his desk, pretending to be all pious and godly while there's something not quite right about all those ledgers, or how it seems fishy that he makes me leave the room when certain people call.

Not that she doesn't already know those things about her husband—she does. It's me knowing them that she wouldn't like. She knows her husband's sins same as Mama knew Daddy's, because that's how it is with married folk. She knows, but she'll protect what's hers. And somehow I knew as she stood there, that that was exactly what she was doing. Protecting what was hers—and sending me a warning.

SEVEN

1995
Hideaway Key, Florida

Chessie—the doll's name was Chessie.

Lily came awake with a start, feeling gritty and drained and a little dismayed that for a second straight night she'd slept in her clothes. She had pored over the notebooks until well past two, devouring entries until she no longer had the heart to read what came next. A dead father, an alcoholic mother who casually abandoned her daughters in order to catch herself a new husband. What was she supposed to make of it all?

Mt. Zion.

She'd never heard of the place, or of Harwood Zell, but Lily-Mae had painted a clear enough picture. How had her mother never spoken of such a horrid place? Or of being abandoned by her own mother? And what of Lily-Mae? She had submitted to the attentions of a predator in order to protect her sister, only to have that sister end up despising her.

It was inconceivable, and yet there it all was, written in Lily-Mae's own hand. And there was more. She eyed the remaining three notebooks, stacked beside Chessie on the nightstand. For as long as she could remember, she had wanted, perhaps even needed, to understand the broken relationship between her mother and aunt. Maybe it had to do with being an only child, one who had always longed for a sister of her own. Or maybe it was a need to understand the mother who had raised her from a distance, who claimed to love her, but had always done so at arm's length. Whatever her reason, it seemed the answer to her questions might be within reach, threaded through the unread pages of Lily-Mae's diaries—if she had the stomach to know the rest. And she wasn't sure she did, at least not before giving her mother a chance to fill in the blanks for herself.

Slipping off the bed, she padded to the old beige slimline phone she had seen on the desk, praying as she lifted the handset that the thing was still working. This wasn't the kind of call she wanted to make from a pay phone. She breathed a sigh of relief when she heard the dial tone, then another of frustration when the answering machine picked up after four rings—her mother's voice, cool and Tennessee-free, promising to return the call at her earliest convenience. Of course. It was Friday. She'd be on her way to play bridge with the ladies at the club.

"It's Lily," she said curtly when the beep finally ended. "I was going through some boxes at the cottage, childhood things of Lily-Mae's. There are some things . . . some questions. I'm sure you know what I'm talking about. Call me at this number as soon as you get my message."

She could only imagine her mother's reaction when she returned home later this afternoon and checked her machine. She wouldn't be happy, that much was certain. When it came to questions about Lily-Mae, Caroline St. Claire was a master of obfuscation, dodging questions outright when she could, and resorting to the smoke screen of innuendo when she couldn't. Well, not this time. This time she would be armed with cold, hard facts. This time she'd finally get the truth. In the meantime, maybe she'd take the new bikini out for a spin.

Twenty minutes later, she was making her way cautiously toward the water's edge, reminding herself for the third time that this part of the beach was private. She wasn't going to run into anyone she knew, or anyone she didn't, for that matter. Sadly, that didn't keep her from feeling ridiculously conspicuous—a ghost-white tourist in a tell-all bikini, grappling with a straw hat she could barely keep on her head.

By the time she finally got her blanket spread out and her beach bag unpacked, she was out of breath, sticky with sweat, and wondering why anyone in their right mind would come to the beach for rest and relaxation. Though she had to admit, she liked the idea of having an entire beach to herself. No noise. No intrusions. Just the sea and the sun. In fact, if she wasn't careful, she could get used to this.

She scanned the shoreline to the north, hazy with sea spray and the shimmer of hot sands, as she began slathering on sunscreen. From beneath the brim of her hat, she was able to make out a man in bright blue trunks, romping with what appeared to be a very large yellow dog. She watched them for a moment, playing catch at the water's edge with a heavy stick, the man hurling the stick far out into the waves, the dog plunging in after it. It was hard to tell who was having more fun.

Wiping the slippery goo from her hands, she eased back onto her blanket, trying not to imagine what her mother would say if she could see her now, stretched out in the sun like some sort of a sacrificial offering. Freckles—the curse of every redhead—were the one lesson her mother had ever bothered to teach her. Freckles were not beautiful. Freckles came from the sun. Therefore, the sun was the enemy.

Caroline St. Claire knew a little something about beauty, though she'd never been the celebrated beauty her sister was. It was one of the few things Lily actually did know about Lily-Mae, that her likeness had once been plastered on billboards and in magazines, the iconic face of some beauty cream or other. And even that, she had learned by accident—if you counted snooping and eavesdropping as accidents. And now she was snooping again, this time in the pages of a young girl's diary.

Rolling onto her belly, she propped herself up on her elbows and reached for the notebook in her beach bag, opening to where she'd left off the night before. She stared at the neatly penned lines, noting the subtle evolution of the handwriting over time. The letters were less loopy in this third notebook, thinner and more elongated, but still sloped noticeably. Even the words felt less childlike. And why wouldn't they? She was telling things no child should ever know, let alone live through. Things even Lily wasn't sure she was ready to know. But she needed to know them. If for no other reason than they had shaped her mother's life, as well as her aunt's, and might finally answer so many questions. About her mother, her aunt, and perhaps even her father.

Her aunt and her father.

The thought bobbed to the surface like a bit of old wreckage, begging to be examined. Was it possible? That Lily-Mae had once been interested in Roland was no secret. Whether her father ever returned that interest, however, had always been less clear. If asked, her mother would say no, but Roland St. Claire was a man, presumably as susceptible to the charms of a beautiful woman as the next red-blooded male—and Lily-Mae had been nothing if not beautiful. Was it possible that more than a flirtation had arisen between them? The kind of thing that smoldered quietly, and made wives and sisters jealous? It would certainly explain Caroline's hatred of Lily-Mae, and might explain Lily-Mae leaving Roland the cottage, as a remembrance of the affection they once felt for each other. But when? Before or after he had married Caroline?

An affair.

It was hard to imagine, and not just because pairing the words *father* and *infidelity* made her squirm. Roland St. Claire wasn't the champagne-and-roses type—or the philandering type, either. He was married to his work, to his trusts and his foundations, too busy conferencing, or organizing, or traveling on business, to get bogged down in matters of the heart. In fact, she often wondered if that was why he had married her mother. In Caroline, he had chosen a wife as romantically detached as himself, a partner who would play the part but never ask for more than he was able to give.

Had she been a compromise, then? A woman who looked like Lily-Mae but would make no demands on his heart? The possibility wasn't at all far-fetched, and it certainly brought the animosity between the sisters into a new light. The question was how to broach these suspicions with her mother.

Lily was still wrestling with the question when she felt a sudden coolness steal across her bare back, as if a cloud had drifted in front of the sun. Shoving back the brim of her hat, she turned to peer over one shoulder. Dean Landry stood grinning down at her, bare-chested and soaking wet in a pair of bright blue board shorts. The yellow dog at his side grinned at her, wagging from head to tail.

Damn.

She had enough on her mind without having to dodge a man whose sole purpose in being friendly was to get his hands on the cottage. She thought she'd made herself clear. If and when she decided to sell, she'd be sure to let him know. Until then, she preferred he keep his distance—and keep his charm to himself.

"Studying for a vocabulary test?" he asked, pointing at the notebook in her hand.

Lily closed the notebook and tucked it out of sight. "It belonged to my aunt. Who's your friend?"

"This drowned rat?" He paused, giving the damp yellow head a pat. "This is Dog."

Lily sat up, frowning. "That's his name? Dog?"

"I figured it was as good as anything else, and he answers to it, so . . ."

"Seriously? You couldn't come up with something more creative than Dog?"

"I suppose I could have, if I'd meant to keep him, which I didn't. He showed up one day at one of the job sites, a mangy rack of bones bumming lunch scraps off the crew. I asked around but no one knew where he belonged, so one day I loaded him in the truck and took him home. The plan was to give him a bath, fatten him up, then palm him off on one of the construction guys, but he sort of got comfortable in the meantime. He doesn't eat much, so I figured why not?"

"How long ago was that?"

"Four years, give or take."

"So maybe it's time?"

"Time for what?"

"To give him a proper name." Lily reached out, giving one blond ear a scratch. "He's a handsome boy. He deserves better than plain old *Dog*, don't you think?"

Another shrug. "Never thought much about it. But honestly, I don't think he cares who he belongs to or what I call him, as long as there's food in his dish. Names are just words we stick on things so we can pretend they belong to us."

Names are just words?

Lily fought to keep her face blank. He'd done it again: dropped another curious one-liner into a perfectly normal conversation. Yesterday it had been about families. Today it was names. Who didn't believe in names, for crying out loud? And as for Dog not caring who he belonged to, one had only to look at that wagging tail and those adoring brown eyes to know exactly who the poor thing belonged to.

She looked up at him, silhouetted against the bright blue sky, letting her gaze linger on broad wet shoulders, a flat expanse of tan, taut belly. After a moment, she dragged her eyes back to his face. She didn't have time for distractions, especially one that looked like Dean Landry.

"Did you need something?"

Dean ignored the question. "You do realize you won't get much sun wearing that hat?"

Lily lifted the hat briefly, pointing to her ponytail. "Redhead, remember? We don't tan; we burst into flames. Or freckles, which, according to my mother, is a far worse fate."

"I see. That explains the SPF fifty-six, I guess. So why drag all this stuff out here if you're not working on your tan?"

"Would you believe I wanted to soak up a little of the local ambiance?"

"Sure I would. Best beaches in the state, right here. But you'll need more sunscreen if you're going to be here three weeks. Sun's pretty intense this time of the year. Nice suit, by the way. Very . . . flattering."

Lily resisted the urge to drag the blanket up around her. He was doing it again. Fishing for answers, hanging around where he wasn't wanted—and flirting. She chose not to play along. "I doubt I'll have much time for sunbathing. I was just taking a break to finish up some reading before I dive into the boxes."

Dean sent Dog off to amuse himself, then dropped down beside her. "So you still don't know what's in them?"

Lily thought about pointing out that she hadn't invited him to sit but decided against it. "Not yet, no. Except for the one I found under the bed yesterday. It was full of stuff from my aunt's childhood—from my mother's childhood, too, I guess. A beat-up old rag doll, a handful of notebooks, and a family photo I've never seen."

"Sounds like a lot of crap, if you ask me."

"I didn't," Lily shot back tersely. "And even if it is crap, it's my crap now, and my responsibility. Whatever it is, my aunt obviously had her reasons for holding on to it. Though I have to admit, this isn't what I expected when I hopped in my car and headed south."

"I'll bet. But I'm confused. She's your aunt, right? Your mother's sister? So how come you got nominated to pack up her stuff? How is this your deal, and not hers?"

Lily's gaze slid to the shoreline, where Dog was playing tag with the waves, the waterlogged stick still clamped between his teeth. How *had* this become her deal? The truth was she'd been asking herself that question since she arrived. Feud or no feud, why wasn't Caroline here, helping sort through the remnants of her sister's life?

Beside her, Dean shifted on the blanket, a subtle reminder that he was still there and still waiting for an answer.

"That's an interesting question," she said finally, and perhaps a little bitterly. "It's my deal because my mother and Lily-Mae hadn't spoken in over thirty years. I don't know what happened between them. My mother refuses to talk about it. And she hates that my father left the cottage to me. We had a huge fight before I left. She didn't want me to keep it, or to even come here."

"Why?"

"I don't know. I think that's why I came, actually. Because she was so dead set against it. It made me want to know what the big deal was. I just had no idea what I was getting myself into."

"Would it have mattered if you had?"

Lily thought about that, about the work that lay ahead of her, along with the very real possibility that at the end of three weeks she wouldn't know anything more than she did right now. Finally, she shook her head. "No, I don't think it would have. I would still have come. I've been fascinated with her all my life—my aunt, I mean—because that's what you do when grown-ups tell you something's off-limits. You obsess until you figure it out. Except I never have. So I guess that's why I'm here. To figure it out."

"Can you do that in three weeks?"

Lily shrugged. "I haven't a choice. I report to Milan at the end of the month."

"You make it sound like a prison sentence."

"I just meant I won't have a lot of free time between now and then."

"What about Paris? Won't you miss it?"

"No," Lily said flatly. "Sometimes you just need to move on—and I did."

"Okay, I'm intrigued. Why?"

Lily shrugged. "I was restless."

"Restless?"

"I wasn't thrilled with work, and there was this guy I was seeing—sort of. Things started to get messy."

"With the job, or the guy?"

Lily looked away, wondering how she'd let the conversation become so personal. "The guy," she answered finally. "But job-wise I was ready, too." She paused, drawing a deep breath and holding it a moment before letting it go. "People hailed my father as a financial genius—the man with the Midas touch—and he was. What they don't know is he only took on projects he could pour his heart into, things he felt really passionate about. I loved him for that. And here I am designing clothes no real woman will ever wear. I swear, sometimes I can't even remember why I went into fashion." She looked up, suddenly sheepish. "Do you ever feel that way? Like you can't remember why you do what you do?"

Dean shook his head. "I can't say I do. I don't need to love what I design. Only my clients do. Nothing against passion—believe me, it has its place—but for me that place has nothing to do with work. Work is a means to an end, a way to keep moving forward, to get to the next thing."

The next thing.

He sounded so cool when he said it, so matter-of-fact. But what if you weren't sure what the next thing was supposed to be? She was about to voice the thought when a low but ominous rumble interrupted. She shot a glance at the sky, noting the bank of dark clouds stacked up on the horizon. When had that happened?

Dog was suddenly at Dean's side, panting anxiously. Dean gave him a reassuring pat, then jerked a thumb at the sky. "Looks like we're in for a doozy. They don't always make it to shore, but this one's coming fast. Best pack up."

Lily wasted no time in gathering her things, tossing them haphazardly into the beach bag. Another rumble sounded, accompanied by a sharp blast of wind. She grabbed for her hat just in time. "What in the world? It was sunny a few minutes ago."

Dean shot her a wry smile. "Welcome to Florida. I'm guessing it must be three o'clock, or pretty close to it. They don't last long, but you can just about set your watch by them. You'll get used to it." He grabbed the other end of the blanket as she shook it out. "We'd better make a run for it. See there, just past the jetty? That's rain, and it's going to be here any minute. It won't hurt you, but the lightning might."

Lily dragged off the straw hat and stuffed it into her bag, then followed Dean's finger to the blurred horizon. He was right. They were about to get soaked—if they didn't get electrocuted first. A fork of blue lightning split the sky, accompanied by a crack of thunder so sharp it shook the sand beneath their feet.

"Your mail," Dean hollered over the rising wind.

Lily shoved the hair out of her eyes. "What?"

"Your mail. That's what I came over to tell you. I have some of your mail at my place, delivered by mistake. I came across it again this morning. Follow me over and I'll give it to you."

Lily glanced at the sky, at the curtain of rain inching steadily closer. "Can't it wait? You just said it's going to come down any minute."

Dean shrugged, a gesture she was already beginning to recognize as habit. "Your call. Most of it's probably junk mail, but it seemed like there might have been some personal stuff, too. I thought some of it might be important."

Lily thought about that, about who might have been sending Lily-Mae mail at the end of her life, and what kind of mail it might be.

Bills, invitations, or a letter, perhaps? She had to admit the prospect was tempting. The journals spoke to Lily-Mae's early years, but here was a chance, albeit slim, to steal a glimpse of the grown-up Lily-Mae. Hitching the beach bag up onto her shoulder, she turned to follow Dean.

EIGHT

Lily felt awkward as she ducked past Dean through the wide set of sparkling glass doors, keenly aware of her half-naked state despite the beach bag clutched tight to her front. How had she not thought to bring a T-shirt, at least? Goose bumps sprang up instantly along her arms. The place was colder than a meat locker.

She lingered a moment on the sisal mat in front of the door, trying not to appear nosy as she brushed the sand from her feet and covertly took in her surroundings. It was clearly a man's home, stark and no-nonsense, with soaring ceilings and lots of glass and leather. The walls were washed a soft blue-gray, trimmed in a clean, bright white, the perfect choice for a house by the sea, but something was off. The place felt stripped down; not a print or photograph to be seen. In fact, there wasn't a knickknack in sight, nothing remotely personal, like a stage set without the props, everything wide open and pared down—impermanent.

Dean was still out on the deck, giving Dog a quick toweling before letting him inside. When the job was finished he closed the doors, shutting out the thrum of wind and sea. Another crack of thunder sounded, this one so sharp it sent Dog scurrying down the hall. Dean watched him go, shaking his head.

"Poor guy. Four-plus years, and I still haven't been able to train it out of him. He'll be under the bed for the next two hours."

"And you say this happens every day?"

"Just about. Especially in the summer. But they usually blow right over."

Lily eyed the clouds with a prickle of foreboding. She was no expert, but she probably had about five minutes to get what she came for and scoot back to the cottage before the sky opened up. "You said something about mail?"

"Mail. Right. Give me a minute."

He disappeared down the hall, returning moments later wearing jeans and a long-sleeved T-shirt with UNIVERSITY OF FLORIDA COLLEGE OF DESIGN, CONSTRUCTION & PLANNING printed across the front. His alma mater, presumably. He tossed her a similar shirt on his way to the kitchen.

"I figured you were freezing. I like it cold, and you're not wearing much."

She was about to say she wouldn't be staying long enough to need the shirt when the sky suddenly let loose, hurling a noisy sheet of rain against the sliding glass doors. Lily let the beach bag slide to the floor with a little huff of defeat. Unless she wanted to make a run for it—which she didn't—she was stuck until the rain let up.

Lily dragged the shirt on over hear head, then folded back the too-long sleeves. The thing swallowed her almost to the knees, but she was glad for the cover.

"It's here somewhere," Dean called from the kitchen, where he was sorting through a stack of papers. "There's a dozen pieces or so."

Lily went to stand beside him, the rough slate tiles cold on her bare feet. It was an amazing kitchen—dark, sleek granite and lots of stainless steel, a rack of shiny pots and pans suspended over the cooking island. There was a bowl of fruit on the counter, another of onions and garlic beside the stove, along with a block of good knives, and a mortar and pestle. Did he actually cook, or was it just for show? Judging from the living room's blank walls and barren furniture, she decided it must be the former. This man didn't do anything for show.

"Ah, here it is. I was wrong—eleven pieces."

Lily took the stack from him, shuffling through the envelopes almost greedily. Most were white, the generic sort with cellophane windows. Several had been stamped across the front with red ink: PAST DUE. Electric, gas, newspaper subscription. Others were addressed to RESIDENT or OCCUPANT. She thumbed past these, disappointment mounting until she came to the postcard at the bottom of the stack—an oblique shot of the Eiffel Tower on a rain-drenched day. It was stamped *Postes Française, Paris, 26 septembre 1994*—less than a month before Lily-Mae died.

There was a single line scribbled across the back, badly blotched, as if it might have gotten wet somewhere along its travels. She had to squint to make it out—*We'll always have Paris.*

A postcard from Paris. Lily considered the possibilities. An old lover, almost certainly, and one with a fondness for old movies. She hadn't realized people still sent postcards. It made her sad to think this one had traveled all the way across the Atlantic, only to be delivered too late.

Dean peered over her shoulder. "Something important?"

"Something . . . interesting," Lily corrected. "A postcard to my aunt. From Paris." She passed him the card, waiting a moment while he looked it over. "It's not signed."

"With a line like that, the sender wouldn't need to sign it, would he? She would have known who it was from."

"She never got it."

"Obviously. It's been sitting in that drawer since—" He broke off, scanning for a postmark. "Wow, since last September. Sorry. I meant to drop all of it off at the post office, but it fell through the cracks." He handed it back. "Any idea who might have sent it?"

Lily shook her head. "None. But I like thinking that she had a lover, that at the end of her life someone cared for her."

"You got all that from a line on a postcard?"

Lily's eyes widened. "That *line* is from *Casablanca*—only *the* most romantic movie of all time. What else could it mean?"

Dean made a face, a blend of irony and annoyance. "I know where it's from. As I recall, the guy doesn't get the girl at the end of that one. How is that romantic?"

"You're kidding, right? The whole movie is about the sacrifices people make for love, how love transcends time, endures all things."

Dean snorted. "You actually believe all that hoo-ha?"

Lily blinked at him, miffed, though she wasn't sure why. "Are you always so . . ."

"What?"

"*Blunt,* I guess, was the word I was looking for. You just blurt out whatever you're thinking, whether it's appropriate or not. It's like you have no filter."

He shrugged unapologetically. "It's a valid question. Why not ask it? Besides, I'm curious. Do you?"

"Do I what?"

"Believe what you just said—about love transcending all things?"

Lily set down the postcard and turned to stare out the window. Beyond the window, the beach was a warped and watery blur, the steady thrum of rain against the glass strangely melancholy. She thought of Lily-Mae, of Catherine Earnshaw, wandering through storms, bereft.

"I don't know," she said at last. "For some, maybe. I've never seen it myself, but someone must have, or people wouldn't make such a big deal out of it. Or maybe it's like the unicorn—a beautiful idea that's purely mythical."

Dean opened the fridge, pulled out two beers, twisted off both caps, and handed her one. "I vote for the myth. We believe it when we're young, because we want to. And then we grow up. Some of us sooner than others."

Lily took a slow sip of her beer as she processed Dean's last statement. "You grew up sooner, I take it?"

"You might say that. My mother left the week I turned thirteen. Took off with some guy she met at the garage after she banged up our car."

"I'm sorry."

Dean waved off the sentiment as he tipped back his bottle. "I was fine, but my dad fell apart."

The blithe response took Lily by surprise. "It must have been hard on you both," she said quietly, studying his face for some sign of a chink in his armor. If there was one, he hid it well.

When he spoke again his voice was strangely flat, as if he were talking about a stranger. "He never got over it. For a while I think he actually believed she was coming back. Then, when he finally figured it out, he started dragging out the vacation slides and the wedding photos. I'd come home and there'd he'd be, sitting in the dark, smoking and crying. After a while, he stopped caring about anything. To this day I'm not sure he knows I've moved out."

Lily took another sip of beer, mostly because she didn't know what to say. Something in his manner had changed, as if he'd flipped a switch and turned something off. It wasn't the first time she'd sensed it, but she was beginning to understand now. He'd been abandoned as a child, physically by his mother and emotionally by his father, and he was most certainly not fine about it, no matter what he liked to pretend.

"Is he alive?" she asked gently.

"He lives in Delray Beach, on the other side of the state."

"And your mother? Is she alive, too?"

Dean's shoulders bunched briefly. "No idea. We never heard from her again. My father couldn't have divorced her if he wanted to. Which he didn't, of course."

"So they're still married?"

"Maybe. I really don't know. She may be dead."

"You're not . . . curious?"

"Curious?" He repeated the word with something like surprise. "No, I don't think *curious* is the right word for what I am."

"Angry, then?"

"I'm numb," he said simply. "I quit giving a damn a long time ago."

"You're sure about that?"

"The rain's letting up," he noted, with a nod toward the window.

"Right. You don't want to talk about it."

"Only because there's nothing left to say. How about I whip us up a late lunch instead? You can tell me about Milan."

Lily set her beer in the sink, then crossed the room to retrieve her beach bag. "Thanks, but I really can't. I've got three weeks and a cottage full of boxes, remember?"

"We could grab dinner later on, then? Boxes or no boxes, you have to eat."

Dinner? Like a date?

Lily groped for an excuse. She didn't have time for a date. Lily-Mae's notebooks were waiting. And the postcard from France. Just the thought had her sifting through the possibilities. It might have been sent by someone she met on holiday, a dashing Frenchman who had instantly fallen victim to Lily-Mae's beauty. The message was in English, but that didn't necessarily exclude a Frenchman . . .

"Dinner, then?"

Lily blinked at him. "What?"

"I asked if you wanted to grab dinner." Dean ducked his head, looking sheepish suddenly. "One of the reasons—okay, the *real* reason—I asked you to come over this afternoon was to invite you to dinner."

"And the mail?"

"Was just an excuse."

"I see."

"Don't be mad. You should come, get a feel for where you are, meet some of the locals, listen to some music. Besides, I just spilled my life story, so you sort of owe me."

He had switched on the charm again, flashing that dangerous smile. She hated to admit it, but it was actually working. Or maybe she just didn't feel like eating alone.

"Are we talking casual?"

"Very. I'll take you to the Sundowner. It's just a beach bar, but the food's great, and there's usually a pretty good band on the deck."

"What time?"

"How does seven work? I need to run a set of plans over to a client for approval."

Lily checked her watch. Her mother ought to be home by now. "Seven's fine. It'll give me a chance to wash off all this sunscreen, and then make a few phone calls."

Dean flashed another smile. "It's a date, then."

"It's dinner," she corrected as she slid the door open and stepped out onto the rain-soaked deck. "Not a date. Just dinner."

NINE

It was Friday night, and the Sundowner was jammed. It wasn't hard to see why. Situated right on Beach Street, the restaurant offered a sweeping view of the coastline, and out back, a wide wraparound deck sprawled out over the sand, dotted with large yellow umbrellas and a canvas-covered bandstand.

Inside, the place was exactly what it should be, from the resin-coated tables studded with suspect bits of sunken treasure, to the net-draped walls and piped-in strains of Jimmy Buffett's "Son of a Son of a Sailor." An array of framed photos and newspaper clippings offered glimpses of the Sundowner's long and storied history, including several taken after the hurricane of 1920, when it seemed the bar had nearly been swept off the beach.

Dean paused to speak to the twentysomething brunette tidying a stack of laminated menus at the hostess stand. "We're just going to the deck, Haley."

Haley looked up with an air of distraction, then grinned when she saw Dean. "Sure thing. But just so you know, Salty's in one of his creative moods."

Dean groaned. "God help us all. The last time he was in one of his *creative* moods I ended up with a headache that lasted two days."

Lily felt the light pressure of Dean's hand on the small of her back as he steered her through the crowd and out onto the deck. She squinted as they stepped out into the breezy sunshine, feeling a little jolt of pleasure. It was livelier here, the air awash in music and the mouthwatering aroma of fried seafood. They waited a moment for a high-top at the end of patio to clear, then quickly snagged it.

Dean raised his voice to compete with the oozy strains of "Tupelo Honey" coming from the bandstand. "I thought we'd start with a table. We can join the gang at the bar later, if you're up for it. Are you hungry?"

"I am, as a matter of fact. What's good?"

"Two questions: Do you do spicy? And are you allergic to shellfish?"

"The spicier, the better. And no, I'm not."

"Perfect. What are you drinking?"

"Tanqueray and tonic, extra lime."

"No, no. Try again. You're not in Manhattan now. You're in paradise. That calls for an appropriate drink."

"What do you suggest? Wait, let me guess—something with an umbrella in it, served in a hollowed-out coconut?"

Dean gave her a withering look. "Don't be snarky. It doesn't suit you. Okay, maybe it does, but remember, you're on vacation. I was thinking about one of Salty's specialties. How about a Drunken Sailor?"

"Is that the drink that gave you the two-day headache?"

"Come to think of it, yeah. Okay, maybe what we need is some expert advice." He paused, waiting until he caught the bartender's eye, then waved him over to the table. "This is Salty. He's our local libations expert. He also owns the place."

Salty looked to be in his early sixties, with a disheveled mane of salt-and-pepper hair, and a goatee to match. His face was tanned to the color of leather, his ice blue eyes fanned on each side with well-worn creases. He was also missing most of the ring finger on his right hand.

He nodded at Dean before turning his attention to Lily. "And who's this?"

"My neighbor, Lily St. Claire."

"Neighbor? Since when?"

"Since the day before yesterday."

Salty extended a hand. "How do you do, Lily St. Claire?"

Lily took the proffered hand, liking him instantly. "I'm great. So is your place."

Salty scanned the crowded patio, pride of ownership written all over his face. "Yeah, well, it keeps me off the streets. What's your pleasure?"

Dean stepped in before Lily could answer. "That's why I called you over. We're having a discussion about the proper drink to order at a beach bar. Lily here was about to order a gin and tonic, but I explained that she can't come to a place like this and order something boring. I thought maybe you could suggest something."

"I don't do girlie drinks," she told Salty, shooting a scowl in Dean's direction.

"Would you try one for me—on the house?"

Lily feigned an eye roll but nodded. "All right, for you. But no umbrella."

"Throw in a Corona for me," Dean added. "And an order of shrimp."

Lily lifted a brow as Salty moved away. "What, no fruity drink for you after all your lecturing?"

Dean grinned. "It comes with a lime."

There they were again: the charming smile, the amusing quip.

Quite the package if a girl was looking—which she most certainly wasn't. Still, it was turning out to be a pleasant evening, so pleasant she actually found herself relaxing, forgetting the mess and the mystery that awaited her back at the cottage. The view of the sea, the brine-scented air, the music and the crowd, eclipsed everything else. If she wasn't careful she'd forget she wasn't on vacation.

They didn't have to wait long for Salty to reappear, a beer in one hand, a martini glass of something pink and slightly frothy in the other. He set the beer down in front of Dean, then handed Lily the glass with a bow and a flourish.

"There we are, one Pink Flip-Flop for the lady."

"A pink what?"

"Flip-Flop. It's the specialty of the house. My own concoction."

Lily eyed the sugared rim; a girlie drink if ever she'd seen one. "What's in it?"

Salty shook his head. "Not until you taste."

Lily did as she was told, and was pleasantly surprised as she licked sugar from her lips. "Wow, that is good. Now tell me what's in it."

"Parrot Bay rum, three kinds of fruit juice, and one more secret ingredient. Now drink up. I shook you a double."

"Why? You didn't even know if I'd like it."

"Because, Lily St. Claire, Pink Flip-Flops only come in pairs."

Grinning, Lily lifted her glass again. "I guess I'd better get sipping, then."

The band had broken into "Kokomo," and the entire crowd seemed to be singing along, heads bobbing as they sipped their beers and soaked up the last of the day's sunshine. Lily settled back in her chair, reveling in the rightness of it all, in the slowed-down pace and the mellow feel of the waning day, content to simply sip her drink and do as the natives did. She didn't want to think about postcards right now, or journals, or unsent letters. Right now, she wanted to be right where she was.

The food Dean ordered finally arrived. "Sunset Shrimp," Salty said, setting the basket in front of her, along with a stack of napkins and Lily's second Pink Flip-Flop. "Another specialty of the house—fresh from the gulf, lightly battered, then tossed in a mango-chili jam." He paused to fire a quick wink at Dean. "Let me know if you lovebirds need anything else."

Lily leaned in as Salty moved away. "He's a bit of a character, but I like him."

"Used to be a Miami cop. Now he owns this place and writes crime novels."

Lily paused, a shrimp hovering on the end of her fork. "Crime novels?"

"Yup. Whodunits, set right here on Hideaway Key. Pretty successful, too, from what I'm told. He likes to joke about being the island's number one cliché, but we've got a lot of clichés here, so the title's actually still up for grabs."

"Really. Like who?"

"Oh, I expect you'll meet a few tonight. We're all clichés in one way or another, but we seem to get more than our fair share here."

Lily's eyebrows shot up. "You think you're a cliché?"

"I'm a thirty-eight-year-old bachelor with commitment issues, so yeah, a little."

"And what about me?"

Dean chuckled as he speared a shrimp and neatly dispatched it. "A trust fund princess? What do you think?"

There'd been no malice in his answer, but it stung just the same. "I'm sorry I asked."

"Don't be. Like I said, we all have our thing."

"And yours is commitment issues?"

He tipped his Corona back for a sip, then gave her one of his shrugs. "They're not as much of an issue for me as for other people."

"For women?"

"It's not a phobia," he added almost defensively. "It's a choice. One I made a long time ago."

Lily pushed away her empty glass and reached for the second. "I get it. No complications. No strings."

"Does that make me a terrible person?"

"It makes you a smart person."

Dean set down his beer, appraising her with a new light in his eyes. "You, too?"

Lily nodded, trying not to think about Luc. "Afraid so. Also by choice."

"Somehow, you don't sound as sure as I am."

"I was in a relationship with someone. It got . . . intense, so I ended it. Badly."

"Were you up front with the guy?"

"Luc—his name was Luc. And yes, I was. He knew I wasn't looking for anything permanent. He just kept forgetting. Things would ramp up, start getting serious, and I'd have to bring him back to earth. For a while things would smooth out, then all of a sudden he'd start dropping hints again, talking about honeymoon spots, or what our kids would look like. I just couldn't keep hurting him—so I ended it."

"Badly."

"Yes. Very badly."

Dean was quiet for a moment, staring at her and chewing thoughtfully. "You need to stop beating yourself up," he said finally. "You're allowed to want what you want. If the guy kept pushing after you were straight up about what you wanted, he can't blame you. And you shouldn't blame you, either."

Lily nodded gloomily. This was starting to feel like a date—or a therapy session. "Can we talk about something else?"

She reached for her glass, surprised to find it empty. When had that happened? Dean noticed, too. He waved Salty over, ordering another round and a crab ceviche to share. The band had taken a break, promising to return when they were rehydrated. The sudden quiet felt awkward. Lily feigned interest in a gull tottering hopefully up and down the deck railing, relieved when Salty finally arrived with their next round of drinks and an enormous martini glass heaped with crab, tomato, and cilantro.

"Perfect timing," he said, setting down their food and an extra stack of napkins. "Show's about to start."

Lily peered over his shoulder, but the bandstand was still empty.

"No, no, not that show." Salty jerked his head toward the bandstand. "The real show." He pointed toward the beach then, to the bloodred disc sinking toward the edge of the sea.

Until that moment Lily hadn't noticed that the noise level had dropped to almost nothing, or that virtually every eye in the place was trained on the horizon. It was a thoughtful, reverent kind of quiet, like being in church, but outdoors. All along the deck, as well as along the bar, patrons had turned their gazes to the glorious spectacle taking place on the horizon. *Awe,* Lily realized with a jolt of something she couldn't begin to put a name to. Awe for something that happened every single day.

For the next ten minutes no one at the Sundowner moved or spoke. Out on the beach, people stood at the water's edge, arm and arm, hand in hand, children perched on their father's shoulders, all watching, waiting, as an orb of liquid fire slid steadily lower, turning the clouds to flame and the sea to quicksilver. How long had it been since she'd watched a sunset, treated it like a miracle? Had she ever?

Lily watched until the last sliver of crimson had melted into the sea, surprised and delighted when the crowd burst into applause, accompanied by raucous cheers, and even a few whistles. Her eyes stung with a sudden rush of tears. She blinked them away before turning to Dean.

"Is it always like this?"

"Every night. Best show on the island, and it's absolutely free."

Before she had time to think better of it, she closed her hand over his. "Thank you," she murmured over the slowly dying applause, embarrassed by this sudden gush of emotion. He'd planned it, of course, but she didn't care. In fact, the evening might just go down as one of the best dates ever—if it were a date, which it definitely wasn't.

TEN

Dusk settled softly over the beach, cooling the air and casting long blue shadows over the deck. The dinner crowd had gradually thinned, replaced with guests looking for a taste of weekend nightlife. Dean picked up his beer and the forgotten ceviche as the band reappeared, motioning for Lily to grab her drink.

"The gang's starting to show up. Let's go meet a few people."

Lily grabbed her glass and trailed after him, waiting while he dragged a pair of stools toward the end of the bar. She waved to Sheila, pleased to see a familiar face in the crowd, then glanced at the man to her right. He was sturdily built, with a dark tan, a day's worth of scruff, and a University of Alabama ball cap pulled low on his brow. As Dean approached he held out a hand.

Dean shook the hand, then gave the man's back a hearty slap. "Nice to see you getting out again, Captain. I thought you might still be licking your wounds."

The man's smile evaporated instantly. "It was one damn point, son. And it was six months ago. You think you might be shutting up about it anytime soon?"

Dean grinned like a cat toying with its prey. "One point in an SEC

Championship Game, Bubba. A game, I'll remind you, my Gators won. So *never* is your answer. I'm never going to shut up about it."

The captain sighed and rolled his eyes. "This is why you're thirty-eight and live alone—because you're not a nice person."

Dean ignored the remark. "Speaking of alone, where's your other half?"

Bubba craned his neck, peering over the bar. "Talking to Haley, I think. I swear to God, they're like sisters when they get together. I can't pull them—" He broke off abruptly as his gaze settled on Lily. Lifting his cap, he smoothed down a fringe of sun-blond hair, and then tugged the cap back in place. "And who's this? Don't tell me you're here on an actual date, Deano?"

"*This* is Lily," Lily supplied before Dean could open his mouth. "And no, he's not. We're neighbors."

"Ah, should have known better." He held out a hand. "Eric Hall. My friends call me Bubba, though. Or Captain. I run the dolphin cruise out of Hideaway Marina."

Lily noted the calloused palm as she accepted his hand. "Nice to meet you, Captain."

"Captain Bubba's actually a marine biologist," Dean interjected with a too-bright smile. "Has a degree and everything, from the University of Alabama. But he doesn't like to talk about that."

Bubba hung his head in exasperation. "And . . . here we go."

Lily had no idea what they were talking about but couldn't help feeling just a little sorry for Bubba. On impulse, she cut her eyes at Dean, summoning her best Alabama drawl. "It was one damn point, son. When are you going to let it go?"

Bubba snorted as he yanked off his cap, using it to give Dean a swat. "You need to keep this one, son. I like her."

Dean cocked an eye at her. "You're supposed to be on *my* side."

"Why?"

"Because I'm buying the drinks."

Lily smiled, batting her lashes prettily. "I'm a trust fund princess, remember? I can buy my own drinks."

"Yeah, well, just for that I'm not sharing the ceviche." He turned, eyeing Bubba with mock severity. "And as for you—here comes Drew. You might want to knock off the flirting before you wind up in even more hot water than usual."

Bubba's brows shot up, the picture of innocence. "Who's flirting? I was being polite. It's how civilized people act, not that you'd know."

Lily scanned the crowd for some sign of Bubba's wife or date, but all she saw was a man in madras shorts and Titleist ball cap elbowing his way through the crowd.

"Drew," Dean said when the man finally reached them, "please control the Captain, would you? I believe he's got designs on my date."

"She's his neighbor, not his date," Bubba corrected with another eye roll. "Yes, I know. Everyone, conceal your shock. Dean's flying solo—again. Lily, this is Drew, my better half."

Ah . . . Drew. As in Bledsoe—not Barrymore.

Lily smiled as Drew lifted his Titleist cap and smoothed back his hair in the exact same way Bubba just had. He wasn't at all what she had expected, but the longer she watched the two of them together, the more she saw why they fit so perfectly. With their deep-set blue eyes and close-cropped blond hair, they could as easily have been mistaken for brothers as lovers. She had heard about couples who'd been together so long they started to look alike, finished each other's sentences, and even adopted each other's mannerisms, but she had never seen it for herself—until now.

Bubba waved Salty over and ordered a round for the bar as the conversation returned to football, and next season's prospects for winning something called the SEC. Lily tried to follow the conversation but soon gave up, happy to sip her third Pink Flip-Flop and simply observe the social dynamics of Hideaway's locals.

Dean handed her a fork and placed the ceviche within sharing distance, still sparring noisily with Bubba about division rivalries and out-of-conference strength of schedule. Drew seemed less interested as he tucked into his hot wings and chatted with Salty about proposed improvements to the Gulf Sands golf course, but occasionally his hand would stray toward Bubba's, the contact so slight it might almost have been accidental.

Lily looked away, surprised by the pang of envy that had suddenly taken root just south of her ribs. Sheila must have been watching them, too. She gave Lily a smile that was warm but a little wistful.

"We all want the same thing, don't we?"

Lily was about to protest but thought better of it. "I guess. Sure."

Sheila's eyes drifted down the bar. "So, you're here with Dean?"

"Sort of. He's my neighbor."

"Lucky girl." Sheila's scarf tonight was blue and green paisley, tied gypsy-style over her shoulder-length chestnut curls. Beaded hoops of lapis and jade jangled softly as she spoke. "A little advice—move fast. Every unattached woman in Hideaway Key has eyes in that direction."

Lily stole a glance at Sheila's ring finger—bare. "Does that include you?"

"No, sugar." Sheila shook her head, setting her earrings tinkling like little bells. "Once, maybe, but not now. I'm afraid those days are over for me."

Something in Sheila's tone caught Lily's attention, not sadness exactly, but a kind of resignation that seemed out of character. The moment stretched uncomfortably, the cautionary strains of "Desperado" bleeding into the silence, making Sheila's words more poignant somehow. There was a story here, she was sure of it, but it was Sheila's story, and none of her business.

As if sensing Lily's discomfort, Sheila picked up her glass—one of Salty's pink specialties—and drained it, then turned a too-bright smile on Lily. "The skirt looks amazing, by the way. You didn't tell me you had such great legs. Next time we'll go shorter."

Lily glanced dubiously at her bare legs, about to reply when a sound that could only be likened to the squawking of an angry crow rose above both the band and the crowd.

"Sweet Mother of Mercy, I thought I'd never get out of the shop tonight."

"Brace yourself," Sheila whispered behind her hand. "It's Rhona."

"Rhona?"

There was no time for Sheila to answer. Rhona descended in a cloud of patchouli and vanilla, silver bangles jangling. For a moment Lily couldn't even blink. The woman was like nothing she'd ever seen, draped in folds of bright tropical print, close-cropped white hair standing out from her head like a cloud on a windy day. But that wasn't the best of it. Behind her left ear, fluttering like the plumage of some exotic bird, bloomed a single red hibiscus.

"It never fails," she rattled, without so much as a look in Lily's direction. "I'm just about to turn off the sign when three woman strut in wanting a reading. Three of them, at six o'clock!" Boosting a stool from a nearby high-top, she dragged it over to the bar and plopped down heavily. "I mean, who does that at six o'clock?"

Dean grinned, then elbowed Lily. "Told you we had our share. Rhona is the local fortune-teller."

"She's certainly . . . colorful."

"Yeah, in more ways than one. She's a hoot, actually. But she can get a little out there sometimes." He grinned and winked, as if to say *Watch this*, then leaned forward to holler down the bar. "Rhona, are you telling us the greatest seer on Hideaway Key didn't know three women were going to show up at her door at six o'clock?"

Rhona swiveled her white head in Dean's direction, brandishing a finger that nearly caught Lily in the eye. "It's a good thing you're better-looking than you are funny, sir. I've got housecoats older than that joke." She paused then, as if noticing for the first time that Lily was seated between them. "Good Lord, girl, you're the spitting image of a woman who used to live here on Hideaway. She's dead now, but oh brother, she was something else. The stories I could tell—"

Lily cut her off with an extended hand. "Hi. I'm Lily St. Claire, Lily-Mae Boyle's niece."

Rhona stared at her, openmouthed. After a moment she seemed to recover herself, accepting Lily's hand with a creeping smile that was slightly unnerving. "Well, of course you are. I'm Rhona. Rhona Shoemaker. And ignore your date. He's a nonbeliever."

"He's not my date. I just live next door."

"So, you're living in your aunt's place, then, over on Vista?"

"Yes. I'll be there for a few weeks while I clean the place out. Did you really know her?"

Lily suddenly became aware of Dean's knee tapping hers with growing insistence, but she chose to ignore the warning. "So you knew my aunt?"

"Well, I don't know if you could say I knew her, but I knew who she was. We all did. She was a big deal around here, so pretty and so famous. And so sad."

Lily seized on the word. "Sad?"

Another bump from Dean, harder this time, accompanied by an unmistakable glower. Even Sheila was shaking her head behind Rhona's back. But it was too late. Rhona had already swiveled around to face Lily, eyes glittering.

"We lived in the bungalow across the street. It's not there anymore, but back when it was we had a bird's-eye view of your aunt's place. It wasn't all grown-up back then, like it is now. We could look across the street and see smack into her windows."

Drew ducked behind his beer glass, shoulders hunched uncomfortably.

Bubba groaned and shook his head. "Rhona, hush that up."

Rhona's eyes hardened sharply. "Could we help it if the woman left her blinds open? She obviously didn't care if folks knew what she got up to at all hours."

Sheila set her glass down hard, sloshing some of its contents onto the bar. "For Pete's sake, Rhona! The woman's dead, and this is her niece."

Rhona's lower lip jutted petulantly. "Then it's probably nothing she doesn't already know."

The argument continued to escalate while Lily sat numbly on her stool, head jerking back and forth like a spectator at a tennis match. Everyone was talking at once, and all seemingly bent on keeping Rhona from being heard. And yet, despite the noisy protests and the band's boisterous rendition of "Love Shack," Lily actually did manage to catch a word here and there, and they weren't particularly nice words. In fact, they were words her mother might have used.

Men at all hours . . . something to hide . . . drank herself to death.

Lily was still trying to digest what she'd heard when she saw Dean stand abruptly and begin counting out a handful of bills. "Ready?" he asked tightly, as he slid the money across the bar to Salty.

Lily blinked at him, not sure what was happening. Were they leaving? Because of Rhona? Dean said nothing more, just stood there waiting. Finally, she slid off her stool, mumbling her good-byes as she gathered her purse. As she turned to go Sheila caught her by the wrist, pulling her close.

"Sorry about all that, sugar. She doesn't mean any harm. She just doesn't know when to keep quiet. It's a family thing."

Lily nodded with a pasted-on smile, but couldn't help wondering what was going on. She had known this handful of people for less than an hour, and yet they seemed hell-bent on silencing Rhona Shoemaker. What was it they didn't want her to hear?

And speaking of Rhona, where had she gotten to? Scanning the length of the deck, and then the thinning crowd of restaurant patrons, Lily finally caught sight of the red hibiscus disappearing down a short hallway marked RESTROOMS.

"I need to make a pit stop before we go," she told Dean on impulse. "Go on. I'll meet you at the truck."

The truck was running by the time she got out to the parking lot, a cool sea breeze wafting in through the open windows. Lily belted herself in and waited for Dean to put the truck in gear and pull out, but he made no move to leave.

"You shouldn't listen to anything Rhona says about your aunt," he said finally. He had both hands on the wheel, his eyes locked straight ahead. "The woman doesn't know what she's saying half the time."

"You're saying she's crazy?"

He turned finally, his face all hard angles in the moonlight. "I'm saying she's the kind of woman who's only too glad to tell what she knows, even if she doesn't really know it. Her mother was a notorious gossip—Dora was her name. They say she hurt a lot of people by running her mouth, and there's a little bit of that in Rhona, too. Which is why you need to take anything she says with a grain of salt. Better yet, steer clear of her altogether."

"So, the things she was saying tonight about Lily-Mae—none of it's true?"

He sighed, half shrugging, half shaking his head. "I don't know. I wasn't here then. I just know Rhona likes to talk, and that she isn't always right when she does. Every word she said in there could be true. Or it could all be lies. I'd just hate to see you base your opinion of your aunt on anything she says."

"It's nice of you," Lily said quietly. "Trying to protect me. Thanks."

For a moment she wasn't sure he'd heard her. He was staring out the window, as if focused on something miles away. Finally, he nodded, then dropped the truck into reverse. "Gossip can be a vicious thing—especially when it's true."

Lily eyed him as he backed out of the parking lot, his face unreadable in the soft blue glow of the dashboard lights. He'd meant the words kindly, but there had been an unmistakable edge to his voice that made her wonder if he might be speaking from personal experience. Had there been rumors about his mother, gossip that had been especially painful for a young boy to hear?

It seemed likely, and would certainly explain his words of caution. But it was different for her. Dean had known his mother, and loved her presumably, while Lily-Mae would always remain a stranger. There were no illusions to shatter, no feelings to hurt. She wasn't emotionally invested in her aunt's past, only curious, which was why, despite Dean's warnings, she was going to have lunch with Rhona Shoemaker tomorrow and see what else the woman did or didn't know.

Until then, she'd keep trying to reach her mother and throw herself back into the notebooks, not that they would shed much light on the grown-up Lily-Mae. They'd been written long before the hiding and drinking and men at all hours. Long before Paris, too. But for now, they were what she had.

ELEVEN

November 23, 1955
Mt. Zion Missionary Poor Farm

I wish I could say I don't remember.

I wish I could say it, but I can't. If I live a hundred years, or even a thousand, I'll always, always remember—and wonder if there was some way I could have stopped what happened. If I had run, or screamed . . . or killed him.

I didn't do any of those things, though. I didn't do anything.

Zell was stretched out in the chair behind his desk when I walked in, fuming on one of his cigarettes while another one smoldered in the ashtray behind him. It's a habit he has, lighting a new cigarette before he's finished the last one. Sometimes he has three going at one time. I didn't care about his habits right then, though. I was more worried about the way he was looking up at me through all that smoke.

He was smiling, not the pious smile he wears for his flock, but a sharp little half smile that made my throat thicken and my blood go cold. That's when I remembered it was the second Wednesday of the month, and that on the second Wednesday of the month Sister Ruth went into Ransom to see the doctor. He was always friendlier on those days, always patting me on the knee and forgetting to take his hand away, or brushing up against me like it was an accident when we both knew it wasn't. But today was different somehow. I could see it in his eyes, like he'd made up his mind about something, and that something had to do with me.

I turned away, grabbed the first stack of papers I could find, and scurried to the filing cabinet, praying, praying, that I was wrong. I heard the creak of leather, the sound that meant he was getting up out of his chair, then the cold snick of the door being locked. A moment later he was behind me, reeking of sweat and stale smoke.

"We're friends, aren't we, Lily-Mae?"

I stared down at my shoes, trying to think how to answer. I wasn't his friend, and I didn't want to be, but I knew that was the wrong thing to say. I nodded instead, and kept fumbling with my papers. I thought if I just kept busy, if I kept my head down, maybe he'd forget whatever it was he'd made his mind up about.

It didn't work. I could still feel his eyes on me, the weight of them cutting between my shoulder blades, paring me like an apple, right down to my core. I closed my eyes when he touched me, a single finger traced slowly along my cheek.

"Very good friends, yes. The best of friends."

His voice was silky and raspy all at once, a breathy crooning that made my legs start to tremble. And then, before I could think how to stop it, it was happening. There was no pretending, today, as his hands began to roam, no mistaking his meaning when he pressed his hips to mine, whispering things that made my skin crawl.

I heard a voice in my head—a voice like Mama's—screaming at me to get away, but there was nowhere to go, no route of escape. I opened my mouth, ready to scream, when I felt the flat of Zell's hand against my cheek, the crack of it so unexpected that for a moment white lights danced behind my eyes. And then he was smiling again, stroking the cheek where he'd just left his handprint.

"Hush now, and be a good girl. I won't hurt you. We're friends, remember. Good friends."

He pulled me to his chair and dragged me into his lap—like Daddy used to do to Mama when he'd come home with liquor on his breath and winnings in his pocket. His face was so close I could see the place on his chin where he'd nicked himself shaving, and the sweat in tiny beads along his upper lip.

"Yes. Yes. Such a good girl. Such a beautiful child."

Bile scorched up into my throat as he began to fumble with the buttons of my blouse, his fingers sticky as they plunged inside, groping and pinching until tears sprang to my eyes. If he noticed, he didn't care. Without a word, he shoved me off his lap and sprawled me back onto the desk, sending a pencil cup clattering over the edge and onto the bare wood floor. I squeezed my eyes shut as my sweater was pushed back, the rest of my buttons greedily undone.

And then, for one desperate moment, I thought I heard a noise, something or someone at the window. But when I opened my eyes there was no one there—only Zell with his suspenders dangling around his hips and his trousers gaping open.

No one was coming to save me.

I was shaking so hard I thought I might come apart as he raked up my skirt and pried my knees apart. Time slowed then, like a moving picture running at half speed, and suddenly it was as if I had stepped out of my skin and was watching it all happen to some other girl. And then, because I didn't want to watch it happen—not even to that other girl—I squeezed my eyes shut again, and willed myself far, far away, out of that room and out of my body, back to the old tire swing in front of our house, barely aware of my head thumping against Zell's big black Bible as he battered his way into me.

When he was finished I slid from the desk and pulled my clothes together, dimly aware of the stickiness between my thighs, and the

urgent need to scour every last trace of him from my skin with a bar of Sister Ruth's strong lye soap. He was fumbling with his suspenders, mopping his face with the limp handkerchief he always kept in his pocket, doing his best to avoid my eyes. I was glad. I knew if he looked at me he would see the hatred I felt for him at that moment—the hatred I will always feel.

I had edged all the way to the door when he seemed to notice me again, and took me by the wrist. "Fornication is a sin, Lily-Mae. Doubly so for women, who were made to be man's downfall. We must pray together, and beg forgiveness for yielding to the temptations of the flesh."

The Bible says that sinning in your heart is the same as sinning in deed. If that's true I committed murder at that moment. I wanted to scream, to rage at him that I had nothing to pray about, no sins that needed forgiving—that the weakness, the vileness, was not mine, but his! But the words wouldn't come. They were stuck in my throat, almost choking me as he dragged me to my knees and began to pray in his Sunday-morning voice. His fingers were still around my wrist, squeezing until my hand began to tingle and go numb. And there I stayed—for Mama's sake, and for Caroline's—pretending to pray to a God I want no part of.

I don't know how long I stayed in the shower afterward.

I only know it wasn't long enough, that there will never be enough showers, or days, or tears to wash away the stain of Harwood Zell. His smell might be gone from my skin, his seed and my blood scrubbed from my thighs, but no amount of scrubbing will ever erase what he's done.

Afterward, when I was alone, I forced myself to look at my body in the bathroom mirror, at all the places Zell had had his hands. Like a bruised piece of fruit, I expected the damage to show, for the spoiled places to be mottled and black. They weren't, and for that at least I was grateful.

I skipped supper. I couldn't bear the thought of seeing him in the mess hall, of listening to him say grace in that pious, quaking voice of his, as if he hadn't just broken half the commandments. Instead, I went for a walk, out to the pond behind the cow barn. It isn't much of a pond, really, just a triangular-shaped gouge in the earth, filled with muddy water and cow dung. But it reminds me of home. I didn't care that it was freezing and almost dark, or that I'd forgotten to bring my coat. I was alone, which was all I wanted. I gathered a handful of stones as I stepped to the water's edge. It was a game Caroline and I used to play, to see who could throw the farthest. I let her win most of the time, because she was younger, and because she pouted for days when she lost at anything. But I didn't want to think about Caroline just then, or about Mama, or home. It all seemed too far away, too lost.

I could feel the tears burning in my throat, but I didn't want to cry. If I started I might never stop. I tossed the first stone, watching as the dark water swallowed it up, imagined it sinking to the cold, quiet bottom—wishing I could sink there, too. Instead, I hurled another stone at the pond, farther this time, and harder. Then another, and another, flailing blindly at the water's inky surface as the rage came again, threatening to drown me with its invisible waves. I kept throwing until I had spent my stones and my strength, and then, emptied, sank to my knees in the muck, keening it all out at last.

I was frozen through by the time I returned to the dorm, wanting nothing but the warmth of my cot and the escape of sleep. I heard the usual chatter as I approached the door, muffled voices leaching out around closed windows, almost happy sounds now that the day's work was over. But the chatter died as I stepped through the door, a heavy hush that grew thicker with every step I took toward my cot.

And then I saw it—the nest of small objects at the center of the blanket—a tangle of ribbons, a pair of butterfly barrettes, a copy of Anne of Green Gables. *And Chessie. All things I had passed on to Caroline, some of them from Zell, and now she had given them back. I scooped them up, but I knew it was too late. The others had already seen, and like me, were wondering what it meant.*

But Caroline was nowhere to be found. Finally, just before lights-out, she appeared, her hands and lips blue with cold, her chin sticking out the way it does when she's angry. I waited for her to launch into one of her tirades, to wail and gnash it all out of her system. But this felt different somehow, colder, and in a way I can't explain, more final, as if something between us had been severed. For a moment I wondered if she knew about Zell and what he'd done. But that was impossible. No one knew, or would ever know—Caroline, least of all.

She wouldn't look at me, and didn't utter a single word as she stripped out of her dress and dragged on her nightgown, just crawled into bed and turned her back to me. It hurt to see her turn away, especially now, when I needed her most. Then I remembered how young she is, and that she's supposed to lean on me, not the other way around. She'll calm down. She always does—usually in the middle of the night, when she wakes up and remembers where she is.

Long after lights-out, I lay awake, listening to the wind rattling the windows, waiting for the familiar creak of Caroline's cot springs. It never came.

November 26, 1955
Mt. Zion Missionary Poor Farm

Zell has gone away.

Not for good, but for three full weeks, which is at least some small mercy. He left the morning after, lit out all of a sudden for a revival in Knoxville no one knew anything about—including Sister Ruth, if the whispers are to be believed. And there's been plenty of whispering going on of late, most of it about me, and why I've suddenly been sent back to the kitchen.

I don't care. Let them whisper. I was so relieved not to have to go back to Zell's office I nearly cried when I was told. Sister Ruth has been keeping a close eye on me. She's wondering if I'm the reason her husband has left so suddenly. I wonder that, too, if it was guilt that drove him away, if he was ashamed of what he'd done. Not that it can possibly matter now. Like Mama used to say, what's lost is lost, and what's done is done. Please, God, let it be done. Please let him be finished with me. But in my bones I know he isn't.

Making a deal with the devil. That's what Mama called it the day I walked in and found her on the couch with a man she met on one of her shifts at the truck stop. She said with Daddy not coming back we were in trouble, and that sometimes a woman had to make a deal with the devil in order to protect her angels. I suppose that's what I've done, too—with Zell—made a deal with the devil to protect Caroline. I wonder if it's what Mama had in mind all along when she dragged that promise out of me, and then drove off.

Maybe not in so many words, but it's what she would have done, too. I know that now, but wish I didn't. The thought of it—a deal with the devil—sickens me. Men don't have to make those kinds of deals. They're always on the other end, the receiving end—the devils holding all the cards and setting all the terms.

I try not to think too much about Mama these days. It'll be Christmas soon, our third at Mt. Zion, and we haven't had a word from her, not at Thanksgiving, and probably not at Christmas, either. I know she isn't coming back for us, that she's sick—or worse. I don't say any of this to Caroline, but then, we don't talk much these days.

She spends her time with the other girls, the ones who shoot me dirty looks and talk behind my back. Maybe she's just growing up, outgrowing her need for me, but it feels like something else, like maybe she's heard the talk about me and Zell and believes what she's heard.

I still haven't breathed a word to her about what happened, and I never will. She's too young to know about such things, and even if she weren't, I'm not sure I could ever bring myself to say them out loud. It's my way of protecting her, of keeping my promise, by pretending I'm fine, and that nothing has changed.

Everything has changed, though.

All I think of now is leaving this place, of waiting until everyone's asleep and slipping away, of disappearing down that dirt road, of being gone when the sun comes up. I could, too, if I made up my mind to do it. There's no fence, no gate to keep us in. We're free to go whenever we choose. And every cell in my body screams to go, to put this place—and Harwood Zell—behind me. I'm strong, smart. I could get a job, two if I had to. I could find a place to stay, and a way to feed myself. But it isn't just me. How would I take care of Caroline?

All this time I've been trying to keep my promise to look after her, to keep her safe until Mama comes back. Only she isn't coming back. I know that now, and that the real reason I cling to that promise is because it's my way of holding on to the woman who asked it of me. It doesn't change anything. Caroline is still mine to look after, and until I can work out how to do that on my own, I'm stuck here, at the mercy of Harwood Zell.

TWELVE

1995
Hideaway Key, Florida

Lily was still rattled as she drove to meet Rhona Shoemaker for lunch. The more she learned about Lily-Mae's childhood—and her mother's—the more stunned she was that it had remained hidden at all. One thing was becoming clear: her mother's animosity toward Lily-Mae had begun long before Roland St. Claire entered either of their lives.

She had managed to get through the fourth notebook after Dean dropped her back at the cottage the night before, adding several new questions to the growing list of things she'd ask her mother if she ever managed to get her on the phone. She had tried again, just before leaving to meet Rhona, but as usual, the machine had picked up. Caroline was being either extremely petulant or extremely evasive. It wasn't going to work, though; sooner or later she was going to have to pick up the phone. Right now, Lily wanted to hear what the local fortune-teller had to say.

Rhona was waiting when she arrived, seated on the deck in the shade of an enormous patio umbrella, a glass of iced tea sweating in one gnarled hand. The flower in her hair today was yellow, her voluminous muumuu printed with green and yellow birds.

Lily ducked into the seat across from her with an awkward smile, Dean's words of warning suddenly playing in her head.

"Thanks for agreeing to meet me, Rhona."

"After all the fuss last night, I'm surprised you asked."

"I never knew my aunt. She and my mother had this sibling rivalry thing going on, so there was never much talk about her in our house—at least not nice talk—so nothing you say about her is going to surprise me. I'm just on a fact-finding mission."

"Why?" Rhona asked, swirling her tea glass. "Why now? And why from me? People around here'll tell you, if they haven't already: I get as much wrong as I do right."

They had told her, but she wasn't about to share that with Rhona. "Because there *is* no one else," she said finally. "My mother won't talk about her, and my father's dead. I just want to know what you know."

Or think you know.

Lily grabbed the menu as the waitress approached, and after a quick scan ordered a salad. She waited while Rhona dithered, then finally settled on a crab cake sandwich and fries. When the waitress moved away, Rhona folded her hands beneath her chin, leaning forward almost conspiratorially.

"I was young when your aunt moved in across from us. And pretty naïve. Most of what I remember is stuff I overheard my mother and Gran saying. And the rumors. There were lots of rumors."

"Such as?"

"Oh, silly things, mostly—like her being in the witness relocation program for testifying against some New York gangster. We didn't know much about her, except that she was from New York, and was sort of famous. Back then—around here at least—New York meant two things: glamour and gangsters. My mother had her pegged as both. It didn't help that she kept to herself so much. We'd go weeks without laying an eye on her. She used to have her groceries delivered, her liquor, too. She didn't even try to make friends. That made folks think she was uppity."

"Gangsters? Seriously?"

Rhona shrugged. "My mother had a whole scenario in her head, how your aunt was a moll for some big mob boss, that she'd run away because she'd decided to go straight. She had a vivid imagination, my mother, as I'm sure you've heard."

"People didn't really believe that, though, did they?"

"Some did, sure. The ones who wanted to. Others had their own theories."

The waitress reappeared, this time with their food. Rhona went quiet while the plates were handed out, the glasses topped off.

"What kinds of theories?" Lily prompted when they were alone again.

"That she was a high-priced call girl. That all the talk about her being a famous model was just a cover. Or that maybe she started out that way, and then switched over."

"To a prostitute?"

"Not the common sort," Rhona assured her hastily, as if that somehow made the rumor more palatable. "She would have been one of the expensive ones, the kind who could afford to pick and choose." She popped a fry into her mouth, then licked a dab of ketchup from her thumb. "For the record, my mother never believed that."

"No. She just had her pegged as a gangster's moll."

"It was only because of that man showing up."

"What man?"

Rhona was fiddling with her sandwich, carefully extricating the crab cake from its bun. Lily waited until she was finished.

"Rhona, what man?"

"Who knows? He showed up late one night in a fancy car, all black with dark windows. She let him in, then threw her arms around him and kissed him."

"Was this one of the nights she left the blinds open?"

Rhona scooped up a bite of crab cake, chewing thoughtfully.

"Rhona?"

"Not for long. But he stayed the night because the car was still in the driveway in the morning. In fact, he stayed for several weeks. People would see them out together now and then, always arm in arm. Thick as thieves, Gran used to say. He was always dressed up in a hat and one of those suits with the stripes, always flashing around a lot of money, too—like they do in the movies."

"So you naturally assumed he was a gangster."

"Well, it was mostly my grandmother. He was a pretty thing, blond hair and nice white teeth. My mother thought he might be a movie star, though she couldn't remember ever seeing him in a movie. But I think Gran liked the idea of him being the dangerous sort."

"Did you ever hear his name mentioned, or figure out who he was?"

Rhona continued to pick at her crab cake, dissecting out bits of green onion and herding them to the edge of her plate. "No. And we never saw him again after that. My mother thought it must have been her husband."

Lily set down her fork and folded her hands on the edge of the table, wishing she had taken Dean's advice more seriously. So far, all she'd heard was a mash-up of rumor and innuendo, and now the woman had conjured a husband out of thin air.

"Rhona, my aunt never married."

It was Rhona's turn to look surprised. "She most certainly did. My mother saw it in some society paper. There were pictures of her and everything. She kept up with things like that. Mama just assumed it was that golden boy with the fancy clothes, since he was the only one who ever stayed any length of time. The others . . . well, I don't know really. I never saw any of the others. Just heard about them. Everybody did. Coming and going at all hours, they said."

Lily wasn't listening. Her mother had never said a word about her sister marrying. In fact, she had suggested just the opposite, gloating in unguarded moments about Lily-Mae's spinster status. Was it possible she had married without Caroline's knowledge? Yes, of course it was. Caroline was hardly likely to have been on the guest list.

"But then, you can hardly blame the men for coming around. Moths are always drawn to a lit candle."

Lily glanced up from her plate, realizing with an awkward start that Rhona had been talking the whole time and was now waiting for some sort of a response.

"I'm sorry, what?"

"I said your aunt was beautiful, and that it wasn't her fault that men flocked to her, though, like I said, I never saw them—except for Golden Boy, of course. We all got a look at him, since he was around for most of the summer. But then he disappeared. She should have held on to him. Rich as Croesus, by the look of his car."

Lily's eyes narrowed thoughtfully. "You never saw *any* of them?"

Rhona waved a hand as she folded a particularly long French fry into her mouth.

"Not with my own eyes, no. Mama did, though. And just like that she was everybody's friend. Everybody wanted to know the latest."

Lily nodded, digesting the implications, but decided to leave it alone. "What ever happened to the man with the fancy car? Does anyone know?"

Rhona had been pulling her sandwich bun to pieces while they talked, creating a tidy pile of scraps on one side of her plate. She looked up, brushing crumbs from her fingers. "As far as I know, no one ever saw him again. The cottage was shut up for a while, though I can't remember now if that was before or after he came. I do know your aunt disappeared for a while. Everyone wondered where she'd gone. When she finally came back she was alone."

Lily set down her fork, her appetite suddenly gone. She felt stupid now, and more than a little disappointed. She'd been hoping for insight, and actual facts. Instead, she'd spent the last hour listening to the muddled memories of a woman who got her *facts* from the infamous Dora Shoemaker, Hideaway Key's most notorious gossip. And she couldn't say she hadn't been warned. The worst part was that Rhona's memories, as fragmented as they might be, still seemed to confirm Lily-Mae's dubious reputation.

Rhona was busy scooping bread scraps into her napkin, careful not to leave a crumb behind. Lily watched her gnarled fingers work, folding the napkin into a tidy little bundle, then stowing it away in the pocket of her dress.

"For the birds," she told Lily, patting the pocket. She pointed to a sign nailed to the railing a few feet away. PLEASE DON'T FEED THE BIRDS. "I'll go down on the beach when we're through."

"Are we through? I mean, is there anything else you can tell me? Anything about how she died?"

Rhona shook her head, sending the yellow hibiscus petals fluttering. "Can't help you much there. Mama sold the house after I got married, so I kind of lost track. I heard she died last year, but not how or why. The money was on her drinking herself to death, but I don't think anyone knows for sure. They found her in bed, that much I do know. They say she was a rack of bones." Rhona slapped a hand over her mouth, as if suddenly aware that she was being indelicate. "I'm sorry. I haven't got an ounce of tact in me. Never have."

A rack of bones. Lily pushed the image away, doing her best to keep her face blank. "It's fine, really. Like I said, I never knew her."

Rhona smiled, a sharp, knowing smile that narrowed the corners of her eyes. "Right. Because you're just here on a fact-finding mission."

Lily nodded. "Can I ask you one more thing? Last night you said something about Lily-Mae being beautiful, but sad."

Rhona pushed back her plate, folding leathery arms on the edge of the table. "You could just see it in her, or at least I could. My mother didn't notice, or Gran, either, but I could always tell that something had happened to her that left her scarred up, especially after she came back. I always felt a little bad for her. All of us poking around all the time, trying to learn her story. People have a right to their suffering."

Lily didn't know what to say. The woman's memory might be faulty, her sources less than reliable, but there was nothing wrong with her powers of observation. Lily-Mae had been through something that left her scarred up.

"Thank you for meeting me today, Rhona, and for telling me all this."

She meant it, too. Rhona hadn't painted a particularly pretty story, but at least Lily had some idea about the kind of life her aunt had lived while here. As she signaled their waitress for the check, she thought about Lily-Mae's self-imposed exile, trying to imagine the kind of sadness that could cause a woman to shut herself away from the world. She couldn't, not really. But if a childhood filled with horror and a town filled with gossipmongers didn't justify a life of seclusion, she didn't know what did.

THIRTEEN

Sheila was unpacking a box of sunglasses, arranging them on a tall plastic spinner, when Lily walked in. Her face brightened when she saw Lily. "Let me guess," Sheila said, laughing. "You decided you couldn't live without those strappy little sandals you were looking at the other day."

"Actually, I had to come into town, so I thought I'd pop by and say hi."

"Well, then, hi. How goes it at Sand Pearl Cottage? How's Dean?"

Lily wasn't sure which question to answer first. She had phrased the two as if they were somehow connected. "He's fine, I guess. You saw him last night. And the cottage is, well, the cottage."

"And what else?"

Lily's brows lifted a notch. "What else?"

"You've got that look, the one that says your body's here but your head's somewhere else. What's up?"

Lily tried not to let her surprise show, wondering if Sheila wasn't the real clairvoyant. She hadn't come to buy anything, or even to browse. She had *popped by* because she wasn't ready to go back to the cottage.

had lunch with Rhona today. I just left her."

Sheila clucked her tongue. "And she told you things?"

Lily nodded. "You've heard the stories. Everyone has. It's why you were all trying to hush her up last night. But I needed to hear what she had to say. All my life I've wanted to learn more about my aunt, and now that I have I don't know what to think."

Sheila laid a hand on Lily's arm. "Oh, sugar, don't take it to heart. Rhona's a bit of a crackpot. She's been known to be a little—let's call it unreliable."

"Yes, I know. Dean told me. But it's not just the things she said. I ran across some of Lily-Mae's journals at the cottage and I've been reading about what she went through as a child." She paused, closed her eyes, shook her head. "She had her reasons, Sheila. If what people said about her back then was true, she had her reasons. Maybe not good ones, but she went through some terrible things."

"Of course she did, honey. We all have reasons for everything we do. The good stuff and the bad. We do the best we can from where we are, with what we know. That's life."

Lily managed a smile, already feeling better. "I knew I came to see you for a reason, but I didn't know you were a Zen master."

Sheila rolled her eyes. "Honey, what I know you can't learn in any monastery. You have to earn it, one scar at a time."

It was the second time Sheila had mentioned scars in the course of a normal conversation. "You think we learn from our scars?"

"I do, actually. At least I know I've learned from mine, though God knows I fought it tooth and nail. Let me tell you, you can do a lot of thinking when you've hit rock bottom and you're all alone. How's Dean, by the way?"

The abrupt change of subject was jarring. "I already told you. He's fine."

"He's a good guy. He's got some issues, but who doesn't? You should make a move in that direction if he's your type."

"I just met him!"

"Yeah, well, life is short. Trust me, if you don't go after what you want you'll wind up alone and empty-handed."

She'd said it with such gravity, such knowing. "That sounds like experience talking."

"Breast cancer," Sheila said simply. "Five years ago."

"I'm sorry." Without meaning to, her eyes slid to Sheila's chest.

"Both," Sheila said without blinking. "No reconstruction, but they make great bras nowadays."

Lily glanced at the stack of folded pink shopping bags on the counter beside the napping Sir Galahad. Suddenly, a light went on. "Sassy Rack?"

Sheila smiled slyly. "You guessed it. I was still in my defiant phase when I came up with the name. It was kind of an in-your-face choice, which is pretty much how I was after it was all over."

"And now . . ."

"So far so good. Which is why I said what I said about life being short. You never know, honey. So don't pass up things you might regret later—like Dean."

"I'm only here for three weeks. There's no point—"

"You've never heard of a summer romance?"

"I don't have time for a summer romance. Besides, I'm not interested."

Sheila arched one slim brown brow. "You have seen him, right—the tall, dark, handsome architect who lives in that big blue beach house next to your aunt's cottage?"

"It's not him. Well, maybe it's a little bit him. But the real reason is I'm not looking for anything right now. I've got my hands full with the cottage, and then I'm off to Milan."

"What's in Milan?"

"A job at a very prestigious design house. I design clothes."

Sheila's eyes went wide. "Get out of here! Seriously?"

"I've been in Paris, working for Sergé Leroux, but then this offer came up. Like I said, it's a really prestigious house. A dream job, really. I couldn't turn it down."

"Was someone holding a gun to your head?"

Lily shook her head. "I didn't mean it like that."

"Maybe you did. Sometimes we say what we mean without meaning to. I know it's none of my business, but for a girl who just got offered a dream job you don't sound very excited."

"Everything's just happening so fast. My father, the cottage, and now Lily-Mae. I haven't had time to catch my breath."

Sheila's look said she wasn't buying it. "You know, a minute ago I warned you about passing up things you might regret later. But I forgot to tell you that it works the other way, too. You should never do something you're not over the moon about."

"More experience?"

"Maybe. My point is, we only get one life. It's up to us to fill it up with things we love. That goes for people, too."

"If this is about Dean—"

"It's about whoever. And whatever. When I got sick, I got stupid. There was a man—we'd been together for years. He was a great guy, so great I couldn't bear the thought of him seeing me sick and all scarred up. So I ran him off. Not all at once, but it didn't take long. Then came the chemo and radiation. It was so awful, and I was so sick and alone. Everywhere I went there were all these women. Women with breasts. Woman with hair. Women who didn't look like walking mummies. I wanted to go somewhere, anywhere, and hide. But there was nowhere to go. I almost quit. I didn't want to go on with it. I just wanted everything to be over. One of the chemo nurses must have sensed it. She gave me a card for a survivors' group. I went, and that night I got smart again. I realized what an idiot I'd been, and how much I had thrown away. It was too late to fix a lot of it, but I could get on with my life, and I did—on my terms. You get me, sugar?"

Lily blinked at her. She didn't, actually.

Sheila's smile was kind, but a little sad, too, as she began gathering up the small plastic bags the sunglasses had come in. "Life is precious. That's what I'm saying. And you shouldn't throw away a single minute of it. Especially not on a job you don't want—even if that job *is* in Milan."

Lily shrugged, feeling more adrift than ever. "I've always wanted to do something big, something that really matters. Maybe this job is finally it."

"I agree with every word of that, honey. What you do with your life does have to matter—but only to you. Nothing else is important. You get to decide what's big. You, and *only* you."

Lily smiled, a sad smile that made the center of her chest ache. "You sound like my father. He was always telling me to listen to my heart, to follow my own North Star."

"Sounds like a wise man."

"He was," Lily said quietly. "Thanks for sharing. I didn't mean to dredge up bad memories."

Sheila waved off the apology. "In case you haven't noticed, I've moved on. Sometimes things happen and you think it's the end of the world. You rail at fate and you curse the gods. And then one day you're all raged out, and you realize everything is just the way it's supposed to be, that life is just one long chain of lessons and there aren't any accidents. Things—lessons—come into our lives for a reason."

Sheila's words continued to echo in Lily's head long after she left the shop. Was it true? Was everything the way it was supposed to be? If she let herself believe that, it meant that Hideaway Key was where she was supposed to be, at least for now, and that inheriting Sand Pearl Cottage had been no accident.

FOURTEEN

Lily felt a pleasant sense of accomplishment as she gathered up the armload of grimy paper towels and stood back to survey her handiwork. It had taken half a roll of Bounty and thirty minutes of elbow grease, but the glass doors finally sparkled.

She had made a conscious decision to take a break from the notebooks, to immerse herself in physical tasks and give her mind a rest. She had started with the bedroom, careful not to disturb any of Lily-Mae's treasures as she stripped and remade the bed, then cleared a drawer in the bureau for her own things. She couldn't live out of her suitcase for three weeks. When she finished there she moved on to the kitchen, emptying cabinets, washing dishes, scrubbing counters. She did the same in the bathroom, then ran a load of laundry. The place still looked like a warehouse, but it would do for a few weeks. Nothing left now but to get started on the boxes.

On impulse, she yanked down a carton from the nearest stack and dropped down beside it on the floor. It was nothing but newspapers, she saw as she pulled back the flaps, yellowing editions of the *New York Times* dating as far back as 1957. There seemed no rhyme or reason why they'd been kept, no sequential dates or common thread among the headlines to explain why they might have been worth saving.

Curious, she wrestled the next box down from the stack, delighted to discover that she had stumbled onto a treasure trove of vintage fashion magazines—*Vogue, Harper's Bazaar, Charm, Mademoiselle,* and *Vanity Fair,* all dated between 1950 and 1960. Her heart beat a little faster as she lifted out the top issue. She really should press on, she told herself, stay focused on what she was supposed to be doing, but vintage fashion had always been her passion. She couldn't very well set them aside without at least flicking through a few. Besides, she'd been thinking of trying a few retro pieces. Maybe she'd pick up some ideas and hit the ground running when she got to Milan.

Forty minutes later, Lily reluctantly set aside the May '58 issue of *Bazaar,* ready if not eager to get back to work, when she saw something that made the hairs on her arms prickle to attention—a woman who could have been her mother, who could almost have been her, gazing up in full color from the cover of *Vogue* magazine.

It was Lily-Mae, of course, breathtaking in a sheath of emerald green silk. She was looking straight into the camera, her sea green eyes heavy-lidded and beckoning, her head tilted slightly, spilling waves of red hair over one creamy shoulder. It was almost impossible for Lily to wrap her head around. Somehow, inconceivably, a poor girl from Mims, Tennessee, had made it all the way to the cover of *Vogue.*

She was surprised when the image began to blur in a rush of tears. She dashed them away, still staring at the cover photo. There was no disputing that Lily-Mae and Caroline were sisters. And yet, the longer Lily studied the image, the more she began to notice subtle differences. Lily-Mae's jaw was softer, her cheekbones higher and more delicately sculpted. And there was just a bit of a pout to Lily-Mae's lower lip, the kind of bee-stung fullness women now paid big money to attain. Caroline's mouth had always been thin, and tended to turn down at the corners, as if a lifetime of bitterness had etched itself into her features.

But there was something else, too, that Lily couldn't put her finger on, something dark and quiet lurking behind that camera-ready smile. *Sadness?* The word startled her when it came. Was she only imagining it? Because of what Rhona had said at lunch? She stared at the cover again. No. It was there, beneath all the beauty and glamour: a shadow hiding behind the eyes, invisible perhaps to the casual glance, but laid bare by the camera.

This was what Rhona had seen, and what her mother and grandmother hadn't, the sadness that was always with her, even at the height of her career. The more Lily thought about it, the more inconceivable it seemed that a girl like Lily-Mae, who, aside from her beauty, had never had a single advantage, had managed to reach the pinnacle of her profession. That she had was a fact, but no one started out on the cover of *Vogue*. How had she gotten there?

A light went on as she glanced at the magazine-strewn floor. Suddenly, she knew why Lily-Mae had saved them. She was there, somewhere, in every single one of them. This time, when Lily began turning pages, she wasn't looking for fashion details; she was looking for a face. She found it, too, after a bit of careful searching, smaller ads in the earlier issues, near the back and shot mostly in black and white, selling hats and gloves, the occasional wristwatch. But as the dates advanced, so did the size and prominence of Lily-Mae's photos, modeling Dior, Chanel, and Pierre Balmain. There were head shots, too, glam ads for lipstick, soft drinks, and something called Pearl-Glo Beauty Cream.

It was like thumbing through a glossy time-lapse of her aunt's career. It hadn't lasted, though. Something had happened, something that sent her here, to Sand Pearl Cottage, to live out her days alone—and to die. Perhaps that's what all this chaos was really about—a lifetime, tidily boxed in preparation for the end. Had she known she was sick? Dying? The unsent letter seemed to indicate that she had.

How awful it must have been, awaiting death all alone, writing letters she never meant to send.

God, she needed a glass of wine. Two, actually, if she was going to keep dredging up those kinds of thoughts. In the kitchen, she pulled a bottle of chardonnay from the fridge. She was still hunting for a corkscrew when a quick tap sounded on the glass doors. She whirled toward the open doors to find Dean standing there.

"I thought I'd try knocking this time. I didn't mean to scare you."

"You didn't. I was just . . . I didn't hear you come up the steps."

He pointed to the wine bottle still in her hand. "Happy hour?"

"Something like that. It's been a bit of a day."

"Did I catch you at a bad time?"

Lily shrugged, torn between telling the truth and being polite. She opted for polite. "No, you're fine. What's up?"

"I just came by to apologize about last night. It got kind of weird when Rhona showed up, and then the whole lecture when you got in the truck. Let's just say I wasn't at the top of my game."

Lily smiled uncomfortably at the mention of Rhona. She'd rather he not know how she'd spent her afternoon. "No need to apologize. I had a nice time. A great time, actually. I think I needed to get out and get away from all this." Lily paused, waving her arm at the newly created mess. "As you can see, I haven't made much progress."

Dean briefly scanned the living room. "Wow."

"Yeah, I know. I made it worse."

"I'll say. On top of the plumbing and electrical issues, I think it might qualify as a fire hazard now, too. Are those magazines?"

"Yes. Fashion magazines, with pictures of my aunt in them. It was so amazing. I was going through them, not really paying attention, when all of sudden I looked down and there she was, staring up at me from the cover of *Vogue*. I couldn't believe what I was seeing. I knew she was a model, but I had no idea she was such a big deal. My mother skipped over that part."

"Maybe she was jealous."

"Maybe." Lily reached down to retrieve one of the magazines. "That's her," she said, holding up the copy of *Vogue*. "Lily-Mae Boyle."

Dean whistled softly. "I can see why they'd put her on the cover. She's a knockout. You look just like her, by the way, but then you probably already know that."

"I look like my mother, who looks like her sister." She sighed as Dean handed back the magazine. "She really was beautiful, though, wasn't she? She just had . . . something. And who'd ever believe it—a poor kid from Mims, Tennessee, wearing Dior on the cover of *Vogue*?"

"I thought you didn't know anything about her."

"I didn't when I got here, or at least not much. But I found a set of notebooks in a box under her bed. Diaries, I guess you'd call them, from when she and my mother were girls. I've been reading some pretty awful stuff over the last two days. Things that affected my mother, too, though she's never breathed a word about any of it."

"And what did your mother say when you asked her about it?"

"She hasn't said anything. She's ducking my calls."

"Oh."

"Right. So here I am, trying to piece it together on my own. It's like being caught between a treasure hunt and a ghost story. It's mind-boggling."

"Which explains the wine."

"Pretty much, yeah."

"What if I told you I have a better cure for what ails you?"

Lily eyed him warily, not sure she liked where this was going. "Such as?"

"A walk," Dean said simply.

"A walk is going to cure what ails me?"

"A walk out there will." He hiked a thumb toward the open doors. "The sea. The sand. And a nice long walk. I promise, there's nothing better for a boggled mind. Besides, I deserve a do-over."

"Will this walk of yours include another sunset?"

"That's up to you."

Something about his answer, soft and slightly husky, made Lily hesitate. Maybe this wasn't a good idea. She eyed the wine bottle on the kitchen counter as she weighed her options. Gulp half a bottle of chardonnay and dig around in a few more boxes, or take a walk in the sea air to clear her head?

"Okay, you sold me. Give me a minute to throw on some shorts."

"Or you could just put on that little turquoise swimsuit."

Lily arched a brow at him. "Will we be swimming?"

Dean grinned, feigning sheepishness. "No, probably not. But you can't blame a guy for trying."

FIFTEEN

It was the time of day Lily liked best, when the sun began to soften and slide, painting everything with a warm, golden patina. There was a fresh breeze blowing in off the gulf, warm and salty where it kissed her bare skin. It was good to be outside, to walk along the shore with the sun on her shoulders and the warm, wet squelch of sand between her toes.

It was good to have company, too. They strolled side by side, silent and in no particular hurry, shoulders brushing now and then as they navigated the incoming waves. The truth was she had been relieved to look up and see Dean in the doorway. For all her curiosity, she was finding the excavation of Lily-Mae's past more daunting than expected. It was a prickly business, dredging through old memories, but it was doubly so when the memories belonged to someone else, when every discovery begged a new question, instead of offering answers.

Dean halted, shielding his eyes to watch a pair of kiteboarders skimming dizzily over the waves. Lily moved on a few paces, then stopped, too, bending to pluck a shell from the sand. It was perfect in her palm, creamy white, with pale pink striations that reminded her of a sunrise. On impulse, she tucked it into her pocket, thinking of the jar of shells on Lily-Mae's bureau. Perhaps she'd start one of her own. Three weeks wasn't much time, but it would be fun while it lasted.

"So, tell me about being a fashion designer," Dean said, surprising her. She hadn't heard him approach. "How old were you when you knew it was what you wanted to do?"

Lily shoved a handful of hair off her face, then shrugged. "I can't remember when I didn't know. When I was little I used to cut up my mother's old dresses to make clothes for my dolls. It drove her crazy. She kept buying me all these doll clothes and I kept giving them away. No doll of mine was wearing off-the-rack. I don't know where it came from. Maybe it's some recessive fashion gene from my aunt. What about you? How did you decide to become an architect? Were you designing beach houses at age eight, out of erector sets and Lincoln Logs?"

"Hardly. I didn't know what a beach house was when I was eight. I grew up in a three-bedroom ranch, the same one my father still lives in. When I was seventeen I went to work as a mason's apprentice, and I fell in love with stone. That's when I knew I wanted to design houses—the kind that would still be standing in fifty or a hundred years."

"Really?"

"Yeah, why? What did you think I was going to say?"

Lily abandoned her hair to the wind and resumed her pace. "It just sounded funny coming from a guy who wants to knock down a house he built last year." She shot him a pointed look. "*And* my aunt's cottage."

"To build a *better* house, I told you. I can show you the plans if you want."

Lily stopped again, facing him with hands on hips. "Can I just tell you—if this is your idea of a do-over, you seriously need to think about going back to charm school."

He grinned at her, clearly unscathed. "What can I say? I'm an enigma."

"I thought you were a cliché."

"Oh, I'm that, too. And I cook. Which reminds me—I bought a couple of salmon steaks this afternoon. We could throw them on the grill, whip up a nice salad, eat out on the deck. I'll even throw in that sunset."

"You bought *a couple* of salmon steaks?"

Dean managed to look sheepish. "Yes. One for me, and one for you."

Lily sighed for effect. "Yesterday, it was the mail. Today, a walk. Do you ever do anything without an ulterior motive?"

"Almost never. But seriously, this is the real do-over part. Say yes."

Lily hesitated. Dinner, two nights in a row. It sounded like a bad idea. Although certainly better than the can of clam chowder she'd planned to open. Besides, she couldn't remember the last time a man had cooked for her. If it started getting weird she'd just leave. It wasn't like she'd have far to walk.

He was impressive in the kitchen, Lily had to give him that, keeping up a steady stream of conversation while he diced vegetables and whipped up a lime-butter sauce for the fish. Dog thought so, too, shadowing Dean's every step in case he was called upon to clean up any drops or spills.

"Maybe you should have been a chef instead of an architect," she told him as she watched him snip several sprigs of dill onto a cutting board. "You're pretty handy with a knife. How did you learn to cook, by the way?"

"When your mother takes off you learn pretty quick how to feed yourself—and your father. Plus, it relaxes me. I come home at the end of the day, put on a little music, sip a little wine. Which reminds me."

Stepping to the fridge, he pulled out a bottle, then dug out a corkscrew and a pair of glasses. A few minutes later, he pressed one of the glasses into her hand.

"It isn't French, but it's good. A buddy of mine owns a place out in Napa. He's only been producing a couple of years, but he seems to know what he's doing. Not that I'm an expert. I just know what I like."

Lily ventured a small sip. It was good. And after ten years in France she *was* something of an expert. She watched as Dean stepped out onto the deck with the salmon steaks, laying them down on the hot grill with a delicious hiss.

"Can I at least set the table?"

"No, you cannot. I'm taking care of it. You just sit there and drink your wine."

It only took him a few minutes to gather what he needed and carry it to the small bistro table outside. Then he was back in the kitchen, rinsing lettuce for the salad.

"Onion or no onion?"

"What? Oh, no onion." She watched as he began tearing the bright green leaves into a bowl. "Honestly, this is too good to be true. If I had waited for Luc to cook, I would have starved to death."

"You two live together?"

"No," she said a little too sharply. "He wanted to, but I was afraid he might—"

"Get the wrong idea?"

Lily nodded. "He did that a lot. He always had to make things so complicated."

"How long were you together?"

"Four years, on and off."

"On for him, off for you?"

Lily cocked her head at him. Not because it was an odd question, but because it described perfectly the somewhat tempestuous relationship she'd had with Luc. "Mostly, yes. It always felt like we were out of sync. Probably because we were. He was a good guy, a great guy, but we wanted different things. He was looking for the swing set and the white picket fence, and I'm not." Lily took a long sip of wine, then stared into her glass. "I know it sounds funny, but those things have never been on my radar. Maybe because I didn't grow up that way myself. The only relationship I've seen close up was a disaster—enough of one to know it isn't going to happen to me."

"Your parents divorced?"

"Worse. They stayed together."

Dean's hands stilled over the tomato he was seeding. "You know, I don't think I've ever thought of it like that. Sounds like we both got the fuzzy end of the parental lollipop."

Lily waved the remark away, not wanting to give the wrong impression. "It wasn't traumatic, just . . . strained. My father was wonderful, but he stayed gone a lot—business travel—though I don't think he minded. I missed him terribly, but part of me knew how unhappy he was at home. My mother wasn't—isn't—an easy person to live with."

Dean reached for the wine bottle and topped off both their glasses. "Well, aren't we a pair. Though I must say, it's nice to meet a woman who isn't so distracted by her biological clock that she can't have a little fun." He picked up his glass and took a quick sip. "Grab the salad and come outside. I need to turn the fish."

Lily stared after him a moment as he disappeared, then grabbed the bowl and her glass and trailed out after him. The sun was going down in earnest now, a flat red disc set against a blushy pink horizon. Moving to the railing, she watched it slowly sink, no less captivated than she had been the night before.

A moment later, Dean was beside her. "Every one is different."

"Sorry?"

"Sunsets. Every one is different. You can stand in the same place, day after day, and they never look the same twice. That's what keeps it fun—the surprises. You never know what to expect, so you keep watching. It isn't predictable. Or complicated. You just take it as it comes."

His voice had changed subtly, taking on a hushed, silky quality that might have been reverence for the sunset but felt like something else entirely.

He was looking at her when she turned to face him, his expression unreadable in the dying sunlight. Had she imagined it? Their eyes met, holding briefly before she dragged her gaze away. No, she hadn't. There *was* a question there, an invitation—one without complications.

But there were *always* complications, weren't there, no matter what was said at the outset? Guilt, hurt feelings, self-recrimination. Three weeks of fun hardly seemed worth the risk.

"I'll be gone in three weeks, Dean."

He leaned close, letting his lips brush the curve of her cheek, his words breathy and warm against her skin. "I wasn't proposing."

"It isn't . . . It's not a good idea."

But Dean was undaunted, continuing to blaze a maddening trail along the soft underside of her jaw. "Since when is a little fun between two interested parties a bad idea?" He paused to trace two fingers along her collarbone, coming to rest lightly at the base of her throat, and the tiny pulse that beat there. "We are two interested parties, aren't we? Or am I reading it wrong?"

No, you're not reading it wrong.

Lily cleared her throat as she stepped away from his touch. "You'd better go check on the fish."

SIXTEEN

December 21, 1955
Mt. Zion Missionary Poor Farm

Zell has come back.

For a while I thought I might be safe, that he might have come back a changed man—repentant, like Paul after Damascus. At least in the kitchen I'm out of his sight. I don't mind shucking corn and scrubbing pots. As long as I don't have to go back to the office. I still see him, of course, pious in his shiny black suit as he goes about God's business. He's skittish now, careful not to meet my eye in the mess hall, or from his pulpit on Sunday mornings—so careful I think his wife has started to take notice.

She seems to be everywhere these days, forever lurking and finding fault. If I've left too many eyes on the potatoes, or dribbled gravy on the stove, she's there to scold with a finger in my face. I'm even convinced she has spies snooping after me—a pair of girls who never liked me very much, and stick together like glue. I feel them watching me, catch their eyes sliding away when I turn suddenly in their direction. It takes everything in me not to fly at them both, to blurt out the whole disgusting truth and shock them into letting me alone. I want to, but I don't. I know better than to say anything they could take back to Sister Ruth.

Besides, I haven't been feeling well lately. I'm wrung out all the time, and light-headed, like any minute I might melt into a puddle. Yesterday, while I was scraping the plates, I thought I was going to have to run for the door and heave up my breakfast. Even Caroline has noticed. I told her I was fine, and not to worry, but deep down I can't help worrying a little. I think about Cindy Price, about her dying, and wonder who would look after my sister if anything happens to me.

I've heard the stories, people lying in their own filth with no one to clean or feed them, people going in with some small ailment and never coming out again. Maybe that's because there's no doctor, or even a real nurse, just Sister Doyle, who used to travel with her husband's healing show until they threw him in jail for fleecing an old woman out of her life savings. And there's no real medicine, just wives' tale remedies. It's just goose grease, turpentine, and castor oil—and the laying on of hands, for all the good that does. No matter how sick I get, I'm never going there.

But now I have something new to worry about.

This morning, I was scraping grits from the breakfast bowls when word came that Zell wanted me. It was Sister Ruth who brought the news. For a moment I thought about throwing myself into her arms, about blurting out the truth and begging her to help me. But there wasn't much point. I could see it in her face, in the pitiless gray eyes she swept over me, like I was something to be scraped off her shoe. She knows, and always has, what her husband is all about—and knows, too, that there's nothing she can do to stop it. If there were, she would have already done it. I nodded and wiped my hands, feeling almost sorry for her. It must be awful being married to a brute like Zell, though I can't think of a woman who deserves it more.

Caroline stood close by, watching as I stripped out of my apron and squared my shoulders, the venom on her face shocking as I moved past her and out of the kitchen. I knew what she was thinking—that I was deserting her again, leaving her to fend for herself—like Mama had done.

When I stepped into the office Zell was waiting with a present in his hands, a parcel wrapped in tissue and tied with bits of ribbon.

"Merry Christmas," he said, fixing me with one of his oily smiles.

When I didn't move, he gave the ribbon a tug, then folded back the layers of tissue. I shrank back as he pressed the gift into my hands—a peach sweater with tiny pearl buttons sewn down the front. I stared at it, wondering where he thought I would ever wear such a thing.

He was looking at me, watching my face and waiting for me to say something—thank you, probably—but I couldn't form the words. I didn't want his presents.

"I wanted you to have something nice," he said, "something . . . grown-up." He took a step toward me, and then another, until I felt the edge of the desk against my backside. "I missed you while I was gone, Lily-Mae. Did you miss me?"

I wouldn't answer. Not to that. He could push me down on the desk and take what he wanted. There was nothing I could do to stop him. But he couldn't make me say I had missed him. Could he not see that I despised him? That I had wished him dead a hundred times while he was gone? A thousand?

He reached for me then, taking my chin in his hand, forcing it up until I had no choice but to look him in the eye. "I've been kind to you, haven't I, Lily-Mae? And to Caroline? Do you think I'm that kind to all the girls here?"

The room started to wobble, and I felt my hands go clammy. I wanted to say I thought he was kind to the pretty ones, but didn't give a damn about the rest, but I knew better. I let him keep talking, trying to ignore his free hand, on my waist now, skimming higher with every word.

"There are lots of girls who'd like to be my pet, who'd like the presents I give you. I could do that, you know: choose someone else to help me here, someone else to do favors for. How old is your sister now, Lily-Mae? She's growing up nicely—a pretty little thing, just like you."

The room began to turn and shift. "I . . . missed you, too, Brother Zell."

He smiled then, because he could see that I understood. "Yes, I thought so."

His hand slid up to cup my breast, squeezing until I nearly cried out. He was hurting me and he knew it. And then his mouth was on mine, pulpy and slick as he shoved me back onto the desk, and I reached for the rope of the old tire swing.

January 17, 1956
Mt. Zion Missionary Poor Farm

The sickness has gotten worse. So much worse that there are times I'm sure I must be dying. But there's a part of me—one I've refused to listen to—that has always known I wasn't sick, that knew what was wrong with me was worse than sick—worse, even, than dying.

One morning I was brushing my teeth when the sickness came again. I nearly buckled when it hit me, holding on to the sink for dear life until I had retched myself empty. When I straightened again, Sister Ruth was there in the mirror, reflected back at me in all her rigid rage, and I knew, suddenly, what a fool I had been to deny the truth—that Harwood Zell's baby was growing in my belly.

For a moment I thought I would be sick again. But there was no time. Before I could grab hold of the sink again she had me by the arm, whipping me around until we stood face-to-face.

I didn't see the slap coming until it rocked me back against the sink. A second one came quickly on its heels, stinging the other cheek. I tasted blood, coppery and hot at the corner of my mouth.

"Whore!" she screamed, drawing back for another slap.

I dodged it, but she latched onto my sleeve, shaking me until the teeth rattled in my head. Spots danced in front of my eyes. She was the only thing keeping me on my feet. "It wasn't my fault," I choked, begging her, begging God—begging anyone who could hear—to believe me. "I didn't want him to. He forced me!"

"It's a lie!" she bellowed, giving me another savage shake. "You've been throwing yourself at him since the day you got here, sashaying after him with that red hair of yours, you . . . harlot!"

I was dimly aware of the crowd gathering outside the door, of a sea of curious faces peering in at us, and wondered if Caroline was among them, watching this awful spectacle. I sagged to the floor when Sister Ruth finally let go, half blind with shame, with tears that wouldn't stop. She kicked me then, and kept on kicking me, with all the hatred that was in her, trying to kill me, to kill the baby. And suddenly I didn't care anymore. The world had grown fuzzy and cold, the lights over my head shrinking, fading, until, finally, they were gone.

I woke with my stomach heaving, choked by the mingled stench of urine, sweat, and unwashed sheets. I was in a room with three empty cots, and a sign on the half-open door that read "Quarantine." Turning my head, I retched drily onto the stained mattress. They had taken me to the infirmary.

I had no idea how I came to be there, only why I was there. Gradually, sounds began to penetrate, ragged snores and heavy groans from the beds in the other room, the drone of flies against the windows, and from somewhere behind me, the hiss of female voices. I couldn't make out what was being said, but I recognized one of the voices as Sister Ruth's.

Dear God . . . have I lost the baby?

My eyes stung with sudden hope. Ashamed, I turned my head and blinked away the tears. To be free of it, to be spared the shame, the hideous reminder. It was wrong to hope for such a thing, but I did hope for it.

And then suddenly there was a woman hovering over me, a large, square-built woman with shoulders like a man and a face like God's own judgment—Sister Doyle. She was standing beside the cot, arms folded, looking me over like she was sizing me up for a roasting pan.

"How far?" she grunted.

I blinked up at her, trying to make sense of the question.

"She doesn't show yet," came Sister Ruth's cold voice from somewhere behind the bed. "I want it taken care of. Now."

Sister Doyle nodded gravely. "I'll get help, then, and we'll be done with it."

I had no idea what they were talking about as Sister Doyle disappeared, or what they were in such a hurry to be done with, but something in Sister Ruth's tone filled me with dread. I craned my neck, trying to find her, to demand to know what they meant to do with me, but a fresh wave of sickness drove me back to the mattress.

Sister Doyle returned with two heavy-boned women I had seen before but never spoken to. They were careful to keep their eyes from mine as they approached, looking at their hands, their shoes, anywhere but at my face. I still didn't understand when Sister Doyle pulled a handful of rags from her pocket and handed two to each woman.

They fell on me then, without a word, as if it had all been prearranged, dragging my arms above my head, winding rags about my wrists as they lashed me to the bed frame. I railed and thrashed, suddenly, hideously aware of what they meant to do, but their weight and their strength were too much for me. Soon my legs were bound as well, my knees bent toward my ears, spread wide apart.

When they finished with their knots the heaviest woman lay across my belly, pinning me to the mattress, exposed and helpless. A wadded sheet was shoved under my hips, but I was left uncovered. Sister Ruth stepped to the foot of the bed then, her face twisted with a kind of grim satisfaction as Sister Doyle pulled something long and slender from the pocket of her stained apron. It looked like a knitting needle, shiny and sharp in her thick fist.

"Don't," I pleaded in a voice I no longer recognized as my own. Girls died from what they were about to do. They got infections, or they bled to death. "You can't do this!"

Sister Ruth stepped forward, her face drawn, and white as chalk. She trembled as she reached for me, winding her fingers through my hair, twisting until my eyes began to water and our gazes locked. A vial was pressed to my lips, forcing them apart. I choked as the bitterness trickled down my throat.

Sister Ruth bent down then, her breath hot against my ear. "Do you think you're the first? That there haven't been others like you? Maybe not as pretty, but there have been plenty, and more than one has ended up tied to this bed. You're not special."

I stared at her, groping for words, but my head was fuzzy suddenly. How could I make her understand? I didn't want her husband, and I didn't want this child. But I didn't want what they were about to do, either. There were ways—other ways. I could go away, give up the child as soon as it was born. But my tongue was too thick and the words wouldn't come.

I felt the grip on my hair ease as Sister Ruth turned to Sister Doyle. They muttered something, but the words seemed to melt and run together. When the whispering ended Sister Doyle gave a nod to the woman sprawled on top of me, then moved to the foot of the bed, face hardened, needle poised. Terror swirled up into my throat, panic mixed with bile and the beginnings of a fresh scream—a plea for help from a God who wasn't there. Then a rag was shoved into my mouth, and Sister Doyle went to work.

February 10, 1956
Mt. Zion Missionary Poor Farm

For days—I can't say how many—I lapsed in and out of something like sleep, sweating and tossing in a darkened room, dreaming of blood-soaked sheets, of towels wadded thickly between my legs. And then, when the bleeding was finally over, the fever came. I remember little of those days, only the memory of sweat-drenched sheets, and a feeling like drowning as water was forced past my lips.

I was alone when I woke, dazed, and so dry I could barely pry my lips apart. Finally, a woman in a red and brown kerchief poked her head in, startled to see that my eyes were open, then backed out hastily.

Moments later, she returned with broth and a pan of cool water, going about her business without words or pity, then left me again, alone behind the closed door of the quarantine room. There was something she knew but wouldn't say. I could see it in her face as she turned away from my questions. As she slipped out with lowered eyes, she said Sister Doyle would be in to talk to me when the time came.

Time ground slowly while I waited for Sister Doyle, the hours so long and empty I thought I might go mad. Instead I lay there, sifting through my feelings, trying to muster some kind of sadness or rage, but all I felt was numb. The child—Zell's child—was gone, and it would be a lie to say that I was sorry. But the taking of it, the sheer brutality at the hands of those so-called godly women, will be with me always.

And then Sister Doyle finally came, filling up the doorway with her square frame and dour face. Her expression was set, hard as granite, with no hint of sympathy. "You're better," she said gruffly, leaving no room for an answer. "It's time to talk about things."

"Things," I repeated, my voice rusty from disuse.

"Your little difficulty has been seen to, Lily-Mae, but you gave us a rough time of it there for a while. I'm afraid there were complications . . . damage."

Damage. *The word should have alarmed me, but didn't somehow. Perhaps because I had no inkling of what she was about to say. Or perhaps because I did, and the prospect stirred no regret in me.*

"In cases like yours, it's doubtful there will ever be children." The words dropped from her mouth like hard little stones, and for just a moment her eyes skittered away, avoiding mine. When they finally found me again I could see that her resolve was firmly back in place. "Do you understand?"

I managed a nod against the pillow, wanting her to go away. Sister Doyle studied my face, waiting for tears, for grief, but I felt none. Her words could not wound me since I had already decided no man would ever be allowed to touch me again. So where was the loss? I was aware of my numbness, of the cold, hollow space where my grief should be, but wasn't. My heart was empty and locked down tight. Zell had seen to that the first time he laid his hands on me.

"God has seen fit to let you live," Sister Doyle said gravely. "But only just. You would do well to remember that, and to lay down your wicked ways."

For a moment something like fury flickered in my chest. I stared at her with her condemning tone and her unkind eyes, longing to tell the pious Sister Doyle that it was not my wickedness that had brought me here, but that of the saintly Brother Zell. But there was no time to say any of that. She was heading for the door.

She paused when she reached the doorway, her thick hand resting heavily on the knob, and in that instant I felt those hands on me again, gripping my knees, forcing them apart—and I hated her. Not for what she had done to me, but for what she believed about me, that somehow I deserved all of this.

"You'll be here a while yet, until you're stronger."

"My sister? Can I see her?"

"That would be unwise. She hasn't been told of your . . . condition. She knows only that you were taken with a violent fever and have been in quarantine."

I let the words sink in, feeling tears prickle against the backs of my lids. For the first time, I felt relief. She'd been told only part of the truth, though I suspect leaving out the rest had been Sister Ruth's idea. Not to save me any shame, but to protect her husband. I didn't care about the why *just then, only that Caroline should never know the truth.*

"Is she . . . being looked after?"

Sister Doyle squared her already square shoulders and glowered at me from across the room. "All the girls at Mt. Zion are looked after."

I wanted to laugh, to scream, to throw the words back in her face. But she was gone, leaving me alone with my thoughts in the creosote-scented gloom.

February 17, 1956
Mt. Zion Missionary Poor Farm

A full week passed before I saw Sister Doyle again. She came to tell me I was being allowed to leave the infirmary, and that I was to report straight to Zell's office. If she noticed my horror she gave no sign, just slipped back out and left me to dress on my own. No one spoke to me as I walked out the front door, but I could hear the whispers as I passed between the rows of cots, could feel their eyes, hurling their questions between my shoulder blades. They wanted me to feel shame, to feel dirty. But I didn't. I didn't feel anything at all.

After being cooped up so long it should have been good to step outside into the sunshine, to breathe air that didn't smell of urine and disinfectant, but I barely noticed as I made my way across the winter-bare yard, past the dorms, and the mess, and the chapel. I was too worried about why Zell wanted to see me. Almost from the moment I had awakened from the fever, I had been imagining what it would be like when I finally returned to the dorm—and to work. I would go back to the kitchens now, or to the laundry. Not to Zell's, surely. Not after everything that had happened. He would find some other girl to file his papers. The thought made me a little sick, and sorry for whoever he would choose next, but at least it wouldn't be me. Sister Ruth would see to that. She despised me, but had reasons of her own to keep me safe.

As I reached the outer door to Zell's office I faltered, stunned by the sight of my reflection in the gritty pane of glass. I barely recognized the face staring back at me, pale as biscuit dough with a pair of hollowed-out eyes, cheekbones stark beneath my too-thin skin. I was a ghost, a shadow of the girl I had been only weeks ago. Part of me was glad. I wanted Zell to see what he had done, to feel ashamed, to be sorry. So sorry he would never come near me again.

I didn't think to knock when I reached the inner door. I don't know why. But when I pushed into the office Caroline was perched on the corner of Zell's desk, legs crossed at the knees and swinging coyly.

They didn't hear me come in. I stood there, rooted to the spot, trying to think what to say. Finally, Zell looked up, past Caroline and straight at me, the hint of a smile on his face. Caroline turned then, eyes glittering with something like satisfaction as they settled on me. She didn't look fourteen anymore. She was wearing lipstick and the peach sweater Zell had given me—the one I had buried at the bottom of my footlocker so I would never have to see it again.

"What are you doing here, Caroline? You shouldn't be here."

Horrified, I watched her turn to Zell, offering him a much-too-grown-up pout. The effect was ridiculous, like a child playing dress-up. Where on earth had she learned such a thing?

"I've been helping out while you were sick," she said with a triumphant little smirk. "Brother Zell said I could."

I was trembling all over, my fists clenched to keep from dragging her off the desk and shaking some sense into her young empty head. The little fool! She hadn't a clue what she was doing, or where it could lead—if it hadn't already. The thought of him touching her—of Sister Doyle touching her—nearly made my legs buckle.

"It's lunchtime," I managed through numb lips. "And time to wash your face."

Caroline's eyes narrowed briefly before turning a honeyed smile to Zell. "Do I have to?"

Zell got up, but made no move to come from behind the desk, just stood there with his thumbs hooked in his suspenders, running his piggy eyes over my sister, slow and thoughtful. "For now," he said at last, with a smile that chilled me to my bones. "We'll talk again tomorrow."

His eyes fell on me the moment Caroline closed the door, tallying the devastation he'd inflicted. "Poor Lily-Mae," he crooned. "You've been ill, haven't you?"

I flinched at the question, at the causal words we both knew were a lie. He knew. I could see it in his face. He knew everything, and he wasn't one bit sorry. As I stood there, Sister Ruth's words came floating back. I wasn't the first. I wasn't special. How many had come before me? And how many would come after?

"Why was my sister here?"

He smiled blandly as he came from behind the desk, hands clasped behind his back. "You were gone. I needed help."

"I don't want her here. I don't want her helping you!"

The words had burst out of me before I could stop them, but Zell's smile never wavered. "Well, now, I don't suppose I'll be needing Caroline now that you're well again. And I'm glad you are well." He frowned suddenly, as if a thought had just occurred. "I wanted to come and see you, Lily-Mae. I wanted to, but it might have spoiled our little secret." He paused, raising his pale brows a notch. "It is our little secret, isn't it, Lily-Mae? Ours and no one else's?"

He wanted to know if I had told anyone, or planned to. He lit a cigarette, then stood stroking his suspenders. When I said nothing, he continued. "I ask only because there are some who wouldn't understand. They might . . . kick up a fuss." He paused long enough to blow out a plume of smoke. "It would be a pity for you and Caroline to have to leave Mt. Zion because of a little misunderstanding. Assuming, of course, that your sister was allowed to go with you."

My head snapped up, my insides slowly turning to ice. "What?"

"She's only a child, after all. The authorities might not think you were fit to care for her. They might think her better off here, under proper supervision, than with a sister who had recently suffered . . . health problems. They would want my opinion, Lily-Mae, naturally, and I'm afraid I couldn't lie, even for you. I would hate to be placed in such a position."

I was speechless as I digested the threat. If I told anyone what he had done, he would see to it that I was tossed out of Mt. Zion—and that Caroline would not be allowed to go with me. I wanted to believe he was lying, that he could never be cruel enough to separate sisters. But as he stood there waiting for me to say something, I knew I needed only to cross him to find out.

He reached for my hand then, giving it a pat. "I'm glad we un-

derstand each other, and that we're still going to be . . . friends. It would be a shame to see you and Caroline separated."

That's when I knew he meant for us to carry on as before. Not just the work, but all of it. "But your wife!" I blurted, suddenly desperate. "She knows you—"

Zell turned away, stepping to his desk as calmly as if we'd been discussing the weather. "I've seen to my wife," he informed me casually as he picked up an envelope and coolly slit it open. "She won't bother you again."

The words settled in my belly like a cold stone. Because I knew without Sister Ruth to stand in his way, this nightmare would never end. I wouldn't be free of Zell until he said I was. And then there was Caroline, foolish, headstrong Caroline, eager to take my place, though she was too young to know what that meant.

I stood there, rooted to the floor, saying nothing as I watched him begin to count out a fat stack of bills. It wasn't the first time I'd seen him do it. He was always getting envelopes like that, counting out cash, and then locking it up in the small metal box he kept in his desk. Only this time, I found myself paying attention. Because an idea—a mad, desperate, impossible idea—had already taken hold of me.

SEVENTEEN

1995
Hideaway Key, Florida

Lily spooned sugar into her mug and stirred, still vaguely numb. The previous night, after dinner with Dean, she had returned to the cottage to finish reading the last of Lily-Mae's notebooks. She'd had to push herself to make it to the last page, sickened by the images the entries conjured: rape, forced abortion, unending intimidation. Her skin crawled at the thought of Harwood Zell—a predator hiding behind a collar and a Bible—forcing himself on a helpless girl.

She'd only kept reading because she was convinced that by the last page she would finally know how the nightmare ended. Unfortunately, she was wrong. There had been no closure—no escape from Mt. Zion, and no justice for Harwood Zell. That they *had* gotten away was a fact. It was the *how* that remained a mystery. How long had Lily-Mae been forced to endure Zell's disgusting attentions? And how had she finally managed to get herself and Caroline away? In the absence of additional journals it seemed only her mother knew the answers to those questions.

Lily eyed the phone but didn't move. What was the point? She'd lost count of how many messages she'd left, all of which had gone ignored. Still, it was the only avenue open to her. Mug in hand, she marched to the phone and punched in her mother's number, nails tapping while she waited for the inevitable beep to end.

"Mother, pick up," she finally snapped, imagining Caroline stubbornly entrenched on the couch, listening to every word. "I know you're there, and I know you can hear me. You might as well answer. I'm just going to keep calling until you do." She waited a moment, counting to ten and listening to empty silence. She was about to hang up when she heard the receiver lift on the other end.

"Mother?"

"Yes, I'm here."

"I knew you were. Why haven't you called me back?"

"Because"—she sighed wearily—"there's nothing to say."

"Nothing to say? I just finished reading the most hideous things imaginable, things that happened to your sister, and to you. There's plenty to say."

There was the familiar plink of ice being dropping into a martini pitcher, the rasp of a lighter being struck, the sound of smoke being exhaled. "I have no idea what you're talking about, Lily."

"Mt. Zion, Mother. I'm talking about Mt. Zion, and what happened there. How could you not tell me any of that?" The line went quiet a moment. "Mother?"

"How do you know about Mt. Zion?"

"I found a stack of notebooks under Lily-Mae's bed. More like diaries, actually, from when the two of you were there. She wrote about what your mother did . . . and what Zell did."

"They were about Mt. Zion? That's all there was?"

"All?" Lily was incredulous. "Abandonment isn't enough? Rape isn't enough? There was a baby, Mother. Did she ever tell you that? And what they did to her? My God, it was barbaric."

"What would it have changed?"

"What would it have *changed*? Nothing, I suppose. But Mt. Zion was a part of your life. Why would you keep it a secret?"

"I didn't keep it a secret. I chose not to share it. It's not the same thing. And it's my right, don't you think? Not to share things I'd rather keep private?"

A thought suddenly occurred, one Lily was shocked to admit she had never even considered, one that might explain years of silence. "What he did to Lily-Mae . . ." She faltered as she tried to form the words. "The rape. He didn't hurt you, too, did he?"

"Rape? Is that how she wrote it down?"

Lily felt mildly stunned. "What other way could she have written it? She was a girl, and he forced himself on her."

"She was seventeen, Lily. Hardly a child."

"I read it, Mother, every disgusting word. About Zell and his horrid wife, and about the child. They held her down and forced her to have an abortion, then botched it so badly they almost killed her. Are you saying that didn't happen, either?"

"I'm not saying those things didn't happen, Lily. I'm saying they might not have happened the way my sister chose to remember them."

Lily let the words sink in. "So you're saying it was a lie? That she made the whole thing up, then wrote it all down in a book no one was ever supposed to see? Why bother?"

There was a pause, then a huff of impatience. "God knows what went through that woman's mind. She had a knack for concocting stories. She could look you straight in the eye and lie without blinking. I've seen her do it."

"But why this? Why make up a story about Zell?"

"She liked men, Lily. All kinds of men. Rich men. Powerful men. Other people's men. And when she got caught it was always someone else's fault. You can't take anything she wrote in those notebooks as fact. But if it did happen, it was only what she had coming to her."

"Mother!"

"Zell was a man. She threw herself at him. What did she expect him to do?"

"Not rape her, for God's sake! How can you even think something like that?"

"You don't understand her. You can't."

"No, I don't. I never have. You've never been willing to talk about her, and now that I'm starting to discover things on my own, you're telling me she was some sort of pathological liar. At this point I don't know what to believe."

"So now I'm the liar."

"That isn't what I said, but you've got to admit this is all a little bizarre. Daddy leaves me a beach house, and when I get here it's full of Lily-Mae's things. Then when I ask you about something she wrote you shut me down, just like you always do. And I'm just supposed to take you at your word. Can you see why I might be skeptical?"

"It's over, Lily, done with. She's dead, and I'm finished talking about it. I wish you could be, too. It's time to focus on Milan and let this obsession of yours go."

"Not until I sort through the rest of what's here."

"Throw it out, or just leave it."

There was a tremor in Caroline's voice, as if she were afraid. "I can't do that, Mother. She was my aunt, and for better or worse, I want to know who she was. I'm not asking you to talk about it anymore. I'll work it out for myself."

"You're doing this to spite me." Caroline's voice shook with suppressed fury. "You *and* your father."

Lily stifled a groan. She didn't have time for drama. "It isn't spite, Mother. I'm curious. I've always been curious. Because she's family. You hate her. I get that. But you think that means I have to hate her, too. You've just never told me why. So unless you're willing to talk about it now, I'm going to find out for myself."

"Lily, please—"

"I'm getting off now, Mother. I won't bother you anymore."

Lily hung up more frustrated than ever. She'd been hoping for a little insight into the events in the journal, to be a little closer by the end of the call to knowing the real Lily-Mae. Instead, two distinct but conflicting likenesses of the woman were beginning to emerge: one a sad and selfless martyr, the other a liar and a tease. Which was real?

EIGHTEEN

A bead of sweat traced down Lily's temple as she labeled and set aside another box for giveaway. Stretching the kinks from her back, she eyed the stack of cartons waiting to be taken to Goodwill—old cookbooks, dishes, pots and pans. After four straight days of backbreaking work, it was good to see some progress, and to finally be able to walk in a straight line from the bedroom to the kitchen. But four days of sorting, sifting, and tossing had taken a toll on her muscles—and her mood, which hadn't been great to start with after the confrontation with her mother on the phone the other day.

Other than morning coffee on the deck, she hadn't been out of the cottage in days, opting to stay focused on the tasks at hand. It was hard to believe she'd already been here a week, that one-third of her time on Hideaway Key had already ticked by. Milan was waiting, but there was still so much she hadn't touched, more than she could ever hope to get through in two weeks. But how could she possibly walk away without knowing the rest of Lily-Mae's story?

She didn't have to, though. Not really. It wasn't like she needed the money. If she really wanted to stay, she could. All she had to do was pick up the phone and tell Dario she wasn't coming, that with everything that had happened since her father's death she couldn't possibly leave the States right now. And if she made that call—what then? Would there be another opportunity? Did she even want one?

Beyond the open doors a flash of gull wings caught her eye, silver-white against a blinding blue sky. She watched the bird skim over the water, sinking and then lifting away, effortless on the afternoon breeze. Nowhere to go, nowhere to be. Just free.

Without warning, a pang of grief hit her square in the chest, a sense of loss so keen it made her throat constrict. She missed her father, the comfort of his presence, the sound of his voice, the ability to pick up the phone and ask him what she should do. But she already knew what he would say.

Follow your North Star.

And she had been—or at least she'd been trying. For all she knew, her North Star *was* in Milan. She knew it wasn't in Paris, or in New York. And it certainly wasn't here in Hideaway. How could it be, when the cottage had simply fallen into her lap, a whim of her father? She thought of what Sheila had said, about there not being any accidents, and everything happening as it was supposed to. She didn't know if she believed that or not—or if she even wanted to. What she did know was that if there was any hope at all of clearing the cottage by the end of June she had better stick with it. But first she needed some lunch.

A few minutes later, Lily stepped out onto the deck with a bottled water and a hastily assembled turkey sandwich. She ate standing at the railing, watching the steady progress of a sailboat tracking across the horizon. She was halfway through her sandwich when she thought she heard the faint strains of music. Head cocked, she strained to locate the source of the sound. For a moment it disappeared, snatched away on the breeze, but then it returned—U2's "Mysterious Ways."

Going up on tiptoe, she peered past the screen of sabal palms. Dean was on the patio, bare to the waist and shiny with sweat, a black boom box stationed nearby. He looked to be finishing up for the day, hosing out a large plastic bucket, gathering up trowels and mortar boards. When he was finished he drained a nearby bottle of water, mopped his face, and headed out onto the beach.

Lily watched from the edge of the deck as he jogged down to the shore and, without breaking stride, launched himself into the waves. He disappeared briefly, plunging beneath the glassy blue surface, then bobbed up again seconds later and rolled onto his back, arms and legs extended. He didn't stay long, wading back to shore just moments later, obviously more interested in cooling off than in taking an actual swim. Lily took a quick step back, but it was too late. Dean had already seen her and was waving. There was nothing to do but wave back and hold up her lunch plate in a lame attempt to explain her presence. *I wasn't spying on you. Really, I wasn't. I was just out here enjoying the sunshine and eating my turkey sandwich.*

Back inside, Lily dumped the half-eaten remains of her sandwich in the trash and made a beeline for the desk, rummaging around until she found a phone book. She wasn't ready to dive back into cartons of chipped dishes and souvenir ashtrays, but maybe if she got rid of some of the stuff she'd already sorted she'd have a clearer sense of what still needed to be tackled.

She had just found the listing for the local Goodwill location when she heard a commotion out on the deck. She glanced up to see Dog, grinning his doggy grin from the open doorway. A moment later, Dean appeared at the top of the steps.

"Hey, stranger." His hair was still wet on the ends, and there was a fresh nick on his chin from shaving. "You've been pretty scarce since dinner the other night. I thought I'd better make sure I didn't poison you."

Lily's gaze shifted uncomfortably. She didn't want to talk about dinner, or why she had ducked out the minute they'd finished eating. "I've been keeping my head down."

Dean stepped in off the deck, making a quick survey. "I'll say you have. You can actually move in here now. What did you do with all of it?"

"A lot of it's stacked by the front door. It's household stuff, mostly. I was just looking up the address for the nearest Goodwill."

"And what about fun? What have you been doing for fun?"

Lily rolled her eyes. "Look at this place. I don't have time for fun."

"Haven't you heard? All work and no play makes Lily a dull girl."

"I'm not dull," Lily snapped defensively. "I'm . . . responsible."

"You're also pale. You need to get out and soak up a little sunshine, see what Hideaway Key has to offer. I can help with that."

Lily was ready with a perfectly valid excuse. "I really can't. I need to get those boxes to Goodwill before they close."

"Great. We'll take the truck and drop them off on the way."

Lily eyed him warily. "Why do I feel an ulterior motive coming on?"

"Come on," he coaxed boyishly. "I haven't steered you wrong so far, have I?"

She had to admit, he hadn't. "Okay, where are we going?"

"It's a secret."

"I don't like secrets."

"You'll like this one, I promise. I'll run Dog home and load the boxes while you change. Dress cool. And leave the hat at home."

Lily still had no idea what Dean was up to when he pulled into the parking lot of the Hideaway Marina.

"I forgot to ask. You don't get seasick, do you?"

Lily lowered her sunglasses. "We're going on a boat?"

"If you don't get seasick, we are."

She was still a bit leery as she followed Dean to the ticket window of a small whitewashed shack. She watched him count out a few bills and pass them under the Plexiglas window, then trailed after him down a narrow aluminum dock. Lily smiled when she saw the bright blue letters emblazoned on the hull of the sleek white catamaran. CAPTAIN BUBBA'S DOLPHIN WATCH.

Bubba looked surprised to see Dean as they boarded, then grinned when he spotted Lily. "What are you doing with this guy? Slumming?"

Lily nodded in Dean's direction. "I was bribed, I swear."

"Yeah, I figured. Well, welcome aboard the *Southern Star.* Let me know if he makes a nuisance of himself, and I'll have him tossed over."

Ten minutes later they were skimming over the water, Van Morrison's "Into the Mystic" piping over the speakers. Lily closed her eyes and tipped her face to the breeze, reveling in lyrics she had probably sung a hundred times but never truly listened to. *Smell the sea and feel the sky. Let your soul and spirit fly. Into the mystic.* It was perfect. All of it. Absolutely perfect.

A few miles out, the *Southern Star* slowed to a crawl. Lily turned to scan the receding coastline, white sands and blue water, lazily swaying palms, like something from a postcard. Bubba's voice broke in over the speakers, his dry humor and languid Southern drawl a crowd-pleaser as he welcomed his passengers, gave a brief history of Hideaway Key and Florida's Gulf Coast, then moved on to the various feeding and breaching habits of the bottlenose dolphin.

They didn't have long to wait before the first pod made an appearance, breaching in a silvery, slick arc so perfectly timed it seemed to have been choreographed for their benefit. Cheers and applause erupted around them as the dolphins continued to surface, splashing and posing, while children squealed and cameras clicked. Lily stood gripping the railing, basking in the magic and beauty of the moment. She couldn't remember the last time she felt this way, blissful and alive, as if something that had been bound up for years had suddenly begun to unknot itself.

She glanced down at Dean's hand, surprised to find it closed over hers on the railing, but even more surprised that she felt no impulse to pull away.

"It's all so beautiful," she said dreamily. "So perfect."

"It is."

Something in his voice, a soft, honeyed warmth, let her know he wasn't talking about the scenery. She turned to him, smiling almost shyly. "Thank you for this—for bringing me today."

"You're welcome." He paused to push a strand of hair out of her eyes. "Maybe next time you'll trust me when I suggest something."

Lily looked up through her lashes. "That depends on what you suggest."

A smile tugged at the corners of his mouth, warm and lazy. "I'll be sure to keep that in mind."

It was flirting, Lily told herself as she turned to look back over the water, the kind that didn't have to go anywhere. Harmless, uncomplicated flirting. In two weeks she'd be gone, half a world away, and Hideaway Key would be a memory. So would Dean. Would it really be so terrible? So dangerous? When they both wanted the same thing?

She was no closer to an answer when the coastline finally came back into view, and Bubba came over the speakers thanking his passengers and reminding them to gather up their belongings. A sudden pang of disappointment caught her off guard. She wasn't ready for the day to end. She wanted to stay right where she was, to savor this afternoon, and this feeling, for as long as possible. Unfortunately, all good things came to an end, including cruises—and summers.

Back on dry land, they headed to the Sundowner for drinks. Lily grinned sheepishly at Salty as she ordered one of his infamous Pink Flip-Flops.

"What can I say? I'm hooked."

Salty winked and shot her one of his pirate smiles. "If I didn't know better I'd say Mr. Landry was starting to rub off on you."

"I'm doing my damnedest," Dean said, chuckling as he wrestled a lime wedge down the neck of his Corona. "Got her out with Bubba this afternoon. I think she might have even gotten a little sun. She looks good, don't you think? Like a proper tourist."

Salty gave Lily's drink a final shake, then poured the bubble gum–colored liquid into a sugared martini glass and slid it to her across the bar. "Speaking of tourists—from where do you hail, Lily St. Claire? Not from the South, I'm guessing."

"Then you'd guess right. I'm from New York. Dean tells me you're from Miami. He says you were a cop, and now you write mysteries set here on Hideaway. How fun."

Salty nodded sheepishly as he picked up a glass and towel and began drying. "Keeps me off the streets. Well, that and this place."

"How'd you get started?"

"Like everyone else, I guess. Used to play around with it when I was young, then forgot about it for a while. You know how it goes—gotta make a living. Then, when I left the force, I had all this time on my hands. I started playing again. Next thing you know I had a chapter, then five chapters, then a book. Took three years to write that first one. Like I said—keeps me off the streets."

Dean scooped a fistful of peanuts from a nearby bowl and popped several into his mouth. "He's being modest, Lily. He's actually quite the celebrity. People are always popping in here asking him to sign their books, or to have their picture taken with him."

Lily turned wide eyes on Salty. "Is that true?"

He shrugged, reaching for another glass. "People are fascinated by writers. And the name of my place is right there on the back with my picture, so I'm easy to find."

"Was that on purpose? Putting the Sundowner on the back?"

"It started out as a joke, actually. But my publisher liked the idea of a bar-owning ex-cop writing mysteries."

"Who wouldn't? It's brilliant marketing. I've always been intrigued by mystery writers, how you can take something incredibly complicated and make it look so easy. You weave in all these clues, some real and some not, so the reader has no idea what to pay attention to. And then, at the end, when you lay it all out, it's so perfectly obvious we can't believe we never saw it coming."

Salty grinned. "Literary sleight of hand, my dear. In a good mystery, or any story, really, all the clues are right there under your nose. But only if you pay attention and don't go into a story thinking you know how it ends. That's when you miss things, because your brain is only looking for answers in one direction. If you just stay open and let the clues add up, it all falls together at the end."

Dean snorted. "Easy for you to say. That last one—*Heat in High Places*—had me scratching my head to the very last page. Not to mention keeping me up for three straight nights."

"Better rest up, then," Salty said, grinning. "Detective Hank Petri's next adventure hits the shelves next month, and this time the body belongs to his ex-wife."

"Is Detective Petri you?" Lily asked, growing more fascinated by the minute.

Salty gave a hearty laugh, as if he found the remark amusing. "Not even close. For starters, I don't have an ex-wife. Or any wife. Oh . . ." He paused, holding up his left hand to wiggle his fingers. "And Petri has all his digits."

"Okay, so purely fictional. But how many of your ideas come from actual cases you worked while you were on the force?"

"A few, but only as seeds. Real life doesn't lend itself to well-plotted story lines. It would be nice if it did, but cases rarely wrap themselves up all nice and neat in three hundred and fifty pages. In fact, some of them never wrap up at all. So you have to help things along a little. Or a lot."

Lily ran a finger around the sugared rim of her glass, suddenly thoughtful. "How do you know when they're not going to wrap up at all? I mean, how do you know when it's time to walk away?" She pretended not to feel Dean's eyes on her as she posed the question. "I was just wondering."

"Ah, there's the tough question. I guess when the trail goes cold. You get to a point where the evidence just runs out. But you're never quite ready to let it go. Who's to say you won't turn a corner tomorrow and find something you missed, something that's been hiding in plain sight the whole time?"

Lily was still digesting this when Sheila breezed over, a picture in a lemon yellow scarf and sundress. She threw a tan arm around Lily, dragging her close for a quick hug. "Hey, sugar, you look great. Is that a sunburn?"

"Dolphin cruise. It was amazing. Aren't you working today?"

"I left early. My college girls are back down for the summer, which means I get to knock off early a few days a week. I needed to talk to Salty about the Affair."

Lily's eyebrows shot up. "Affair?"

"Oh, sorry. The Summer Affair. It's this big shindig we hold every year to kick off the summer—like a street fair. There's food and music and fireworks. It's the biggest thing to hit this town all year. Draws folks from all over the state. I usually set up a booth for breast cancer awareness. The money goes to education and screening. I'm trying to talk Salty into throwing in with me this year. I thought we could do a coupon—a dollar from every Pink Flip-Flop goes to the cause."

Behind the bar Salty stood glassy-eyed, his gaze trained on Sheila as he continued to dry the same glass—over and over and over.

"What do you say?" Sheila hollered across the bar. "Can I count you in?"

Salty started like a schoolboy caught dozing. "I'm sorry, what?"

Lily fought to suppress a smile. A moment ago, he'd been a regular magpie, sharing the tricks of his trade with anyone who'd listen. Now, all of a sudden, he couldn't string three words together. Was it possible this sudden reserve had to do with Sheila's appearance? She suspected it might.

Sheila had climbed up on the stool next to Lily's and was grappling with Dean for the peanut bowl. "I was asking if you'd given any more thought to throwing in with me for the Summer Affair. Have you?"

"The coupons." Salty nodded as he filled a fresh bowl of nuts and set them in front of Sheila. "Yeah, sure. Count me in."

Sheila beamed her thanks, then called down the bar to Dean. "What about you, handsome? Have you asked this lovely girl to go with you yet?"

Lily felt a flash of panic. "Oh no, we're just . . . He just . . ."

Sheila sat looking at them both, a hand on her hip. "He's going. You're going. Everyone in Hideaway Key is going. So why not go together?"

"Oh no, really. I'm sure he's already got —"

"No, I don't," Dean said, effectively cutting her off. "I think it's a great idea, actually. You'll need a tour guide, and I know where all the best funnel cake stands are."

"Well, then," Sheila cooed, smiling one of her wide white smiles, "that's all settled. No need to thank me, either of you—unless someone wants to buy me a drink?"

NINETEEN

The morning sky was awash in streaks of lavender and silver, the sea mirror-smooth at low tide. Lily skirted a small tidal pool, careful to keep the rolled cuffs of her jeans dry. Shivering, she tugged the long sleeves of her T-shirt down over her hands. She hadn't expected the breeze to be quite so chilly or the sand to be so cold. Still, it felt good to be up with the sun, to wander the shore before the stars faded and the world stirred to life.

She was surprised to have awakened so early. It had turned out to be a rather long night, and a pleasant one at that. They'd ended up staying for dinner, or some semblance of it—plate after plate of appetizers that kept appearing and then disappearing, shared among an ever-changing group of faces. Sheila had stayed. Rhona had shown up next, thankfully saying nothing about their lunch date. A short time later, Bubba and Drew had joined them, fresh from an anniversary dinner at La Petite Marmite that had apparently left them both hungry and bored to death.

It was a mixed bag of personalities, but somehow it all worked. Lily enjoyed watching the dynamics—the witty couples' banter between Bubba and Drew, Rhona's colorful and inexhaustible supply of anecdotes, and the thinly veiled attraction quietly simmering between Salty and Sheila. Maybe something would finally come to a head on that front while they were working on the coupon deal for the Affair. Lily hoped so. If anyone deserved to be happy it was Sheila.

Lily grimaced at the thought of the Affair, wishing she'd been quick enough to sidestep Sheila's blatant attempt at matchmaking. If anything was to come of this flirtation with Dean—and she wasn't saying anything would—she wanted to be the one calling the shots. When it came to matters of the heart, Sheila's philosophy was quite different from her own. Sheila believed in driving with the top down and the music full blast. Lily believed in driving with the emergency brake on.

It wasn't that Dean wasn't a nice guy—he was. Fun to be with, and definitely easy on the eyes. But he was also the first to admit he rarely did anything without an ulterior motive, and she was fairly certain his motives had to do with getting his hands on Sand Pearl Cottage. Which was why the smartest thing she could do was *keep* the brakes on. Besides, she didn't have time for romance, summer or any other kind. It was going to take every waking moment to clear out the rest of the cottage before she had to leave.

The truth was her concerns weren't so much about Lily-Mae's effects as they were about learning the rest of her story. All the way home last night, and then again this morning, Salty's words had been tumbling around in her head . . . *all the clues are right there under your nose. But only if you're paying attention, and don't go into a story thinking you know how it ends. That's when you miss things, because your brain is only looking for answers in one direction.*

Was that what she'd been doing with Lily-Mae? Looking for answers in only one direction? She paused at the shoreline to stare out over the water, a pair of terns squabbling over breakfast at her feet. Maybe she had. All this time, she'd been working backward, operating on other people's assumptions—her mother's and Rhona's. Was it possible she'd been so busy trying to *disprove* their beliefs that she'd forgotten about trying to *prove* anything else? Maybe what she needed was a fresh perspective, or better still, no perspective at all.

Back at the cottage, she made coffee, swapped her soggy jeans for dry ones, and immediately set to work. She was surprised at the progress she was able to make in only a few hours. The work felt easier somehow, less claustrophobic now that she had room to unpack things and examine them fully. Not that the bulk of what she'd found required much examination. Most of it was unremarkable, castoffs that might have been unearthed in any basement or attic—cameras, clocks, the occasional chipped vase. But she *had* come across a few items of interest, small keepsakes her aunt had collected over the years and had cared enough to hang on to.

She paused to pick through them, gathered now into a tidy pile: a matchbook from someplace called Top of the Sixes on Fifth Avenue, a souvenir ashtray from Niagara Falls, ticket stubs for a showing of *The Unsinkable Molly Brown* at the Winter Garden Theatre. They weren't much, really, random blips on a nebulous timeline, but they were at least tangible, a way of fixing Lily-Mae in the world, a glimpse of life beyond Mt. Zion. Her aunt had dined out, traveled, attended the theatre. Not exactly earth-shattering, but it was more than she'd known when she'd climbed out of bed that morning, and with any luck she'd know more before the day ended.

Resolved, she reached for the next box, smaller than most but surprisingly heavy as she dragged it over and wrestled back the flaps. Her heart skittered as she peered inside at the hodgepodge of old scrapbooks, some leather, some cloth—all bulging with promise. For a moment she actually felt dizzy, breath held as she lifted out one of the albums and laid it in her lap.

She ran her fingers over the cover, grainy green leather embossed with gold around the edges. It was nothing extraordinary, and yet it might as well have been the Holy Grail resting against her knees. Her hands felt shaky as she spread the book open, her breath leaving in a soft rush as she stared down at the young faces of Caroline and Lily-Mae. The first shot was of the sisters on the steps of a crumbling brownstone, stiff and unsmiling in plain dark coats. The trees were bare, the corners of the steps packed with dirty snow. Lily had to squint to make out the caption scrawled beneath—*March 1956 at Mrs. Bingham's.* Only a month after the last journal entry at Mt. Zion.

Lily swallowed a sudden lump in her throat. She had done it. She had vowed to get herself and Caroline away from Harwood Zell, and she had. In fact, unless Lily was mistaken about the license plate on the battered Buick in the corner of the shot, she had managed to get them all the way to New York. The observation was quickly shelved as Lily spotted the shadow stretching across the cracked slate walkway. Who had taken the photo?

The question continued to niggle as she paged through the rest of the album, poring over the details of each and every photograph, as if some hidden clue might suddenly jump out and answer all her questions. She knew better, of course. Especially since most of the photos were of Caroline: Caroline in a wide straw boater looking sullen beside a giant Easter Bunny; Caroline modeling a shiny new pair of skates; Caroline in bathrobe and curlers, hanging tinsel on an emaciated-looking Christmas tree. But where were the pictures of Lily-Mae? For a woman who had eventually become a celebrated model, she had certainly managed to steer clear of the camera.

Finally, she resurfaced in the second album, though almost always as part of a crowd, a group of five or six faces that quickly became familiar to Lily, attending picnics, dances, days at the beach, though never *quite* happy. There was no missing the guarded expression in those beautiful eyes, the wary, almost skittish smile when she was forced to look into the camera. But then, after what she'd been through, Lily supposed she had a right to that.

And then on the last page she found a shot that felt different: Lily-Mae posing in a swimsuit—with a man. He was older than Lily-Mae, but handsome in a Robert Redford sort of way, with striking eyes, a long, squarish jaw, and a shock of wavy blond hair. He was standing with his arm around Lily-Mae's bare midriff, but that wasn't the surprising part. The surprising part was that Lily-Mae didn't appear to mind one bit. In fact, she looked almost happy.

Intrigued, Lily studied the photo. There was water in the background, a small dock and a few boats, and below, in a hand Lily knew only too well, the words: *Jasper and me. Palm Beach, 4th of July, 1957.*

Who was Jasper?

Rhona's so-called Golden Boy? One of Lily-Mae's many other men? The sender of the postcard from Paris? All of the above? Or none? Whoever he was, Lily-Mae was clearly comfortable with him. Gone were the shadows, the restless counterfeit smile, replaced with trust—and perhaps something more.

A crack of thunder jolted Lily back to the present. Glancing up from the photo, she saw that it was raining, and apparently had been for some time. She'd been so engrossed in the photographs she hadn't noticed. A look at her watch confirmed what she already knew. Dean was right; you really could set your watch by the afternoon storms. She had managed to work straight through lunch, too absorbed in the photographs to register the gnawing in her belly. She considered breaking for a quick bite but decided to push on instead. She could eat later. Right now, she was more interested in learning more about Jasper.

Reaching back into the box, she fished out the remaining three scrapbooks and laid them in her lap, surprised to find them all covered in the same dark blue cloth. They were smaller than the others, and not like scrapbooks at all. It took a moment to realize what she was holding—but only a moment.

TWENTY

March 11, 1956
Mt. Zion Missionary Poor Farm

I knew we were leaving the day I found Caroline with Zell. I didn't know how, or when, I only knew it had to be soon. A plan was already churning in my head, how we could get away, what I would need to do to keep us fed. I just didn't know how to get Caroline to go along with any of it. She barely spoke to me anymore. What if she refused to go? A year ago, I wouldn't have thought such a thing possible, but now I could imagine her doing almost anything to spite me.

Unless I could find a way to make her want to go.

And then, one morning while I was sitting through Sunday service, it came to me: the one thing that might sway her. I was sitting in the back pew, where I always sit on Sundays, listening to Zell thunder on about honoring thy father and thy mother, and suddenly I knew what I had to do.

One day after mail call, I asked Caroline to slip away with me to the pond. I told her I had a secret that no one else could hear—a secret about Mama. It broke my heart to see her eyes light up when I said it, but I knew it was the only way to get her away, to keep her safe.

Later, at the pond, I told her I'd finally had a letter from Mama, that she'd sent money and wanted us to come to Richmond to live with her. I told her Mama had married a fine man with lots of money, and that she wanted her girls back, that she wanted us to be a family again, but that Zell wouldn't let us go if he knew.

Her lip began to quiver, her beautiful green eyes shimmering with tears. For two and a half years she had waited to hear the words I was saying. Only I knew they weren't true. Still, I made myself keep talking. I told her we would need to slip out one night after everyone was asleep, and then run away, and then we would be with Mama.

Caroline's eyes went as wide as quarters as I told her my plan. She was afraid, but promised to be brave when the time came, to do whatever I told her and not complain. Anything, so long as we could be together again with Mama. We pinkie swore then, and she threw her arms around my neck. And just like that, she was my Bitsy again.

I spent the next week working out the details, watching closely and biding my time, running exactly how it would work over in my mind until I knew every move we would make, every place where the plan might hit a snag. I rehearsed it my head like a movie, running it forward, then backward, then forward again, knowing full well we would only get one chance—knowing, too, what would happen if we failed.

And then one day there was nothing to do but go.

I waited until supper, when I knew the grounds would be empty, to slip out of the mess. I kept my head down as I hurried across the yard, trying not look furtive as I snuck past the dorms, then sidled up to the office door at the back of the chapel. I didn't bother trying the knob. I knew it would be locked. Zell was always careful to lock up when he left. But he wasn't always careful about where he kept his spare keys.

I had run across them months ago, at the back of a drawer in the filing cabinet, had even seen him use them a few times when he lost track of his regular set, which he did nearly as often as he lost track of his cigarettes. It had been surprisingly easy to slip them into my coat pocket the previous day. I waited for him to get up from his desk and go down the hall to the bathroom, and then I took them. I had no idea which key went to what, but I knew the three I needed were somewhere on that ring.

It was full dark by the time I reached the office door. My hands shook as I fumbled the key ring out of my coat pocket and began trying them one at a time. None of them seemed to work. Dread turned to desperation at the thought that all my careful planning would come to nothing. And then, finally, the seventh key slid home.

The reek of stale smoke hit me as I ducked inside. I froze, struck suddenly by the sheer madness of what I was doing—and by a sickening certainty that it couldn't possibly work. Too many things could go wrong, like getting caught in Zell's office in the pitch-dark, taking money that didn't belong to me.

What would happen to Caroline then?

Could it be any worse than what would happen if we stayed? If I decided to abandon my scheme, confess to Caroline, that the letter from Mama had never existed? I couldn't do it. I had told a terrible lie, one that would eventually break my sister's heart, and there was no way to take it back. The least I could do was make it count for something.

I moved to the desk, calmer somehow, once I had made the decision to see the thing through. I was clumsy in the dark, holding my breath until I finally found the key to the center drawer.

The strongbox was where it usually was. Even in the dark I found the last key easily, smaller than the rest, and stubby. My stomach lurched as the latch sprang open, a cold snick in the quiet. I didn't stop to count what was there, just scooped out the stack of bills, folded them into my pocket, and returned the box to the drawer. On the way out, I grabbed the single key that hung on a peg near the door—the final key to freedom.

My heart was thundering as I stepped back out into the night, my hand sweaty around the clump of stolen bills in my pocket. It felt like a lot. I hoped it was, because it was going to have to feed us until we landed somewhere and I could find a job.

I wondered, as I crossed toward the dorm, how long it would take for someone to miss us, how long before Zell discovered the empty lockbox and was told about the truck. It wouldn't take him long to put it all together, and even less time to call the police when he did. I just hoped Caroline and I were miles away when he did.

The few things we were taking—shoes, and a change of clothes, my journals, the Bible Mama gave me, and Chessie—were already bundled into a pillowcase, and waiting in my footlocker. All that was left was to give Caroline the signal and wait until everyone was asleep. Waiting was the hardest part, lying in the dark after lights-out, listening for the stillness to settle over the dorm, and then the heavy breathing sounds that meant the others had fallen asleep. I was terrified that I would fall asleep, too, and miss our chance, or that Caroline would balk when the time came.

Hours crept by before I felt sure the coast was clear. Even then I pretended to go to the bathroom, checking each cot as I passed. No one stirred. Tiptoeing to Caroline's bed I shook her awake, a finger to my lips to remind her to keep quiet. Her eyes opened drowsily, then went wide when she realized it was time.

It took only a moment to slip into our coats, and for me to ease the lumpy pillowcase from my footlocker. The door squealed softly as I pulled it open. I held my breath, praying. When nothing happened, I stepped out into the cold, Caroline close on my heels. And then we were running, tearing toward the old barn behind the chicken coop, the night a blur as we pounded barefoot over half-frozen ground.

The battered delivery truck gleamed like an old ghost in the open doorway of the barn, the most welcome sight I had ever seen. I hissed at Caroline to get in, then dug the key from my pocket and scrambled up behind the wheel, grateful for all the times Daddy let me drive back from town so long as I didn't tell Mama he'd drunk too much.

My heart plummeted when I turned the key, the reluctant grind of the engine echoing the death of all my hopes. Caroline's eyes met mine, glittering with panic. I tried a second time, and then a third, nearly sobbing when the thing finally coughed, then churned to life. I felt small behind the wheel, and couldn't see two feet in front of me with the headlights off. Caroline's hand clutched my arm as the front gate came into sight. I blinked back tears as we passed beneath the painted wooden sign I had first glimpsed more than two years ago.

"Is this the way to Richmond?" Caroline asked as I turned off the dirt road and onto a two-lane stretch of pavement.

I nodded, but said nothing. The truth was I didn't know and I didn't care.

I wondered what time it was as the road ground away beneath us. There wasn't another car in sight, but I kept one eye on the mirror as I drove. I expected to see lights at any moment—flashing red ones, mostly—but none came. After a while, Caroline drifted off to sleep, huddled for warmth in her oversize coat, knees tucked to her chest.

Reaching over, I tucked the corners in around her bare ankles, wishing I had made her put on her shoes. My own feet were so numb I could barely feel the pedals anymore, and the steering wheel was like ice in my hands. The truck had no heat, or at least none that I'd found. I held tighter to the wheel, trying to stop myself from shaking. It didn't help. Soon I was trembling so violently that my teeth were knocking together, and I thought I might shake apart. Finally, I had to pull over.

I turned off the headlights and sat there in the dark, clutching the wheel while the spasms racked me, and the reality of the last few hours sank in. I was grateful Caroline was a sound sleeper. I wouldn't have wanted her to see me that way, or to see me roll down the window and get sick down the side of the truck. Eventually, the shaking stopped, and the urgency to keep moving retuned. I had no idea what time it was or how soon it would be light, but I knew the farther we were from Mt. Zion when our empty beds were discovered, the better our chances of not getting caught.

Caroline stirred but didn't wake as the truck bumped back onto the pavement. I envied her. I was so very tired. But there was still so much to do. I needed to decide where we were going, where we would live, how I would find work—and how I would ever make Caroline forgive me when she learned that I had lied to her.

I had no idea where we were, only that we were still in Tennessee, somewhere along a bare stretch of Highway 70, when the truck began to sputter.

The coughing and bucking woke Caroline with a start. "What's happening?"

"I don't know. Something's wrong with the truck."

I managed to get us off the road before it died completely, noting with a pang of dread that the sky in front of us was beginning to show the first blushes of pink. East. We'd been heading east. Only now we weren't heading anywhere. Frantic, I scanned the dash for the fuel gauge, and felt my belly plummet. After all my careful planning, I had never thought to check the gas gauge.

I fought back tears as I reached for the pillowcase and quickly untied the knot. "We're out of gas," I said flatly, handing Caroline her shoes. "We're going to have to walk."

Her eyes rounded. "Walk where?"

"To a gas station."

"I don't see any gas station."

"I don't, either, but there has to be one up ahead somewhere."

"But I'm tired."

"I'm tired, too," I told her wearily. "But the truck won't go without gas. The sun is coming up. We need to hurry."

"Then we'll have to walk back?"

"Yes. We'll have to walk back and put the gas in the truck."

"Can't I just wait here while you go?"

I thought about that. I would make better time on my own, but I didn't dare leave her alone. What if Zell came looking and spotted the truck? Or the police. "I'm sorry, Bitsy, but we need to stay together. They might already be looking for us—to take us back."

I let the words dangle, their meaning plain. If they found us, we would never make it to Richmond—or Mama. That's all it took to make Caroline put on her shoes. I checked to make sure the money was still in my pocket, slung the pillowcase containing all our worldly goods over my shoulder, and started walking east.

Caroline did her best to keep up, poor thing, but after a while she began to lag behind. I had no choice but to slow my own pace, but as the sky continued to brighten and the stars began to dim, I found myself growing more and more anxious. I had hoped to be out of Tennessee by morning, but that wasn't going to happen. All we could do was keep putting one foot in front of the other.

I was worrying about how I was going to find breakfast for Caroline when I heard the hum of tires behind us. I froze, my legs nearly buckling when I turned to see headlights on the horizon. Finally, dread turned to panic and I grabbed Caroline's arm, dragging her back from the road, toward a thick stand of trees. I thought I might be sick again as we huddled there, watching the lights grow larger and brighter by the minute. If they had spotted the truck on the roadside they would know to look for us on foot.

I nearly wept with relief when the car drove past, its black and gold plates clearly not local. But as we stepped from the shadows the car stopped, its back-up lights flashing on. I tried to drag Caroline back to the trees, but she wouldn't move, her eyes big as quarters as she watched the approaching lights. I shook her savagely, desperate to get us away, but she seemed not to know I was there.

My mind scrambled for a story as the car drew near, some plausible way to explain what we were doing on a dirt road out in the middle of nowhere, wearing nothing but our nightshirts and coats. And then, almost before I knew it, the car was in front of us, a blue four-door Plymouth coated with miles of yellow dust.

The driver poked his head out, squinting one eye as he looked us over. "Something I can do for you ladies?"

I was afraid to trust my tongue. I shook my head instead, praying he would just drive away.

"Hell of a place to be walking all alone, and pretty cold, too. I'd be happy to give you a lift someplace."

I felt Caroline's hand tighten on my arm. Her eyes lifted to mine hopefully. Even in the thin morning light I could see that she was exhausted, her eyes shadowed, her lips blue with cold. Against my better judgment, I weighed our choices. I had no idea how much farther we'd have to go before we found a gas station, and then we would have to walk all the way back to the truck. We would lose hours of valuable time. And if they were looking for us, they'd be looking for a stolen delivery truck, not a blue four-door Plymouth.

The man was still staring, clearly waiting for an answer. He seemed to know I was looking him over, but didn't seem to mind. "I promise I'm harmless," he said at last.

There was something foreign about his voice, something hard and sharp I couldn't quite place, but his smile was pleasant enough. "I saw a truck on the side of the road a few miles back. That belong to you?"

"No," I answered abruptly. "We're on our way to Richmond."

His eyebrows shot up. "Richmond's an awfully long way."

"Our mother's there," Caroline chimed almost cheerfully. "We're going there to live with her."

The man smiled indulgently. "I see. You know, I could get you there a whole lot faster, and save you a lot of shoe leather, if you hop in. I'm going right past there."

I glanced around sharply, my heart smacking against my ribs as I spotted a fresh pair of lights on the horizon. It took everything in me not to grab Caroline by the hand and break into another run. I could feel the man watching me, his eyes shifting between us and those lights.

"Get in," he said firmly.

And so we did, with me in the front and Caroline in back. I held my breath, as he put the Plymouth in gear and pulled away. I saw him watching the mirror, felt him watching me, too, as the distance between us and the new set of headlights quickly closed. I expected to see the flash of red lights at any moment. Instead, the car came alongside, then blew past us. I closed my eyes and breathed what would have been a prayer—if I believed in prayer.

When I opened my eyes he was studying me again. We went several miles before he finally spoke. "You don't have to hold on to that the whole time, you know. You can put it in the back."

I looked down at the lumpy pillowcase, clutched tight against my chest, and shook my head. I felt safer somehow holding on to it. I wondered what he must think of us, two girls walking down an empty road at dawn, with the hems of our nightgowns peeking from beneath our coats, and everything we owned stuffed into a single pillowcase. It was a wonder he had stopped at all.

"I'm Jasper Mitchell," he said. "I'm on my way back to New York. I left California a few days ago."

I knew it was an offhand way of getting me to tell him my own name, but I didn't. Instead, I thanked him for picking us up, then turned my face to the window. It wasn't long before I heard Caroline's soft, rhythmic breathing coming from the backseat.

"So, Richmond . . ." Jasper said, trying to sound casual. "Your mother's there?"

I nodded, still staring out the window. The sun was full up now, and I could see small farmhouses in the distance, mailbox posts along the road.

"What part of Richmond? I've got friends there."

My mind went blank suddenly. I knew nothing about Richmond. I had simply pulled it out of the air to make the lie about Mama seem real. "I'm not sure," I stammered thickly. "She only just moved there."

I wasn't the least bit convincing, but it must have satisfied him because he didn't ask any more questions. We drove in silence for a while, Caroline snoring in earnest now, just behind me.

"Look," Jasper said quietly, when we had gone a few more miles, "I don't know what kind of trouble you're in, but I can see that it's something." He waited for me to answer, but must have seen that I wouldn't. "Your mother isn't in Richmond, is she?"

The lines on the road became a watery blur as we sped on. I shook my head. "My sister thinks she is. I lied so she'd come with me."

"So if you're not on your way to Richmond, where are you headed?"

"Somewhere . . . anywhere far away."

"You're running from something—from someone?"

I nodded, brushing a tear from my lashes. I wanted to tell him it wasn't my fault, that I hadn't done anything wrong, but that wasn't true anymore. I had stolen money, and a car. "We had to leave," I said instead.

"You weren't . . . You don't need a doctor, do you?"

A fresh well of tears stung my eyes at his kindness. I shook my head, my throat too tight to speak. For the first time since climbing in the car, I let myself look at him. He had the look of a boy, blond-haired and blue-eyed, with a full lower lip and straight white teeth, but the faint creases at the corners of his eyes told me he'd seen much more of life than a boy. His suit, too, had seen its share of life—shiny at the elbows and threadbare at the cuffs. I think it was that suit that finally made me trust him.

"My name is Lily-Mae," I said, at last. "My sister is Caroline."

"Well, Lily-Mae, I think your sister has the right idea. We've got a lot of road ahead of us, and you look like you could use some sleep. Why don't you close your eyes? We'll talk some more after you've gotten some rest."

He smiled then, as if we were old friends, and for the first time in what felt like years, I felt the knot in my belly relax.

The next time I opened my eyes we were pulling into a parking lot dotted with trucks and shiny metal campers. I sat up, blinking at the enormous arrow-shaped sign over the door. Dixie's Truck Stop Diner.

"Sorry," Jasper said, pointing to the dash. "I wanted to let you sleep, but the needle was heading for E. Besides, I thought you might be hungry."

My arm was numb from being curled beneath me. I tried to rub the blood back into it. "Where are we?"

"We crossed over into Virginia about an hour ago."

The words brought a small flutter of relief—we were out of Tennessee—but it reminded me, too, that I would soon have to tell Caroline the truth. I peered at her in the backseat, still asleep, bless her. But after what she'd been through I wasn't really surprised. I shook her gently, until her eyes drifted open, muddled with sleep and confusion.

"Are we here? Are we at Mama's?"

"No," I said, biting my lip as I caught Jasper's eye. "We just

stopped to get something to eat. Sit up now, and button your coat. It's cold out."

Jasper saw to the empty tank, then parked the car. I grabbed the pillowcase as we got out, and threw it over my shoulder. Heads turned as we stepped into the diner. I didn't begrudge them their stares. How could I, when I was wearing a nightgown under my coat?

We found the bathroom while Jasper ordered food. I tried not to look at my reflection as I stood at the sink, at the cheekbones that were still so sharp, the eyes that were still so shadowed, the face of a stranger—or an escapee from the local asylum. I finger-combed my hair—I didn't own a brush anymore—and splashed my face with cold water, then traded my nightgown for the one set of clothes I had to my name.

Jasper was waiting with two greasy white bags. We piled back into the Plymouth, devouring our hamburgers before we'd reached the edge of town. When the scenery became sparse, Caroline folded up in the backseat, and was soon snoring softly. I thought about doing the same, but knew I wouldn't sleep. The bleakness of our situation was beginning to sink in.

"Maybe it's time we talk about where you and your sister are heading," Jasper said solemnly when we'd been driving a while. "I'll drop you wherever you want, but I've got to tell you, I don't like the idea of you and your sister on your own in a place where you don't know anyone. It isn't safe. Do you even know how you'll get by?"

I snuck my hand into my coat pocket, comforted by the wad of stolen bills there. "I have some money. And I'll get a job—two, if I have to. I can wait tables, or wash dishes. And I've worked in an office."

He eyed me skeptically. "It's an awful lot for one set of shoulders. Isn't there anyone you can go to? Relatives? Friends?"

"It's just Caroline and me. There's no one else."

"What about me?"

I turned to look at him. I didn't understand.

"I could be your friend, Lily-Mae—if you let me."

My heart went cold beneath my ribs. Zell had wanted to be my friend. For an instant, I forgot Caroline was asleep in the backseat, forgot we here hurtling down the highway. Not again. Never again. My hand crept to the door handle.

"You don't have to be afraid, Lily-Mae. It wouldn't be like that." He reached for my arm, then seemed to think better of it. "I mean help. Nothing more."

"What kind of help?" I asked warily.

"I could get you a little work—not a lot to start, but some—and help you find a place to stay. A safe place. If you want to come to New York."

"Why would you want to help me?"

"Because someone needs to, and it might as well be me. I could tell you stories, but I won't. Let's just say I've seen too many girls, good girls, get in over their heads. I'd hate to see that happen to you, or to Caroline. You seem like a nice kid, one who could use a break."

It took a moment for the words to sink in, and then a few more for me to realize he meant them. Still, I tried to tamp down the glimmer of hope they had sparked. "What kind of work?"

"Modeling." He fished around in his jacket until he came up with a tattered business card. "It's what I do. Scout for models."

I stole another glance at his suit, at his shiny elbows and shabby cuffs.

He grinned when he caught me looking. "Okay, so it's been a little slow lately, but I've got an eye for faces. That's why I was in California. I was out there scouting new faces. Who knew I'd find one on the side of the road?"

"I'm not a model," I told him, handing back the card.

"No, but you could be. I'm not saying you couldn't do with a little fattening up, and maybe someone who knows what to do with that hair of yours, but I promise you, you've got the face. Redheads are the rage right now. Like I said, it wouldn't be much to start. It's hard breaking in, but once you did—if you did—you could really be set."

"But I don't know anything about modeling."

"No one does in the beginning. You'll learn. If you don't like it we'll find you something else. In the meantime, you'll have a little money coming in. And it sure beats washing dishes. So what do you say, want to come to New York and be my meal ticket?"

I had no idea what a meal ticket was. I only knew I didn't feel afraid when Jasper Mitchell said it. I didn't care about making it big, as long as I could keep us safe and fed.

"All right, I'll go with you to New York."

I turned to look at Caroline, huffing softly in the back, and wondered what she would say when she woke up and realized we weren't in Richmond.

March 21, 1956
New York, New York

Caroline has sworn never to forgive me, and I'm starting to believe her.

We were nearly to Fredericksburg, a good hour past Richmond, when she finally woke up. Her hair was matted flat on one side, her eyes still heavy with sleep, when she poked her head up into the front seat.

"How much farther to Richmond?"

I felt Jasper's eyes slide in my direction. I'd had hours, days even, to think of a way to tell her, but now that it was time I couldn't find the words. It was too awful a thing to admit, too terrible to say out loud. And yet I had to.

"We're not going to Richmond," I blurted, quickly, like yanking off a bandage.

She blinked at me, groggy at first, and then wary. "Why not?"

"There was never a letter from Mama, Caroline. The money. Richmond. I made it all up. It was the only way I could be sure you'd come with me."

"No!"

Her eyes filled as the words finally hit home, head shaking in denial as she slowly absorbed the truth. I had betrayed her, and in the cruelest way imaginable. Before I knew what was happening, she was flying at me over the seat, howling and clawing like a wounded thing. Jasper pulled off the road, but by then she'd gone limp against the seat, a shuddering heap of anguished sobs. I let her cry. She had a right to her tears.

Finally, she went quiet, the worst of her rage spent. I reached for her, but she flinched away, eyes shiny with hatred as they lifted to meet mine.

"Don't you touch me!"

"Caroline, I know you're angry, but I swear, I only did it to protect you. I had to get you away from there, and I was afraid you wouldn't go."

"Take me back. I don't want to stay with you!"

Tears prickled along the backs of my lids. I blinked them away. I needed her to understand. "We're not going back, Caroline. Not ever."

"You were jealous! That's why you did this! You were mad because Brother Zell was starting to like me!"

"That isn't true. Caroline, listen to me. I know you're too young to understand, but you have to trust me. Zell isn't a nice man. He did things to me—bad things—and I was afraid he would do them

to you, too. He said he would take you away from me if I ever told anyone what he did. That's why we had to sneak away, and why I had to lie. Because I was afraid for you."

"It's a lie! You're just a liar! I want Mama!"

My heart bled as she pulled her knees to her chest and began to cry again. Jasper was looking at me, his eyes full of pity. He understood what I was trying to tell Caroline, even if she didn't. I looked away, tears flowing before I could check them. A moment later, he pressed a neatly folded handkerchief into my hand.

"Go ahead and cry it all out," he said as he cranked up the car and pulled back onto the highway. "God knows you've earned it."

That was two weeks ago, and she's barely uttered a word since. She doesn't understand why I lied, doesn't believe I was only trying to protect her. She doesn't believe me about Zell, either. Still, I don't regret my decision, or anything I did in those last days at Mt. Zion. I'll never regret keeping the promise I made to Mama.

TWENTY-ONE

1995
Hideaway Key, Florida

Lily stood and stretched, working the stiffness out of her neck and shoulders. It would seem she'd read the entire day away. At some point she had switched on a light, just enough to see the pages in front of her, but the rest of the cottage was dark now and felt faintly gloomy. She switched on a few lights on her way to the kitchen, stomach grumbling as she peered first into the fridge and then into the cabinets in search of dinner. Unfortunately, everything required more time and effort than she was willing to invest. In the end, she settled for a box of Wheat Thins and a glass of chardonnay, and carried them out onto the deck.

The darkness was strangely comforting as she eased into one of the plastic chairs and perched her bare feet on the railing. The night was damp and unusually still, the sky a moonless stretch of indigo punched full of stars.

Lily sipped her wine, barely tasting it. The past few days had yielded any number of intriguing discoveries, many of which she was still trying to comprehend. For instance, how did a girl of seventeen find the courage to pull off what Lily-Mae had, knowing full well what would happen if even the smallest detail went awry?

She could only imagine what it must have been like, expecting to be caught at any moment with her hands in Zell's cash box, waiting in the dark for the other girls to fall asleep so she and Caroline could slip out unseen, stealing a truck, walking miles in the cold and dark, constantly looking over her shoulder, terrified Zell would come after her, find her, bring her back.

And yet, it was the lie that had haunted Lily-Mae most, the fear that Caroline would never forgive her for such a heartbreaking falsehood. Obviously her fears had been well-founded. Lily couldn't blame her mother for feeling betrayed. She was only thirteen at the time, a child who believed she was about to be reunited with the mother she hadn't seen in nearly three years, only to have her hopes dashed by the one person she thought she could trust. But Caroline wasn't a child now. She was past the age of childish hurts, wise enough in the ways of the world to understand that Lily-Mae had simply done what she felt she needed to do in order to protect them both. She didn't, though, and clearly never would. It was all just water under a very long and bitter bridge.

And yet, Lily couldn't shake the horror of it. She would rather not have been reminded there were men like Harwood Zell in the world, and that Lily-Mae had fallen prey to one. Thank God, at least, for Jasper Mitchell. Without him there was no telling where the girls would have ended up. He had come to their rescue with his Plymouth and his offer of work, but where had it gone after that? Lily closed her eyes, conjuring his likeness from the Palm Beach photo, smiling and golden-haired. Friend? Lover? A husband, perhaps?

It was a question for another day. There were two more journals to get through, but she was finished for the night, content to sip her wine, empty her head, and munch her Wheat Thins in the dark.

"Lily?" Dean's voice drifted up softly from the beach. "What are you doing sitting up there in the dark?"

"I'm having dinner."

A moment later he was standing at the top of the stairs, Dog panting happily at his side. "It's a little late for dinner. Everything okay?"

"Sure." She held up her wineglass. "Just taking a break."

"That's your dinner? Wine?"

"I've got crackers, too. I was too tired to fix anything."

"Let me guess—you've been digging through boxes all day."

"Some. But mostly, I've been reading. I came across more journals."

"Anything interesting?"

Lily fished a cracker from the box, nibbling thoughtfully at one corner. "*Intense* is more the word I'd use. I can't understand it. All these years I've been asking questions, and never once has any of the stuff I'm reading come up."

Dean settled back against the railing, arms folded. "Sharing your emotional aches and pains isn't always cathartic, Lily. Sometimes it's just painful. Maybe she couldn't talk about it."

"Even to me?"

"Especially to you. Have you spoken to her yet?"

"Yes, for all the good it did me. She claims my aunt made it all up."

"That's a little odd, isn't it? Do you think she did?"

Lily let her head fall back with a sigh, staring up at the stars without seeing them. "There's nothing about my mother's relationship with Lily-Mae that isn't odd. And no, I don't think she made it up. It's too awful."

"Do you want to talk about it? You don't have to, but if you need someone to listen . . ."

Lily hesitated, not sure she did want to talk about it. But maybe it would do her good to get it out. "When my mother and Lily-Mae were kids, their mother left them at a poor farm. She dropped them off and just drove away. Lily-Mae was fourteen and my mother couldn't have been more than eleven. They were there almost three years."

"Is a poor farm what I think it is?"

"Yes, it's exactly what you think it is."

"Jesus."

"That isn't the worst part. The man who ran it—Zell was his name—had a thing for young girls. He forced himself on Lily-Mae. Then, when she turned up pregnant, they forced her to have an abortion. When she finally came to they told her she'd probably never be able to have children."

Dean swore softly in the darkness.

"When Zell set his sights on my mother, Lily-Mae decided it was time to go. She lied to get her to go along with her plan when the time came. She said there was a letter from their mother, and that they were going to live with her. Only there was no letter. Apparently, my mother has never forgiven her. I think that's why she refuses to believe what's in the journals."

"That's a long time to hold a grudge."

"Yes, it is," Lily said softly. "Lily-Mae risked everything to protect my mother, only to end up hated and dying all alone in this godforsaken cottage. I just don't understand. They were family—all each other had."

"Wow. This has really gotten to you."

Lily drained the rest of her wine and set her glass on the railing. "It's just so sad."

Dean stepped away from the railing and dragged over a chair. "Maybe she wasn't alone. There's no way to know for sure."

But she did know. *They found her in bed . . . They say she was nothing but a rack of bones.* She couldn't tell Dean that, though, without telling him she had ignored his warning and spoken to Rhona. And she wasn't up for that discussion.

Standing abruptly, Lily ducked inside, returning a moment later with a fresh glass and the bottle of chardonnay. "There was a letter," she told Dean as she pressed the glass into his hand and began to fill it. "One Lily-Mae wrote but never sent. I think she must have known she was dying when she wrote it. It was . . . sad." She refilled her own glass, then dropped back into her chair with a sigh. "There are two more journals. God knows what's in them."

Dean had been about to take a sip. He paused, peering over the rim of his glass. "Have you ever considered not reading them?"

"Not reading them?"

"Look, it's none of my business, and as you might have guessed, families aren't exactly my area of expertise, but it seems to me that dredging up all this family history is getting under your skin. It's swallowing up time you could be using to have fun, but worse, it's messing with your head. It isn't too late to step away, you know, just toss all this stuff out and forget it. If we worked together we could get it all done in a day, and then you'd be able to enjoy the rest of your time here."

"We've had this discussion, Dean. I can't do that."

"So you're just going to keep sifting through it all, dredging up a dead woman's past? And then what? You can't change any of it."

"I know."

"Then why put yourself through it? My father did the same thing. After my mother left he spent years raking through old snapshots and birthday cards, and it didn't change a thing. He wasted his life mourning someone who was never coming back."

"This isn't the same thing, and you know it. And your father wasn't mourning because he thought it would bring your mother back. He was mourning because he didn't know how to go on without her, because losing her left a hole in him he knew he could never fill."

Dean stood and wandered back to the railing, his gaze fixed on the invisible horizon. "Well, you're right about that last part. She hollowed him out but good."

"I'm sorry."

He shrugged but didn't turn. "No need."

It was a habitual gesture, one she'd seem him make at least a dozen times, but something about this time was different. She rose and went to stand beside him. "Why do you do that?" she asked softly. "Why do you try to pretend your mother leaving was no big deal when it isn't true?"

"Who says it isn't?"

"I do. You were thirteen. Your life was turned upside down. It's normal to be affected by something like that."

He responded with another shrug.

"Look, I know a little something about this. Your dad checked out after your mother left. My mother never bothered to check in. I know how it feels to grow up with a parent who's *in* your life but not *really* a part of it, one who wouldn't dream of missing a bridge game at her club but can't seem to remember the date of the school play. Or your birthday. So I get it. All of it. Why you don't bat an eye when you talk about knocking down a house you built with your own hands, why there aren't any pictures on your walls, why your dog doesn't have a name. It's easier to cut and run when you don't let yourself get attached, so you make yourself a moving target. It makes you feel safe, because it feels like there's nothing to lose."

Dean cleared his throat but kept his eyes on the horizon. "Maybe you should take up psychiatry instead of fashion."

The words were laced with amusement, but there was something else, too, something that told her she'd hit too close to home. "I'm sorry. I shouldn't have said all that. It was just, well . . . kindred spirits and all."

He did turn then, though his face was lost in shadow. "Kindred spirits?"

"You're not the only one with commitment issues. With you, it happens to be houses and dogs. With me, it's relationships and jobs. I've had four jobs in ten years, and I'm about to move on to number five."

"Right, Milan."

"Yeah, Milan—I guess."

Dean dropped his arms to his sides, clearly relieved that the conversation had shifted to safer subjects. "I thought it was definite."

"It is. But I've been thinking. Maybe I shouldn't go. There's so much to still do here. Way more than I can ever finish by the end of the month."

"I thought this was your dream job. You'd throw it away for a bunch of boxes?"

"I said it was *a* dream job; I never said it was mine. I'm not even sure I know what my dream job is. I always thought when I did find it I would know, that it would feel like coming home or something. Comfortable. Right. But so far, nothing has. I don't want to make another mistake."

He was quiet for a long moment, studying her face, or what he could make of it in the dark. When he finally spoke, the edge had returned to his voice. "A minute ago you said something about making yourself a moving target."

"Yes."

"In my experience, there's a lot to be said for that philosophy. It keeps people from getting hurt—and I don't just mean me. If you don't get attached, you can't lose anything. If you don't make promises, you can't break them. But you did promise to go to Milan, didn't you?"

Lily tipped her head back, confused. "Is this about the cottage, about me leaving Hideaway so you can knock it down?"

"No, it's not about the cottage." He paused, huffing heavily. When he spoke again she could hear the smile laced through in his words. "Okay, maybe it's a little bit about the cottage." He reached for a stray strand of hair then, the one that had been tickling her cheek, and tucked it gently behind her left ear. Any other time the gesture would have felt quite intimate, but now it felt almost paternal, like something her father might have done when he knew she was upset about something. "All I'm saying is, don't get too hung up on the idea of home. It doesn't pay."

Lily continued to peer up at him, wishing she could read his eyes—and his mind. "No complications?" she whispered.

"No complications."

He kissed her then, like she knew he would, a slow and patient plundering that made her mind go blank and her knees go weak. She was vaguely aware of his hands in her hair, of her body melting into his, and then, of the voice in her head reminding her that she was on dangerous ground. There was no such thing as *no* complications.

TWENTY-TWO

Summer was clearly in full swing in sunny Hideaway Key, the sidewalks bustling with strolling couples and boisterous families, its streets lined with cars bearing out-of-state plates. Lily had to circle the block three times before finally finding a parking place, then had to walk two blocks back to Sassy Rack.

Galahad was the first to notice her as she stepped through the door, executing a sinuous figure eight around her ankles in way of greeting. Sheila shot her a quick smile and a wave before turning back to her customer at the shoe rack. The shop was surprisingly busy for midweek, but then so was the entire town.

"Can I help you find something?" Lily turned to find an almond-eyed brunette smiling at her over an armload of swimsuits.

"Oh, no, thanks. I just popped in to see Sheila, but I can see you're busy. I'll come back later."

"Like fun you will." Sheila was already making her way over. "What's up, buttercup?"

"I came into town to scrounge for boxes, and thought maybe you could get away for lunch. I didn't expect you to be so busy."

"It's summer, sugar. The whole town's hopping."

"I noticed. We can do it another day."

"Don't be silly. Even entrepreneurs have to eat. Just let me finish up, and we can head out. Penny and Jess can handle things for an hour."

Lily browsed while Sheila wrapped things up with her customer. The shop might be small, but its bright merchandise and breezy sophistication made it a pleasure to explore; everything was carefully chosen, right down to the jewelry, hats, and sunglasses, and all displayed with Sheila's special brand of panache.

A few minutes later Sheila was at her side, purse in hand. "Ready? There's a yummy Cuban café around the corner if you're in the mood. Best mojitos in town, but don't you dare tell Salty I said so."

Café Paradiso was abuzz with a healthy lunch crowd. Wedged between a bank and a dry cleaner, the place might have gone unnoticed if not for bright red umbrellas and festive music spilling out onto the sidewalk.

Sheila waved to one of the waitresses, then several other patrons as they wove their way to the last open table. She seemed to know everyone. A dusky-skinned girl named Vida delivered glasses of ice water and a basket of something called *mariquitas*: thinly sliced plantain chips drizzled in warm garlic sauce. On Sheila's recommendation, Lily ordered an ice-cold mojito and a Cuban sandwich, with a side of black beans and rice.

"Well, this is nice," Sheila said, picking up a plantain chip as Vida disappeared with their orders. "So much better than the ham sandwich I'd be scarfing down in the back room if you hadn't shown up."

"It's a great little place, and I needed to get out. I was going a little stir-crazy."

"Still wading through the mess?"

"Sadly, yes. I've made some progress, but there are still two rooms I haven't even touched. Not counting Lily-Mae's bedroom. I just can't make myself go rooting around in there. It's one thing to go through things I know she hasn't touched in years, but raking through her bureau and nightstand . . . It feels invasive somehow. And God knows how I'm going to get it all done. I'm going to have to work day and night to finish."

Sheila scowled at her across the table. "I hope that doesn't mean you're thinking of backing out on your date with Dean."

"It isn't a date, but actually—"

"Don't you dare. Not after I went to all the trouble of setting the two of you up. You look too good together to blow this."

"What does that mean?"

"It means the two of you fit. Think how pretty your children will be."

Lily was about to sip her freshly delivered mojito, but set it back down again. "Children? It was a kiss. One kiss in the moonlight. Well, actually, there was no moon, so I guess you'd have to call it a kiss by starlight, but really, it didn't mean . . ." Lily let her words trail as she realized what she had just walked into.

It was Sheila's turn to set down her glass. "You kissed him?"

"He kissed me. At least I think he did."

"Honey, if you have to think about it, one of you was doing it wrong."

"Okay, then he kissed me. But it didn't go anywhere."

"Why the hell not?"

"Because I stopped it."

Sheila sighed. "Of course you did."

"It felt weird. Scary weird. One minute we were having this heavy conversation, and the next we were kissing."

"Was it fun?"

Lily picked up her glass, eyeing Sheila over the rim. "Was it . . . fun?"

"Yeah. You know, sexy, hot . . . *fun*."

"Yes, but that isn't the point."

Sheila's lips curved wickedly. "Honey, that's *exactly* the point."

"It's a bad idea, Sheila."

"Not from where I'm sitting, it isn't. The man is gorgeous. He builds houses with his bare hands, cooks, and, judging by the color of your cheeks right now, kisses like a Greek god. Seriously, as your self-appointed romance guru, I don't know what you're waiting for."

"I'm not waiting for anything. It just doesn't make sense. I'll be in Milan in a couple of weeks, and he'll be a continent away."

"Maybe not."

Lily smiled, amused by Sheila's determination. "We've known each other less than two weeks. You think he's going to Milan?"

"I'm saying I don't think *you* are. I don't think you even want to. And why should you? There's nothing there for you."

"There's a job, Sheila. One I've already accepted."

"So unaccept it."

"Why would I do that?"

"We talked about this the other day, Lily, about not doing things you're not over the moon about. Are you over the moon about Milan?"

Lily bit her lip, reluctant to say it out loud. "No," she said finally. "I'm not."

"Well, then, there's your answer."

Lily glanced down at her lap, toying with her napkin. "I was watching you earlier, back at the shop. You love it, don't you?"

Sheila smiled, a soft, almost fond smile. "It saved my life. I told you what it was like after I was diagnosed. I gave up, and I ran away to Hideaway. I chose it because of the name—I wanted so badly to hide back then—but then I fell in love with the place, with the sun and the sea and the quiet. And little by little I started to heal. I stopped running away from it, stopped mourning what the doctors had taken from me, stopped believing I wasn't enough because I didn't look like the women in the magazines, and just decided to love this new me, scars and all. And then the most amazing thing happened. I met other women who were going through the same thing.

We were all miserable and sick, fighting like hell to get through the next treatment. We were soldiers on a crusade, but we'd forgotten we were women. That's why I got into clothes. I wanted to remind my friends—and me, too, I guess—that we were still beautiful. Sassy Rack sprang from all of that."

"It's an incredibly brave story."

Sheila shrugged. "We've all got one. They come in different shapes and sizes, but at some point we're all called on to stand up and fight something that scares the hell out of us."

Lily couldn't help thinking about Lily-Mae, about all the things that must have scared the hell out her, and how she'd faced them without flinching. Compared to Sheila and Lily-Mae, her problems were small. In fact, she couldn't even think of anything that scared the hell out of her.

Vida returned to drop off their meals and top up their waters. Lily bit into her sandwich, moaning her approval. "This is delicious."

"I know. I love this place, but I never think to come here by myself. So, what about you? What made you fall in love with clothes?"

"I don't know, really. From the time I was able to hold a crayon I was drawing dresses, and then trying to make them for my dolls. I was a horrible seamstress, and still am, but the designing part came naturally."

"So, you could just dream up something while we're sitting here, just sketch it from an image in your head?"

"Yeah, I guess I could."

Sheila foraged in her purse until she found a pen, then handed Lily a clean napkin. "Go on, design me a dress."

Lily took the pen and napkin reluctantly. "Anything in particular?"

"Nope. Just any old dress."

Fifteen minutes later Lily handed back the napkin. Sheila stared at it, openmouthed. "Are you kidding me? You just came up with that this minute, right out of thin air?"

"It's just a concept," Lily said, waving off Sheila's enthusiasm. It wasn't much, just a pleated A-line with a nipped waist and keyhole bodice, but she had to admit she'd have worn it herself in a minute. "The detail's no good, but a napkin isn't exactly ideal."

"I love it. It's got a great vintage feel."

"It's all those old *Vogues* of my aunt's, I think."

Sheila sighed as she set aside the napkin and returned to her lunch. "I'm so jealous. I've always wanted my own line for the shop, exclusive stuff with my own label. Unfortunately, it wasn't meant to be. Give me a pattern and a Bernina and I can make magic, but when it comes to creating anything from scratch I'm a total washout."

"I have a classmate who started her own label. It took a ton of work, and a fortune to get it off the ground, but the last I heard she was doing well."

"Well, that leaves me out. I don't have a fortune, just a little dress shop that already keeps me busier than I need to be. That reminds me, I need to get back. Let's grab a Cuban coffee for the road, though. I need all the caffeine I can swallow to keep up with Penny and Jess."

TWENTY-THREE

Lily turned her gaze to the sky, eyeing the sullen gray clouds beginning to pile up out over the sea. It would rain soon, but she didn't care. She wasn't ready to go back in yet. The entire week had been a blur, unpacking and repacking, sorting and discarding, box after box after box, until she was convinced she'd go mad if she didn't step away. And she was right. A brisk walk along the shore had been exactly what she needed.

She was on her way back from the mailbox when she spotted the hot pink sticky note stuck to the front door. Peeling it free, she squinted to decipher the hastily scrawled words. *I stopped by with a surprise for you, but you didn't answer the door. Call me, or come by the shop. Sheila.*

Lily checked her watch: two thirty. They must have missed each other while she was out on the beach. Dragging out the phone book, she found the number for Sassy Rack and dialed. Sheila answered.

"Hey, it's Lily. I got your note. What's up?"

"I've got something for you. Your car was there when I came by, but no one answered, and I didn't want to just leave it."

"I took a break and went for a walk. So what's this surprise?"

"I'm not telling you over the phone. Your choice. You can pop over here, or I'll stop by the cottage after I close up."

"Well, now you've got me curious. I don't think I can wait until six. I need to pick up a few things at the market anyway. I'll come to you."

An hour later, she pulled into a parking space down the block from Sheila's shop. Sheila was waiting with a glint in her eye and a bright pink shopping bag on the counter.

"So what's the big mystery?" Lily asked without preamble. "You've got me so curious I almost ran a red light getting here."

Lily took the bag, dangling now from the tip of Sheila's index finger. "It isn't baby clothes, is it—for all the pretty children I'm supposed to be having?"

Sheila gave her an innocent shrug but refused to say a word.

Lily removed the carefully wrapped parcel and laid it on the counter, peeling back delicate layers of tissue until a soft puddle of cobalt blue crepe de chine came into view.

"A dress?" She lifted it up to examine it more closely, then gasped. "Not a dress—*the* dress. Sheila, how did you do this? It's only been three days!"

Sheila was absolutely sparkling. "I told you, I'm a wiz with patterns. I found a couple of patterns that were close and then borrowed. I used the skirt from one, the bodice from another, and pieced it all together. The bodice was tricky. I had to pull it apart twice and start over, but I think it's pretty close."

"It's amazing, and the color is divine. No wonder you were so secretive."

"Try it on."

Lily took the dress to the fitting room and slipped into it, still marveling as she checked Sheila's handiwork in the mirror. The fabric was perfect—the movement, the drape, the work, all superb. There was a collective sigh as she stepped out of the tiny cubicle to face three eager faces.

"Sheila, I absolutely love it. I still can't believe you did this."

"I went shorter than the sketch to show off your legs. I thought you could wear it on Friday—to the Affair."

"Oh no. It's way too dressy."

"Stay right there." Sheila disappeared briefly, returning moments later, hands full of accessories. "Watch," she said matter-of-factly. "All we need to do is dress you down a little."

Lily had no choice but to submit as Sheila went about the business of dressing her down, working with deft hands and a catlike smile. A handful of minutes later, there was a filmy scarf tied about her waist, a pair of whispery silver earrings dangling from her ears, and beaded sandals on her feet.

"There now. All you need to do is pull your hair into a perky little ponytail and you're ready to go. Hot dogs instead of caviar."

Like Penny and Jess, Lily stood in awe at the transformation. "It looks like a completely different dress. I *could* wear it Friday."

"You'll certainly get Dean's attention. And don't roll your eyes. You weren't planning on wearing a gunnysack, were you? Tell the truth."

Lily's cheeks warmed. Actually, she had given more attention to her Friday-night attire than she cared to admit. "No, not exactly."

"I didn't think so. Now get out of it so I can wrap it up again."

A few minutes later, Sheila had wrapped up the dress, as well as the scarf, earrings, and sandals, and set the bag on the counter. Lily reached into her purse for her wallet, but Sheila stopped her.

"Don't even think about it. It's a present from me to you."

"But the fabric alone—I can't let you do that."

"Oh yes, you can. Besides, you never know when I might ask you a favor."

Something about the way she said it caught Lily's attention, as if she might be getting ready to ask for a kidney. "A favor?"

Sheila's eyes slid meaningfully toward her salesgirls. "I was thinking about knocking off early. How about a drink?"

Lily knew something was up when they arrived at the Sundowner and Sheila sailed past the bar, heading instead for a quiet table along the railing. A waitress stopped by for their order, then disappeared. After several minutes of stilted chatter about the weather, Lily decided it was time to get down to brass tacks.

"So, what's the big mystery? You said something about a favor."

Sheila clasped her hands together so tightly her knuckles went white. "That's right, I did. I was going to . . . You know what, never mind. Let's just enjoy our drinks."

"Sheila, you're starting to freak me out. Just tell me what you need."

"Okay." Sheila took a deep breath, unfolding then refolding her hands. "I need you to tell Izzani to jump in a lake and go into business with me instead." Once she'd gotten the first part out, she seemed to pick up speed. "I haven't been able to think about anything else since you drew that sketch at lunch the other day. You designing. Me selling. I know I'm small-time, and this isn't Milan, but we could have so much fun, Lily. So much fun."

Lily didn't know whether to be relieved or stunned. "Sheila, I'm flattered, really, but I can't. I'll be happy to help in any way I can while I'm here, but after that it would have to be long-distance."

Sheila's effervescent smile vanished. "So you're taking the job?"

"Probably, yes. But even if I didn't I wouldn't be here."

"What's wrong with here?"

"Nothing. But it isn't where I belong. There's nothing here for me. I'm not sure what I'm looking for, but whatever it is, I won't find it as long as I'm hiding out at the beach. The way I see it, Milan's as good a place to look as any."

Sheila sipped her Pink Flip-Flop thoughtfully. Finally, she put her glass down. "Can I ask you something?" she said, licking sugar from her lips. "Why are you so hell-bent on making a life choice in the next ten minutes? I mean, you're not exactly living from paycheck to paycheck."

Lily understood the question. It wasn't the first time she'd been asked; her father used to ask her the same thing. And now she would tell Sheila what she always told him. "Everyone assumes that because I'm Roland St. Claire's daughter and have all this money, I'm perfectly satisfied to just be that. It never occurs to anyone that I might *want* to work, *need* to work. Not for the money, but for me. I've spent my whole life trying to live down my last name, and confound people's assumptions. I want to do something that makes a difference, Sheila, and prove I'm not just a trust fund princess."

"Who calls you that?"

"Dean, for starters."

"Oh, honey, I'm sure he was just joking."

"Maybe he was, and maybe he wasn't. I've got the best education money can buy, and a résumé longer than my arm. What does it say that I'm almost thirty-six years old and still don't know what I want to be when I grow up?"

Sheila pondered the question a moment, as if weighing her answer. Finally, she put down her glass and folded her arms on the edge of the table. "Have you ever thought you might be asking the wrong question? You took this Milan thing because you need to prove something, and not just to other people. You want to do something big, something meaningful, but I wonder if the real reason you keep moving is because you're afraid that if you hold still you might actually bump into yourself."

Lily traced a thoughtful circle around the base of her glass. "I told Dean once that he purposely made himself a moving target."

"Maybe you were talking about yourself, too."

"Maybe." Lily looked up, ashamed suddenly. "God, I'm sorry, Sheila. I didn't mean to turn this into a pity party for me. We were talking about the shop."

Sheila perked up. "Does that mean you changed your mind?"

Lily smiled but shook her head. "I don't think so, but you've made me think about some things. You're good at that, you know?"

"I just call 'em like I see 'em, sugar."

"I can help you get started," Lily said, happy to steer the conversation back to business. "I've only got about ten days left, but we can collaborate on the kind of line you're thinking about. I can play with a few sketches, give you some branding tips, help you put together a business plan. Before I go I'll hook you up with the people you need to make it work. "You can do this on your own, Sheila. You don't need me. But if you do, I'll only be a phone call away."

"A long-distance call," Sheila pointed out drily.

Lily couldn't help laughing. "So reverse the charges."

Sheila laughed, too, as she raised her glass, tears sparkling in her eyes. "Thank you, Lily. You've made me think about some things, too."

Lily opened her eyes, suddenly and inexplicably awake. Beside the bed, the clock read five thirteen, blue numbers glowing coolly in the dark. She lay there a moment, eyes closed, listening to the muffled rush of the sea beyond the windows, waiting for sleep to retake her. When it didn't, she padded to the kitchen in the early-morning gloom and pulled a bottle of water from the fridge.

Resigned to starting the day a full two hours earlier than planned, she brewed a pot of coffee, then filled a mug and carried it onto the deck, folding herself into a chair with her knees tucked up beneath her T-shirt. The sky was beginning to lighten, the stars gradually winking out. There was something almost reverent about the beach in the chilly predawn hours, when the wind was still and the sea smooth, before the sun had shaken the world awake. Except she *was* awake.

Or maybe *restless* was a better word, as if she had forgotten something she was supposed to do, or somewhere she was supposed to be. She racked her brain as she sipped her coffee, but kept coming up empty. And then suddenly she knew. It wasn't something she was supposed to do. It was something she *wasn't* supposed to do.

Milan.

Lily set her mug on the railing and did the math on her fingers. Five thirty Eastern Standard Time meant eleven thirty in Milan. If she called now she could catch Dario before lunch, and have it over with. Sheila was right. There was absolutely no reason to take a job she wasn't *over the moon* about. She wasn't going to starve, and it was high time she stopped giving a damn what anyone thought about her last name or her trust fund. Sooner or later her North Star would show up—she hoped. In the meantime she'd enjoy the summer and take her time clearing out the cottage.

In the kitchen, she refilled her mug, waiting for the little voice in her head to chime in, to tell her she was out of her mind, that trust fund or no trust fund, this was a bridge she couldn't afford to burn. But the voice didn't come. Nothing did, except a startling flood of relief.

Before she could change her mind, she dug Dario Enzi's number out of her planner and dialed, rehearsing her lines while she waited for his receptionist to put her through. Her stomach knotted when he finally picked up.

"Dario, hi. It's Lily St. Claire."

"*Buongiorno*, Ms. St. Claire. How good to hear from you. We're all very excited that you're going to be joining us."

Lily bit her lip, took a deep breath, and plunged ahead. "Well, that's the thing, Dario. I'm afraid something's come up, and it looks like handling my father's estate is going to take a little longer than I anticipated. I had hoped to get everything wrapped up by the end of the month, but there have been a few . . . complications. I'm afraid there's no way I'll be able to be there by the date we agreed upon. In fact, it looks like I'm going to be stuck here for most of the summer. I'm sorry, really. You've been so patient—"

"Take all the time you need, Ms. St. Claire."

Lily went quiet, running his response over in her head in case she'd gotten it wrong. "I'm sorry?"

"I said to please take all the time you need. I know how it is when a parent dies. My own mother died last year. So much to go through. And who knows what you find."

"Oh, Dario, I don't expect you to hold the position for me. You've been so kind already. I totally understand that you'll need to fill the spot."

"Ms. St. Claire, we've been chasing you for more than a year. A few more months isn't going to make much difference. Take the summer, and handle what you need to handle."

Beyond a promise to keep Dario updated, Lily barely remembered the rest of the conversation as she hung up the phone. She hadn't prepared herself for the possibility that they would give her more time. She also hadn't prepared herself to say no.

But maybe it was for the best. She had managed to buy herself enough time to finish up the cottage without closing the door on Milan. Now she could take the summer to properly investigate the remaining boxes, and perhaps find answers to the questions she'd been asking her whole life.

TWENTY-FOUR

March 22, 1956
New York, New York

This city scares me to death. It's so cold, and loud, and dirty. It snowed again yesterday, an icy, wet slush that coated the sidewalks and turned the streets a muddy gray. I don't think spring will ever come. Not that it matters. They've cut down all the trees and paved over all the grass. And I've never seen so many cars, always in a snarl, blaring horns and sirens at all hours, so that it's impossible to find a moment's peace. But I can't say I miss home. There was never much to miss, and what little there was is getting harder and harder to remember. I'm happy to let it go.

Jasper found us a rooming house on West Forty-fourth, a rundown brownstone with warped wood floors and drafty windows. Our landlady is Mrs. Bingham, a square-faced widow who runs the house like a battleship and doesn't allow men after dark. Except for Jasper. She likes Jasper, because he brings her black cherry ice cream every Saturday night—and because everyone likes Jasper.

He's been so good to us, kinder than I can ever repay. He's found me work, just like he promised. It isn't much—some shots for a pinup calendar—but it helps stretch the little bit I earn at the lunch counter. They paint up my face and pile up my hair, then dress me up in silly outfits. I shuddered when I saw the pictures. I looked cheap and smutty, like the women back in Mims who used to hang around the Orchid Lounge on Friday nights. I didn't even recognize myself—and maybe that's just as well. Jasper says I won't have to do them for long, that he's shopping my face around and better jobs will come along soon.

In the meantime, I'm hoarding my tips, helping Mrs. Bingham with laundry and cooking to get us a cheaper rate, and pinching pennies wherever I can. Zell's money is beginning to dwindle. It seems there's always something to buy, clothes and shoes for Caroline, and things for school: milk money, bus money, money for notebooks and pencils. I try not to think about what will happen when it runs out completely. Mrs. Bingham seems fond of me, but not fond enough to let us stay for free.

It's hard to think about the future, but harder still not to think about it. There's so much I want to do for Caroline, so many things she's done without that I'd like to make up for. I can't bring Mama back, but I can make sure she has a better life than Mama ever managed to give her.

May 14, 1957
New York, New York

Caroline seems happier now that we've left Mrs. Bingham's. She likes having her own room, and a bathroom we don't have to share with strangers. She's at a new school now, and has made a few friends. She's still angry with me about Mama. She doesn't say so, but it's there in her eyes when she looks at me. Only time will heal it now. There's nothing left for either of us to say.

I've been doing catalog work since New Year's, for Sears and Roebuck mostly. It's steady and the pay was enough to let me quit my job at the lunch counter. I think things must be going well for Jasper, too. I've noticed him wearing new suits, and last week he took me with him to look at new cars. He's got his eye on a shiny black sedan. He says if things go the way he's hoping he'll have a big surprise for me soon.

He's been taking me out a lot lately, to restaurants and nightclubs—to show me off, he says. He's always shaking hands with someone, introducing me to people whose names I can't remember. I smile and nod, but it all makes my head spin, like I've stepped into a world where I don't belong and never will. Sometimes I look around—at the fancy food and fancy plates, at more forks than I know what to do with—and I find it hard to believe that a little more than a year ago I was eating supper from a battered metal tray.

Sometimes I feel Jasper's eyes on me, as if he can read my thoughts. He smiles and touches my hand. He wants so much for me to be happy, to relax into this new world, but I can't. There's a shadow that's always with me, of Mt. Zion and Harwood Zell, and the dread that one day I'll look up to find him standing in front of me.

June 28, 1957
New York, New York

The most preposterous thing has happened. My surprise, the one Jasper has been dangling in front of me for months, has finally come to pass. I've been signed as the new face of Pearl-Glo Beauty Cream. I was so stunned when he told me he had inked the deal, as he put it, that I nearly fell over in a faint. To think of my face in magazines, and plastered on billboards all over the country, was more than I could comprehend.

Still, it was the money that came as the biggest surprise. We have a car now, and a television set, and more clothes than we can ever wear. It looks like there will even be enough for the private school Caroline's been asking to go to this fall. I'm not sure I like the idea of her going away to school, but all her friends are going, and after everything she's been through it's hard to deny her anything. And maybe some time apart will help to heal the rift between us.

She's certainly not happy with me now. And I can't really blame her after all the nonsense about the billboards. She was annoyed enough when my face started popping up all over New York, but she was positively mortified to learn that both the local news and the morning papers had nicknamed me "The Face That Stopped Traffic."

It wasn't my fault. Two days ago, a man on his way home from work ran into the back of another car on Fifth Avenue, who then ran into another car, who then ran into another. Before it was over eleven cars were involved, snarling traffic for more than an hour. When the police asked the driver why he wasn't paying attention, he pointed to my face, splashed across the sign over Bond Clothing.

Now that's all anyone's talking about. One of the papers called—the Mirror, *I think it was—asking if I would let them take my picture with the man. I told them no, and not to call again. Jasper says his phone has been ringing off the hook with offers, including one from* Vogue, *which he immediately accepted. Mine rings, too, but the offers are of a different sort. I don't know who they are, or how they got my number, but they're not the kind of thing I want Caroline exposed to.*

Thankfully, she's gone to the mountains with her best friend's family for most of the summer. I'm going away, too. Jasper thinks it's a good idea for me to get out of the city, to give the fuss time to die down. He's taking me down to Palm Beach for the Fourth, as soon as the Vogue *shoot is finished. We'll be staying with his friends the Gardiners, who I met once at a dinner party. Old money, Jasper calls them, part of the Mayflower Brigade. I'm not sure what any of that means, except that they have a lot of money, and probably never had to get their hands very dirty. I'm still not comfortable around people like that, but anything's better than staying here and listening to my phone ring.*

I'm starting to worry about Jasper, though, and whether this trip is wise. I'm afraid his feelings are beginning to stray beyond friendship. I catch his eyes on me sometimes, when he thinks I'm not looking, and see a kind of longing there. Not like Zell, but the kind of tenderness most woman dream of seeing in a man's eyes. He's never made any sort of advance, but sometimes I sense he wishes for something more. I feel bad about that. I do. For his many kindnesses, to me and to Caroline, I owe him more than I can say. Sadly, what I suspect he wants isn't something I have to give—to him or any man.

July 1, 1957
Palm Beach, Florida

Jasper said he was bringing me to Palm Beach for the peace and quiet, but there's nothing remotely quiet about this place, not even in the supposed off-season. There are endless rounds of parties, luncheons, dinners, outings to tennis and golf clubs where no one seems to play either tennis or golf, but everyone seems to do a tremendous amount of gossiping and drinking.

Still, it's lovely here, like something right out of a postcard, all swaying palms and pretty people, so different from anywhere I've ever dreamed of being. But I'd be lying if I said I was enjoying it. I can't seem to manage a moment to myself. I'm forever being trotted around for introductions, like I'm some kind of movie star—or a freak from the circus—all because some silly man couldn't keep his eyes on the road. It's all so exhausting. I just wanted some peace.

Instead, I feel like a goldfish trapped in a great big bowl, swimming alone with no way to get free.

I didn't know there would be other guests. It never occurred to me that rich people opened up their homes like hotels. But when you have a house like this one I suppose it is rather like a hotel. I can't begin to say how many bedrooms there are, but there's a patio with umbrellas, a pool surrounded with wicker lounge chairs, and hovering men in starched white uniforms, ready to tend our slightest whim.

There are two other couples down from the Hamptons, who apparently travel in Jasper's new circle, though I've somehow escaped meeting them until now. The women are cool but curious. The men are curious, too, but far less cool. The wives keep commenting on my accent—a drawl, they call it—which I didn't know I had until one of them pointed it out. They think I'm charming, like Scarlett O'Hara or Blanche DuBois. But those aren't real people. I'm not sure these women know the difference.

I dread their questions—who my parents were, where I grew up, what schools I attended, their casual references to places I've never been, or ever hope to go—Paris, and Venice, and Majorca. Honestly, I've spent most of my time here wanting to crawl under the nearest piece of furniture.

There's another man who's just joined the party, a banker who arrived two days ago. A last-minute addition, it seems, since a Mr. Charles Addison was abruptly cut from the guest list after it became known that he'd gone and gotten himself engaged to some twice-divorced film star. Apparently, he is what they call persona non grata among polite society, though I must confess I was at a loss to understand why his fiancée's past marriages should be held against him, until it was explained that a man who kept such low company couldn't help but cast an unsavory shadow over them all. I couldn't help but wonder as I slowly sipped my cocktail what kind of shadow they would think I cast had they known about my past.

At any rate, his place at the Gardiners' table was smoothly filled, and with a man who has apparently made quite a name for himself by buying and selling some hotel chain or other. Everyone was excited when his name came up. I, of course, had never heard it. I wasn't looking forward to meeting anyone new, or enduring a fresh round of interrogation, but he put me at ease the moment we were introduced.

He's pleasant-looking, built square and tall, with a watchful face and startling blue eyes—eyes that seek me out often, sliding across dinner tables, and crowded rooms. They don't make me uncomfortable, only curious about what sort of man he is, and why, unlike the others, he doesn't feel the need to grill me about my past and my pedigree.

The more closely I watch him, the more I see he's like me: reserved, and perhaps less than thrilled with the company. There's a power about him, a quiet self-assurance I find myself drawn to, perhaps because I wish I could be like him. He seems to care little what others think. His opinions aren't swayed, no matter how much he's disagreed with, though he somehow manages never to be disagreeable.

Tonight after dinner, we were playing cards, the men enjoying their scotch, the women sipping coffee, trying not to wilt in their fancy evening attire, when Celia Gardiner asked out of the blue if my parents were still alive. I froze, groping around in my head for an answer. What could I have said about Mama? "I don't know" was hardly an answer to give a woman like Celia. I was still fumbling for something to say when Mr. St. Claire invited me to take a stroll out on the patio. I believe I could have wept with relief at the chance to escape that room.

I felt Jasper's eyes follow us out the large double doors, sharp with disapproval, but just then I didn't care. It wasn't him being dissected for amusement, picked apart and studied like some pecu-

liar quirk of nature. I can't say whether there was malice behind their questions or not. I only know I was weary of being their curiosity piece, something to fill the empty hours between lunch and cocktails, dinner and cards.

Outside, the night was like magic, the air heady and thick with the scent of Celia's potted gardenias, the sea beyond the low wall of rough coral stones shimmering smooth and gold beneath a fat three-quarter moon. We walked quietly for a time, taking several turns around the pool before settling on the seawall, our hips barely touching. I can't say why I wasn't afraid to be alone with him, only that sitting there with him in the dark, listening to the quiet pulse of the sea, felt like the most natural thing in the world.

"Ghastly woman, Celia," he said finally. "Doesn't have a clue when she's stepping over the line."

I didn't know what to say to that, so I said nothing.

"Her husband's a decent sort, though, a real straight arrow. We do a lot of business together, or I would never have agreed to come down for the week. I was looking forward to meeting you, though."

"Me?"

"The Face That Stopped Traffic? How could I not?"

I blushed, grateful for the darkness. "I didn't know they told anyone I'd be here. Jasper thought I needed a break. I thought we were going to be the only ones here."

"Jasper seems rather protective of you. He's your agent?"

"Yes. And my friend."

He turned to look at me, those blue eyes of his shining in the moonlight. "Is he anything more?"

"No," I answered, surprising myself with the quickness of my response. "He's been good to me, and to my sister. I don't know where we'd be now if he hadn't come along when he did. We owe him everything. In fact, he probably saved my life."

I still don't know how I could have admitted such a thing to a stranger, but at that moment Roland St. Claire didn't feel like a stranger. There was no judgment in his eyes when he looked at me, no need to pry into my story. He was just there, beside me, almost touching, but not. And I felt safe. Not the way I did with Jasper, but deep down in a place I thought I'd never feel safe again.

"People come into our lives for all sorts of reasons," he said after a few moments of quiet. "And there are all kinds of ways to save a life." He touched my hand then, the barest of touches, and for the first time in longer than I can remember, I didn't want to pull away.

TWENTY-FIVE

1995
Hideaway Key, Florida

Lily was pouring a glass of iced tea when Dean poked his head through the open sliders. In his board shorts and T-shirt, he looked more like a surfer than an architect, tall and tan, and ruggedly windblown.

"I just stopped by to say I'll see you at six."

"Six?"

"We had a date, remember?"

"Oh God. The Affair. I forgot it was Friday."

Dean eyed her curiously. "Is everything okay? You look a little frazzled."

"I guess that's as good a word as any. I've been reading again. Please don't roll your eyes. I just stumbled across my father's name in one of Lily-Mae's journals and it jarred me a little."

"Jarred, how?"

"I always assumed Lily-Mae and my father met through my mother. But it turns out Lily-Mae saw him first."

Dean's brow creased. "Saw him first? As in . . . called dibs?"

"Not exactly, but a little bit, yeah. My mother always made it sound like it was Lily-Mae who did the encroaching, but after what I just read it looks like it was my mother who horned in."

"Your mother obviously won the war. Does it really matter who came first?"

"No, I guess it doesn't. It's just that it sounds like Lily-Mae fell for him pretty hard, and long before my mother ever entered the picture. But somehow my mother ended up marrying him."

"Sounds like your classic love triangle to me, but with sisters."

Lily shook her head, uttering a sound that was half sigh, half groan. "Every time I read a new entry I learn something that makes me scratch my head—or just plain depresses me."

"All the more reason to stop reading. How about a swim, instead?"

"Don't you ever work?"

"I do, actually. My office just happens to be at home. I've been at it since five thirty. Which is why I thought I'd take a swim. Come with me."

Lily glanced at her watch. "I can't."

"Can't swim?"

"Of course I can swim. But it's after four, and apparently I've got a date tonight." She paused to glance up at him, offering a smile that was just short of coy. "A girl needs time to tart herself up properly."

Dean shot her a roguish grin. "I've never met a woman who could tart herself up properly in under two hours, but something tells me this time it might be worth the wait."

Dean arrived promptly at six, knocking on the front door instead of coming up the back steps like he usually did. Lily tried to ignore the butterflies in her stomach as she finished smoothing on a coat of shimmery peach lip gloss and went to let him in. The evening was already off to much too official a start for her liking: full makeup, a fancy dress, her date coming to the front door. If he was holding a corsage, she was calling the whole thing off.

"You look amazing," he said as she stepped aside to let him in. *No corsage—thank God.*

Lily grinned, batting her eyes. "Not too tarty?"

Dean ran his eyes over the length of her, slow and appreciative. "No. Just tarty enough. That's some dress."

"Thanks. It's one of mine. Sort of. Sheila and I whipped it up a few days ago."

He circled slowly, whistling softly. "Impressive. And I think you're actually getting a bit of color." He paused, running a fingertip over the crest of her bare shoulder. "What are these?"

Lily glanced at his finger, resting lightly on her skin. "Freckles. I told you—the curse of redheads. That's what I get for not wearing my hat."

"I don't know that I'd call it a curse. A redhead without freckles is like a beach without sand. They just go together."

Lily eyed him dubiously. "A beach without sand? Did you just make that up?"

"As a matter of fact, I did. At least I think I did. Aren't I charming?"

"Hmmm, maybe a little too charming. Something tells me you've had lots of practice."

"Not as much as you'd think, and never with a redhead." His finger began to move again, featherlight along her bare shoulder blade. "I don't suppose you'd consider a game of Connect the Dots before we go?"

Lily suppressed a shiver and looked up at him through lowered lashes. "I'll get my purse."

Beach Street had been blocked off well in advance of the festivities, with orange and white barricades stationed at each end of the four-block strand, clogging smaller side streets with rerouted traffic. For nearly a week, trucks and equipment had been pouring into town, heightening the anticipation for tourists and locals alike. According to Sheila, there wasn't a vacant hotel room in all of Hideaway Key, and local business owners were positively beaming.

Dean had to circle several times before finally finding a parking space several blocks away. Lily was surprised at the crowds already milling along the sidewalks, parents with children, teens traveling in small packs, young couples holding hands, all clearly ready for opening-night festivities.

Dean paid for their tickets, then helped Lily put on her neon green armband before donning his own. The excitement was contagious as they stepped through the gate. Lily's eyes widened as she took it all in, mesmerized by the noise, lights, and bustle that had transformed a sleepy little beach town into a full-fledged carnivàle. Everywhere she looked there were tents and booths, snack trucks and food stands. Even the air played a role in the magic, spiced with the delicious aromas of hush puppies, fried clams, and conch fritters.

"Well, this certainly smells better than any fair I've ever been to," Lily said, her mouth already watering.

"Wait until you taste some of it. It's all caught local, right off the boats. You can't get much fresher than that. What do you want to try first?"

"I'd like to walk a little first, unless you're starving. I want to see everything."

They strolled at a leisurely pace, content to flow with the crowd until they made their way to the end of the street, where a large bandstand had been set up. Based on the sheer volume of instruments and equipment, whatever was scheduled to go on later was going to be a fairly big deal. Lily glanced up at the banner hanging over the bandstand: DEEP BLUE UNDERGROUND WELCOMES YOU TO SUMMER AFFAIR 1995.

Beside the bandstand, an enormous sandwich board listed events scheduled over the next four days—blue crab races; an appearance by Susie Potter, the newly crowned Miss Hideaway Key; an oyster-shucking contest; and a conch chowder cook-off, as well as a variety of other bands and singers.

"And will you be entering the oyster-shucking contest?" she asked, teasing.

"No, but I did consider the chowder cook-off. I make a mean conch chowder, if I do say so myself. The secret is sautéing the bacon and peppers together before they go in, so the flavors marry. The entrants are mostly restaurants, though, which makes it hard to win. The judges like rewarding local business, and I don't blame them. It's a big deal to be able to put 'Winner of Summer Affair Conch Chowder Cook-off' on your menu. I think Salty's won it three years running. The money's on him making it four."

"Can I just say . . . I find your culinary skills a little intimidating. I don't think I've ever known a man who is a better cook than I am."

Dean seemed surprised. "You cook?"

"I'm not winning any chowder cook-offs, but I won't starve. I'm a wiz at takeout, though. And I make a mean turkey and brie sandwich."

"Great, next time I'm in the mood for kung pao, I'll know who to call. So, what do you say: do you want to walk some more, or have you worked up enough of an appetite to sample some of the local fare?"

"Let's eat something, then walk some more. I need to find Sheila, and say hello."

They found a shady place along the seawall to sit, sharing a basket of fried shrimp from one truck, nibbling honey-drizzled hush puppies from another, and washing it all down with cups of ice-cold limeade from a third. It might just have been the best meal Lily had ever eaten. Not only because the food was amazing but because of how and where she was eating it: sitting on a stone wall overlooking the sea. And the company wasn't bad, either.

"So, dessert?" Dean asked when the food was gone.

"Lord, no," she said, licking the last traces of honey from her fingers. "I'm stuffed after that. Let's go look for Sheila. I promised I'd stop by."

They turned around, heading back the way they had come, pausing now and then to watch children take their chances at the game booths, tossing balls or darts or bright plastic rings. There were lots of local artists, too, selling candles and soap, watercolor seascapes and sculptures carved from driftwood. Everywhere she looked was a new feast for the senses.

They found Bubba in his small booth, passing out brochures and registering out-of-towners for a chance to win a free cruise. Drew was there, too, selling T-shirts and handing out stickers to passing children. They hung around, chatting for a few minutes, until the crowd began to thicken.

As they moved on, it quickly became obvious that the entire business community of Hideaway Key was here, including Rhona, who was in full fortune-teller regalia, head adorned with not one but two fluttering pink hibiscus. She caught Lily's eye as they passed, raising a hand in greeting.

Sheila's booth wasn't hard to spot, either, with Sassy Rack's signature pink logo splashed across an enormous vinyl banner. Sheila was busy filling a wicker basket with tiny pink ribbons. She lit up when she saw them approach.

"Well, hey, you two!" Sheila leaned across the booth to plant a kiss on Lily's cheek. "You look gorgeous, honey. But then you always do. So, what do you think? Is it living up to the all the hype?"

"So far it's been amazing. The kid stuff, the art, the food—my *God*, the food!"

"Just wait, the band's about to crank up. Then things will really start hopping. So, how's your date? Is he behaving himself?"

Lily eyed Dean with an air of speculation before finally breaking into a grin. "He fed me, so yeah. So far, so good."

"And he told you that you look amazing?"

"Hello," Dean barked, feigning exasperation. "I'm right here. And yes, I did tell her she looked amazing. I was charming. Go ahead, ask her."

Lily was about to respond when a voice boomed down the street from the direction of the bandstand, officially welcoming everyone to Hideaway Key's fortieth annual Summer Affair. A collective cheer went up when the music started, the crowd shifting in unison like a school of minnows, flowing toward the sound.

"Go," Sheila hollered over the music. "Get a good spot down front. We can catch up later."

The band was surprisingly good for a local group, playing just the right mix of '70s and '80s, Top 40 and easy rock. It didn't take long for the crowd to get warmed up and into the action. Packed shoulder to shoulder, they were soon singing and dancing, fists pumping in unison to the lights and music as dusk settled softly over Beach Street.

Eventually, the music took a more mellow turn, and the crowd seemed only too happy to follow the band's lead. Lily felt a little thrill of pleasure when the lighters began to pop up, arms swaying in time to Seals and Crofts' "Summer Breeze." Several couples even started to slow dance. Dean noticed, too, and held out his arms.

"Care to?"

Without thinking, she stepped into Dean's outstretched arms, flustered by the unexpected rush of warmth as they connected. She was glad for the dark, and for the crowd pressing in on them. It felt safer somehow, less intimate. And yet she couldn't deny liking where she was at that moment, held lightly against his chest, chin tucked into the delicious-smelling crook of his neck.

The spell evaporated as the song came to an end, and applause erupted around them. Lily stepped back, eyes everywhere but on Dean.

"Thanks. That was nice. I mean fun. That was fun."

"We'd better get moving."

"We're going?"

"Not going, no. But we need to grab a spot on the wall before the fireworks start. If we don't move fast we're going to get caught in the stampede."

Grabbing her hand, he hauled her through the crowd and then back down Beach Street, slowing just long enough to wave to Salty, who was with Sheila now, in her booth, hands stuffed into his pockets like a child who'd just been summoned to the principal's office.

"They look good together," Lily observed as she and Dean moved past.

"Who?"

"Salty and Sheila."

Dean slowed, then stopped, glancing back at the booth. "Seriously?"

Lily laughed and kept on walking. "What it is with men? Do you guys come equipped with some sort of clueless gene? You've known them longer than I have. How have you not seen it? Sheila turns three shades of pink every time Salty looks in her direction, and Salty, our local wordsmith, can't seem to put a sentence together if she's within earshot. I'm telling you, something's brewing there, and I'm pretty sure it has been for a while."

Dean pointed to the spot along the seawall where they had eaten earlier. "We should have a great view from here. I'll go grab us something to drink."

A few minutes later, he returned with a pair of bottled waters, handing Lily one as he dropped down beside her. "So . . . Sheila and Salty?"

"I'm pretty sure."

"You and Sheila seem to have become fast friends."

"We have. She's so amazing—and after everything she's been through."

"The cancer?"

Lily nodded. "I can't imagine going through something like that and coming out as strong as she has. It makes me think about how easy I've had it my whole life."

"Because of your father's money?"

She nodded again, this time with a sigh. "I've never had to worry about anything. All my life, whatever I wanted was always within arm's reach. Cars, clothes, the best schools. Doors opened because I was a St. Claire."

"You make that sound like a bad thing."

"Not bad, maybe, but it changes the way people see you. They assume I don't have anything to contribute, that I can't *do* anything because I've never had to."

"Who cares what they assume?"

"I do. Or did. I've spent my whole life making sure people knew I wasn't one of *those* girls."

"What girls?"

"You know. Bratty. Entitled."

Dean chuckled. "This from the girl I had to practically trick into slowing down to watch a sunset."

Lily was still searching for a retort when the first plume of fireworks exploded out over the beach. A sudden hush fell over the street, then a collective sigh, as every neck craned, eyes trained eagerly on the sky as the show began in earnest. A single languid missile arced upward, nearly invisible until it bloomed into a profusion of pink and white and gold. A shared gasp went up, followed by another sigh as willowy arms of light slowly trailed back toward earth.

She smiled when Dean took her hand, but her eyes remained fixed on the sky, exploding again and again in a breathtaking display of color and light, illuminating upturned faces and the beach below. Lily couldn't help reveling in it all, in the hypnotic plumes of color pulsing against a velvety black backdrop, in gold and silver blooms erupting like man-made stars, then raining down like glitter from the sky.

The air filled with a smoky haze and the acrid tang of sulfur as the finale came, a magnificent flurry of light and sound that shook the ground and set the night sky ablaze.

There was a brief silence at the end of the show as the tendrils of smoke began to shred and drift, followed by a raucous burst of whistles and applause.

Lily stood, reluctant to leave. The crowd was already beginning to thin, pleasantly dazed as it straggled en masse toward the gates at the head of Beach Street. Dean still had hold of her hand as they turned to follow the horde.

TWENTY-SIX

By the time they turned back onto Vista Drive Lily was so relaxed she felt nearly boneless, drunk on limeade, fresh air, and small-town charm. She felt a pang of disappointment as Dean pulled into his drive and cut the engine. She wasn't ready for the night to end. Nor, apparently, was Dean. Neither of them moved, content to sit quietly, listening to the soft rustle of palms, the chirp and twitter of night things.

"So, are you tired of me yet?" Dean asked finally, sliding the keys from the ignition.

"I'm not sure how to answer that."

"I thought maybe we could take a walk."

"On the beach?"

"Well, we could stroll around the cul-de-sac if you'd rather, but I like the beach better."

Lily chuckled as she reached for the door handle, glad for the levity. She felt like she was back in high school, being driven home after prom, that awful will-he-or-won't-he tension churning in her belly like a swarm of nervous bees. She followed him down a manicured path that ran alongside the hibiscus hedge, then across the stone patio behind his house, pausing when he did to kick off her sandals. When he linked fingers with her and led her out onto the beach, it felt like the most natural thing in the world. The sand was chilly on the soles of her bare feet, the breeze off the water balmy and sweet.

It was a perfect night for a walk, the sea quiet, a wedge of pale moon shimmering on the dark, silky surface. They strolled along the shore in easy silence, content to savor the moonlight and the deserted stretch of beach.

Lily breathed the night air like a tonic. After the noise and the hubbub of downtown, the quiet was like heaven, but there was something she needed to tell Dean.

"I, uh . . . I decided I'm not leaving for Milan at the end of the month."

"Oh?"

"There's too much left to do at the cottage. I knew I'd never be able to get through it before I left, so I called and told them I wasn't going to be able to make it. They gave me the rest of the summer."

"Wasn't that a bit risky? What if they'd said they were going to give the job to someone else?"

"Actually, that's what I expected them to say, but they didn't bat an eye."

"You must really be something."

Lily laughed. "I must be."

"I thought you said this was the kind of job that made careers."

"I did, and it is. It's right up there with Chanel and Dior."

He stopped walking and turned to face her. "And you were willing to risk that to stay here? We must have made quite an impression on you."

"Yes," she said softly. "You have."

"So now what?"

"I just wanted you to know that my plans had changed. I know you're interested in buying the cottage, so . . ." Lily let the words trail off. He wasn't asking about her plans for the cottage, and they both knew it.

She was still groping for the right thing to say when his mouth closed over hers, tentative at first, and then growing more sure. His lips tasted faintly of honey as they moved over hers, his teeth nipping at the tender underside of her lower lip. She was aware of the soft rasp of his chin, of his hands moving through her hair, of something warm and dangerous uncoiling in her belly.

Once again, it was Lily who broke the kiss, teetering backward as her heels sank deep into the sand. "We shouldn't," she said hoarsely. "I shouldn't."

"Wasn't I doing it right?"

Lily could hear the smile in his voice and couldn't suppress one of her own. "You were doing fine. Better than fine, actually. I'm just not sure it's a good idea. I've got enough on my plate with the cottage, and I've just promised to help Sheila get a private label off the ground for the shop. My days are going to be pretty full."

"And what about your nights? Are they going to be full, too?"

"Dean, I don't have time for—"

"Let me guess—complications?"

Lily sighed. She hated the way it sounded when he said it, like a trite brush-off. "I was going to say I don't have time to get . . . involved, but it amounts to the same thing."

"It doesn't have to be involved. We can keep it nice and simple, have some fun, enjoy each other's company."

"Every time I try to keep things simple, they end up anything but."

He traced a finger along her jaw, his touch so light it made her shiver. "We've had this conversation, Lily. I'm not looking for complications any more than you are. I like simple. I'm good at simple. I don't see what the problem is. I like you. You like me. There's obviously chemistry here. I know you feel it, too."

"I do," Lily said quietly. "It's just that in my experience, chemistry has a way of exploding in your face, and I don't have the energy to sweep up the pieces right now. Yours or mine."

"What if I could promise there won't be any pieces?" His lips touched hers again, a flurry of small caresses that left her reeling. "I'm not talking about picking out china patterns. I'm talking about a couple of months. No strings. No messy endings. When it's over, it's over."

Lily tipped her head back, already feeling her resolve beginning to thaw as her eyes drifted up to meet his. "And no one gets hurt?" she whispered hoarsely. "You go your way, and I go mine?"

He smiled, cupping her face in both his hands, one thumb stroking gently along her cheek. "To Milan, or anywhere else your little heart desires."

This time Lily surrendered to the warm, thorough plundering of his mouth, the feel of his hands through the fabric of her dress, strong and insistent as they skimmed along her curves, allowing the hunger at her center to yawn and stretch itself awake.

"Stay," he murmured against her mouth. "Stay with me tonight."

Lily nodded a little dizzily, not realizing until that moment just how badly she had wanted him to ask. They didn't speak as he led her back up the beach. There was nothing left to say, nothing left to decide.

Upstairs, in the bedroom, Dean threw open the balcony doors, letting in the moon and the sea, then slowly unzipped her dress, allowing it to slide down her body and puddle at her feet. Lily felt the first hard stirrings of longing as he stripped out of his clothes and lay down beside her, the primal need to merge, to consume and be consumed.

But Dean was in no hurry, holding her off when she would have pulled him down with her, plumbing hollows and curves with maddening slowness, the weight and feel of him, of hands and breath and pulse, so very real and good. Sighing, she closed her eyes, abandoning herself to his touch and the sounds of the sea, the slow and steady push and pull, a rhythm as deep and old as time.

TWENTY-SEVEN

Dean was waiting out on the deck when Lily got out of the shower, the small patio table set for two. "Your breakfast awaits," he said warmly, handing her a glass of orange juice. "French toast, bacon, and coffee."

Lily sipped her juice, feeling self-conscious in wet hair and one of his oversize T-shirts. "You didn't have to go to all that trouble."

"It wasn't, I assure you. Bread, a little milk, a couple of eggs, and some vanilla. Voilà, breakfast. Cream in your coffee?"

Lily sat, spreading her napkin in her lap with more care than was necessary. "No, thanks. Just sugar."

Dean dropped down across from her, studying her closely as she spooned sugar into her mug and stirred. "So," he said, lifting his own, "let's just get it out of the way so we can both relax. Last night was amazing."

Color flooded Lily's cheeks as she picked up her fork, but the truth was, other than a brief moment of disorientation, she had awakened feeling as languid as a cat, well stretched, and just a bit dreamy.

"Yes, it was . . . amazing."

He waited until she'd taken her first bite before crumpling a strip of bacon into his mouth. "Unfortunately, at the risk of sounding like a heel, I have to run out on you this morning. I know. I know. Really bad form. But I didn't know we were going to . . . well, you know. I've got a meeting with clients who are in for the weekend from Chicago—the Newmans. It's probably going to take several hours. It's their first beach house and they have no idea what they want."

Lily waved off the apology, ignoring the faint nigglings of disappointment. "Seriously, no worries. My day's full, too. I was hoping to get started on the back bedroom, and then I've got a bunch of calls to make, a little long-distance legwork to help Sheila with the new line. She'll be glad to hear I'm staying through the summer."

Dean reached for her hand, lacing his fingers through hers. "I'm glad, too, for what it's worth. The rest of it can wait. The cottage isn't going anywhere, and now we have the summer."

It was on the tip of her tongue to ask what could wait, but then he spoke again. "Maybe we can do something later, grab some dinner, then see what's playing at Screen on the Green—if you're free, that is. Or we can just play it by ear. Whatever's good for you."

Lily suppressed a smile. He was trying to sound casual and unassuming. It was the dance of new lovers, deliciously awkward, terrifyingly unsure. "Dinner sounds great, and I'm not sure what Screen on the Green is, but I like the sound of it."

"Good, then it's a date."

Breakfast was delicious, savored along with easy conversation and the warmth of the morning sun. When their plates were empty Lily stood and began clearing, carrying their dishes inside to the sink. Dean followed her to the kitchen, stepping in to turn off the tap before the sink could fill.

"You don't have to do that. I'll get it later."

"I don't mind. It's the least I can do after you made me breakfast."

"Well . . . I kind of need to hop in the shower."

Lily's eyes widened. "Oh, right . . . so I should take off. Let me just change, and I'll get out of your way."

Dean grabbed her arm before she could slip past, a grin playing at the corners of his mouth. "Boy, did you ever read that one wrong. I wasn't hinting around for you to scram, silly. I was hinting around for you to join me." He leaned in then, touching his lips to hers. "Last one to the shower's a rotten egg."

Hours later, Lily was still trying to quash images of the shower that had nearly made Dean late for his meeting with the Newmans. Getting there on time might well have cost him a speeding ticket, but at least he'd be smiling when he arrived.

She'd been doing a bit of smiling herself, too. Giddy to the point of distraction, she had quickly abandoned her plans to work in the back bedroom, opting instead to concentrate on Sheila's new project. As Dean had pointed out at breakfast, the cottage wasn't going anywhere. Why not spend at least one day doing something she enjoyed?

Planner in one hand, coffee mug in the other, she stationed herself at Lily-Mae's black enameled desk, ready to tackle her first order of business. Flipping to her address book, she began scribbling a list of industry contacts who might be able to provide Sheila with knowledge or resources, then carefully starred the names of those who owed her favors. She wasn't above cashing in a few IOUs to help a friend. It was Saturday, so she wasn't likely to catch many people in the office, but she did have a couple of home numbers, and she could leave messages with the rest to help get the ball rolling.

Six phone calls, and a page and a half of notes later, Lily was feeling quite pleased with herself, and eager to share what she had learned.

Sheila glanced up from the counter when she walked into the shop, looking vaguely distracted.

"I didn't expect to see you today."

"I came by to talk about the line, if you have time. I made a few calls this morning and put together some information."

Sheila blinked at her, clearly trying to wrap her head around what she'd just heard. "Already?"

"We can do it another time if now isn't good."

"No. Now is perfect. It's been slow all day, and the girls are here. I just didn't expect you to work so fast."

Lily grinned, affecting an exaggerated curtsy. "What can I say? You're a wiz on a Bernina. I'm a wiz on the phone. Seriously, though, have you got time? I was so excited I didn't think. Maybe we should schedule some time away from the shop."

"Are you kidding? I've got nothing *but* time. Everyone in town's down on Beach Street, shucking oysters and meeting Miss Hideaway Key. Come on back. I could use a little distraction right about now. Penny knows where to find me if she needs me."

In the stockroom, they picked their way past clothes racks, display props, and mannequins in various stages of undress, finally arriving at a card table littered with salt and ketchup packets.

Sheila grinned sheepishly as she swept the pile of condiments into a nearby trash can. "Step into my office."

Lily dropped into one of two folding metal chairs, pulled her notepad from her purse, and primly clasped her hands before her. "I have news."

Sheila eyed her warily. "Good news or bad news?"

"I'm not leaving for Milan at the end of the month."

Sheila's face went blank for a moment. "You're not . . . What happened?"

"I called and told them I needed more time."

"And they were okay with that?"

"They were. Which means I have all summer to help with the new line—unless you've changed your mind?"

"Changed my mind? Are you crazy? This is great news. Not as great as you not going at all, but I'll take it."

Lily decided to leave the part out where she had actually intended to scrap Milan altogether. It had been a silly idea anyway. The summer was all she needed to wrap things up and get Sheila headed in the right direction. When it was over she'd let Dean have the cottage, and board a plane for Milan, off to chase her North Star—again.

"I thought we'd start by running through the process from start to finish, the steps you'll need to take and in what order. I also put together a list of contacts you'll need, people who can help you get things done. You might want to take notes. It's a lot of detail."

Sheila rose just long enough to scare up a pen and legal pad, then dropped back into her chair. "Okay, fire away."

They spent the next two hours brainstorming, covering everything from trademark registration to branding schemes, logo design to prototypes and manufacturing. Sheila scribbled frantically, undaunted as she moved to a second page of notes, and then a third.

"What about the clothes?" Sheila asked finally, rubbing a thumb over the crease between her brows. "When do we get to talk about the clothes?"

"Ah yes, the clothes." Lily smiled patiently. Sheila looked tired, and a little overwhelmed. "Finally, we come to the fun part. The first thing you'll need to decide is what you want the line to say, how you want it to feel. Elegant? Casual? Trendy? Where you want to set your price points, and how narrow or broad you want your appeal to be. In other words, who do you see wearing it, and where? As soon as we nail that part down I can get started on the sketches."

Lily turned to a fresh page on her legal pad, ready to begin jotting down Sheila's thoughts. But Sheila was no longer paying attention, her eyes fastened vacantly on a cat calendar thumbtacked to the wall.

"Sheila?"

"I'm sorry—what?"

"We were talking about your ideas for the line, about the actual clothes."

The crease had reappeared between Sheila's brows. She rubbed it away. "I'm sorry. I was somewhere else for a minute. The clothes. Right. I've been thinking about that, and as much as I loved the blue dress—I mean, really loved it—I don't think it's where we should start. I was thinking we should keep it more casual, at least in the beginning. You don't mind, do you?"

"It's your line, Sheila. I don't get a vote. But if I did, I'd say stick with an island feel—not Hawaiian print, but comfortable, breezy. Lots of color, in light fabrics that move well and won't wilt in the heat. I've already got some ideas."

"Oh, good. Besides, that dress would never look as good on anyone else. It was made for you. Dean certainly seemed to like it. By the way, you skipped right over last night. So . . . how was it?"

Lily turned her attention back to her notes, placing check marks beside several items for no reason at all. "It was good. Nice."

Sheila peered at her closely. "Just nice?"

"The food was great. The artisans were amazing. The fireworks were out of this world. There."

"You sound like a Chamber of Commerce ad. What about Dean?"

"He thought the food was great, too," Lily shot back without batting an eye. "Now can we please get back to business?"

Sheila's eyes narrowed suspiciously. "What's with you? You're all squirmy, and you keep looking at your watch like you've got a date, or . . ." She stopped abruptly, blinking twice before her face lit with understanding. "Something happened last night."

"Oh, Sheila—"

"Knock it off, sugar. You're not fooling me. Spill it."

Lily sighed as she laid down her pen and pushed the pad away. "I spent the night at his place."

"Oh my God, I knew it! I knew something was different about you today. You're all lit up. So . . . tell!"

Lily groaned. If she didn't set the record straight—and fast—Sheila would be making rice bags before the night was out. "Okay, before you get all excited, this isn't the movies, and no one is riding off into the sunset with anyone. It's an attraction, a flirtation—not some grand passion. We laid down some ground rules. No strings. No complications."

Sheila snorted. "Have you notarized the contract yet? Because I'm pretty sure it's not binding until it's notarized."

"Oh, ha-ha. A few days ago you were pushing the idea of a summer romance pretty hard. Now I'm doing it wrong?"

"As a matter of fact, you are. The whole point of a summer romance is that delicious sense of not knowing, that silly soaring feeling you walk around with all day because you have no idea what's going to happen next, and you don't care."

"Like you and Salty?"

Sheila's eyes widened unconvincingly. "What do you mean?"

"You like him."

"Everyone likes Salty."

"I have eyes, Sheila. I see how you look at him. So why aren't you practicing what you preach? Why is a summer romance a good thing for me, but not for you?"

"Well, for starters, sugar, you've got two things going for you that I don't." Lily was about to protest when Sheila pointed to her breasts. "And even if I was interested—which I'm definitely not—Salty's a great guy, with plenty to offer. He doesn't need to settle for . . . well, for someone like me."

Lily could have kicked herself. Sheila was so beautiful, so strong and so vibrant, that she sometimes forgot about the surgery, and the trials she had passed through on her way to becoming who she was now.

"God, Sheila, I'm sorry. I didn't think. I shouldn't have—"

Sheila shrugged, giving Lily's hand a pat. "Forget it, honey. Life goes on. Maybe not all of it, but most of it. I love my life, my business, my friends. I don't need to find *the one* to be happy. But you're not me. You've got your whole life ahead of you to go out to find yours—whoever he is."

Lily shook her head, sighing. "I know you mean well, Sheila. I also know you believe in soul mates and fairy tales, but I don't. Maybe because no one I know has ever come close to finding what you're talking about. God knows my parents never did. So how are you supposed to know—I mean, *really* know—when you've found *it*?"

"You just do, honey," Sheila said quietly, her eyes suddenly shiny. "You know when you realize that you're absolutely terrified. When you're convinced you're going to smash yourself to pieces, and you're still willing to leap—because the thought of plunging off a cliff and breaking yourself wide open is still better than playing it safe alone."

Lily let the words settle in her chest, trying to imagine what it would be like to feel that way, reckless, defenseless—exposed. Just the thought of it made her shudder.

"Thanks, but no thanks. Sounds way too scary for me."

"Yeah, well . . ." Sheila stood abruptly, her face suddenly close to crumpling. "I guess I'm an expert on scary these days."

Lily studied her face, seeing what she hadn't before. "Something's wrong."

"It's nothing. Just being silly, is all."

"Why don't I believe you?"

Sheila hesitated a moment, then eased back into her chair. "My annual is coming up in a few weeks, that's all, and it always freaks me out. I start running all these scenarios in my mind. What if they find something this time? What if I have to go through all that again? Or worse, what if I don't come through it? It's part of the deal. You try to pretend it's not there, but it is—the feeling that there's this time bomb ticking in your chest, waiting to go off just when you've put your life back together."

Lily's heart ached for her. She couldn't imagine living with something like that always hanging over her head. "Have you ever had a recurrence?"

"No. I've been lucky. The chances are much lower after a bilateral, but I can't help it. The thought of being some statistical anomaly scares the hell out of me. I think the drive is actually the worst part. My oncologist is in Tampa, which may not seem far, but I can tell you it's a mighty long drive when you're by yourself and scared to death."

Lily laid a hand on Sheila's arm, waiting until their gazes met. "What if you weren't by yourself this time?"

"I wasn't angling for company, honey. I go through this every year. I'll be fine."

"When's the appointment?"

"Three weeks from Tuesday, but seriously, I can't let you waste a whole day like that just to drive me to the doctor. I'd feel like a big old baby."

"Just think of us as Thelma and Louise."

Sheila managed a shaky smile. "I'll be Susan Sarandon."

"Which makes me Geena Davis. I can live with that. In the meantime, I want you to go through that list I just gave you, and write down any questions you have. I've got to run. I've got a date."

The old twinkle returned to Sheila's brown eyes. "Well, that's progress, I guess."

Lily was disappointed to find Dean's truck still gone. His meeting must be running long. Still, it wouldn't be a bad thing to have a little quiet time to process the last forty-eight hours. A lot had happened in a dizzyingly short period of time: her job plans had changed substantially, she had just agreed to become the de facto consultant for a fledgling design label, scheduled a road trip to Tampa, and plunged headlong into a relationship with a man she'd known less than a month.

Restless, she wandered through the cottage, wondering how her life had taken so many sharp turns. Until a few months ago she'd been living in Paris, sleeping with a man named Luc, and working for Sergé Leroux. Now none of those things were true—and she didn't miss any of it. How was that even possible? Wasn't it natural to feel something when you left whole parts of your life behind? Regret? Nostalgia? Something?

Lily-Mae had obviously felt them. Why else would she have held on to so much of her past? Wandering though her aunt's room now, she again found herself fascinated by the sheer number of keepsakes, small personal items kept carefully close—books and tiny trinkets, the jar of shells on the bureau. And there were the journals, of course, a kind of living memory. She had planned to take a break from reading them, to channel her energies into clearing out the clutter and helping Sheila with her new venture, but suddenly she felt the pull of those pages keenly.

TWENTY-EIGHT

July 5, 1957
Palm Beach, Florida

I no longer know what to wish for. A week in this place—with these people—has drained me, and a few days ago I was close to begging Jasper to take me back to New York. But there's Roland now, whom I never ever counted on, and whom I scarcely know what to make of. Since the night he rescued me from Celia Gardiner's bridge table we have become almost inseparable, slipping out onto the beach in the afternoons, wandering the gardens at dusk.

Jasper is sullen these days, making small but pointed remarks about how often Roland and I seem to drift away from the others. He's worried—or so he claims—that our host and hostess will think me ungrateful for their invitation, and that the other guests will question my manners. He doesn't seem to understand how little I have in common with any of them, or that the quiet moments I spend with Roland are the only pleasure I've found since arriving.

I'm afraid things came to a rather unpleasant head last night. I had just excused myself from yet another hand of cards when Jasper followed me out onto the patio. He seemed surprised to find me alone. The truth is, I was waiting for Roland, hoping he had seen me slip away and would follow me out.

"I must say, I didn't expect to have you all to myself. I seldom do these days."

He was scolding me, lazily swirling the glass of scotch dangling from his fingers, not his first by a long shot. I let the remark pass, choosing to say nothing. I don't like it when he drinks too much, something he seems to be doing more and more lately.

"So where is the illustrious Roland St. Claire this evening? Off buying or selling something, no doubt." He sounded petulant, like a child pouting because the boy next door had more toys than he did.

"Why do you dislike him so? He's been good company for me, nothing but kind, a perfect gentlemen."

"And I haven't been those things to you? All these weeks and months, I haven't been good company?" His voice was slightly slurred, but his face was hard. "Have I ever been anything but a gentleman?"

"Of course you've been a gentleman, Jasper. And kind, and thoughtful, and so very generous. You've been a good friend—the best friend I could ever have wished for."

"Then why? I've been right here all the time—waiting for you to see me, to look at me the way you look at him. It never occurred to me that you wouldn't someday. But now, when I see you with him, I don't know what to think. Is it his money?"

I felt my cheeks go hot, but did my best to bite my tongue. "I don't know anything about his money, Jasper. I don't know how much he has, or a thing about how he made it, and I don't care. Until a few days ago I didn't even know his name. But I know it now, and I can't help the way I feel when I'm with him. I won't apologize for it, either."

He tossed back the last of his scotch, eyes glittering as he put down his glass. "And that's it? You just turn your back . . . after everything?"

"Everything?" I breathed the word out, like I'd just been punched.

It was the scotch, I knew, but his words cut too deep to ignore them. "You're saying I owe you? You think because of everything you've done for me, for Caroline, that I owe you . . . that?"

Jasper closed his eyes, swaying a little. "I'm sorry, Lily-Mae. I didn't mean it to sound like that. I guess I just thought friendship and gratitude would eventually . . ."

The words dangled in the gardenia-scented air, an apology, a plea.

"Jasper, I'll always love you. You rescued me, then helped put me back together. You made sure I had a roof over my head, that I was safe and could afford to feed my sister. The day we met, you became my friend, my rock. And that's what you'll always be, but nothing more. There's nothing either of us can do to change that."

"And St. Claire," he asked thickly. "Is he more?"

"I don't know. After Zell, I didn't think anyone could ever be. I didn't think I could ever feel that way about a man—any man. But Roland is different. I don't know how or why. I just know I trust him."

"Well, then"—Jasper made a stiff little bow, teetering as he straightened—"it appears you've made up your mind, and I'm the odd man out."

I watched as he turned on his heel and stalked back inside, hating that I had hurt him, but knowing I had done the right thing. I owe Jasper Mitchell everything—including honesty.

July 8, 1957
Palm Beach, Florida

I'm afraid we've caused a bit of a scandal. And if I've learned anything over the past week, it's that nothing delights Celia Gardiner and her elegant circle of ladies like having something—or someone—to chew on. I expect everyone in Palm Beach has already heard the news, perhaps even the papers, but somehow I don't care.

I wonder if Caroline will hear, and if she'll believe it. It all happened so fast I can scarcely believe it myself. Last night in the drawing room, just after dinner ended, we were all standing about, having a tug-of-war about whether to play cards, or music, or both, when I felt Roland touch my arm.

"We could leave," he said close to my ear as he pressed a glass of something cool and fizzy into my hands and smoothly steered me away from the others. "Just walk out the front door."

I looked up at him, trying to read his face, though I really didn't need to. I could tell by his voice that he meant what he was saying and was waiting for me to say something. Instead, I sipped my drink without tasting, my eyes straying to where I'd last seen Jasper nursing another scotch with Robert Gardiner. He caught my eye briefly before looking away.

"Did you mean what you said last night—out on the patio? That you trust me?"

I blushed furiously. "I didn't know—"

"I wasn't spying. I came after you when I saw you leave the table, but Mitchell had beaten me to the punch. Did you mean what you said?"

I nodded, mortified that he had overheard my confession.

"I know a place, Lily-Mae. An out-of-the-way place on the other side of the state. No dinners, no parties, no smiling until your cheeks ache. Just the sun and the sea, and us. If we leave now we could be there by morning."

Jasper was inching closer, watching us sullenly. At that moment I couldn't think of anything I wanted more in the world than to run away.

"What will they think when they find us gone?" I asked, but only for something to say. I didn't really care what they said. I had already made up my mind.

Roland threw back his head and laughed. "What will they think?

Why, the worst, of course. And then, when all the meat's been gnawed off that bone, I suspect our hostess will take credit for bringing us together. She ought to be able to milk that for the rest of the summer."

The thought of being the center of more gossip brought a pang of uneasiness, a tiny voice whispering in my ear that I must be mad to even be considering such a thing. Then I looked into Roland's eyes, and the voice went quiet.

No one saw us leave the house. It took less than twenty minutes to throw my things into my suitcase and meet Roland out on the driveway. I smiled nervously as I climbed in beside him. It was the second time in my life that I had bolted a place at night, but this time I wasn't afraid.

July 12, 1957
Hideaway Key, Florida

I could feel something let go as we drove across the bridge and left Palm Beach behind. It was as if, for the first time in more than a week, I could finally breathe. We rode with the windows down, the warm night air tearing through the car. I had no idea where we were going, and I didn't care.

Still, I couldn't help thinking about Jasper, wondering what he would think when he learned I was gone—that we were gone. I didn't feel guilty, or only a little. From the day Mama left Caroline and me standing on the steps of Mt. Zion, I have lived my life always worrying about someone else. Mama. Caroline. But Jasper wasn't my responsibility. Just this once, I wanted to do something, to have something, that was just for me.

I was sticky and windblown by the time we crossed the narrow iron bridge onto Hideaway Key. There were no neat rows of palms to greet us, no manicured hedges or stately Spanish homes, just a painted wooden sign welcoming us to Florida's best-kept secret. I smiled as we passed by the sign. Hideaway Key. Even the name was perfect.

Dawn was still hours away when we turned down a narrow lane, then pulled to the end of a crushed shell drive. My belly clenched when Roland turned off the engine. For a moment we sat perfectly still, steeped in the buzz and chirp of night things. Finally, he touched my hand.

"If you've changed your mind we can turn around, and I'll take you home."

"To New York?"

"Yes, if that's what you want. I have no expectations, Lily-Mae. None. I don't know who or when, but I overheard enough the other night to know someone hurt you, which is why I'll never ask you to do anything—to give anything—that you don't want to. If you want to leave at any point, all you have to do is say so."

The thought of changing my mind had never occurred to me, but Roland's offer brought tears to my eyes. "I want to stay. With you."

Roland got our bags from the trunk. I followed him up onto a small porch, waiting nervously while he fished a key from under the mat. "It's not much," he told me as he unlocked the door. "Certainly nothing like the Gardiners', but it suits my needs when I want to get away. It belongs to a friend of mine who never uses it anymore. I'll call him in the morning and let him know I'm here."

There was a faint whiff of mustiness as we stepped inside, and the heavy quiet of a place long shut up. I was too anxious to notice much as I trailed Roland from room to room. I was still trying to grasp what I had done, waiting for the reality of it to register—a beach cottage in the middle of the night with a man I barely knew—but nothing in me regretted the choice. I had no idea what would happen next, and for the first time in my life I didn't care, so long as it was with Roland St. Claire.

He let me choose between the two bedrooms, then carried his bags to the other. He was moving so carefully, watching me so closely, as if I were a deer who might spook and skitter off into the woods. I touched his hand, a question in my eyes.

"The sun will be up in a few hours." His voice sounded thick, unsteady. "We should both get some sleep."

"I'm glad I came," I whispered.

"I'm glad, too. I don't know how I found the nerve to ask. I just knew I had to get away. I hate house parties, especially Celia's. I usually make some excuse to leave early. That's what I planned to do this time, too. Then I met you. All of a sudden I couldn't make myself go."

His eyes met mine, a long, lingering gaze that made me go warm and soft inside. My heart battered my ribs as the moment stretched. He felt it, too, the invisible current that had thrummed between us almost from the moment we met.

"What I said in the car, Lily-Mae, about trusting me—I meant it. You can. But if you ever feel like you can't, I want you to say so."

Before I could reach for him, he cleared his throat and stepped away to open the windows, letting in a breath of salt air and the distant rush of the sea. Then he placed a kiss on my forehead and was gone.

I lay down fully dressed, knowing I wouldn't sleep, and listened to the waves sighing softly beyond my window. The sound was no longer strange to me; I had grown used to it at the Gardiners'. But it sounded different here, somehow, like music. The next time I opened my eyes the room was full of sunshine.

I held my breath as I crept out of my room, as if I were somewhere I didn't belong. The tiny living room was splashed with light, the doors to the deck thrown open. Roland was there, standing at the railing, the breeze ruffling through his sandy hair. As if sensing me, he turned.

I smiled shyly, not sure what to say, then moved to his side. His arm slid around me, drawing me close. We stood there for what felt like a long time, savoring the closeness and the glorious quiet of the empty beach below.

"Thank you for last night," I said, finally breaking the silence. "For your . . . chivalry. Other than Jasper, I haven't known many chivalrous men. And even he . . ."

Roland stepped in to finish my thought. "Even he wanted something from you?"

"Jasper's a good man, Roland. And a true friend. What you heard the other night on the patio—he didn't mean it the way it sounded. He was hurt."

"He was also half in the bag. The man drinks too much for his own good—and yours."

"Yes, he does, but he was there for me when no one else was. Please don't think badly of him."

Roland nodded, but the crease between his brows made me wonder if I'd really convinced him. "I'm afraid there's no fancy breakfast this morning," he said, changing the subject abruptly. "We'll have to fend for ourselves. I know a place in town with good coffee. Then, if you like, I'll show you around the island."

I can't remember ever enjoying a day more. It was all so easy, so relaxed and unrushed, as if Roland had planned every moment for my enjoyment. And perhaps he had. He seemed to take great pleasure in my happiness, lighting up each time I laughed or expressed delight in something he had taken pains to show me. After breakfast we poked around downtown, visited a few shops and local landmarks, stocked up on sundries, then bought shrimp from a tiny seafood market and a bag of oranges from a roadside stand.

It's still hard to believe how comfortable we felt together, as if we'd known each other all our lives. And yet there was a delicious newness to it all, moments when our eyes would meet or our hands would touch, when we might have been a pair of newlyweds. I felt almost giddy, but tentative, too, as if someone had suddenly granted me the right to be happy but might snatch it away at any moment.

Later on, back at the cottage, we listened to the radio while we fixed dinner—ice-cold shrimp and a salad we threw together—then ate outside on the deck. We had oranges for dessert, giggling like children as the sticky-sweet juice ran down our chins and arms. Roland joked about our modest meal, but for me it was like heaven.

I felt almost sad as the day began to wind down, like the last pages of a fairy tale where you dread the story's end because you want it to go on forever. I kept waiting to be pinched, to wake up with a start and realize that none of it was real. But then he would take my hand, or smile at me, and I knew I wasn't dreaming at all, that somehow this perfect day, this perfect man, was very, very real.

After dinner, he led me down onto the beach and we walked, savoring the first blush of sunset as the sky was slowly set aflame. We stood, arms locked, watching the sun slide away, a ball of red fire melting into the sea. Then he turned and kissed me.

He tasted of oranges and the wine we'd drunk with dinner. The combination was heady. A desire I never realized I could feel leapt to life in my belly as my mouth opened to his, my limbs suddenly liquid as the kiss drew me closer and closer to something I should have been afraid of, but somehow wasn't. Finally, I surrendered, melting into Roland until I could no longer tell where I ended and he began.

I don't know how long he held me like that, how many times he kissed me or I kissed him. After a while it all became a sweet, warm blur. I only know our hands remained twined as we turned and walked back to the cottage, and that there were no more questions between us as we stepped inside, just a bone-deep need where there had once been only fear.

August 30, 1957
Hideaway Key, Florida

There's no use pretending it isn't true. I have lost my heart to Roland St. Claire. There, I've said it—or at least written it. Perhaps I should have been more careful, more guarded with my emotions, but in a million years I couldn't have guessed such feelings would ever take root in me. I thought myself immune, too scarred to ever let anyone get close enough to love. And yet, Roland has found his way in.

I have fallen in love with Hideaway, too, with its wide white beaches and smooth blue sea, its unhurried days and dreamy nights, all blurring together like something from a dream, had I been able to dream such happiness was possible. What was meant to be a week has somehow stretched into seven, waking each morning with Roland beside me, up with the sun to comb the beach for shells, basking away long lazy afternoons, drunk on salt air and sunshine, taking evening swims beneath a ghost-white moon, in a sea that seems to belong to only us. Nowhere to be. No eyes to pry. No link at all to the outside world.

I've thought several times about calling Caroline in the mountains, to tell her where I am and what I've done, but somehow I can't make myself dial the number. How can I explain running off in the middle of the night to a place I've never heard of, with a man I barely know?

And what of Jasper? I should have at least phoned him to let him know I was safe, and to apologize for leaving the Gardiners' so abruptly. I should have, but I didn't. After our conversation on the patio I'm not sure I could bear another sullen conversation about what I do and do not owe him. Even now, all these weeks later, I can't help wondering if that night has forever tainted our friendship. I suppose I'll know soon enough.

Tonight will be our last night at the cottage.

As I write this, most of my things are already packed, only a few stray items still waiting to be stowed for the long ride home. But as I sit here on the edge of the bed, I find I haven't the heart to finish it off. Instead, I linger with my jar of shells, lifting them out one at a time, holding each one in my palm, summoning behind my closed eyes, the exact color of the sunlight and precise hue of the sea on the day it was discovered. I've been using them to mark the days, adding a new one to the jar after each of our long morning walks along the shore. If Roland thought me silly he never said so. There are forty-nine shells now, each one whole and perfect and precious—forty-nine perfect shells for forty-nine perfect days.

I can hear Roland now, moving about the cottage, locking doors and checking windows, the sound of the cottage being shut up as our last precious moments together slowly tick away. I'm sure he's anxious to get back to his work. I haven't had the heart to ask what happens when we return to New York. Probably because I already know the answer. I have no claim to him, no right to feel as though I'm losing something that belongs to me. There have been no promises between us, no declarations made or asked for—nor will there be.

At thirty-six, Roland is already both wealthy and powerful, a man who moves in influential circles and must choose his companions wisely. His friends are important people, pedigreed and polished. I'm not fool enough to think a girl like me, a girl from Mims, Tennessee, without education or family name, could ever fit into his world. His future is too big, too promising, to include someone like me. We have had our time—our mad, reckless, blissful time—

but that time is winding down now, as I always knew it would. He will return to his life, and I will return to mine.

The thought of it makes my throat thicken. It's a hard thing to sample paradise and know you must give it up, and yet I wouldn't trade this bittersweet ache for a single shell in my jar.

August 31, 1957
Hideaway Key, Florida

There are moments we can't begin to dream of, twists of fate so wondrous and sweet they somehow make up for everything that has come before, all the grief and pain blotted out in an instant with the asking of a single question.

I was out on the deck bidding farewell to the beach, my bags waiting by the front door to be taken to the car, when I felt Roland's hands on my shoulders. I didn't hear him step outside, and had to dash tears from my eyes. I'd been trying all week to be brave, to mask my sadness behind a carefree smile, to maintain some shred of dignity at the end of things, but the effort had worn me too thin.

Suddenly, Roland's touch was more than I could bear. I stepped away before he could turn me into the circle of his arms.

Frowning, he reached for my hand on the railing, twining his fingers with mine. "You've been quiet these last few days, Lily-Mae. Is everything all right?"

I nodded, not trusting my voice. Everything in my body longed to throw myself against him, to memorize just one last time the touch and taste and feel of him, to hold tight to those final few moments and seal them away in my memory, proof that, for a time at least, I was his. Then later, when better able to bear the loss, I would unwrap them, carefully and tenderly, like the precious things they were, and hold them up to the light.

His fingers squeezed mine, a reminder that he was still waiting for an answer. I cleared my throat, tight with unshed tears. "It's just that these last few weeks have been so perfect it's hard to think about going back." I glanced away, out over the sea, swallowing past the razors in my throat. "I don't know how to thank you, Roland, for this summer. I'll cherish it always."

His fingers went slack suddenly, slipping through mine as he stepped away. "It isn't your thanks I was looking for, Lily-Mae. But then, that isn't your fault; it's mine. The instant I saw you I knew I was on dangerous ground. I knew better than to get involved with someone like you. You're nothing like the women I know. You're . . ." He paused, shoving his hands deep into his pockets. A tick appeared along his jaw. "Damn. I swore I wasn't going to do this. Do you have any idea at what I'm trying to say, Lily-Mae?"

Someone like me. The tears came in earnest as I absorbed the words, spilling over my lashes and onto my cheeks. "Yes," I said softly. "We're different people, with different lives. We've had fun, but now it's over. I understand."

Roland's head came around sharply, his eyes wide as they found mine. "That's what you thought I was trying to say, that this summer has been some kind of fling, and now I'm done with you?" He pulled me to him, eyes suddenly soft as he ran a finger along the curve of my cheek. "You little fool. I was trying to say that I've fallen in love with you—that I want to marry you."

The mingled sounds of the sea and wind suddenly went quiet, as if the world itself had suddenly stopped turning. "Marry . . . me?"

"Yes, Lily-Mae. I want to marry you. I think I have since the moment I first saw you in Celia Gardiner's drawing room. I just never dreamed someone like you would ever look in my direction. Am I a fool to hope you might say yes?"

Someone like me. The very words that made me cry only moments ago now made my heart want to soar—and yet I didn't dare let it. I took a step back, hating the flash of pain in Roland's eyes as I pulled away. "I love you, Roland, but we both know I don't fit in your world. You've heard my story, how and where I grew up, what Zell did, and then his wife . . ." My voice began to fray. I glanced away. "You don't need that in your life. You need a proper wife, one who can make you proud and give you a family, one who doesn't panic every time she's asked about her past. I can never be that wife. You may not think it now, but one day when the newness was gone, you'd wake up regretting you ever asked me. And I don't think I could bear that."

Roland closed the distance between us in two quick steps, taking my hand when he reached me. "The only thing I'll ever regret is hearing you say no."

I closed my eyes and pulled in a deep breath, trying not to think of Charles Addison and his tainted orphan. "How can I say anything else, Roland? You're an important man, with important friends. You can be so much, do so much with your life. I'd only stand in your way. My past would—"

"I don't give a damn about your past, Lily-Mae. It's your future I want. You're the strongest, bravest woman I've ever met. That's what I need in my life—that, and nothing else. I love you, Lily-Mae Boyle, and always will. A moment ago you said you loved me. Did you mean it?"

I nodded, barely able to speak. "With all my heart."

"Then I'll ask again—am I a fool for hoping you'll say yes?"

I couldn't help it; I threw back my head and laughed. "You were a fool for not asking me sooner."

Even now, as I write this, I feel a fresh round of tears beginning to well, joy mingled with disbelief. Roland St. Claire has asked me to be his wife, and I have said yes.

September 10, 1957
Paris, France

We were married on a Tuesday afternoon at a tiny chapel on the outskirts of Hideaway Key. I wore a simple sheath of cream-colored silk—not a wedding dress, but close enough—and a tiny hat with a beaded veil. My bouquet was a handful of roses purchased from the local florist, and hastily bound with creamy silk ribbon. And for a wedding present, Roland has bought me the cottage, so we can come back as often as we like, and relive our first blissful days together.

It all happened so fast I barely had time to call Caroline with the news. She was stunned at first, but quickly warmed to the idea when she recognized Roland's name. I pretended to ignore her snide remark about my knack for wrapping a man around my finger, but it stung a little that she couldn't simply be happy for me. I had hoped spending the summer away would soften her feelings toward me, but apparently it hasn't. Roland noticed my mood as I hung up the phone, and asked if everything was all right. I told him it was. He wouldn't understand, as I did, that it was just Caroline being Caroline. Besides, I wasn't letting anything spoil this time for us.

And then, almost as quickly as the wedding was accomplished, we were on our way to Paris, where every day has been a fresh whirl of beautiful places, sumptuous food, and shopping trips that leave me dizzy as glass after glass of champagne is pressed into my hands, and high-cheeked models stroll about for my pleasure. Dresses, gowns, lingerie, hats, gloves, handbags, and jewelry. Nothing is too good or too expensive. I've worn nice things before, have reveled in the feel of good lace and fine linen, but never in a million years have I dreamed of owning such exquisite things myself. I confess, it makes me a little uncomfortable, like a child playing dress-up with her mother's best things—things that are too good for her. It's all so much—too much, really—but when I protest, Roland reminds me a man should be allowed to spoil his wife.

And spoil me he does. We lunch in cafés with tables right out on the sidewalk, sipping café au lait and nibbling pastries filled with sweet almond paste. Evenings are spent at the opera, theater, or ballet, then followed by late suppers served under sterling. We sleep late each morning, waking slowly to make love while the Parisian sunshine streams in through the balcony windows.

It's all been lovely, so lovely that at times I have trouble believing any of it is real. It's as if I have been set down in the middle of someone else's dream, and will soon awaken in my narrow cot at Mt. Zion. Those are the times I find myself reaching out to touch Roland's hand to be sure this is all real, that he's real.

TWENTY-NINE

1995
Hideaway Key, Florida

Married.

Lily closed the journal, too stunned to move. It was too much to comprehend. But even more stunning than the actual marriage was the fact that her mother had kept it secret all these years. And so had her father. She did the math on her fingers, ticking off the months between Lily-Mae's last journal entry and the date of her parents' marriage in November of 1960—roughly three years.

Lily-Mae had predicted that Roland would wake up one day regretting that he had ever asked her to marry him. Had her prophecy come to pass? Or had it all just happened too fast? A summer romance, a cottage by the sea, lazy days and passion-filled nights, but in the end they had been little more than strangers, two very different people brought together by circumstance and moonlight. Perhaps their differences had simply proven too much to overcome. It wasn't hard to imagine. And yet Caroline, a product of the same world as Lily-Mae, had managed to hold on to Lily's father for more than thirty years, and without any sign of the affection Roland and Lily-Mae had shared.

Lily rose and went to the bureau, taking down Lily-Mae's jar of shells and carrying it back to the bed. With special care, she spilled them onto the spread, lining them up in neat little rows, counting as she went. *Forty-nine perfect shells for forty-nine perfect days.* And more than thirty years later they were still here. Their marriage might not have lasted, but one thing seemed certain: Lily-Mae had never stopped loving Roland St. Claire.

At long last, she was beginning to form a picture of Lily-Mae's life, though it was still hazy in a lot of places, and not at all what she'd expected. Unfortunately, there were no more journals, which meant there was no way to fill in the blanks. And there were a lot of blanks that needed filling. Like how her parents ended up married. There had been no mention of how they'd gotten together. Had Caroline thrown herself at Roland as she had done with the odious Zell, desperate to possess something that belonged to Lily-Mae?

Lily was still contemplating the possibility that her mother had purposely set out to destroy her sister's marriage, when she heard Dean call her name.

"Back here," she called back to him. "In the bedroom."

He appeared seconds later, handsome in khakis and a crisp blue oxford. "What's all this?" he asked, eyeing the bedspread littered with shells.

"It's forty-nine days."

"Sorry?"

"They belonged to Lily-Mae," she explained as she began gathering the shells and returning them to the jar. "I've been wondering about them since I got here. Now I know."

"And?"

"She used them to mark the days. One for every walk they took together."

"Who's *they*?"

"Lily-Mae and my father. They spent a summer here once—and then they got married."

"Married? Are you sure?"

Lily nodded. "It's all right there in her journals. The last entry is about their honeymoon. It was before he met my mother, and it didn't last long if my math is right."

"And then what?"

"I don't know. There aren't any more journals. They divorced, presumably, and he married my mother."

"Wow." Dean dropped down on the bed beside her, scooping up a stray shell and handing it to her. "Are you okay? I mean, it's a weird thing to find out, isn't it—your father being married to both your mother and your aunt?"

"It's very weird. But what's even weirder is that no one ever told me. I've always known there was something, some secret having to do with Lily-Mae that my mother couldn't bear for me to know, but I could never have guessed this."

"I don't think anyone could. I take it you haven't talked to your mother yet?"

"Just the one time. When it comes to Lily-Mae, my mother has never been very cooperative, and it's been worse since my father died. I'm betting she never counted on these journals turning up."

"I still don't understand your mother making a big secret of it. Your father was married to her sister for a couple of years. What's the big deal?"

"You have to understand my mother, but I wouldn't hold your breath. Even I don't understand her. Maybe she didn't want anyone to know she wasn't my father's first choice. Or maybe she didn't want anyone to know she was the one who broke them up."

"You think there was a little extracurricular activity going on?"

"I don't know, but my father certainly didn't waste any time between weddings. Three years after he asked Lily-Mae to marry him he was saying 'I do' to my mother."

"Ouch. That is pretty fast."

Lily rose from the bed to return the jar of shells to the bureau. "It's only a hunch, and not a very nice one, but it does add up."

"Maybe, but it's a pretty touchy subject to bring up with your mother. How do you think she's going to handle it?"

Lily pressed the heels of her hands to her eyes, trying to quell the dull pain that had begun to throb there. "The same way she always does, by making me feel guilty for even asking. She'll talk around it, or talk over it. Anything but answer my questions. We've been playing the same game for thirty years."

Dean stood and reached for both of her hands, twining his fingers through hers. "We talked about dinner earlier, maybe catching a movie. Do either of those still sound like a good idea? Or I could whip us up something over at my place, and then we can curl up on the couch and find an old movie. It doesn't matter to me. I just think getting away from all this for a while might be a good thing."

Lily looked down at their hands, at Dean's long tan fingers twined with her own, and was surprised by the flurry of emotions the sight conjured. Lifting her gaze to his, she smiled gratefully. "An old movie would be great."

They made omelets together—mushroom, ham, green pepper, and Swiss. Lily handled the chopping with reasonable efficiency, while Dean manned the pans with all the skill and technique of a breakfast chef. They were delicious, but tasted even better eaten on the couch with *To Have and Have Not* playing on the classic movie channel.

Dean loaded the dishwasher, then poured them each a glass of merlot, settling in beside Lily to watch the rest of the movie. She wouldn't have guessed it, but apparently, he was quite the classic movie buff, able to quote almost every line verbatim, including Bacall's famous whistle scene, which he mimicked in fine comic fashion, after dragging his bangs down over one eye.

"I think you missed your calling. You nailed her. Though I have to say, I never would have figured you for a classics man."

"I'm not sure how to take that."

"I just meant you seem more like a *Die Hard* or *Lethal Weapon* kind of guy."

"Again, I'm not sure how to take that." A smile touched his lips briefly. "My mom and I used to watch the old black-and-whites. We'd do all the voices, accents, the whole nine yards. Her favorite was *Gone with the Wind.* She did a pretty mean Scarlett, but my Rhett needed a lot of work." Again, the smile came and went. "After she left I kept watching. I'd leave the TV on all night. It made me feel like she was still around, like she'd just gone to the store and would be back any minute. Silly, huh?"

Lily reached up to brush the bangs back out of his eyes, her fingers lingering in the soft waves of his hair. "No, not silly—sweet. It was a way to keep her with you."

"I knew she wasn't coming back. I pretended for a while, for my dad, but I always knew."

"I'm sorry."

"You don't need to be. It was a long time ago."

Lily studied him through lowered lashes, impassive as he sipped his wine, though perhaps just a little too impassive. "You're doing it again," she said quietly. "Do you really think people stop loving just because someone's not there anymore? Or because the years keep piling up?"

Dean stared into his glass, slowly swirling the contents. "I think they can—if they let themselves. You don't?"

"I honestly don't know. Lily-Mae loved my father, but something happened to separate them. They'd been apart for nearly forty years, and yet those shells were still on her dresser when she died. She never stopped loving him. Was that because she didn't let herself stop, or because that's just how it works?"

Dean shrugged. "Can't help you there. In case you haven't noticed, love isn't exactly my area of expertise."

"Not mine, either." Lily raised her glass with a sigh. "Here's to hopeless cases."

Dean lifted his glass in return. "May we always stick together."

Lily smiled as they touched glasses, aware, as their eyes met and held, of a sudden warmth blooming just south of her ribs. On impulse, she leaned over and touched her lips to his.

There was the sensation of melting as their mouths connected, a dreamy, languid surrender as his arms came around her and the kiss warmed, sweet, unhurried. And then, from some dim corner of her mind, there came a whisper, a female voice not her own, but familiar somehow. *This is how it began for me, too.* But it was too late to pull back, too late to retreat from the line they had crossed last night—and too late to safeguard against complications.

THIRTY

1995
Hideaway Key, Florida

Lily gnawed the end of her pencil as she eyed her latest sketch, a gauzy slip dress with a button-down front and slightly dropped waist. It was coming along, but there was something about the straps that was still wrong. She glanced at the stack of finished sketches on the sofa, twelve so far—wraparound skirts and dresses, casual suits, smart little capris in bright, summery prints. She still found it hard to believe how much work she had managed to produce in only two weeks.

Maybe it was all the salt air, or the constant shushing of the sea, nature's own white noise, that had helped her tap her creative juices. But the truth was probably much simpler—as simple as being happy. Since *To Have and Have Not,* she and Dean had spent every night together, eating breakfast on the deck every morning before going their separate ways for the day, then coming together as the sun went down, to prepare dinner and share their day.

She had been pleasantly surprised when he offered the use of the spare drafting table in his studio. It was an amazing space, with lots of light and a stunning view, much more optimal for working than Lily-Mae's cramped little writing desk. She had gladly accepted, but it felt awkward at first, encroaching on his creative space, but he assured her that barring any annoying habits, such as humming, whistling, or gum-cracking, he would barely know she was in the room. He had even given her a key, so she could let herself in and out as she pleased.

Today, however, she was making do with Lily-Mae's desk at the cottage, as Dean was currently finishing up a rather tricky set of plans for the Newmans of Chicago, and she didn't want to risk posing even the tiniest distraction. It was just as well. Her to-do list included another attempt to contact her mother, and on the off chance that she was successful in reaching her, she'd prefer to have a little privacy. Sadly, though not unexpectedly, this morning's call had yielded the same results as all her other recent attempts.

In truth, she was almost relieved when the answering machine picked up. Yes, she wanted answers, but right now she was more interested in keeping her head down and finishing the preliminary sketches. Anything to help keep Sheila's mind off Tampa. Which reminded her, she needed to call and firm up what time they would need to leave in order to make Sheila's appointment.

Sheila answered after two rings. Lily smiled at her chirpy greeting. "Hey, Thelma, it's Louise. How goes that list?"

"Getting longer by the minute. I had no idea there'd be so much involved."

"Getting cold feet?"

"Not on your damned life. My mama didn't raise no quitter."

"Thata girl. I'm telling you, you can do this." Lily paused, reluctant to steer the conversation onto sensitive ground. "Anyway, I was calling to find out what time we're going to need to leave next week. I have no idea how long the drive is."

"Oh." And just like that, the chirpiness was gone. "My appointment's at two, and it's about a three-hour drive. Maybe ten thirty, to give us a little leeway?"

"Ten thirty, it is. Let me jot it down." Lily reached for her planner, then realized she'd left it at Dean's. "Hang on, let me grab something to write on." Pulling out the right side drawer, she rummaged for a notepad but had to settle for a rumpled manila envelope instead. "Okay, ten thirty, it is."

Lily was taking down directions to Sheila's house when she noticed the postmark in the upper right-hand corner of the envelope. *New York City, NY. July 12, 1960.* But what really caught her attention was the return address. *Stephen Singer, Attorney-at-Law.* Peeling back the flap, she shook the contents out onto the desk. Sheila was still talking, rattling off lefts and rights, but Lily had stopped listening, too busy trying to decipher the neatly typed legalese dissolving the marriage of Mr. and Mrs. Roland St. Claire.

Lily ended the call as quickly as she could, promising to call back and firm up, then sat staring at the pages in her lap. There was a date stamped in red ink across the bottom. She did the mental math, July to November. Her father had divorced Lily-Mae in July, then married her mother just four months later.

She was still processing this latest revelation when she noticed the small scrap of newsprint on the desk. It had obviously been in the envelope with the divorce decree. She picked it up, squinting to make out the faded print. It was an article from the *New York Globe.*

Billboard Bride Just Another Pretty Face For Wealthy Financier

---

If speculation is to be believed, billboard sensation Lily-Mae St. Claire, née Boyle, and wealthy financier husband, Roland St. Claire, appear to be headed for divorce. No word yet on the cause of the split, but

> rumor has it there's been more than one blowup about a certain someone closely connected with the couple. The St. Claires married secretly in September, and have been seen together often in public, giving their best impression of wedded bliss, though it now appears all may not be well in paradise. To date, no details are available with regard to the size of any possible settlement, but with Roland St. Claire's name on the court documents, the price tag is certain to be a hefty one. Stay tuned, readers: this one is liable to get nasty.

Lily stared at the clipping, the words blurring and shifting behind an unexpected film of tears. What must it be like to have your private heartache splashed across the tabloids, to have your pain used as entertainment for the masses? The article contained no facts, but it offered plenty of speculation and innuendo. Her father, painted as a wealthy playboy. Nebulous hints about a nameless third party. Gleeful speculation about the possible size of the settlement. That the author had been hinting at the possibility of a love triangle was hard to deny. The glaring question was, who was the third party? Given what she'd read in the journals and the haste of her parents' marriage, it was hard not to imagine Caroline as the culprit.

Lily sighed heavily as she slid the clipping and divorce papers back into their envelope. Another discovery, and a whole new set of questions. And the only person alive who had the answers wasn't picking up her phone. Lily was tired of sleuthing, tired of running into brick walls, and clues that weren't clues at all, just new blind paths down an already maddening maze.

If only things worked out like they did in Salty's novels, clues falling into place right on schedule, everything wrapping up all nice and neat by the last page. They weren't falling into place, though.

There were no more journals, no more scrapbooks, nothing left to go on. And with what she now suspected, about her mother *and* her father, she wasn't sure she actually wanted to know any more. She hated to admit it, but maybe it was time to take Dean's advice and let it go.

And yet the idea of giving up rankled. She had come all this way, spent all this time. What was it Salty said about giving up on a case? *Who's to say you won't turn a corner tomorrow and find something you missed, something that's been hiding in plain sight the whole time?*

Hiding in plain sight.

Was it possible? Had she missed something that was right under her nose? She'd been through most of the boxes, read all the journals, thumbed through all the scrapbooks. But then, those things didn't really qualify as *in plain sight.* What she should be looking for was the kind of thing she might have already looked right past, something that blended into the background.

With fresh determination, she went to Lily-Mae's room and simply stood in the doorway, trying to see it as she had that first night—a woman's life crammed into one small room. It seemed wrong, impossible actually, when that life had been so big, so filled with love and loss. She thought of the small box discovered beneath her aunt's bed, family photos and a battered rag doll, cherished things from childhood, the jar of forty-nine shells, a precious reminder of the only time she had been happy. But the rest of it was different, boxes filled with fragments of a past that was neither cherished nor precious, things she must have been only too glad to pack away and forget. It was the things she kept here, in this tiny bedroom, that Lily-Mae had treasured enough to keep close. If there was something, anything, it would be here.

Stepping into the room, Lily let her gaze wander. She had already made forays into the bureau, closet, and nightstand, even the steamer trunk at the foot of the bed. There was no need to look again. What she was looking for, if it was there at all, was going to be out in the open, perhaps . . . on a bookshelf.

Lily held her breath as she stepped to the bookshelf. It filled one corner of the room, six shelves of thick, dark walnut lined top to bottom with an awkward jumble of scarred leather spines. Slowly, methodically, she began scanning titles, some familiar, some not, but all shabby from use. And then she saw it: a single volume in smooth brown calfskin tucked unobtrusively between Woolf's *A Room of One's Own* and Whitman's *Leaves of Grass*, its dark leather spine devoid of either author or title.

There was a little skitter in her chest as she slid the volume free and carried it to the bed. The pages were warped in places, and mottled with a gummy brown substance, as if something had spilled nearby and splattered. Still, the words were legible enough once she managed to tease apart the sticky pages. Her heart leapt at the sight of Lily-Mae's elegant hand, as familiar now as her own, but there was something different about the writing here, a spidery quality to the lines not present in any of the other entries. Then she saw the date scrawled across the top of the page—*June 13, 1993*, more than thirty years after the last entry she'd read.

THIRTY-ONE

June 13, 1993
Hideaway Key, Florida

I've been to the doctor again today.

They didn't bring me into a treatment room this time, no exam tables or needles. Instead, they led me to one of the consultation rooms, where there was a desk and a pair of armchairs. That's when I knew.

I didn't have to wait long. He told me he was sorry, more sorry than he could say, and that after all he has seen of death he still finds it all so very unfair. I told him not to worry on my account. I stopped taking life personally years ago. I almost felt bad for him as he said the words. And almost relieved for myself. I won't have to go through that anymore.

There's not much left of me now, barely enough to cast a shadow, though I have never mourned the loss of my beauty. It's been said that beauty is both a blessing and a curse. That has been doubly true in my life. Aside from allowing me to provide for Caroline, it has never brought me anything but trouble and heartache.

Perhaps that's why I never cared about the scars, or the bits of flesh the doctors cut away while I slept, or even the ravages that came after, with the drugs and radiation. I did not rail against fate when my hair began to fall out by the handful, or when the flesh began to fall from my bones. It is only the loss of myself that I regret, the start that comes each time I look in the mirror and fail to recognize the woman looking back at me.

The woman Roland once loved is gone.

Which is why I would not see him when he tried to come. I could not bear for him to see me this way, to have him look at me as if I were a stranger, wearing clothes that hang on me like a scarecrow, a scarf wrapped around my ruined head like one of those eccentric silent-movie stars.

There's been no one to see, no one distressed by my steady decline. Even Jasper is gone now, thanks to the drinking. Not that he ever stayed long when he did come. There's a kind of freedom in that, in being left alone, allowed to decay without having to be brave. They tell me there are other things to try, other places to go, other opinions to be had, but I've said no to them all. I have a year at most, but probably less. If there was a reprieve to be had, the sea would have granted it by now, as it has somehow managed to do at every broken place in my life. Healing, refuge, forgiveness were all to be had here in my cottage by the sea. But not this time. It's time to make plans, to gather my things about me and wait.

I've been told what to expect, how things will . . . progress. There is no need to suffer, they tell me, no need to be brave when the end draws near. There are pills to dull the pain, pills to ease the way. There are places, too, where one can go to die, lying in a strange bed, surrounded by strange faces. I told them no, of course. The thought of dying anywhere but here is unthinkable. I thanked him then, thanked them all. I will not be seeing them again.

I'll need to call Stephen tomorrow, to tell him how things stand. There are affairs to be gotten in order, arrangements to be made, and tales to tell while I can still bear to tell them.

July 27, 1993
Hideaway Key, Florida

My things arrived from storage last week. I forgot how much I left behind when I left New York, and how very little I've missed any of it. But it's here now, box upon box of it, crammed with bits of my past, the good thrown in with the bad. So many things for such an empty life. It took four days of rummaging to finally find what I was looking for, and then another two days to be sure what I meant to do was right.

I still don't know, but I've sent them just the same, with a note for Stephen that they are to be forwarded on to Roland. It was more of a job than I thought it would be, more . . . emotional. I thought I had made my peace with all that happened back then, but I find I have not, and will not, until the truth is told at last. I must trust Stephen to help me with that.

I've told him how things are with me, that I'm not long for this world. And by now he has surely told Roland, though I suspect he's known of my illness for some time. Why else would he have tried to see me after so many years of silence? I don't blame Stephen for being indiscreet, or if I do it's only a little. He never could keep anything from Roland.

It's too late to change anything now, to unravel the mess we've made and fill the empty places we carved in each other's hearts. But perhaps it's not too late to tell the truth and to forgive. Before I leave this world I want him to know why I left him—why I had to leave him.

Perhaps I've left it too late, but I cannot leave this world without at least trying to set things right. My anger has burned to ash, the wounds closed, if not quite healed. I would do the same for Roland, if I can. It's not pity I'm after, only understanding.

October 24, 1993
Hideaway Key, Florida

The end can't be far off now; a bit sooner than expected, perhaps, but there it is. And what does it matter? There is nothing to keep me here. I've heard nothing from Roland, no word that he received the package I sent, no word of any kind. I suppose it was too much to hope for after all that has passed—too much time, and too much pain.

Still, I did hope.

I have tried not to take the pills they gave me, but the pain is so much worse now, and they help me sleep. And when I sleep I forget. I dream sometimes, of Caroline and me, of the little pond behind our house and the tire swing in front where we used to play together, back before Mama took us to Mt. Zion. I dream of Mama, too, and wonder what kept her from coming back for us, or if she ever really meant to come back at all.

I was angry with her for so long, angry with all of us, if truth be told, at Mama, at myself, at Roland and Caroline. But now, at the end, I see what a waste it has all been. The hurting and hating, the bleeding and blaming, has all been for nothing—has changed nothing. Neither will forgiveness. But it's time to forgive.

It doesn't come easily, though, this forgiving business. It is not the heart's way to turn a blind eye when it has been dealt a sharp blow. Instead, it nurses the wound, and guards against the next, always, always remembering. Forgiveness, then, is a choice we must make, with hearts exposed and eyes wide open, for the sake of our souls, for the sake of peace. It is only Zell I cannot forgive. Zell, and perhaps myself. There is much I regret from those earlier days, but little I would do differently. One thing only, in fact. But I cannot think of that now.

Memory can be a cruel companion, regrets crashing over us like waves, flooding in, pulling back, until the sand shifts beneath our feet, and we're left staring at our truths, bloated and terrible after so many years.

Each night I close my eyes, wondering if it's for the last time—hoping it will be. Death will be a mercy when it comes, the blank relief of that other world, where the soul goes dark and memories are no more. But each night, while I toss and dream, the moon changes place with the sun. Another blue sky. Another day of heavy heartbeats. Another day of waiting. And yet there is just a little relief.

How strange this tug-of-war is, between living and letting go, when the soul longs for relief but the body clings to the pain, clawing for one last breath even as the water is closing over our heads, the seductive pull of freedom, the stark terror of loss.

In truth, it is only the cottage I'll regret leaving. It has been my refuge for so long, and is even now, despite its long decline. It is like me, I suppose: shabby and spare, wearing thin after years of neglect, but lovely still, if you don't look too closely and the light is just right.

I unearthed some of my things from the boxes and put them out. It's good to have one's things about, like old friends come back after a long journey. It pains me to think of it all being shut up when I'm gone. As I write this I'm looking at my jar of shells, each one precious still, tangible proof of those perfect days, and that perfect summer. I meant to fill it once, with more shells and more days, but life has a way of putting up detours, throwing you so far off course it becomes impossible to recover one's way. And so my little jar will remain unfilled. The time for collecting shells is past.

Soon I will take my leave, my heart quiet at last. But beyond my window the sea will go on beating, keeping its secrets and mine. It won't be long now.

THIRTY-TWO

1995
Hideaway Key, Florida

Lily brushed away the tears that had been falling steadily for the last half hour, still shocked by the sight of the blank page glaring up at her from her lap. Her heart had broken open as she read about Lily-Mae's last days, steeped in sadness, and at war with her memories, struggling to forgive and be forgiven. But it was nothing compared with what she'd felt when she turned the page to find that the entries had abruptly run out. The implication of the remaining blank pages had been too terrible to ignore. So glaringly final.

It wasn't the fact of Lily-Mae's death that had rocked her. She'd been prepared for that. Rather, it was the manner of it, the fact that she had died alone, and with such a heavy heart. She had written of secrets kept and lies told, of a longing for forgiveness, but never once had she named her crimes, as if even in her final days she couldn't bear to commit them to paper.

But even more curious was the huge gap of years between the last batch of journals and the one she'd just finished. It seemed unlikely that a lifelong journaler would simply stop recording the events of her life, then resume again more than thirty years later. Nor did the latest entries read as though she had just resumed her writing. If that was the case, if Lily-Mae hadn't actually stopped, where were the rest of the journals? And what had happened during those in-between years?

At least she finally had an explanation for all the boxes. Lily-Mae had had her things brought out of storage and delivered to the cottage, and she'd done so with a specific purpose in mind: to look for something and then send it to Roland.

A deathbed confession? One last chance for absolution? It was possible. In fact, the more Lily thought about it, the more convinced she was that she was right, and that the unsent letter had, in fact, been meant for her father.

This time, when she dialed her mother's number she was ready with a different set of questions. Not that it mattered. As usual there was no answer, just the familiar sound of her mother's voice on the machine.

You've reached the St. Claire residence . . .

"Mother, this is getting ridiculous. Please pick up the phone and talk to me. I need to know about Daddy and Lily-Mae, about why they divorced, and if Daddy received a package from Lily-Mae before she died." She waited, listening to empty air. "Mother, I mean it. I'm not going to stop calling. Sooner or later, you're going to have to talk about this."

Lily waited again, but to no avail. Finally, she banged down the phone, frustration threatening to boil over. The woman couldn't just go on ignoring her forever. Or maybe she could. *Why?* was the question. Refusing to talk about her sister was certainly nothing new, but dodging phone calls from her own daughter was starting to feel a bit manic.

Was it possible her father's death had taken more of an emotional toll than she believed? It was hard to imagine, until she remembered that her mother had lost not only a husband but a sister as well. Two losses in as many years. It would certainly explain the marked increase in her mother's gin consumption. Not even the stoic Caroline St. Claire could absorb two such losses and remain unscathed.

The thought brought an unexpected pang of remorse. She'd been so absorbed in the mystery, so hell-bent on getting answers, that she'd never stopped to think her tenacity might go beyond mere annoyance for her mother. After thirty-five years she was used to her mother's theatrics, especially when it came to Lily-Mae, but this felt different, more dire, almost ominous.

Suddenly, she saw her mother's avoidance in a new light, not as a prolonged act of passive aggression but as a desperate attempt to keep painful doors securely bolted. And with each new phone call and demand for information, Lily had been rattling the keys in those rusty old locks, threatening to throw the doors wide.

All this time she had assumed there was something in Lily-Mae's past her mother didn't want exposed. Now she had to ask herself if Caroline's bizarre overreaction to her father leaving her the cottage might not be about her *own* past, and the fear that some unflattering bit of evidence might come to light—like the fact that she swooped in to marry her sister's husband before the ink on the divorce papers was even dry.

Or maybe it was the fact that despite strenuous efforts to blot her sister out of existence, Lily-Mae had remained a part of Roland's life, if only from a distance—that he had loved her first, last, and always. Caroline had never been keen on playing second fiddle. It must have been doubly hard coming in second to her own sister. Better to hide the facts, perhaps even rewrite history, than have the truth known. It must be rather inconvenient to learn that Lily-Mae had poured her heart out in a series of journals, and then left them to be found when she was dead.

She thought briefly about picking up the phone again and confronting her mother with this new theory, but in the end, she decided to leave it alone. If her mother didn't call back this time, which she almost certainly wouldn't, Lily would have to accept the fact that she simply wasn't going to.

THIRTY-THREE

1995

Hideaway Key, Florida

Lily tipped her head back and closed one eye, watching the bright yellow kite lift away and then dive, tail fluttering gaily against a low leaden sky. She couldn't help smiling as she watched Dean down by the shore. She thought he was kidding when he'd invited her to go kite flying after breakfast, but there he stood, looking all boyish and windblown, grinning happily as he wrestled the wind for control of his Hi-Flier.

The day had dawned gray and sullen, with a sharp wind swirling in off the water, the fringes of a tropical storm that was currently lashing the Texas coast. Perfect kite weather, or so Dean said. She wouldn't know. She'd never flown a kite in her life, or seen one flown, for that matter. One thing was certain: he was having fun, and so was Dog, romping in and out of the softly breaking waves.

She was glad now that she'd let him convince her to take the day off. She'd been in a bit of a funk since reading the last journal, unable to shake the thought of such a sad and lonely end. She had tried immersing herself in work, spending long hours at Dean's spare drafting table, playing with new ideas, fine-tuning old ones, but it hadn't worked.

Lily-Mae was always with her, her losses and her sorrows, and that last terrible blank page. Her aunt had loved one man all her life, and had clearly never *stopped* loving him, even after he turned around and married her sister. How had she managed to endure so much and yet love so deeply? The question still baffled Lily.

The more she knew, the more obvious it became that *happily ever after* was just a clever marketing scheme devised by people who sold diamond rings and honeymoon packages. Lily-Mae had believed it, though, and for a time she and Roland *had* lived happily. It was the *ever after* part that eluded them.

Without meaning to, Lily's eyes found Dean at the water's edge. They were starting to get comfortable, or at least she was, falling into the kinds of routines couples shared. Who slept on which side, who stacked the dishwasher, whose turn it was to do the shopping, the kinds of things that had always roused a vague sense of panic when she was with Luc—and were usually followed by a hasty retreat.

Only this time she didn't want to retreat. How was that possible? She'd been clear from the outset. They both had. No strings. No complications. But somewhere along the way something had changed, something she couldn't or wouldn't name, and it was starting to scare the hell out of her.

Dean's eyes found hers, as if feeling the weight of her gaze. She glanced away quickly, afraid her face might give her away, and caught Dog's eye instead. He turned and trotted in her direction, tracking clots of damp sand onto her blanket. He had grown rather attached to her over the last few weeks, and she to him. So fond, in fact, that she had mentally renamed him Chester. She hadn't told Dean yet. It was one thing to clutter a man's bathroom with scrunchies and shower gel. It was quite another to rename his dog.

Restless, she stood and wandered to the water's edge. The day had grown warm in spite of the cloud cover, the air thick with a haze of salt and blowing sand. Her breath caught as she waded into the waves, briefly shocked by the chilliness as they closed around her ankles, then slid up her calves. She stood there a moment, hair streaming in the breeze, struck once again by the stark beauty of the sea and sky, by nature's palette of blues and grays and greens.

She wasn't aware that Dean had approached until she felt his arms close about her waist. Instinctively, she relaxed against his chest, letting her breath sync with his, content to remain quiet in the circle of his arms. She tipped her head back and smiled, sighing when his lips pressed warmly against her shoulder, then began to trail along the curve of her neck. She couldn't say for certain whose doing it was, but a moment later she found herself facing him, mouth opening hungrily to his.

"This is a whole lot more fun than kite flying," he murmured throatily.

Lily drew back just a little, offering a languid smile. "I'm glad you think so. Care to take a swim?"

"That depends."

"On what?"

"On whether or not you plan to wear this." Without warning, he reached for the knots at both her back and nape and gave them a swift, simultaneous tug.

Lily was too shocked to even protest as the top of her bathing suit slithered free.

"It's a private beach, remember?" he said grinning wickedly. "But if it makes you feel better, I'll let you keep the bottoms . . . for now."

He grabbed her hand then, tugging her with him into the water. Lily gasped as the cool waves broke against her flesh, but she quickly warmed when he drew her close, twining her legs around his waist. She offered no resistance as his lips found hers, her arms tight about his neck, fingers lost in the damp waves of his hair. It was a heady combination, warm salty kisses set against the primal rhythm of the sea, slippery limbs and eager hands, like serpents moving quietly beneath the waves. This time when Lily shivered it had nothing to do with the temperature of the water.

It wasn't until the first cold patter of rain began to fall that the spell was finally broken. Lily turned her face to the sky, laughing giddily. Dean grabbed her hand and dragged her toward shore, scooping her bathing suit top off the wet sand as they made a mad dash for the house.

The sky opened in earnest as they made it inside, hurling sheets of noisy gray rain against the windows. Lily barely noticed as they tumbled into the shower and then into bed, picking things up precisely where they'd left off on the beach, in a heated frenzy of warm breath and wet limbs, heedless of the afternoon storm raging outside.

The rain had stopped by the time they finally collapsed in a sated tangle. They slept for a time, then ate dinner in bed—leftover pasta and salad, washed down with a good red wine. The storm had moved out, leaving the horizon washed in pearly hues of pink and gold, the air damp but cool as it wafted in through the open doors.

Beside her, Dean was propped against a bank of pillows, using his sheet-draped lap as a desk, a legal pad on his knees, a pencil tucked behind one ear, and a calculator in hand as he tweaked the final proposal numbers for the Newmans' new beach house. Lily pretended to work, too, toying with ideas for an elaborate silk sarong that had been floating around in her head for days. But her mind refused to cooperate, her attention straying beyond the bedroom window, where the sun was beginning to slip toward the sea. Another day nearly gone.

Had Lily-Mae felt like this as she lay beside Roland all those years ago? Had she longed to halt the sun in its tracks, to stretch each day and make it last? In her journals she had spoken of time winding down, of knowing each day that her time with Roland was ticking away—that every day they had less.

The words had touched her deeply when she read them, but now, in the afterglow of a day well spent, they struck her even more keenly, because somewhere along the way they had become her feelings, too. Summer was half gone. In a few weeks she would leave Hideaway Key, long before she ever filled her own jar of shells. She was beginning to understand why Lily-Mae had kept the jar, a tangible reminder of happy days that had sped by far too quickly.

Had it been worth it? A lifetime of heartache in exchange for a few weeks or months of bliss? Or had she come to regret the choices that left her heartbroken and alone? Sheila's words suddenly drifted into her head, unbidden. *You know when you realize you're absolutely terrified. When you're convinced you're going to smash yourself to pieces, and you're still willing to leap.*

"Where are you?"

Lily started and pulled her eyes back to Dean's. "I was thinking about Lily-Mae."

"Of course you were."

Lily ignored the gibe. "I was wondering if she would have married my father if she knew how things would turn out, if she would have let herself love him the way she did, knowing it wouldn't last."

"And what did you decide?"

"I think she would have. I don't think it's the kind of thing you have a say over. You don't decide to love someone, you just do. She loved my father, and that was that."

Dean frowned. "That's a bit fatalistic, don't you think? Especially for someone who doesn't believe in all that nonsense. Besides, to hear you tell it, she left him. Your father was the one who got burned, not your aunt."

Lily shrugged. "Yes, she did, but she must have had her reasons. I don't know what they were. I'll probably never know. But if you had read the last journal you'd understand. She never stopped loving him."

"So, love is sacrifice? Not exactly a ringing endorsement, if you ask me."

His sarcasm was hardly new, but for some reason it irked more than usual tonight, perhaps because it came at the end of such a perfect day. "Sheila says you know it's love when you're terrified of losing everything, and you're still willing to take the leap, because going over a cliff together beats playing it safe alone."

Dean shook his head, a combination of annoyance and amusement. "Well, now, there's a testimonial if I've ever heard one."

"I think it's romantic."

There was an awkward moment of silence as Dean's pencil hovered above his legal pad. Finally, he poked the pencil back behind his ear and folded his hands over his abdomen. "I thought you were the no-complications girl. Now, suddenly, you're all moony about lovers holding hands and jumping off cliffs?"

"It's just a figure of speech," Lily shot back drily. "It's about staring heartbreak in the face and not blinking, about being committed no matter the cost. My father told Lily-Mae once that she was the bravest woman he'd ever met. Maybe he was more right than even he knew. She was living a fairy tale, the kind every girl dreams of when she's growing up—a man who adored her, clothes, money, travel—and she just walked away. You can't tell me she didn't have a damn good reason. I just wish I knew what it was."

"Maybe she met a mechanic."

Lily stared at him, not sure if she should feel guilty about blundering onto a prickly topic, or annoyed that he could be so cavalier when he knew how she felt. In the end, she decided to go with guilt.

"I'm sorry," she said quietly, laying a hand on his arm. "I didn't mean to drag up old memories."

Dean pulled back from her touch, his eyes already back on his legal pad. "Forget it. Everyone's entitled to an opinion."

Lily blinked at him, surprised by his frosty tone. Did he think she'd been trying to draw him into a conversation about their relationship, or nudge him toward some sort of declaration? The thought made her queasy. She thought of Luc, of the offhand remarks that had frequently found their way into conversations, how she would do her best to sidestep them, and then, when that didn't work, how she would seize on the first thing she could find to start an argument. Is that what this was? Some kind of karmic role reversal?

"I really am sorry," she said again. "I know you don't understand why I care about all this. I'm not even sure I understand it myself. But if it bothers you, we don't—"

"I'm going to Chicago for a few days," he said gruffly, cutting her off midsentence. "I leave the day after tomorrow."

Lily stared at him, trying to wrap her head around the startlingly blunt announcement.

"Chicago?"

"To meet with the Newmans," he explained, erasing something he'd just written. "It's a big job. A pretty lucrative one, too, if things work out the way I'm hoping with the home and land package I've worked up. I just need one more face-to-face to finalize the details. It shouldn't take long, a week at most." He glanced up then, a crease between his brows. "Is something wrong?"

"I'm just surprised, is all. You didn't say anything."

"Didn't I?"

"No, you didn't." She cringed at the sound of her own voice, teetering on the edge of petulance, but couldn't seem to help herself. "It's not a big deal. I'm just surprised you didn't remember to tell me when you booked your flight."

Dean flashed her a distracted look. "Sorry. I guess I'm telling you now. The timing works pretty well, actually. You'll be in Tampa with Sheila the day I leave. This way you won't need to hurry back. You could stay overnight, enjoy a girls' night out in Ybor City. I thought a little downtime might be a good thing."

Downtime. As in taking a break. As in needing some space.

Lily looked away. She'd used the word often enough to know what it meant.

"Sure. Why not."

If Dean noticed the sudden change in her mood he hid it well, engrossed once more in his numbers and notes. Lily did her best to return to her sarong, but was too distracted to concentrate. Was she imagining it—the feeling that the ground had suddenly shifted beneath her feet? She wanted to think so, but the warning signs were too glaring to ignore. She'd been using the same technique for years—lashing out, then clamming up, retreating behind the safety of work.

And what if she was right, and this impromptu business trip was exactly what it looked like—a way of putting some distance between them? She had no claim on his time, or his comings and goings. They had agreed; no strings, no complications, each free to go their own way when the shine began to wear off. And yet, the thought of him availing himself of the escape clause in their relationship filled her with dread.

"Are you going to work much longer?" she asked tentatively. "I thought we could watch a movie or something."

"You go ahead," Dean mumbled around the pencil clamped between his teeth. "I've got more numbers to crunch."

Lily waited, hoping he would look up. He didn't. It was as if she had suddenly become invisible, a houseguest who had overstayed her welcome. Had there been some sign she missed, some signal she should have picked up on? A few hours ago she had been in his arms. But there was a difference between *making* love and *being* in love. God knows she'd always been careful enough not to confuse the two. Until now.

THIRTY-FOUR

1995
Hideaway Key, Florida

Lily checked her watch, relieved to see that she was actually running ahead of schedule. Sheila was already a basket case about her doctor's appointment. The last thing Lily wanted to do was add to her stress by being late.

She had spent last night at the cottage rather than at Dean's, using the excuse that she wanted to finish up a few last-minute sketches for Sheila before they hit the road. He hadn't seemed to mind. In fact, he barely seemed to notice when she slipped out after dinner, leaving him to his blueprints and his calculator. It felt strange sleeping alone again—and waking alone.

Funny how you could find yourself missing something you didn't realize had become a part of your life, how the absence of a face or a touch could leave an ache at the center of your chest. There had been no sense of loss when she and Luc finally parted ways, only a wave of relief that she wouldn't have to go on hurting him. The thought that Dean might be feeling the way she had back then—guilty and vaguely claustrophobic—made her cringe. The sensible thing, the merciful thing, would be to end it now, to back away quietly and let him move on, an honorable surrender that would leave her pride—if not her heart—intact.

And what better time to part ways than when they were already heading in different directions—her to Tampa, him to Chicago? They'd wrap things up when he got back. It would all be very civil, a cool handshake, and then he'd make himself scarce while she collected her toothbrush and conditioner from his bathroom. In the end he would be relieved, just as she had been with Luc.

She checked her watch for the umpteenth time: ten after ten. He had promised to stop by on his way to the airport, but part of her hoped he'd forget. She'd just as soon skip the awkward good-bye and let the thing die cleanly. And yet here she was, dragging her feet on the off chance that he *would* show up.

Annoyed with herself, she crossed to the desk, about to call Sheila, when he stuck his head through the open sliders. He was wearing his client clothes, neatly pressed khakis and a pale blue oxford.

"Good. I caught you. I was afraid we'd missed each other. I wanted to say good-bye."

Lily busied herself with gathering her purse and sketches from the desk. "I thought we already had."

"You left in such a hurry last night. There's something I wanted to tell you before I left, something I probably should have said days ago. I've been—"

Lily cut him off before he could get the rest out. Knowing what was coming was one thing; hearing it said out loud was quite another. "You don't need to explain, Dean. I've been thinking about it, too. I'll be on a plane to Milan next month, and you'll be here with your blueprints. Why put off the inevitable?"

"Really?"

"Really. I'm okay with it."

Dean's eyes narrowed as he studied her face. "Are you sure? Because you don't sound okay. You sound like something's wrong."

Lily pasted on what she hoped would pass for a smile. "I'm fine, really. I just don't want to be late picking up Sheila."

"You're sure?"

"Sure, I'm sure." But she was already backing away, determined to maintain a safe distance. "Have a good flight, and good luck with . . . everything."

"I wish you had stayed last night. We could have talked about this, instead of me just dropping it in your lap before I hop on a plane. I feel like such a heel. I know how you feel, and that this isn't easy for you." He fished a scrap of paper from his pocket and held it out to her. "Here's where I'm staying. Call me tonight when you get back and we'll talk."

Lily blinked at him. What more was there to say? Still, she took the note and stuffed it into her purse as she walked to the door, knowing she wouldn't use it. "Well," she said, swallowing past the sudden ache in her throat, "you've got a plane to catch, and I really do need to get going."

Dean followed her out, then trailed her down the drive to her car. He stepped toward her as she opened the driver's-side door, a hand on her arm as he leaned in to kiss her. Lily managed to step away in time, so that his lips just grazed her cheek.

"Good-bye, Dean."

He frowned as he watched her slide behind the wheel. "Call me tonight. We'll talk."

Lily reached for a smile as she turned the key in the ignition, wishing she had paid more attention in Mrs. Wittstein's drama class. "Have a safe trip," she said, fighting to keep her emotions in check as she began backing down the drive. "And please keep Sheila in your thoughts."

THIRTY-FIVE

1995
Hideaway Key, Florida

Sheila was waiting on the front porch when Lily pulled up, pretty as a picture in a buttery silk skirt and top. She flashed one of her signature smiles as she bounced down the steps and out to the curb, but Lily could still see the anxiety shadowing her soft brown eyes.

"This really is sweet of you," she said a little breathlessly as she belted herself into the passenger seat and tugged a pair of cat-eye sunglasses down from the top of her head. "Seriously, I don't know how to thank you."

Lily waved away her thanks. "Sorry I'm late. Dean came by, and it took a few minutes."

Sheila eyed Lily over her shades. "I thought you were staying at his place."

"I was."

"Why don't I like the sound of that?"

"I stayed at the cottage last night. I had some work to finish up, and Dean had an early flight this morning. He's on his way to Chicago to meet some clients."

"Oh, honey, you never said anything about him going out of town. You should have gone with him. I'm perfectly capable of driving myself to the doctor."

Lily kept her eyes fixed on the road. "Yeah, well. He sort of forgot to tell me he was going. Besides, no way was I bailing on you."

"Is everything okay with you two?"

Lily groaned inwardly. She'd been dreading this part. "Actually, we're done."

"Done? What does that mean—done?"

"It means just what you think it does. It was time, so we ended it."

"He ended it, or you ended it?"

"Let's just say I beat him to the punch. He came over to tell me this morning, before he left town, and I sort of... helped things along."

"I don't understand. You've been practically living together the last few weeks."

"And now we're not."

"And you're okay with that?"

Lily did her best to keep her face blank. Sheila had her own worries. She didn't need anyone else's. "Why wouldn't I be? We both knew it was going to end sooner or later. This is just sooner."

"But you two seemed so cozy."

"That's the problem. It got a little *too* cozy. Everything was great. It was like we were playing house, and then bang, all of a sudden I realize I'm not just playing anymore. I don't *do* that."

Sheila dragged down her glasses, fixing Lily with a hard stare. "You don't *do* that?"

"We've had this conversation, Sheila. I don't believe in all that gooey stuff. And neither does he. We had a deal. No expectations for either of us."

"Oh, right. I almost forgot—the no-strings clause."

"Go ahead, make fun. But it works for me."

"Sure, when you don't care about the guy. But that isn't the case this time, is it?"

Another silent groan. Why hadn't she just said everything was fine? "I'm not good at the romantic-bliss stuff, which is why I believe in setting rules. I don't want to hurt anyone. It just never occurred to me that I'd end up hurting myself. I don't know how it happened, or when. I just know that it did, and now I have to make it un-happen."

Sheila let her head fall back against the headrest and laughed. "Sugar, love doesn't work like that. It's not a switch you can flip on and off. It's hardwired into your DNA, like your heartbeat or your breath. You don't *decide* to do it. You just do it."

"But it wasn't part of the plan."

"You had a plan?" Sheila remarked snidely. "An actual plan?"

"Sheila, my life isn't here. I'm leaving next month. That's the only reason I started this thing with Dean, because knowing I was leaving made it safe. Only it turned out not to be safe at all."

"Well, sugar, I'm afraid that's just the way the cookie crumbles. You love him. Pretending you don't isn't going to change it. Neither will running away to Milan, or anywhere else, for that matter. Maybe you should think about holding still for a change, and see what catches up with you."

Lily stole a glance at Sheila, sitting with her arms folded smugly. "Did you say . . . what catches up with me?"

"That's what I said. And I didn't mean Dean, although it still applies. You keep talking about where your life is and where it's not. The only thing you're sure of is that it isn't in Hideaway. So if it's not here, where is it? New York? Paris? The truth is, I don't think you know. I'm not even sure you want to."

Lily's eyes went wide. "What's that supposed to mean?"

"It means that if you decide—if you finally commit to something or someone—you've got to find a way to make it work. You can't just run out when things get tricky. There are no promotions in love, sugar. Or in life. You pick and you stick. That's it."

"And you think I'm afraid to do that?"

Sheila's brows shot up. "Aren't you?"

Lily pondered the question, recalling the words she had recited to Dean only a few nights before. *You know when you realize that you're absolutely terrified . . .*

"The truth?"

"Only thing worth saying out loud, sweetheart."

"Well, then, the truth is I'm terrified."

"Good," Sheila said, with a slow, sly grin. "Now we're getting somewhere."

Lily was both relieved and surprised when Sheila let the subject drop, although something told her she hadn't heard the last on the subjects of Dean and Milan. For now, though, she seemed content with Lily's grudging admission. Or maybe the lull in their conversation had to do with the fact that they'd just merged onto I-75 north and the reality of where they were going had suddenly crept back into Sheila's thoughts.

Lily had to admit to feeling a bit uneasy herself. Lily-Mae had died from cancer, and while there was no way to know for certain that it had been breast cancer, the mention of scars and missing bits of flesh painted a vivid enough image. She had undergone surgery, endured chemo and radiation, and it had still taken her. It was true that years had passed since Sheila's diagnosis and treatment, but there was a reason women had to go for tests every year. Cancer came back.

By the time Sheila finally stepped back out into the waiting room, Lily felt like she had been holding her breath for hours. Sheila stood clutching her handbag and a handful of paperwork, her face unreadable.

Lily rose from her chair but made no move to go to her. "So?"

Sheila's eyes suddenly filled with tears. She wiped them away, spluttering until she finally found her voice. "I have to wait for some more tests to come back, but she says my scans looked clear, and she didn't see anything that concerned her."

"Oh, Sheila, that's wonderful!"

Sheila nodded, blinking back fresh tears. "It's not an all clear, but she says she feels good about the preliminary results, and she'll call me the minute she gets the rest."

To Lily's surprise, she found her own eyes welling. She blinked the tears away, in between bursts of relieved laughter. "We're going out to celebrate. You name the place."

Sheila smiled, though she was clearly still a little shaky. "Well, if it's my choice, I think I'd like to go home. I was thinking we could stop by the Sundowner if it's not too late when we get back."

"The Sundowner, it is."

Lily matched the grin with one of her own, her heart filled with gratitude, and a silent prayer that the rest of Sheila's tests came back clean.

THIRTY-SIX

It was well past ten when Lily finally dropped Sheila off and returned to the cottage. She was exhausted as she slid the key into the lock and pushed inside. She hadn't remembered to turn on a light before leaving, and didn't turn one on now. Instead, she made a beeline for the deck, throwing back the wide glass doors and stepping out into the darkness.

The night air greeted her like an old friend, moist and briny, and awash with sound, familiar in a way that suddenly made her heart ache—like a homecoming. Lily inhaled greedily, filling her lungs as she stared up at the night sky. Only a thin white sickle of moon hung out over the water, the stars shining bright in their heaven.

Was it out there—her North Star? Her father had promised her it was. Dozens of times. Hundreds of times. If only he were here now to tell her again, and point the way. She missed him terribly. And yet she felt strangely close to him at that moment, as if he were out there somewhere among all those stars, looking down at her. Perhaps he was. He was the reason she was here, after all.

You keep talking about where your life is and where it's not . . . if it's not here, where is it?

Sheila's words had been in her head all day, perhaps because they were far too close to the truth for her liking. She stood quietly with them now, breathing them in and out, letting them course through her veins. Maybe Sheila was right. She had been running for so long, but never toward something, only away. Maybe it *was* time to hold still and see what caught up with her, even if that something wasn't Dean. It would be awkward with him living next door, for a while at least, but eventually they would work it out, perhaps even become friends. And even if that didn't happen, it was time to stop running away from things that made her squeamish, and learn how to work through them instead. She'd be a fool to let an ex-lover stand in her way if Hideaway was truly where she was meant to be. And she was beginning to think it was. Was it possible her father had known, when he left her Sand Pearl Cottage, that her North Star was right here?

Yes. The answer was yes.

Strange. There had been was no thunderclap, no blinding white light, just the sudden realization that somehow, while she wasn't looking, this place, with its beach, and its cottage, and its sunsets, had quietly become a part of her. Home. And the beginning of a new story—her story.

She'd call Dario in the morning and tell him she had changed her mind—again. He would understand. Or maybe he wouldn't. It didn't matter. And then, when Dean got back from Chicago, she would have to tell him her plans had changed, and in a way he wasn't likely to be at all happy about. He had signed up for a summer romance, the kind where the lovers happily went their separate ways at the end of the story, not the kind where they lived awkwardly ever after as next-door neighbors.

But first she would need to figure out how to broach the subject, and assure him that her decision to remain in Hideaway had nothing to do with him or their conversation this morning, that she wasn't nursing some secret hope of a future together. And before she could do that she needed to make sure it was true.

It was nearly eight when the phone jolted Lily awake the next morning. Her eyes were barely open as she fumbled the phone to her ear, her voice still rusty with sleep.

"Lily? Are you all right?"

The sound of Dean's voice was jarring and unexpected. "Yes, I'm fine."

"I thought you were going to call when you got in last night."

"It was late," she answered thickly. "How was your meeting?"

"Oh, they were thrilled when I told them we could move ahead with the new plans, though they were less than thrilled with the new price tag. They were going home to talk it over last night, so we'll see. We're meeting again this morning. So, how was the road trip? And more important, how's Sheila?"

Lily didn't know whether to be relieved or piqued by his chatty demeanor. He sounded like he always did, like nothing at all had changed. "She's relieved, I think," she said, trying to sound equally chatty. "The preliminary tests all looked good, though she's still waiting on a few more results. I'm sure she'll be holding her breath until they're in, but the doctor did say she was optimistic. We stopped off at the Sundowner to celebrate when we got back to town. Bubba and Drew were there. We stayed way longer than we should have. It ended up being a pretty long day."

"You do sound tired, but that's great news about Sheila. So, what's on the agenda for today? Some rest, I hope."

"Actually, I was planning to stop by Sassy Rack. I think we're just about ready to start working on the mock-ups."

"Wow, that happened fast. Do you really think you'll have time to get it all done before Milan?"

Lily bit her lip. She wasn't planning to have this conversation so soon, and definitely not over the phone. Still, he had opened the door. "Actually . . . I was thinking I might hang around for a while."

"Really." The word dangled awkwardly, neither statement nor question, but more of a placeholder while he digested the news.

Lily closed her eyes and took a deep breath, sensing that the conversation was about to take an uncomfortable turn. "I know it isn't what we talked about, Dean, but we can make it work."

"How long is *a while*?"

"Okay, I guess what I should have said is I've decided to stay in Hideaway."

"Indefinitely?"

"Yes."

"And keep the cottage?"

"Well, yes. Of course."

"And what am I supposed to tell my clients? I told them we should be able to break ground sometime in October."

"Your . . . I'm sorry, what?"

"They're expecting to be in the new house by summer."

"What does that have to do with me?"

"I can't build the house if you're living in the cottage, Lily."

Suddenly, with a sickening jolt, Lily understood. "The plans you were working on for the Newmans were for a house you planned to build after you knock down the cottage?"

There was a long pause, then a heavy sigh. "Lily, we talked about this this morning before I left."

"No, we most certainly did not. I told you when I got here that I'd let you know when and if I was ready to sell the cottage, and I'm pretty sure we haven't had that discussion yet."

"Except, we did have it. You said why put off the inevitable. You said you were okay with it. Do you not remember saying those things?"

Oh God.

"I didn't know... I thought we were talking about something else."

"What the hell else could we have been talking about?"

"I thought you were telling me it was time we went our separate ways."

"Time to go our separate ways," he repeated drily. "And you were okay with that?"

"More okay than with you selling my aunt's cottage out from under me. All the number crunching you've been doing, the house and land package—it all hinged on you getting the cottage. And you just assumed that since we were—"

"It did seem like a reasonable assumption to make with you leaving, Lily. We even talked about it. But what you're saying—what you're thinking—that isn't what happened."

"Did you not just tell me you planned to break ground in October?"

"Yes, but—"

"Then that's exactly what happened. All this time, while we've been—you were working an angle."

"The two things aren't related, Lily. And it's a little late to act all broken up, don't you think? This morning you were apparently ready to walk away without batting an eye. You thought I came to dump you an hour before getting on a plane, and all you had to say was you were *okay* with it. You're not allowed to act like the injured party. Forget about the cottage. I'll find them another property."

And just like that the line was dead.

THIRTY-SEVEN

Lily was worn-out by the time she got back to the cottage. She had spent the last three days huddled with Sheila in Sassy Rack's overcrowded stockroom, fleshing out an operating budget for the new line and dodging an endless stream of questions about what had happened between her and Dean. Aside from the third degree, it had been a surprisingly pleasant afternoon, and Sheila had been absolutely thrilled when Lily suggested they donate a portion of the proceeds from the new line to breast cancer awareness.

She didn't know when the idea had popped into her head, only that she was glad it had. She liked knowing they'd be helping women while they were chasing down their own dream, even if that dream might seem small to others. After Paris, it seemed silly to be excited about designing for a fledgling private label. It wasn't chic or couture. It wasn't going to land her name in any glossy magazines, or on the runways of New York. And she was fine with that.

She had placed the call to Dario the minute she hung up with Dean, explaining that she was very sorry, but for personal reasons, she was going to have to pass on the job. She had needed to close the door, firmly and finally, just in case she got the urge to run again.

She hadn't.

Dropping her purse on the desk chair, she kicked off her sandals. She was contemplating a walk, perhaps even a swim, when a knock sounded on the front door. Her heart skittered briefly, before she remembered that Dean always came up the back stairs. The knock sounded again as she padded to the foyer, more insistent this time. Was it Girl Scout cookie season again? Summoning her best polite smile, she pulled back the door and stood staring at the overnight bag clutched in Caroline St. Claire's perfectly manicured hands.

"Hello, Lily."

"Mother," she managed finally. "How did you... What are you doing here?"

"You've been calling day and night for weeks. I thought it was time we got this over with."

"All you had to do was pick up the phone. I never asked you to come."

"I know, but I'm here. Are you going to let me in?"

Lily said nothing as she stepped aside, too stunned for rational conversation. Caroline's first step into the foyer was a tentative one, as if she were stepping into a boat that was taking on water.

"I had to come," she said, almost to herself. "I had to see it for myself."

"Had to see what?"

"Her cottage."

There was a weariness in her tone that was altogether new, something that might almost have been mistaken for defeat. She was also noticeably thinner than she'd been five weeks ago, her perfectly tailored clothes loose now, hanging slightly askew at the shoulders and sleeves. Even her face was different, her cheekbones sharper, her skin sallow and lined beneath the careful layers of her Chanel powder.

"You don't look well," Lily said, keeping her voice carefully neutral. "Have you been ill?"

Caroline's head came around slowly. "Ill?"

"You've lost weight. And you're pale."

"Yes," she answered, letting the overnight bag slide to the floor with a thump. "Yes, I suppose I am. My sister's dead. Your father's dead. How far behind can I be?"

Lily was about to say something snide when she took another look at her mother's face, at the hollowed cheeks and shadowed, almost feverish eyes. How was it possible she had changed so much in only a few short weeks?

Caroline continued her tour as if in a daze, meandering slowly from room to room, halting at last to peer through the doorway of Lily-Mae's bedroom. Lily couldn't help wondering what was going through her mother's mind as she stared at the bed where her husband and sister had first loved and laughed and slept.

"What's going on, Mother?"

Caroline turned briskly, sweeping past Lily without a word. Back in the living room, she stood with her back turned, staring out at the sea. After a few moments she turned, her eyes shiny with tears.

"You wanted answers, Lily. I've come to give them to you."

It was all Lily could do not to roll her eyes. The response had been so laced with foreboding, so ominously and tremulously delivered, that she was tempted to chalk it up to her mother's penchant for drama, but the tears shimmering in her eyes told a different story. Caroline St. Claire did not cry.

"Why now?" Lily asked almost warily. "After all the evasion and unanswered phone calls, why did you decide to show up unannounced on my doorstep?"

Caroline sighed as she looked away. "Because I knew you weren't going to stop asking, and that one day, with or without me, you'd find out what you wanted to know. It's how you've always been, even as a little girl. So I decided I wanted you to hear it from me."

"It's a little late for that, but you're right. I did find out what I wanted to know. Some of it at least. And I found it without your help."

Caroline's chin lifted sharply. "What is it you think you know?"

"Beyond Mt. Zion, and Zell, and all of that horror? I know Lily-Mae and Daddy were married before you ever met him, that they met in Palm Beach and fell in love in this cottage."

Caroline stood very still, pale as marble in the warm pool of sunshine streaming in through the sliding glass doors. "And what else?"

"I know they divorced a short time later—I found the papers in Lily-Mae's desk—and that you were right there to pick up the pieces when they did. And that you and Daddy were married four months later. What I don't know is how that part happened—and how it happened so fast."

Caroline's face remained impassive. "Your father refused to see Lily-Mae after she left him. I volunteered to act as go-between. Is that all?"

Lily stared at her, stunned that she could be so glib. "You volunteered to act as go-between, and then you married him the first chance you got, knowing she was still in love with him, and that he was still in love with her. How can you stand there and ask, *Is that all?* She was your sister. She loved you. She sacrificed herself to protect you. And that's how you repay her, by taking her husband? She died right here, all alone in this cottage, and you couldn't find it in your heart to even go to her memorial."

"May I ask how you learned all of this?"

"I told you. Lily-Mae kept journals. In fact, she kept a lot of things."

Lily stepped away long enough to go to the bedroom, returning a moment later, the stack of black-and-white composition books in one hand and Chessie in the other. Without ceremony, she pushed the rag doll into her mother's hands.

"Do you remember this?"

Caroline stared at the doll with a mixture of wonder and sadness. "Chessie."

"I found it under her bed the first night I was here, along with a picture of your parents, and the notebooks she kept while the two of you were at Mt. Zion. A beat-up old rag doll, and she held on to it all these years—because it reminded her of you. In spite of everything, she never stopped loving you, and you can stand there and ask, *Is that all?*"

"I need a drink."

"I don't have any gin."

"Vodka, then. Or scotch?"

God, she looks almost desperate. "Wine is all I have."

"Then I'll have wine. Please."

Lily went to the kitchen and poured a single glass of chardonnay. Caroline was on the sofa when she returned, the stack of notebooks untouched beside her. She took the glass with shaking hands, downing half its contents in one long swallow.

"You haven't touched the notebooks," Lily observed as she pushed her purse to the floor and dropped into the desk chair. "You really should read them. Maybe they'll help refresh your memory."

"There's nothing wrong with my memory, Lily, I assure you."

Caroline glanced over at them again, the way one might eye a ticking package in a train station. With a loud sniff, she picked up her wineglass and drained it, then rose stiffly to her feet. She looked almost frail as she made her way to the kitchen to retrieve the open chardonnay and a fresh glass from one of the cabinets.

"I don't want any wine," Lily told her flatly when Caroline set the glass near her elbow and began to pour.

"Yes, you do—or you will."

Something in her mother's tone set off a warning bell. "Why?"

"Because I brought you something."

Lily felt a prickle of apprehension as she watched Caroline cross to the abandoned overnight bag and, after a few minutes of fumbling, produce a slightly rumpled shopping bag. She recognized the Saks Fifth Avenue logo the minute she took the bag from her mother's hand.

"I'm not eight anymore, Mother. You can't fix this with presents."

Caroline ignored the remark as she eased back onto the couch. Her hands shook as she refilled her own glass and sipped deeply. "Believe me when I tell you I'm under no illusions that what's in that bag will fix anything. Go on, open it."

For a moment, Lily considered handing the bag back unopened. She wasn't sure what she was holding, but whatever it was, her mother had come twelve hundred miles to deliver it, and it clearly had her scared to death. Finally, she turned the bag on its side and slid the contents out onto her lap.

She recognized them immediately—three of them—smooth brown cowhide with blank spines and gold-edged pages, identical to the one she had excavated from the bookshelf in Lily-Mae's room.

Lily's head snapped up. "Where did you get these?"

"I found them in your father's desk when I was cleaning out his study. A package came for him about a year ago. I assume it's the one you asked about the last time you called. It came not long before she died. I never asked Roland about it. I didn't have to. The address said it was from Stephen Singer, but I knew it was from her the minute he shut himself up in his study with it. I barely saw him for the rest of that week."

"Have you read them?"

Caroline's chin jutted sullenly. "She was my sister. He was my husband. Of course I read them."

"Why send them after all that time? When they hadn't spoken in years?"

"There are three kinds of secrets, Lily. The ones we keep from strangers, the ones we keep from the people we love—and the ones we keep from ourselves."

Lily shook her head, baffled by her mother's cryptic response. "I don't understand."

Caroline closed her eyes, as if her lids were suddenly too heavy. When she opened them again her lashes were damp with unshed tears. "You will when you read what you're holding."

She looked around then, with the faraway gaze of someone lost, until she managed to locate her handbag. With shaking hands, she extricated a silver cigarette case and lighter and, scooping the stack of composition books off the sofa, marched out onto the deck. Lily watched through the open glass doors as she leaned against the railing for support, a Benson and Hedges Menthol clamped between her perfectly drawn lips. Her hands were still shaking as she grappled with the lighter in the stiff sea breeze. Successful at last, she sagged into one of the deck chairs, letting her head fall back as she exhaled a long plume of smoke over her head.

After a moment, Lily turned away, returning her attention to the books in her own lap, Lily-Mae's missing journals. Breath held, she folded back the first cover, staring at the date penned at the top of the page in her aunt's elegant but slanted script.

THIRTY-EIGHT

October 11, 1957
New York, New York

We've been back from Paris nearly a month now, living in Roland's apartment on Fifth Avenue. I'm still not used to the doorman calling me Mrs. St. Claire, but I do so love the sound of it.

The news of our marriage spread like wildfire, thanks to the gossip rags. Celia Gardiner's name appeared in most of the articles, claiming credit for bringing us together. I suppose I shouldn't be surprised, though I do wish they would stop reprinting that silly billboard story every time they mention Roland's name. If he minds all the fuss, he shows no sign, but then I suppose he's used to his share of fuss. It's been nothing but parties since we returned, champagne and caviar and goose liver pâté, a fresh whirl of faces every night, and another list of names to remember.

Caroline is with us now, happy enough to leave her school friends once she heard where she'd be living. It took almost no time for Roland to win her over. He spoils her almost as badly as he does me. In less than a week he had set up accounts for her at all the best stores, and she hasn't been shy in using them. She has become the belle of every ball, her closets overflowing with Park Avenue fashions. I worry at times that she's taking advantage of his kindness, but he doesn't seem to mind, or even to notice, despite Caroline's best efforts to charm him.

I try to tell myself it's her shamelessness about spending Roland's money that makes me uncomfortable, but it's more than that. I've seen the looks she gives him, the way she pouts her lips and bats her lashes to get what she wants—like she did that day in Zell's office. What's worse, she knows I don't like it, and seems to take delight in my discomfort.

I thought by now she would have forgiven me for the lie, that she would have come to see that it was our only way out of that terrible place. She hasn't, though, and it makes my heart ache to wonder how much longer I will have to pay for the sin of trying to protect her—of trying to protect us both.

October 17, 1958
New York, New York

How quickly life can turn to ashes.

I was relieved to be attending the final event being held in our honor—a reception thrown for us by the Barclays at the Hotel Astor. I've grown weary of the parties, of pretending I'm having the time of my life when all I want in the world is for Roland and me to run back to Hideaway Key, where it was just the two of us, and miles and miles of bright blue water.

I felt it the moment we walked into the ballroom: a pang of panic so swift and sharp I nearly turned and ran from the room. Roland felt me tense. He shot me a look, then a reassuring smile. I smiled back, feeling foolish as we made our way to our table, smiling and nodding, pausing now and then to shake hands along the way. A waiter brought glasses of champagne to our table. I sipped without tasting, running my eyes around the room, unable to ignore the warning bells going off in my belly.

I got through dinner somehow, politely sipping my wine, nodding when I was spoken to, laughing when it seemed appropriate, but I don't remember a single bite or word. By the time the plates were cleared I was light-headed from too much champagne, and queasy with the certainty that some unseen threat was lurking nearby.

I slipped away while we were waiting for dessert to be served, telling Roland that I wanted to freshen my lipstick before the inevitable toast to the newlyweds. It was a relief to leave the hum of the ballroom behind, to step out into the carpeted quiet of the hallway.

I didn't hear him come up behind me, but I knew it was him the instant he touched my arm. Part of me always knew, I suppose, that I wasn't really through with Harwood Zell, that someday he would find me. But the sudden fact of him, standing there in front of me—paunchier after nearly three years, but wearing the same shiny black suit, still reeking of cigarette smoke and stale sweat—nearly brought my dinner up into my throat.

His smile widened, clearly relishing my terror. "I've been looking for you, Lily-Mae." His voice was almost obscenely soft, his eyes glittering with something like amusement. "You left in such a rush that we didn't have time for a proper good-bye."

I felt the room wobble. "Why are you in New York?"

"Why, I've come to toast the bride, of course. Mrs. Roland St. Claire—an impressive title, I'd say, for a girl from Mims, Tennessee. Who would have guessed you'd do so well for herself? Thank goodness for the papers, or I never would have known to look for you here tonight. That would have been a shame, wouldn't it?"

"Leave me alone." My voice sounded thin and thready, the voice of the fifteen-year-old me, terrified and once again at his mercy. "Please. Please, just go away."

"Now, Lily-Mae, you know I can't do that. We have unfinished business, you and I. Private business, if you're a good girl, but not so private if you choose to be naughty."

I felt the blood drain from my face. "What do you want?"

"Merely to share in your good fortune. And to conduct a bit of business with an old friend, a friend who just happens to be married to a man on his way to being one of the richest men in the country. Or if you'd like, I could just step into the ballroom and have a word with him myself. In fact, he might actually be interested in meeting me."

I squared my shoulders, forcing my eyes to meet his. "There's nothing you can tell my husband that he doesn't already know."

"Is that so? Well, then, what about his friends—his very rich and powerful friends—do they know everything? Or would your past come as something of a shock to them?"

There was no mistaking the threat. If I didn't do what he wanted he would make sure Roland's friends learned just enough about his new wife to tarnish both his name and his social standing. "What is it you want?"

"Only what belongs to me." His smile slipped back into place, a hideous blend of greed and triumph. "As I recall, you left Mt. Zion with some money of mine. I came to get it back—with interest. I've been waiting a long time for my ship to come in, as they say, and finally, the SS Lily-Mae *is back in port with a shiny new last name."*

I stood there like stone. "How much?"

He patted my arm, his thick fingers sickeningly moist against my flesh. "Don't be silly. I wouldn't dream of talking about anything so vulgar as money when you're all dressed up. Besides, if you stay away much longer your husband is going to come looking for you, and that wouldn't do at all. We'll talk again tomorrow."

The thought of having to see him again, of having to look at his face one more time, made me physically ill. "I can't see you tomorrow. I won't."

Zell was unfazed, his face bland. "If you'd rather, I can just step inside and have a word with Roland." He pulled back the door a crack, and peered inside. "Ah yes, there he is, now, speaking with Senator Clayton and his charming wife, I believe. I'm sure he wouldn't mind if I joined him for a moment."

I was near tears. There was nothing I could do, nothing I could say that would sway him. "Tell me where, and then please go."

"There's a little place just past the corner of Forty-first and Eighth, called the Terminal Bar. Not exactly a fitting part of town for the wife of Roland St. Claire, but you're not likely to run into any of your country club friends, either. Be there at noon."

I nodded, unable to look at him another moment. Then I squared my shoulders, pasted on a smile, and went back to the party. I didn't know what else to do. I couldn't risk Roland coming to look for me and finding me with Zell. He can't know about this, ever. No matter what I have to do or pay, I will never let Roland be hurt because he married me.

October 18, 1958
New York, New York

My stomach was in knots as I approached the entrance to the bar where Zell was waiting, my handbag clutched in front of me like a shield. Men huddled in small groups on the street, drinking from small bottles wrapped in rumpled paper bags. I felt their eyes follow me as I walked past, a curiosity in my good coat and expensive heels.

A wave of dizziness hit me as I stepped through the open door of the Terminal Bar. It was cramped and gritty, little better than a cave carved out between a pawnshop and another, equally seedy bar. Heads turned as I hovered in the doorway, squinting through a haze of grease and cigarette smoke.

Eventually, for better or worse, I was able to make out my surroundings. A battered pool table stood at the center of the room, a burned-out light dangling crookedly overhead. The walls were studded with pictures, boxers and baseball players grinning behind grimy squares of glass. Clumps of last year's silver Christmas garland glittered miserably from the corners of the windows.

My stomach clenched the instant I spotted him, hunched over a small table in the corner, sucking on a cigarette and sipping something amber from a short heavy glass. For someone who professed to be a man of God, he looked surprisingly at home. The bartender looked up from the glass he was drying as I stepped from the doorway and moved toward the table.

Zell smiled lazily over the rim of his glass, then motioned for me to sit. I took the chair across from him and knotted my hands in my lap, waiting. The less I said, the sooner he'd tell me what he wanted.

"Relax, Mrs. St. Claire. Not much chance of running into any of your husband's friends here, unless they like greasy hamburgers and watered-down booze. They don't, do they?"

He was amusing himself—like a bully holding a magnifying glass over an anthill. I just wanted it over. "It's noon," I hissed at him across the table. "What do you want?"

Zell leaned back in his chair, looking me up and down like he used to through a haze of smoke. "My, my. Marriage has changed you, Lily-Mae. What happened to the sweet little girl who used to file my papers and take down my sermons?"

"She grew up," I snapped. I had never wanted to scratch someone's eyes out until that moment. "Now, tell me what you want so I can go."

The bartender appeared before Zell could answer. He stood there for what felt like a very long time, his mouth slack as he stared at me, fumbling with the grimy towel slung over his shoulder.

"Another for me," Zell barked, jolting the man from his fog. "And bring one for the lady."

I waved a hand at the bartender. "Nothing for me. I won't be staying."

"Bring it anyway." Zell barked at the man's back before turning his attention back to me. "You really should order something, Lily-Mae. It's not polite to let a man drink alone."

I ignored the remark, eager to be away from him. "How much will it take to make you leave me alone?"

He drained his glass, grinning hideously as the liquid went down. "Still in a hurry to get away from me?"

"Yes."

"All right, then, ten thousand."

For a moment I couldn't speak. It never occurred to me that he would ask for such a sum. "Ten thousand . . . dollars?"

"That should cover the money and the truck—plus a little extra for my trouble."

It was impossible. "I don't have anything like that kind of money."

The bartender appeared with two glasses. Zell waited until he left to lean across the table. "You've just married a very rich man, Lily-Mae. Or have you forgotten?"

Panic rose in my throat, nearly choking me. "You can't expect me to ask Roland for the money."

"If you're squeamish, I could always ask him."

A rush of tears prickled behind my lids. "Why are you doing this?"

"I'm not a man who lets things go, Lily-Mae. I may get crossed now and then, but I always make sure to settle up. I have an acquaintance, the kind who knows how to find things out. He's been

keeping an eye out, though I must say, I didn't expect you to make it so easy. Imagine my surprise when I got a call saying you'd gotten your picture on some big, fancy sign in New York. It was easy after that. Your name was in all the papers. All I had to do was follow the trail."

"You're not afraid I'll go to the police? Blackmail is a crime."

Zell clucked his tongue disapprovingly. "Blackmail is such an ugly word. I prefer to think of it as business between old friends."

"We aren't friends. We were never friends."

"My price is still ten thousand."

"And if I can't pay you—what then?"

His eyes went steely as he reached into his pocket, then placed small squarish packet on the table between us. "Then . . . this."

I stared at it, confused. It was a packet of playing cards, the kind with risqué drawings splashed across the faces. My fingers were clammy as I fumbled to open the packet. I could feel Zell watching me, waiting for some kind of reaction or recognition.

My breath left my body all at once as I glanced at the first card in the deck—the queen of hearts—horrified at the sight of myself perched on a brightly striped beach ball, wearing nothing but a pair of red high heels. I remembered the pose; it was one I had done for a calendar when I first came to New York. But I'd been wearing a bathing suit at the time, a red one with a large white bow pinned to the front. Only the bathing suit was gone now, leaving me—or a drawing someone had doctored to look exactly like me—completely exposed.

My lips felt numb suddenly, thick and bloodless. "Where did you get these?"

"My acquaintance was kind enough to pass them on to me. Apparently, he's in touch with a certain photographer who was willing, for a small fee, to share some of your, eh . . . work. There are more in the pack if you're interested, a few even more risqué."

"It isn't me," I blurted desperately. "I never posed like that. They've been tampered with."

"So you say. But will Roland's friends care, do you think, when they're eyeing you across some fancy dinner table? Very important man, your husband, a powerful man with powerful friends; philanthropist, international businessman, sits on several boards, political aspirations, too, I understand. It would be a real shame to see all that ruined. And it would be, what with the papers and all. I hear they pay big money for stories about New York royalty." He paused, smirking as he slid the queen of hearts back at me across the table. "Especially when they come with artwork like this."

I gaped at him, stunned by the undisguised glee in his expression, my mind racing back to Palm Beach and poor Mr. Addison, banished by friends and colleagues because of his relationship with a divorced woman. And what were her secrets compared to mine?

"Ten thousand," he repeated, not batting an eye. "Noon, one week from today. Here. Don't cross me, Lily-Mae. I'll do what I say. Your husband's name won't be worth a plug nickel when I'm through."

I stared at him, too numb to find words, let alone form them. I kept hoping to find some flicker of remorse in his eyes, some shred of conscience I could exploit, but I knew better. I'd always known better.

I made it home somehow, sitting stonily in the back of a cab while the driver eyed me curiously in his rearview mirror. He was trying to place my face, to remember where he'd met me. I held my breath as we passed that ridiculous billboard, praying to God he didn't look up. I couldn't have borne that conversation just then, or any conversation, really. I was too busy trying to figure out where I was going to get my hands on ten thousand dollars.

October 24, 1958
New York, New York

They say old habits die hard, and I suppose it must be true. I know I had no right to ask Jasper for help when I dialed the phone—not after the way we'd left things at the Gardiners'. But I truly didn't know where else to turn. He was cool at first, when he heard my voice. I wasn't surprised. We'd only spoken once since that night, when I had finally called to tell him Roland and I were married. He had wished me well, then tersely ended the call. And now, after months of silence, I've asked him to lend me ten thousand dollars.

I wouldn't have blamed him if he said no, but he didn't. In fact, he never even bothered to ask why I needed the money. I only had to tell him I was in trouble. He told me to give him an hour and then meet him at the St. Regis for lunch.

I scanned the tables for familiar faces as I walked in. Thankfully, there were none. It was late and most of the lunch crowd had cleared. Jasper was there, already working on a second martini. He stood as I approached the table, then slid back into his chair. I spread my napkin in my lap for something to do. I couldn't seem to meet his eyes, afraid that if I did I would crumple into a million pieces. It wasn't until the waiter left that he really looked at me, saw the shadows beneath my eyes, the deep crease of fear that had etched itself between my brows over the last several days, that he realized just how much trouble I was in. He reached for my hand, refusing to let it go until I agreed to tell him what was wrong. Dear, sweet Jasper. He always could see right through me.

Before I knew it, the whole story was tumbling out: Zell sneaking up on me at the reception; the winos outside the Terminal Bar; the playing cards and their humiliating pictures. He was furious at me when it was finally all out, for not calling the police, or at least telling Roland. I tried to make him understand why I couldn't do either of those things, that nothing on earth would ever make me risk my husband's good name. I made him swear he would never breathe a word of what I'd just told him to anyone. He thinks I'm being foolish, but he agreed. Then he pulled a heavy brown envelope from the inside pocket of his suit coat and slid it across the table.

I told him I didn't know how I'd ever pay him back, but that I would, somehow. He waved away my promise, a little sloshy after his third martini, and told me to forget it. He has more clients these days than he knows what to do with, and it's because of me. Besides, he was the one who booked the calendar job. Paying to keep the wolves away was the least he could do.

As I was leaving, he handed me a card, crisp ivory stock with his soon-to-be new office address embossed in heavy gold letters. I couldn't help but remember the dog-eared card he had handed me the first day we met, the day he had picked up two sisters on a narrow dirt road somewhere in Tennessee. He's come a long way since then. We both have.

October 25, 1958
New York, New York

What a skilled liar one becomes when necessity requires it, when everything you hold dear is suddenly in peril and panic takes root in your chest. I have kept no secrets from Roland, held nothing back. Until now. But experience has taught me that the lies we tell are often kinder than the truths we conceal—even when the lie comes at a price almost beyond bearing.

One of the hardest things I've ever done was sitting across the breakfast table from Roland this morning, sipping my coffee and pretending nothing was wrong, my nerves worn raw beneath a too-tight smile. It was such a strange secret to be keeping—a rendezvous in a squalid downtown bar, not with a lover but with an extortionist. And yet the need for secrecy seemed just as urgent, as if I were, in fact, breaking one of my marriage vows—not a vow of the heart, but one of trust, which felt worse somehow. I was terrified that he would glance up from his newspaper unexpectedly, and that in that unguarded moment my face would give me away. And then what would I have said?

How could I explain not coming to him the night Zell confronted me at the Astor? Or turning to Jasper—a man he plainly disliked—for the money to buy Zell's silence, rather than confiding in my own husband? I couldn't. Nothing would ever make him understand my silence, or my secrecy.

But I know Roland too well. I know what would have happened had I gone to him the night Zell showed up, what his reaction would be, even now, if he knew Zell meant to blackmail me with his filthy pictures. There would be no stopping him. He would charge in on his white horse to defend my honor, heedless of the cost to his reputation and standing among members of his social circle.

Zell wouldn't think twice about going to the papers, especially if there was money to be had—and when it came to gossip about the rich and powerful, there was always money to be had. There would be a scandal—the kind a man in Roland's position wasn't likely to survive. My husband is a businessman, used to men who operate inside the law and bear some semblance of a conscience. Zell is none of those things. He will hurt me by hurting Roland—if I let him. And I will not let him, cost what it may.

Which is why I had to go through with it, and why I'll hide the truth from Roland, to keep him from riding to my aid, and ruining himself in the process. I had no desire to set foot in that god-awful place again, or to look Harwood Zell in the eye one more time, but I knew I wouldn't hear the last of him until I did.

My stomach revolted at the reek of smoke and stale beer as I stepped through the door of the Terminal Bar, my breakfast churning its way up toward my throat as I anxiously scanned the tables. There was no one I knew, of course—or, more precisely, no one likely to know Roland—but I needed to be sure. The irony didn't escape me as my eyes swept the dingy interior. Yesterday, I had done the same thing when I entered the St. Regis, worried about being seen, and there I was again, this time in a gritty bar on the wrong side of town. The only difference was that this time there was a smart little shopping bag full of cash dangling from my wrist.

Zell was sitting at the corner table again. He stubbed out his cigarette the minute he saw me, his eyes glittering sharply as they fastened on the shopping bag. I placed it on the table in front of him, not sure what happened next.

"Do you want to count it?"

His eyes narrowed shrewdly. "Not if I want to make it out of here with my skin intact, I don't. I'm just going to have to trust you, Lily-Mae, although that hasn't always worked so well in the past. Still, I'm willing to risk it. After all, I do know where to find you—and the esteemed Mr. St. Claire."

"It's all there," I told him coldly. "You've got what you came for, and I'm going."

He caught my wrist before I could turn away, his fingers warm and slippery against my flesh. The memory of another time, another touch, slithered along my spine, sending a surge of bile scorching up into my throat. He was smiling, the familiar oily smile that had always made my skin crawl.

"Now, now, people might get the wrong idea if you just rush off, Mrs. St. Claire. I took the liberty of ordering you a drink just before you arrived. I thought we might . . . talk over old times."

I yanked my wrist free, trying to wipe away the feel of his touch. "We have nothing to discuss, and I don't care what anyone thinks."

"Come now, we both know that isn't true. In fact, you appear to care a great deal, or you wouldn't be here at all. Now sit down and let's drink to old times."

I sat, but only because heads had begun to turn in our direction. The bartender appeared, gaping at me with the same openmouthed expression he had worn the last time. Zell was grinning, clearly pleased to watch me squirm. He lifted his glass, motioning for me to do the same as the weight of curious gazes from around the room continued to mount. Numbly, I raised my glass, my fingers curled so tightly I thought it might shatter in my hand.

"To renewing old friendships," he murmured, his eyes glittering hungrily as he threw back the shot of dark liquid in his glass. He smiled then, a slow, malicious show of teeth. "I've missed you, Lily-Mae."

I sat there staring at my glass, willing myself to put it down and get up, to flee as fast as I could, but something kept me rooted there, like a fly buzzing futilely in a web as the spider steadily advanced.

"Be a good girl, Lily-Mae, and drink up." He paused to light a cigarette, tipping his head back to spew the smoke into the air above his head. "It's impolite not to drink to a toast, especially one between old friends."

"Stop saying that," I hissed furiously. "We've never, ever been friends."

He pretended to be shocked, but smiled a little, too. "How can you say that after all we've been through? And speaking of old times, how is that little sister of yours? Caroline, wasn't it? She wasn't quite the piece you were, but she was coming along nicely the last time I saw her."

A fresh wave of revulsion swept over me as I stared at the un-

touched amber liquor in my glass. It took everything in me not to toss it in his face, to wash the smug smile from those thick, pulpy lips. I was certain it wouldn't be the first time a woman had thrown a drink in a man's face in the Terminal Bar, but I couldn't afford to draw any more attention to myself than I had just by being there.

The room tilted as I pushed to my feet, the overhead lights going briefly dim. I covered the dizziness somehow, holding on to the table as I gathered my handbag. I would sooner have died than give Zell the satisfaction of knowing how badly he'd rattled me.

"Don't rush off on my account," he said, not bothering to conceal his glee. "I was just beginning to enjoy myself."

I spun around to face him, no longer caring that someone might overhear, or what anyone might think. "I've always wondered. Do you believe in hell?"

I expected the question to take him off guard, or to at least make him angry. Instead, his lips twitched with an almost obscene smile. "I'm an ordained man of the cloth, Lily-Mae. Hell is my business."

I blinked as he blurred in and out of focus. There was nothing to say to that, and clearly no way to shame him. The best I could hope for was knowing I would never have to see his face again, and to make it to the door without landing face-first on the floor. But I wasn't to have even that.

"I'll be in touch," he said almost silkily as I stepped away from the table. "The next time I'm in town I promise to look you up."

I didn't bother to turn around. There was no point. His meaning was clear enough. Jasper had been right all along. Zell wasn't going to stop, and nothing I could say or do, no amount of begging or pleading, would ever persuade him to leave me in peace. He would keep coming back for more. Only there wasn't any more. I couldn't ask Roland for money without telling him why, and I couldn't keep borrowing from Jasper. It was only a matter of time until Zell made good on his threats. And then what? I could go to the police, but where was my proof? And by then the papers would already have had a field day. The damage would be done.

The reality of it hit me full force, like an unexpected punch to the stomach as I stumbled, half blind, out into the afternoon sunshine. I staggered into a man in a grimy gray suit as I ducked into a nearby alley and retched up the last traces of my breakfast. In that moment I knew there was only one way to protect Roland's reputation.

December 15, 1958
New York, New York

There is nothing more terrible than knowing you must let go of something you love, living out that last handful of days like a prisoner bound for the gallows, knowing each day brings you nearer to the end. So much lost. Twice in my life I've told a lie that has cost me someone I love. The first was Caroline. The second was Roland.

It took several weeks to finally muster the courage, to carefully choose and rehearse the words until I could say them without tears or hesitation, to look the man I love with my whole heart in the eye and tell him our marriage had been a mistake—that I was leaving him.

I managed it somehow, like a thing carved of stone, cold and impervious as the words dropped like sharp little pebbles from my mouth. I waited, steeling myself for the moment they finally penetrated. I wasn't prepared for the blank look Roland fixed on me, as if I had spoken in some foreign tongue. To my horror, I had to say the words again. Finally, understanding came, along with a soul-wrenching look of betrayal.

For a long time—an eternity of dull, heavy heartbeats—Roland said nothing at all, just stood there staring as my words sank deep and his face began to crumple. There was nothing to do but meet his gaze, and pray for the strength not to waver, but as we stood there looking at each other in all that awful silence I felt my heart tear and begin to bleed, the slow but fatal leaching of all my happiness. I longed to take back the words, ached to blurt out the truth—that it was all a lie, that marrying him, loving him, was the best thing that ever happened to me. But like the first deep thrust of any blade, once struck it was too late for recrimination. There was nothing to do but finish the thing.

"I never meant to hurt you, Roland," I told him, stunned by the coolness of my own voice, as if I had accidentally stepped on his foot or spilled hot coffee in his lap. "I made a mistake. I'm sorry. I don't want anything from you—only the divorce."

He stepped toward me but stopped when I backed away. "And that's it? Just like that, you've decided?"

"Yes," I managed without flinching, though the word cost me dearly.

"I don't understand. I thought we were happy. I thought . . ."

"We were happy, but it was the summer, the cottage. It was all so perfect, so romantic, but now that we're back in New York, things are . . . different."

"Different how? Are you saying you don't love me?"

"Roland, please, don't make me say things that will hurt you. You're a good man, a kind man—kinder than I deserve—but I told you when you asked me to marry you that one day you'd regret asking."

My throat ached as I watched his face, each word landing like a blow.

"I see," he said stiffly. "You're not saying you've stopped loving me. You're saying you never loved me."

"I made a mistake," I whispered hoarsely, the tears I didn't dare shed searing my throat raw. "We both did. In time you'll see that."

"No," he said raggedly. "I won't. Time won't change how I feel. But if you think it will, then maybe you're right. Maybe you did make a mistake. Where will you go?"

I should have felt relieved at the question, a sign that he had accepted my decision, and that soon this agonizing charade would end. Instead, something in me withered, and I felt my resolve beginning to fray.

I said the first thing that came to my mind. "Jasper has found me an apartment."

A fresh wound appeared in Roland's eyes. "You told Jasper you were leaving before you told me?"

"I had to make plans, Roland."

"With Jasper?"

I ignored the insinuation. He had a right to be bitter, even unkind if he chose. "Plans for myself, Roland. And for Caroline. She'll be home from school soon."

"Is that what the two of you were discussing at lunch the other day? Your plans to divorce me?"

I was shocked. Until that moment he'd made no mention of my meeting with Jasper. "How did you . . ."

"You're not exactly invisible, Lily-Mae, especially now that your last name is St. Claire. You can't just meet a man for lunch at the St. Regis and not expect to be recognized. People see things, and they talk. You, of all people, should know that."

If I'd had any doubts about my decision to leave Roland, his words quickly extinguished them. He was right. I knew it. He knew it. And Zell certainly knew it.

"Yes, Roland. I, of all people, should know—do know."

"Jasper must have been glad to hear the news," he said bitterly. "He never did like having to share you. Now he'll have you all to himself again. Like old times."

The words stung, not because they weren't true, but because I could see that he believed they were. "Yes," I said coolly, pretending his words hadn't just cut me to the quick. "Just like old times."

My eyes blurred as he turned to walk away, but I held myself together, not giving way to my tears until I heard the front door slam, and knew I was alone. Then I went to our room and began to pack my things.

That was weeks ago, though I've not been able to write of it until now. Perhaps because doing so would have made it more real, irrevocable somehow when recorded with pen and ink. And yet there's a blessing in it, too, now that it has been written down, the kind of relief that comes with the purging of poisons and the bleeding of wounds.

I do not regret my decision—it was the only way to protect Roland—but at times it's beyond bearing that he could have believed I was carrying on with Jasper. Then I think to myself, let him believe it if he knows me so little. Let the whole world believe it. And they will, too, if the papers have anything to say about it. They're full of facts and figures these days, inviting readers to peer between the lines of half-truth and lurid innuendo, to speculate on the hows *and* whys *of my marriage's untimely demise. They can say anything they like about me now. With the divorce nearly final, I'm no longer a threat to Roland St. Claire, which is all I wanted.*

The details were handled with startling, if chilly, civility. A few signatures and a handful of phone calls from the law offices of Singer and Bladen was all it took to set things in motion. The Manhattan apartment and all its furnishings are to belong to me, along with a monthly allowance for the remainder of my life—and Sand Pearl Cottage.

It's only the last that I care about, as I clearly told the lawyer when I called to give back the rest. But Roland insists on leaving the settlement as is. It's the customary settlement for a man of Roland's stature, or so Mr. Singer has informed me.

In truth, I have no right to the cottage, either, but can't bear the thought of letting it go. I have never cared about money—Roland's, or mine, or anyone else's. I have only ever wanted to be happy, and for a few brief moments I was. It is far more than most get in this life, certainly more than I ever hoped for, a thought I must and will cling to in the years to come.

January 16, 1959
New York, New York

It's the quiet that plagues me most, the terrible, empty silence as I lie down each night, and then awaken the next morning—the silence that reminds me I'm alone. It's been a month since Roland moved out, a month of silent mornings, empty breakfast tables, untouched financial sections. A month is a long time to get used to a thing, but I'm not used to it. I'll never be used to it. Or to how different everything is now.

Every morning I lie here in the near dawn, waiting. As long as I'm still I'm fine, but the moment I stir, it comes with a vengeance, the same awful sickness I remember from that day when Sister Ruth caught my eye in the mirror, when she knew—when we both knew—that I was going to have a child.

In cases like yours, it's unlikely there will ever be children.

Sister Doyle's words have lived with me since the day she spoke them, and yet I'm as sure of the child growing in my belly as I've ever been of anything in my life. Roland's child. Could fate have played a crueler jest?

Roland doesn't know, of course. No one does, except Caroline, and I've only just told her this morning. Until a few days ago I wasn't certain, but now that I am I don't know what to do. The divorce will be final soon. It's almost impossible to believe. A few signatures on a piece of paper, and it will be as if our marriage never happened at all. All that will remain is the child.

A few months ago I would have been overjoyed. Now I'm just numb, and vaguely bitter. I could go to Roland, of course, and tell him everything, explain that Zell had resurfaced, that I had only lied about Jasper to protect him, that I never for one moment considered our marriage a mistake. I could spill it all, and beg his forgiveness. He would give it, too. Of that I'm sure. That's the hardest part, knowing all I have to do is pick up the phone to put things back to the way they were before. But nothing I can say will change the fact that as long as I was in Roland's life his future would be in jeopardy. Zell had made that only too clear. He would say he didn't care, as he did the day he asked me to marry him. But one day he would care. One day when his friends had all turned their backs, and his good name was in tatters, he would care very much. And he would blame me. How could he not?

I went to see Caroline at her apartment. She was surprised when I turned up on her doorstep. We seldom see each other these days, and rarely even speak on the phone unless it has something to do with the divorce. She's been acting as a sort of go-between since Roland refuses to speak to me. I can't blame him after the lies I told about Jasper.

I didn't have to say a word for Caroline to guess my secret. In fact, I had barely unbuttoned my coat. She took one look at me, green eyes narrowed knowingly on my pale face. "How far along are you?"

I was shocked at first, but then, I suppose a sister knows these things. "I'm not sure," I said quietly. It was almost a relief to finally say the words out loud. "I only just guessed myself this morning."

"And you're here because you want me to tell Roland?"

"No. I'm here because I want you to promise never to tell him."

"Are you keeping it?"

I looked at her, not registering the words. "Keeping it?"

"The baby, are you keeping it or not?"

"I hadn't thought—"

"You don't have to, you know. There are ways, discreet ways, to take care of such things. It would all be over before anyone even knew."

I stared at her in horror, the blood draining from my face as her meaning finally penetrated. I closed my eyes, wavering slightly on my feet as my head filled with memories of a narrow cot, of torn sheets being bound about my wrists, of Sister Doyle's face and the sharp glint of a knitting needle.

"No," I choked out. "Not that. Never that."

"Well, if you're squeamish there are other options, places to go and just lay low. You tell everyone you're going to the South of France or someplace, take care of the business, hand over the kid, and no one's the wiser. There's one upstate, run by a doctor and his wife."

A hideous thought crossed my mind. "How do you know about places like that?"

Caroline rolled her eyes, waving away my concern. "Don't be ridiculous, Lily-Mae. I'm too smart to get caught like that. A girl from school went last year. She told everyone she was going to stay with a sick aunt, which didn't fool anyone. The trick is coming up with a plausible cover story, and no one would question you taking a long vacation. Not with the stress of the divorce and all."

I thought about what Caroline was suggesting, of handing my baby—Roland's baby—over to strangers, to never see it again, to never know if it was happy and well. It seemed unthinkable. "I don't know if I could do it, Caroline. Give away my own child."

Caroline took her time as she lit a cigarette, her face thoughtful as she set down her lighter and blew out a long plume of smoke the way the movie stars do. "I thought you said you didn't want Roland to know."

"I did, and I meant it. He can't ever know. I can't risk him calling off the divorce."

"So you want to have the baby but don't want Roland to know. You don't think he's going to figure it out when he hears his ex-wife's belly is the size of a beach ball? Be honest with yourself, Lily-Mae. Roland or no Roland, you can't keep this child. Divorced with a child, and every gossip rag in the country hounding your heels. What kind of life is that for a child? No father, and a single mother who knows nothing about raising children?"

Those last words stung like a slap. I wanted to point out to her that I had all but raised her, and that doing so had cost me a great deal. I wanted to, but I didn't. She was my sister. Whatever I did for her, I owed her. The worst part was I knew she was right. Roland would hear of it. Just like he'd heard about my lunch with Jasper. And what if Zell were to suddenly reappear? He'd made the threat, and one thing I've definitely learned is that Zell's threats are rarely idle. What kind of mother would I make, living in constant dread that his filthy pictures might appear in some paper somewhere? That they weren't actually of me would make little difference.

"This place you were talking about, it's . . . discreet?"

"It's called Saratoga Pines, and yes, it is. They've done it all up like a fancy resort, but really it's for women who've gotten themselves in a fix. It's pricey, but, like I said, no one will ever know."

I stared at her, wanting to deny what she said. I wasn't like those women. I wasn't in a fix—at least not the way Caroline meant—but was there really a difference? I was going to have a baby, one I couldn't keep. The reputation I was trying to protect wasn't mine, but that hardly seemed to matter. A decision had to be made. And so I made it.

THIRTY-NINE

March 21, 1959
Saratoga Pines Resort, New York

I've been at Saratoga Pines several weeks now. The time finally came when I could no longer hide the truth, when questions would be asked, rumors started. Caroline drove me. I told her it wasn't necessary, that I was perfectly capable of driving myself, but I think she was afraid I would change my mind. I very nearly did.

Jasper knows where I am, and why, but I've told no one else. As far as the rest of the world knows, I've gone into seclusion to grieve for my marriage, which is true in more ways than I can count. God knows, I'd rather be anywhere in the world than here, surrounded by doctors and nurses and carefully manicured hedges.

There are others like me here, sad-eyed women who keep mostly to themselves, clinging to their shame and their swollen bellies. A few are here for what the nurses call melancholia, *a polite word for failed attempts with sleeping pills or razor blades. Others act as if they've come for a vacation, gathering each afternoon on the sun-drenched lawns to gossip and play cards or croquet. And still others who are here because of a fondness for things, for drinking and pills, mostly, but for other things, too, that are rarely spoken of, even in a place like this.*

We all have our stories, our mistakes, and our little tragedies. That's why we're here, to erase them or patch them up, and pretend they never happened. We'll go back out into the world when it's over, back to our lives, hiding our scars behind brave little smiles. We'll be fine, *we tell ourselves.* Fine.

Meanwhile, the days stretch before me, punishing me with their memories and their empty hours. Spring has come, soft and green and full of promise, and I must bear it all somehow, knowing how much I have lost—how much I still have to lose. I was happy once, though, which is more than most people get from this life. My one regret, my only regret in all of this, is that I was forced to hurt Roland. One day I will forgive myself for that. One day, but not yet.

July 25, 1959
Saratoga Pines Resort, New York

The baby has come.

It was a difficult birth, but then I knew it would be, an agony of slowly passing hours and far too much blood. I remember thinking toward the end that perhaps I would die this time, and then hoping I would. The child would not need me. No one needed me. I would do no harm by slipping from this world. But I did not.

They asked me, when it was over, if I wanted to see the child, to hold it, but I said no. I turned my head when they took it away. I had to. If I hadn't, I might have changed my mind. I don't even know if it was a boy or a girl. It's better that way, so I won't always be making up names in my head, wondering if she has my eyes, or if he has Roland's smile. We can't miss what we've never had. At least I pray that we can't.

I've conceived two babies now. The first—torn from my body against my will—I did not want. The second—given away of my own free will—I loved and wanted with all my heart. I wonder sometimes, as I lie alone here in my well-appointed room, if having to give up Roland's child is a kind of retribution, punishment for the aversion I bore that first unwanted child. I never wished it ill. I only wished it gone.

But maybe even that was a sin, one that must one day be repaid in kind. Sin or no, it is now my lot to go through this world with empty arms and a heavy heart, searching the face of every child I pass, counting off the years on my fingers, celebrating cake-less, candle-less birthdays.

Caroline is driving up later to take me home—and to make sure I do not falter in my resolve. She's been such a mercy through all of this, coming to visit whenever she could, bringing books, and treats, and bits of gossip from home. I haven't the heart to tell her I care for none of it, that my heart is too bruised for such trivial things.

A few weeks back she brought the final divorce papers for me to sign. I saw the look on her face as I took the pen from her hand. She thought I wouldn't sign them, but I did, aware as my hand began to move that it was the last time I would sign my name as Lily-Mae St. Claire. As soon as the papers were filed with the court, it would be over; I would cease to be Roland's wife.

In the days that followed I found myself wondering if it was done, if the legal ties that bound us had been dissolved once and for all. Surely, I would have felt the severing, like a limb torn from the body, or a heart from a chest. But there was nothing, no instant of knowing, of loss. Perhaps because I had done so much bleeding already.

Caroline reminds me constantly that what I've done is for the best. My head tells me she's right. And yet, a question lurks in the heart, filling that place where my child's name should reside. In a few hours I will leave it behind, unnamed, unseen. But how can I when it's the only bit of Roland I will ever have, someone to cling to when my memories begin to grow bitter and dim? If I do this thing—this terrible, irrevocable thing—what is left?

Sand Pearl Cottage.

The words come to me like the quiet rush of the sea. That's what is left, the place where it all began, and somehow, it must be enough.

December 9, 1959
New York, New York

I have left the cottage, but only to tend to some business. I've come to New York to shut up the apartment. I will not miss it, or this city, either. Perhaps because it's where things ended, and the memories of those days are still too fresh. Everywhere I look there are reminders of our early days, restaurants where Roland and I dined, theaters we attended, hotels where we went to parties. There can be no moving on as long as I'm anchored by such things. And so it is time.

I arrived the day before yesterday. The phone started ringing the moment word got around that I was back. I am no longer the wife of Roland St. Claire, but apparently the money settled on me in the divorce still makes me an attractive guest at dinners and cocktail parties. I turn them all down, of course, making politely vague excuses. How can I accept any invitation where I might run into Roland? Besides, I have no wish to be a conversation piece, the object of curious stares and knowing glances.

This morning, I set out to see Jasper at his office. I was going to take a cab, then decided a walk in the chilly December air might do me good after being shut up for days. I was waiting to cross at the corner of Lexington and Forty-ninth when I spotted a headline splashed across one of tabloids on display at the newsstand—"Millionaire Financier Dumps Bride for Younger Sister."

I snatched the tabloid off the rack, scanning the small print with a sickening knot in the pit of my stomach. The man running the stand barked at me to buy the paper or put it back where I found it. I fished a coin from my handbag with trembling fingers, and dropped it into his outstretched palm.

My vision blurred as I stared at the photograph of Caroline. She was wearing a small hat with a netted veil, her fingers wrapped around a small bouquet of flowers. It could almost have been me standing there beside Roland. And once, it had been. With a sick little lurch, I wadded the thing up and stuffed it into the nearest trash can, then stumbled blindly across the street to the building where Jasper had his office.

He needed only to look at my face as I stepped into the room to know that something was wrong. He must have thought I might faint. He got up from his desk and crossed the room, guiding me to the nearest chair.

"You've seen, then, or heard?"

"In the papers," I told him thickly. My lips had suddenly gone numb.

"I'm sorry, Lily-Mae. I didn't want you to find out like this."

I stared at him in disbelief, not sure if I was more shocked to learn that my sister had married my ex-husband, or that my dearest friend in the world had kept it from me. "How could you not have told me, Jasper?"

"I couldn't tell you what I didn't know myself, Lily-Mae. I read it this morning, the same as you. Before that, I promise you, there wasn't a word of anything, no talk of them being seen together, nothing. I think it must have happened very quickly."

I couldn't help it. I broke into a sob as the reality of it sank deep. Roland, married to Caroline. How had it happened, and when did it start? Before the divorce was even final? While I was at Saratoga Pines?

Jasper stood and crossed to a small cabinet in the corner, and filled a glass with amber liquid. He brought it to me and pressed it into my hand. "Drink it down."

I sipped, choked, then sipped again. Finally, the sobs slowed. "How could she? My own sister? When she knew—"

Jasper snorted, as if he found something amusing. "How could she?"

My head came up sharply, stung by the combination of mockery and disbelief. His face softened when he saw that he'd hurt me.

"Poor, sweet Lily-Mae. You never did see your sister clearly. You told me once about the time you found Caroline in Zell's office, remember? What do you think that was about? She's always had an eye for anything that belonged to you. Hell, she even threw herself at me a couple of times, until she realized you didn't want me—and then neither did she."

I shook my head from side to side, not wanting to believe it. But suddenly I was remembering the day in Zell's office, the sight of Caroline in my clothes, batting her eyes. Is that what she'd done with Roland? Of course it was. I had seen it for myself. But I had looked the other way, made excuses, anything to keep myself from seeing it for what it was.

No wonder she'd been so adamant that I give up Roland's child. She knew as well as I that a child would have bound him to me forever. And her willingness to act as go-between during the divorce, her keen interest in making sure I signed those final papers, had all been calculated. She had pretended it was for my own good, for the good of the child, when all the while she'd been planning, plotting, biding her time, like a hungry spider.

How had I not seen it?

It doesn't matter. They're married. She's won, somehow, with-

out my ever realizing it was a contest. But of course it was. It had always been a contest. Everything had. I saw it now. Now that it was too late.

I thought of the child I had given away, of the sacrifices I had made for both their sakes. I had been a fool, throwing away happiness with both hands in order to protect the people I loved, and this was how I'd been repaid, with deception and cold-hearted betrayal.

I stood stiffly and pushed past Jasper. I had no claim to Roland, no right to say who my sister could love or marry, but I needed them to know what I thought, what I felt. And I needed to know why.

Jasper laid a hand on my arm. "Where are you going?"

"Where do you think?" I replied so flatly that I barely recognized my own voice. "I'm going to pay my respects to the happy couple."

"Lily-Mae, you're in no shape to go anywhere, and certainly not to see Caroline. Besides, they're not in town."

I lifted questioning eyes to his.

"The paper said they've left on an extended honeymoon."

"Paris?" I whispered, flayed raw by the thought.

Jasper shook his head. "Barbados, if the papers are right, and they usually are."

I nodded miserably. I don't think I could have borne it if it was Paris.

"And actually, it's for the best." He had me by the sleeve then, as if he thought I might bolt. "You don't want either of them to see you like this. And what's the point of a big scene? It's done. I know that isn't what you want to hear, but it's the way things are. The best thing you can do right now is go back to the cottage and put some distance between yourself and your sister, and give yourself a little time to absorb it."

As usual, Jasper was right—or mostly right. I did need distance. But the cottage wouldn't be far enough. The truth is, at that moment I wasn't sure there was anyplace on the face of the earth that would be far enough. I just knew I couldn't be anywhere that reminded me of Roland, where I could hear the gossip or see the headlines. And so I picked up the phone and booked the first flight I could get, then returned to the apartment to throw some things in a suitcase. Tomorrow morning, I leave for Rome.

May 3, 1960
Rome, Italy

A letter has found me all the way across the sea. I scarcely know how Stephen knew to find me here. Perhaps Caroline gave him my address. The letter was brief, as most of Stephen's letters are. But this one was handwritten, not typed, as if he had penned it himself rather than dictating it to his secretary. It said only that he was passing along some information that had recently come to his attention, as he believed I might find it of interest, and perhaps even some comfort.

I couldn't imagine what he would be sending me. He had always been kind, but other than the papers I was required to sign from time to time, we have never had many dealings with each other. I was surprised, as I smoothed the creases from the carefully folded photocopy, to see the words "Mims County Register" printed at the top.

It was the face I noticed first. The photograph was blurry, and had been taken before my time at Mt. Zion, but there was no mistaking Harwood Zell. For a moment I felt the ground tilt beneath my feet, my hands suddenly trembling so violently I could barely read the badly blurred headline: "Local Minister Perishes in Mysterious Blaze."

I don't remember exactly what happened then. I remember closing my eyes, feeling tears squeezing past my lids, and then more and more, until finally I buckled to my knees with a silent prayer of gratitude and sobbed myself dry.

Dead.

For more nights than I can count, I have whispered Zell's name—in both my curses and my prayers. I have cursed his name, and yes, I have prayed for him to die. Now it seems both prayer and curse have been answered. No longer will I have to look over my shoulder, or peer around corners, petrified that he'll be there, waiting. I'm free.

The truth of it struck me so hard that I began to cry all over again, shaking until my teeth rattled and my bones ached. Finally, after a time, I quieted and looked about me for the photocopied article I had let slip from my hands.

I remained on my knees as I read, my eyes still gritty with tears.

> *A massive fire swept through Mt. Zion Missionary Poor Farm Thursday evening, destroying several buildings, including two dorms, the administrative offices, an equipment barn, and a portion of the main residence. Perishing in the fire were the Reverend Harwood Zell and his wife, Ruth, along with several unidentified residents housed in the dorms at the time of the fire. Witnesses say the blaze originated in the office building and then spread rapidly to the surrounding buildings, aided by recent dry, windy conditions. The cause of the fire is unknown at this time.*

But it wasn't unknown. Not to me. Suddenly, I was back in that office, looking at him across the desk through a haze of stale smoke, a cigarette dangling from the corner of his lips while another burned down to ash, forgotten in an ashtray on the other side of the room. Finally, his filthy habit had caught up to him.

As awful as it was, I couldn't stop staring at the photos. There were several of the grounds, buildings ravaged to piles of soot and charred timber, and behind the burned-out barn, the graveyard, scorched black as far as the eye could see, its wooden crosses burned away so that there was no longer any way to tell who was buried there, no way to ever find the grave of Cindy Price.

Sister Ruth is dead, too.

Even now, when the news has had time to settle, I try to muster some semblance of pity, or at least horror at the way she died. But all I feel is relief and a vague sense of numbness. There was a time when I could have strangled them both with my own hands. But now, strangely, all I feel is empty, as if losing the object of my hatred has left a hole in me.

Nothing will ever erase the horror of those days, or the shame I have quietly carried with me every day since, but justice has been done at last. Harwood Zell has been baptized by fire, though whether to cleanse him of his sins or prepare him for hell, I cannot say. I know only that he has gone to his God, and I must be content with that.

July 12, 1962
New York, New York

I stayed away from New York as long as I could, but I'm back again on home soil, though, if truth be told, this city has never felt like home. I have only one purpose in returning. I am back to lay my ghosts, to finally close up the apartment and then quit this place for good, to put it and its cruel reminders far behind me.

Not my memories, though. I have learned that that can never be. I thought once that I could outrun them—fool that I was—if I moved fast enough, and often enough. But memories are not stationary. They do not grow roots and stay in one place. They go with us, like shadows, always one step behind, pouncing when the party winds down and the guests start to leave. Or when darkness falls and there's no one there.

I stayed nine months in Rome, in a rented flat overlooking the Campo de' Fiori, where Julius Caesar died and heretics were once burned. It's a marketplace now, filled with flowers most days. In the late afternoon when the sun was high I could smell their mingled scents through my open windows. I made friends and drank wine, learned new ways and new words, content for a time, if not truly happy. But eventually I grew restless, though for precisely what I could not have said. I moved on to Naples, to Procida, where the buildings are the color of Easter eggs, and the sea is everywhere you look. It was lovely, but it made me sad, too, because it made me think of Sand Pearl Cottage, and of Roland.

Almost before I knew what I was doing, I found myself in Paris, hunting ghosts as I traced and retraced each street and bridge and café Roland and I had visited together. It was foolish, I know, but I couldn't help myself. I was drawn to the memories like sharp, shiny objects, knowing full well they would cut and tear, unable to resist their pull. I deluded myself almost happily, clinging to the lie that it might help me forget, like the tolerance one builds to slow, steady doses of poison. Instead, it was like probing a wound with a red-hot needle so that it was never allowed to heal.

I saw Roland everywhere. In every bistro and patisserie, in every park and shop, on every crowded sidewalk, a set of broad shoulders moving through a crowd, a profile glimpsed fleetingly through a café window. My heart would catch, then plummet sickeningly when I realized I'd been mistaken. And what if it had been him? What could that mean to me? He was married again, out of reach.

What a fool I was. Instead of looking forward, I was looking back. As if that ever worked for anyone. And so I came home—or rather, I came here. The apartment is to be packed up, most of the contents placed in storage. I don't want any of it but can't bring myself to dispose of it, either. I find I'm more careful these days about what I throw away.

All that remains are a few loose ends to tie up, which is why I went to see Jasper this morning. I broke the news as gently as I could and invited him down to the cottage anytime he was free to get away. He said he would come, but I'm not sure he will. Things have been different between us since that uncomfortable night at the Gardiners', though he remains my dearest friend. He didn't like my leaving, and tried to change my mind, but I told him my plans were fixed. I leave for Florida the day after tomorrow. I fear it will be a long time before we see each other again.

I was still a little teary when I left his office, and in no hurry to return to the apartment. Instead, I crossed the street and wandered into the park, keeping to the shady side of the walk. With school out for the summer, the park was full of children, playing tag and tossing balls. The sight always makes my heart ache a little, but I smiled when I spotted a little girl in a straw hat and blue gingham dress poised on top of the slide. She squealed with delight as she careened to the bottom, where her father waited with outstretched arms. I watched as he scooped her up into his arms.

Suddenly, I went stock-still. It was Paris all over again, my heart in my mouth at the sight of those familiar shoulders. Only this time it wasn't my imagination playing tricks. The shoulders didn't just look like Roland's—they were Roland's.

The child was still laughing as he swung her up onto his shoulders, her little fingers clasping his ears like a pair of handles as they trotted back to the ladder and he helped her climb back to the top of the slide. I watched from behind a tree as they repeated the process again and again.

It was a physical pain, watching them together, and yet I couldn't turn away. She was beautiful, with Caroline's deep red curls and Roland's easy laugh. Somehow, it had never occurred to me that Caroline would bear Roland a child, that she had it in her to be a mother. But that was absurd. It was what married people did. They made love. They had children. And they took them to the park.

I told myself to go and speak to him, to say hello to his little girl. It was the sporting thing to do, after all: the loser congratulating the winner, putting on a good face, and then departing the field. Only I didn't feel like a good sport. I felt like dying. I don't know how long I stayed there watching, but finally they finished their play. Roland scooped the girl up into his arms, both of them laughing. He seemed happy. I was glad. And heartbroken, too. I watched them go, the pang of loss so keen as they vanished from sight that my eyes filmed with tears.

They're a family now, Roland and Caroline, and their sweet little girl, stitched together not just by law but by the sweet, warm laughter of a child. I must learn to live with that, and with the knowledge that all I ever wanted—all I have been denied—now belongs to my sister. I can't think how I will ever manage it.

July 13, 1962
New York, New York

I woke with a start just before dawn, shivering in a clammy sweat. I thought at first that I must be ill, to be shaking so violently. Then I remembered the dream. It came back to me in snatches, a dizzying jumble of images with no beginning and no end, and yet so vivid I could not push them out of my head no matter how hard I tried.

The scenes kept shifting, as they often do in dreams. One moment I was in the infirmary at Mt. Zion, bound hand and foot to a reeking, stripped-down cot; the next, I was propped on a bank of crisp white pillows in the green-walled surgery at Saratoga Pines. Sister Doyle would appear with her needle, and then the screaming would start, only to turn to laughter a moment later as Sister Doyle melted into Caroline, wearing too much lipstick and the peach sweater Zell had given me.

She was holding a baby in her arms, a look of something I now realize must have been triumph in her eyes. I tried in vain to catch a glimpse of the child's face, but could make nothing out through all the blankets. Aching to hold the child, I stretched out my arms, but Caroline began backing away, her laughter ringing louder and louder as she carried the child farther and farther away, until they both were gone, and only the echo of her laughter remained.

I have never been one to set store by dreams, especially those that come in times of anguish, but as I pushed back the covers and rose to dress I was filled with a terrible knowing. I told myself again and again that my own sister could not—would not—have devised something so despicable. But even as I formed the thought, Jasper's words drifted into my head.

She's always had an eye for anything that belonged to you.

Was it possible Caroline's eye had strayed as far as my child—Roland's child?

It was a preposterous notion, the stuff of Bette Davis movies, but the thought continued to gnaw until I picked up the phone and dialed Roland's office. His secretary answered. She sounded flustered at first, when she heard my voice, but recovered soon enough, managing a bit of chitchat about how lovely Florida must be at this time of year. She assumed I was still at the cottage, and I didn't bother to correct her. I knew I stood a better chance of getting what I wanted if she thought me miles away.

I told her I had found some papers of Roland's and wanted to send them along if she'd be good enough to give me his home ad-

dress. When she suggested I send them to the office, I told her they were of rather a personal nature, and that I wouldn't feel comfortable sending them to his office, and felt certain Roland wouldn't, either. I'm not sure what she thought these fictitious papers might contain, but finally she rattled off the address to his new apartment. I should have felt bad about lying, but my conscience was clear as I hung up the phone.

I took a cab to the address on East Fifty-second Street. I've grown used to lavish surroundings, to swanky addresses with poshy doormen in hats and brass-buttoned uniforms, but even I was startled by the fortress-like luxury of the Campanile. I craned my neck, staring up at row upon row of windows, counting up to the twelfth floor, where Roland and Caroline's apartment was.

I made sure to go early in the day, when Roland would be working, or perhaps even out of town. I had no wish to run into him. I needed only to prove my suspicions, one way or the other. The doorman eyed me up and down, a flash of recognition in his small dark eyes, followed by another of confusion. Finally, he pulled back the door, tipped his hat, and wished me a good day. I think he must have mistaken me for Caroline.

I counted along with the numbers over the elevator door as I was swept up to the twelfth floor, holding my breath all the way. The St. Claires' apartment was the second door on the right. I was still holding my breath as I drew back my hand and knocked. And then Caroline was standing there as the door swung open, her mouth sagging slightly, a glass in her hand.

"Well, well," Caroline said in a voice sticky-sweet with the old Tennessee drawl. "Look who's come all the way up from Florida to see her baby sister. Really, Lily-Mae, a call would have done."

I stared at her framed in the doorway, a beautiful stranger in her pearls and heels and sleek white suit, her hair pulled up in a neat little chignon. "Roland's money suits you," I said flatly, not caring that I sounded like a spurned woman. "But then, I suppose it always did."

Caroline chose to ignore the remark. She pulled back the door instead, stepping aside, an invitation I was suddenly afraid to accept. My legs wouldn't move, my stomach knotting at the thought of confronting my sister with such a ludicrous possibility. I wasn't sure which scared me most, the prospect of being wrong or of being right. I stood there, mute, wishing to God I had rehearsed what I was going to say. I had no idea how to broach such a subject, how to ask such a question.

It was Caroline who finally broke the silence. "You've been down at that little shack of yours, haven't you, somewhere down in Florida? You certainly don't look very tan. Or very rested, poor thing." She paused, giving me a little pout. "Oh no, that's right, we heard you were in Italy or somewhere . . . getting over things. Did it work?"

I was stunned by the contempt in her voice, by the hatred glittering back from those bright green eyes. I had seen it before, I realized with a shock, but had never grasped its depth. Now there was no mistaking it. She turned and walked away, leaving me to follow, or to leave if I chose. Perhaps I should have left, but by then I was past leaving. I had come for an answer, and wasn't leaving until I had it.

I said nothing as I followed her into the living room, feeling almost dizzy as I surveyed my surroundings. The apartment had been decorated to the point of garishness, the windows draped in heavy gold brocade, the walls papered in gold and white stripes, each article of furniture clearly chosen not for its beauty but for its cost. I could feel Caroline's eyes on me as I took it all in, waiting for a look of envy to flicker across my face, but all I could think was that there was nothing of Roland there, nothing at all of the man I knew.

And what of the child? There was no sign of the little girl I'd seen in the park, no toys scattered about, no dolls or coloring books.

"He isn't here, you know," Caroline said, as she crossed to the bar to refill her glass. "So if you were hoping—"

"I didn't come to see Roland," I said coldly.

Caroline paused, a cube of ice dangling over her glass. "Then why did you come, Lily-Mae? To talk over old times? To be friends again?" She let the ice clatter into the glass, then picked up a bottle of Beefeater. "As if we were ever friends."

"We were once, a long time ago. Before . . ."

She whirled around to face me then, sloshing some of her freshly poured gin onto the carpet. "Is that how you remember it? Because what I remember is a sister who thought she was better than everyone else, who always got the pick of everything, and lied without batting an eye if it meant getting her way."

"Caroline, how can you say that, when I—"

I let the words trail off, knowing nothing I said would change her mind. Jasper was right. I never had seen Caroline clearly. If I had, I would have seen the hatred and resentment that had been burning quietly all these years. My vision blurred. I blinked then looked away.

But Caroline wasn't finished. Her eyes kindled almost madly as she waved her glass in the air. "You thought you were such a big deal, such a great big star because people wanted to take your picture, when all you were was poor white trash from Mims, Tennessee—just like me. Well, sister dear, it seems we've traded places. It's my picture they want now. Because for the first time in my life I'm the one with everything. Roland belongs to me now. After years of coming in second, of making do with your hand-me-downs, I finally took something from you."

"Roland isn't all you took, though, is he? There was something else."

For a moment Caroline looked almost frightened, then she swallowed what was left in her glass and squared her shoulders. "That's right. I took the baby, too, your baby. It was a girl, by the way."

"I've seen her. She and Roland were playing in the park yesterday. I wasn't certain at first, but I am now. That's why I came. Where is she?"

Another look of fear flickered across Caroline's face. Turning back to the bar, she splashed more gin in her glass, not bothering with the ice this time. "She's with a sitter, not that it's any of your business. And there's nothing you can do, Lily-Mae. You can't take her. She's mine now, all nice and legal. Roland's attorney made sure."

She was so cold and matter-of-fact, so utterly unrepentant. "Don't you have a conscience, or at least a heart? You took my husband, and then you took my child, and that's all you have to say to me? After everything I did to keep you safe? After Zell, after—" My voice broke, and I had to look away. "Please help me understand how you could do this, Caroline."

"How could I not, when you made it so easy? You were never going to hold on to a man like Roland. You're too noble, too pure and self-sacrificing. So I took him. As for Zell and the rest of it, those were your choices, Lily-Mae, not mine. I never asked you to make them."

"Is that what you've been telling yourself all these years? Yes, they were my choices, and I'd make them again. Because they kept you safe. But it wasn't enough. You wanted more. You wanted what belonged to me—my husband and my child."

Caroline met my gaze without blinking.

"The baby," I went on, scarcely believing what I was about to say. "That's how you got Roland to marry you, isn't it? You dangled her in front of him, played on his emotions?"

She smiled then, a flicker of triumph in her eyes as they held mine. "Roland is an honorable man, Lily-Mae. He'll always do the right thing. I knew he'd never turn his back on the child when he learned what you meant to do."

"How could you?" I asked again, because I still couldn't fathom it. "You swore you'd never breathe a word to anyone."

Caroline shrugged, her conscience obviously unscathed. "I thought the man had a right to know the mother of his child was about to hand the poor thing over to strangers. You can imagine how he reacted when I broke the news. He was afraid it might be Jasper's, at first, but I assured him that wasn't the case. I made him see that the child—his child—deserved all the advantages of the St. Claire name."

"And that you did, too?"

She flashed another smile, this one almost gleeful. "Naturally, the child was going to need a mother, someone who'd love her like her own flesh and blood—which I just happened to be. It cost a pretty penny to arrange it all so quickly, to fix the dates on the birth certificate and rush the paperwork through. Luckily, Roland just happens to have a pretty penny, and he wasn't afraid to spend whatever it took. He wanted to make absolutely certain that there was no way you could ever come back for her after giving her up."

I gaped at her, incredulous. "It was you who suggested giving up the child in the first place; did you tell him that? That you made all the arrangements, and stood over me when it was time to sign the papers?"

She pretended to search her memory a moment, then shook her head. "I don't recall those things ever coming up, no. But really, Lily-Mae, it's for the best. She has real parents now, who can give her everything: a real home, a proper upbringing, and security. You should remember that if you ever think about trying to get her back. The courts don't look very favorably on women who give up their own children, nor do they make a habit of handing them out to divorcées who have affairs with their business managers."

"But that wasn't true! You know why I had to make up that story. Roland would never have let me go if I hadn't. He would have fought for our marriage."

"You think so?" Caroline almost purred. "You're so sure you were the love of his life, Lily-Mae, the only one who could ever make him happy. But did you ever stop to consider how easy it was to get him to agree to the divorce? Or for that matter, how long he waited before replacing you?"

I felt the room lurch and wobble. She was right. Roland had never questioned my confession about Jasper, had never bothered to put up a fight of any kind. He had simply washed his hands of me and, at the first opportunity, had married my sister and taken my child.

Caroline sneered as she saw her words hit home. "It's over, Lily-Mae. I've won."

"Why?" I asked numbly. "Why have you done this?"

"Because it was my turn. All those years, I took your hand-me-downs—your clothes, your books, your ratty old rag doll—but not anymore."

"This is about . . . Chessie?"

"It's about always coming in second, Lily-Mae. About being invisible because you're not the oldest, or the smartest, or the prettiest. But now, for the first time in your life, you get to know what it's like to be the lesser sister."

I shook my head slowly, trying to understand. "How is this different? Roland, the baby—they were mine; now they're yours. How is that not taking my hand-me-downs?"

Caroline's glass came down on the end table so sharply I flinched, her eyes suddenly glittering with a kind of bloodlust. "Because, my dear sister, this time you didn't give me anything. I took it. Because I could, and because it was my turn. Have you any idea what it's like to be your sister, Lily-Mae? To only ever be seen as a kind of shadow?" She paused, smiling bitterly, then shook her head. "No, of course you don't. You were always too busy fending off the men, or smiling for the cameras. Well, now you're getting a taste of it. It's you who's the shadow, you no one sees."

"I never wanted any of it, Caroline. All I ever wanted—"

"Her name is Lily, by the way," she blurted, cutting me off abruptly. "After her aunt. Roland hated the idea, but I insisted. I thought it was a nice touch. Very . . . sisterly."

Lily.

Her name is Lily. At least she'll have that.

We stood there a moment, facing each other in that hideous apartment, but there was nothing left to say. I was out of words, out of understanding, out of tears, or so I thought. There was a noise in the foyer, the opening and closing of a door. I tried to steel myself for what I knew was coming, but it was too late.

Roland went still as he stepped into the room, his face stony as he registered my presence. I could feel Caroline's eyes darting between us, could feel her waiting for me to throw myself into his arms and blurt out my side of the story, that there had never been anyone but him, that I had only lied about Jasper to protect him, that I'd been tricked into giving up my child.

But I didn't do any of those things.

If Roland believed me heartless enough to turn my back on our baby, he deserved no explanation. He'd been only too willing to go along with Caroline's scheme, to think the worst of me and take my child. Well, he had her now, and there was nothing I could do about it. But I'd be damned if I'd stand there like a martyr at the stake.

I was barely aware of my legs as I crossed to where he stood. It took everything I had to look him in the eye. I saw it then, through the shimmer of my own tears, a glimpse of remorse beginning to kindle in the depths of those soft brown eyes, but it had come too late.

I drew back my hand, landing it squarely on his cheek, the blow so sharp it rippled up my arm like an electric shock. I stood there a moment, frozen as the mottled imprint of my palm slowly bloomed along his jaw, then turned and blundered toward the door before the tears began in earnest.

Lily.

My little girl's name is Lily.

FORTY

1995
Hideaway Key, Florida

"How?" The single word was all Lily could manage as she stepped out onto the deck. "How could you have done it?"

Caroline closed the notebook and looked up, her expression carefully blank. "I was wondering when you'd come find me. You've hardly spoken a word in two days."

It was true. They'd been giving each other a wide berth over the last two days, eating in shifts so they wouldn't have to sit down together, Lily keeping to the bedroom, Caroline to the deck.

"Answer the question," Lily snapped, fighting off a fresh wave of tears. "How could you do it—and why?"

Caroline sat stonily. "You read them?"

"Yes."

"Then you know why. It's all there, just like she wrote it."

"That's it? That's all you have to say for yourself? You ruined her life—and Daddy's—because you were jealous?"

Hot flags of color rose in Caroline's cheeks. "I did not ruin your father's life."

"You tricked him into marrying you when you *knew* he didn't love you, when you didn't love him, either."

"I did!" The words burst out of her like a sob. "I did love him."

"I don't believe you."

Caroline was staring at her hands, spinning the almost ludicrous marquise-shaped diamond on her ring finger. "Not in the beginning, maybe. But eventually I came to care for him. But he never saw me. Ever. Just once, I wanted him to look at me the way he used to look at her, like the sun rose in my eyes. But he never did. To your father—to most people, actually—I was never anything but a second-rate imitation of the real thing."

Lily dropped into one of the deck chairs, stunned into momentary silence. It had never occurred to her that Caroline might have harbored real feelings for her father.

"Did you ever tell him?"

Caroline's eyes widened, as if horrified by the very thought. "Certainly not." She fumbled with the silver case, extracting another cigarette. This one lit more easily. "There was no point," she said, pushing a thin pall of smoke between her bare lips. "I knew that only too well. I got him into bed once, early on, but only because he'd had too much to drink and was missing her. I thought if I could make him want me that way, the rest would come." She paused to take another drag, exhaling quickly. "It didn't. He never touched me again. Not once in all these years."

Lily squirmed, eager to steer the conversation to less awkward ground. "That time I found the magazine picture, the time you slapped me—"

Caroline's face crumpled as she looked away. "You called her Mother."

"Because I thought I was holding a picture of you. That's why I said *Mother*—and you slapped me for it."

"You don't understand. You can't." She pressed a hand to her eyes, shook her head. "I was so afraid you'd find out, that I would lose you. Every day, every single day, I expected her to come take you away, to take you both away. I just knew that was how I'd be punished."

"You were afraid of losing me?"

"I may have won your father, Lily, but it wasn't fair and square. One way or another we pay for things like that."

Lily gaped at her, astonished by this unexpected admission.

Caroline smiled bitterly. "You look surprised. Did you think I didn't have a conscience? I knew what I did was wrong. I knew it the minute Lily-Mae slapped your father's face that day. He hated me after that, because I made her despise him, and that was something he could never forgive. If there was ever a chance for us, it died that day. But I still had you, someone who was mine, and mine alone."

"But I wasn't yours. Not really. You only wanted me because Lily-Mae was my mother. I was something you could take from her."

"I'm your mother. I raised you from a baby. You belong to me."

"No, you didn't. Daddy did, when he was home. Or the housekeeper, or the maid, or whoever was around. But never you. And you still don't get it, do you? People don't belong to other people. We're not possessions or prizes, not *things* to be won or traded. You say you loved Daddy, that you loved me, but the truth is we were just things to you, bargaining chips in some childish little game you're still playing."

"I wanted to love you, Lily. I swear I did."

"You never showed it. Not once. Not ever."

"I know." Caroline's voice crackled with unshed tears. "I didn't know how to share you with your father. He loved you so. The way he looked at you was the way he used to look at her: like you were his whole world. He never let me forget you weren't mine. You were a part of *her*, a part of *them*, and there was nothing I could do to change that. I was an outsider in my own marriage. As long as you were there, she was, too."

"So you hated me in her place."

"No."

"Yes, you did. It's why you were so eager for me to go away to school, and then stay on in Paris, and why you waited so long to tell me Daddy was sick and that I needed to come home. I made you uncomfortable because I reminded you of what you'd done. And then Daddy left me this place, and you knew the truth was going to come out."

"Yes," she said, quietly, her voice suddenly faraway. "I knew. I knew the minute Stephen Singer said your father left you this place. I think Stephen knew it, too, and was glad. He never liked me very much."

"And so you came down to Hideaway to head me off at the pass."

Caroline's eyes fluttered closed, a pair of tears tracking slowly down her cheeks. "I came to ask you to forgive me."

Forgive her?

Lily stared at her, at this woman she'd been calling mother for more than thirty years, and tried to imagine the circumstances under which such a thing might be possible. She couldn't. There was no way to go back and change the past, no way to erase the hurt that had been inflicted or repair the lives that had been altered. It was too much to comprehend—and too much to ask.

Lily lifted her chin a notch, forcing herself to meet Caroline's red-rimmed eyes. "After everything I've heard, everything I've read, I don't know if that's possible. I know it isn't possible today, if that's what you were hoping for."

Caroline looked as if she'd been slapped. "But I came all this way. I brought you the journals. You would never have known otherwise. Don't I get credit for that?"

"Credit? For doing what you should have done thirty years ago? This was damage control, and we both know it, Moth—" Lily bit off the word before she finished it.

"You won't call me Mother?"

Lily met her gaze without flinching. "No, I won't. I suppose I could call you Aunt Caroline, but that doesn't feel quite right, either." She was being cruel but somehow couldn't help herself.

Caroline looked down at her lap, absently fingering the book lying closed on her knees. "So, where do we go from here?"

Where indeed? Lily glanced back out over the sea, where a bloodred sun was already beginning its descent, then back at Caroline. Without makeup she looked haggard and unwell, as if the last two days had aged her twenty years.

"I'm going to go scare us up some food," she said at last, knowing full well it wasn't the answer Caroline was waiting for.

Caroline stared blankly. "Food?"

"We still need to eat."

Truth be told, food was the furthest thing from Lily's mind just then, but eating was what families did when they grieved; they sat down together and chewed and swallowed, because when mouths were full nothing needed to be said.

She had scrounged up the ingredients for sandwiches and a salad, and was rinsing a handful of romaine leaves when Caroline stepped into the kitchen and picked up a tomato and knife. Lily watched from the corner of her eye, saying nothing as she began tearing her lettuce into a scarred wooden bowl.

It felt strange, preparing a meal together in the wake of such startling revelations. Maybe because Lily couldn't recall a single time they'd ever done it. Caroline wasn't the domestic type, and there had always been some cook or other to handle meals, though with Roland frequently away on business they had rarely eaten as a family.

As a child she had envied families who sat down together, dinner tables where Mom and Dad shared their day, then quizzed their children about math homework and spelling tests. She had adored her father, but in some tiny corner of her girlish heart, she had blamed him for being gone so much. Now she understood why he'd stayed away. Home must have been an unbearable place.

They ate in the small breakfast room off the kitchen, eating their salad and sandwiches in silence. Lily opened a new bottle of wine, pouring them each a glass. She watched now as Caroline refilled her glass and lifted it with shaky hands.

"Is Lily-Mae the reason you drink so much?" It was a blunt question, and one Lily already knew the answer to, but she wanted to hear Caroline's reply.

"I'm not . . . proud of the things I've done."

"If you felt so bad, why didn't you at least try to make things right? You could have bowed out and let them be together. Or is this shame of yours relatively recent?"

Caroline shot Lily a look of maternal warning, then seemed to remember she no longer had the right. Her shoulders slumped. "I told myself it was because I couldn't bear the scandal, for Roland or myself, but the truth was I kept hoping . . ."

"That he'd learn to love you?"

"He didn't, of course. And then Lily got sick."

"Cancer."

"Yes. In her left breast. They took it off. She went through chemo and radiation, but it must have come back. Roland tried to go to her when he heard, but she refused to see him."

"And what about you? Did you try to go to her?"

"No."

Lily was appalled, though not surprised. "She was your sister. How could you not want to at least say good-bye?"

Caroline blinked, as if surprised by the question. "I didn't know. Your father didn't tell me any of it until . . . after. And even then it was only to throw it in my face."

Lily traced a finger around the lip of her wineglass, recalling the day as if it were yesterday. She'd been home on a break—from work, and from Luc—when her father returned unexpectedly from an extended business trip. He'd been so steely, so coolly matter-of-fact as he relayed the news that Lily-Mae was dead. It never occurred to her that he might be hiding his own raw emotions, rather than trying to spare his wife's.

And then at the memorial, he'd stood so grave and still. She had taken his stoicism as a show of respect, or perhaps lingering anger that Caroline had refused to attend her own sister's service, never suspecting the horrible grief he'd been struggling to conceal. So much made sense now—such terrible, terrible sense. And yet, there were still questions that needed answering, tiny details not mentioned in Lily-Mae's journals.

"How did Daddy learn that Lily-Mae was sick?"

"From Stephen Singer, I suppose. He always knew where she was and what she was up to. I think your father paid him to know. I had no idea she planned to leave him the cottage when she died. I should have guessed, I suppose." She paused, shook her head. "And then your father left it to you. He knew exactly what he was doing."

"You think he wanted me to know the truth?"

Caroline managed a pained half smile. "Can you think of a better way to get back at me than to turn you against me?"

Lily shoved back her plate, not bothering to hide her annoyance. "He would have told me years ago if that's what he was after. God knows, he had the right. What I don't understand is why he stayed with you. After everything you did, why would he stay?"

Caroline flashed another look of surprise, though this one held no malice. "He stayed for you, Lily. Because he knew what would happen if he ever tried to go to her. I would have ruined us all, in any way I could. And I made sure he knew it. He would never have let me hurt you that way—or her."

Lily blinked back a sudden sting of tears. "He had a good heart."

"Yes, he did," Caroline answered almost wistfully. "It was one of the things he had in common with my sister." She glanced up then, her wineglass hovering halfway to her lips. "How does one end up with a heart like that, do you suppose? The kind that always does the right thing, no matter the personal price?"

Lily had no answer. Instead, she took another sip of wine, watching as the last sliver of sun eased into the sea.

"My return ticket is for tomorrow," Caroline said when the silence began to lengthen.

Lily nodded.

"Should I change it?"

"No."

Caroline's face crumpled. "But we haven't . . . settled things."

"Is that what you think we're doing? Settling things? Do you honestly believe, after what I've read—what you've admitted—that I can just let it all go? Water under the bridge? No big deal?"

Caroline shrugged helplessly. "I thought if I stayed—if we talked some more, that we could work it out, and maybe get past it."

"Past it?" Lily repeated, incredulous. "You want us to just . . . get past it? What about Lily-Mae? Do you think she got past it? Did Daddy? Somehow I doubt it. Perhaps mine isn't the only forgiveness you should be worrying about."

Caroline stuck out her chin, lower lip quivering. "There's nothing I can do about them now."

"No," Lily said flatly. "But there was, while they were alive. You've had years to be sorry—and to make things right—for them and for me. But you didn't. It's only now that you suddenly feel so bad. Do you really? Or are you only sorry that it's all come out?"

Caroline sighed heavily as she let her eyes drift out to the beach. "Would you believe me if I said I really do feel bad? I do, by the way, if it's of any use now. Jealousy is a hideous thing, Lily. As bad as any cancer once you let it get hold of you. And I did. I wish there were some way to go back, to do things over. We were close once, she and I. She used to call me Bitsy. Did I ever tell you that?"

Lily's eyes widened in astonishment. "Of course you didn't. You never told me anything."

Caroline's expression was suddenly hopeful. "I could tell you now. Anything you want to know."

Lily pulled in a deep breath, praying for patience. "It's a little late for storytelling, don't you think? And as for getting past all of this, I'm not sure that's ever going to happen. I don't even know what I'm feeling right now. I haven't had time to process anything. But I do know that I don't want to see you for a while."

Caroline's face fell, but she made no further protest. "Will you be coming home before you leave for Milan?"

"I'm not going to Milan," Lily told her flatly. "And I *am* home. I'm staying here in Hideaway. Not because of anything in the journals, but because I think I can be happy here. I at least want to try."

"You're going to live here? In her cottage?"

"In *my* cottage, yes. At least for a while."

"I see."

"No, I don't think you do. I didn't, either, in the beginning. But I think I finally know why Daddy left me this place. He was happy here once. No matter where he lived this was always home for him, like it was for Lily-Mae. Every time something went wrong, every time she sought solace, this was where she came, and where she stayed. Because her memories lived here. The good ones at least."

"I never knew . . ." Caroline said, setting down her empty glass. "What she felt for your father—I never knew it was real. It all happened so fast. Running off together in the middle of the night, shutting themselves away in some shack on the beach, and then a few weeks later, married. Affairs that begin that way don't last. Only theirs did. I didn't want to believe it was real."

Lily arched a brow. "And now that you know it *was* real?"

A fresh tear tracked down Caroline's cheek. "My heart is broken all over again. Is that what you wanted to hear? I thought if I separated them, made them hate each other, that it would finally be my turn. I didn't understand that nothing—not miles, not anger, not even betrayal—could ever really separate them."

"But they *were* separated. You did accomplish that."

Caroline's lower lip trembled, her voice quivering with barely suppressed tears. "I thought so, too, but I was wrong. It was all for nothing. The hurt, the damage—all for nothing."

FORTY-ONE

1995
Hideaway Key, Florida

It was a relief to have Caroline gone. Lily hadn't waved good-bye, though she had gone to the door to watch the rented Buick back out of the driveway and disappear down Vista Drive. Caroline had made one last stand, a final plea for forgiveness as she walked to the door with her overnight bag. Lily's answer hadn't changed. Perhaps forgiveness would come in time, though at the moment it was hard to see how such a thing was possible. It was a strange reality to be faced with, to go from having not one mother but two—one who raised her, and one she'd never known—to realizing, with a rather nasty jolt, that in truth she had no mother at all.

The thought churned up fresh waves of anger in her gut, a nebulous sense of loss, fury at having been lied to, resentment at being cheated of the mother she should have had. Perhaps it was only a girlish fancy, the cotton-candy notion that with Lily-Mae she might have had the childhood she'd always craved, the kind of bond that existed only between mothers and daughters, a friend and confessor, a keeper of secrets. Instead, she had Caroline—distant, resentful Caroline, who after thirty-five years was still as much a stranger to her as Lily-Mae.

But even as the thought came Lily knew it wasn't true. Lily-Mae wasn't a stranger. Not anymore. She had Roland to thank for that. All her life he'd been teaching her lessons, schooling her in the ways of the world and urging her to find her place in it, counseling her to listen to her heart and then follow it. Had he known, somehow, that her place was here? Perhaps not. Perhaps he'd only hoped. But she liked the idea, just the same.

Restless with the weight of these new thoughts, Lily wandered into Lily-Mae's bedroom, hers now, though she still had trouble thinking of it that way. She'd been at the cottage nearly six weeks now, and aside from the letter found between the pages of *Wuthering Heights*, and the journal discovered on the bookshelf, she had barely touched a thing. It had seemed wrong somehow to disturb any of it, like ransacking the tomb of an ancient king or queen, defiling things made sacred by death. Now, suddenly, in the light of Caroline's revelations, everything had changed. The room, and everything in it, belonged to her mother—a legacy of sorts, sacred still, but no longer off-limits.

This time there was no pang of guilt when she opened the closet, no queasy sense of voyeurism as she ran her gaze over the mother lode of vintage suits and dresses, remnants of a bygone era when ladies wore hats and carried hankies. She couldn't resist touching them, fingering a silk sleeve, a beaded neckline, wondering where they might have been worn, and why Lily-Mae had chosen to hold on to them. Sentiment perhaps, memories that clung to clothes the way good perfume did, lingering long after the wearer cast them aside. Eyes closed, she inhaled deeply. It was still there, or at least the illusion was, as it had been the first time: the faintly mingled scents of lavender and lily of the valley. Like a memory, but not, because that was impossible.

When she'd had her fill of the closet's treasures she moved on to the trunk at the foot of the bed. Like the closet and bureau, she had given the contents a quick peer when she first arrived, but she had ventured no further. She'd been on a different mission then, and to tell the truth, just a bit squeamish about rooting around in a dead woman's things. Now she had no such qualms.

Folding herself down onto her knees, Lily raised the lid and stared at the nest of tissue-wrapped parcels, so neatly arranged that she almost hated to disturb them. In the end, curiosity won out. Her belly fluttered as she lay the first package in her lap and gingerly folded back the layers of crinkly paper.

It was a nightgown, creamy lace, delicate as a web, with a chain of tiny satin rosebuds sewn along the neckline and straps. It weighed almost nothing in her hands, so sheer she could see the outline of her fingers through the fabric. Squinting, she made out the label—La Maison Blanche, Paris, France.

We'll always have Paris.

She'd nearly forgotten the postcard but thought of it now—mailed just weeks before Lily-Mae's death—with a pang of grief even she hadn't expected. That her father might have sent it had crossed her mind, but now there could be no doubt that he'd been the one to pen that brief but poignant line, a bittersweet reminder of their honeymoon. Only Lily-Mae had never received it. She had died never knowing that Roland was half a world away, still thinking of her.

Delving back into the trunk with renewed reverence, she brought out what she was now certain had been Lily-Mae's trousseau. Each article had been carefully preserved in the same silver paper: lacy peignoirs and silk camisoles, satiny slips and whisper-sheer stockings, all of the highest quality and all seemingly never worn. And yet she'd kept them, stashed away like bits of treasure, artifacts from a time and place that no longer existed.

She felt a prickle of anticipation as she reached for the last parcel—larger than the rest, and tied with a strand of pale blue ribbon. Her breath caught as she peeled back the paper folds and saw the sheath of creamy silk. There was a hat, too, a slightly rumpled pillbox with a finely beaded veil, along with the mummified remains of a small posy of flowers.

Lily held her breath as she set the flowers aside and picked up the hat, plucking it back into some semblance of shape. On impulse, she placed the pillbox on her head, adjusting the angle and then smoothing down the veil before stealing a look in the dressing table mirror. A shiver passed down her spine as she stared at her reflection, the kind that comes with recognizing a perfect stranger, a face you've never seen before but somehow know as well as your own.

She was aware, as she shed her shorts and T-shirt, that what she was about to do might be considered morbid, even gruesome. She didn't care. Before she could change her mind she was slipping the silk sheath over her head, letting it slide down her body with a sigh. The fit was surprisingly good, a bit roomy in the hips, perhaps, but otherwise the dress seemed to have been made for her. She was hesitant at first, to look at herself in the mirror, then found that she couldn't look away, startled to see herself as Lily-Mae must have looked the day she married Roland.

It was a queer feeling, as if she had stepped into another time—and another life.

And then, before she knew to brace herself, the strain of the last few days was crowding in, all the emotions she had been carefully holding at bay suddenly spilling free, a hot rush of tears blurring her vision and scorching up into her throat, shuddering through her until there was nothing to do but bury her face in her hands and give way to them.

"What in God's name—?"

Lily snapped her head around, startled to find Dean in the doorway. "What are you doing here?"

His gaze wandered pointedly over the floor, taking in puddles of lingerie and rumpled sheets of tissue. "I think I'm the one who should be asking that question. What is all this, and why are you crying? What's happened?"

Lily wiped at her eyes with the heels of her hands, but the tears kept coming, welling again and again, no matter how many times she blinked them away. "Nothing. No, that's not true. My mother—no, *not* my mother—Caroline showed up."

"Your mother showed up . . . here?"

"She isn't . . ." Lily paused, pulling in a ragged breath. "My God, I can't believe I'm saying it out loud. She isn't my mother. She was never my mother."

Dean stared at her, clearly baffled. "She was . . . I'm sorry . . . what?"

Lily took another swipe at her eyes, frustrated that she couldn't seem to get her emotions under control. "She was going through my father's desk after he died, and she found some of Lily-Mae's journals. Lily-Mae must have sent them when they told her . . . when she learned she was dying. Anyway, Caroline decided to bring them to me."

Dean shook his head, as if what she was telling him refused to translate. "I don't understand. How is Caroline *not* your mother? And why would she show up now, when she couldn't be bothered to answer any of your calls?"

Lily dragged in a breath, then let it out slowly. "She said she wanted to be here when I found out."

"Found out what?"

"That Lily-Mae was my mother."

"Jesus . . ."

Lily pressed on, afraid the tears might start again. "She and Roland were already split when she realized she was pregnant. Caroline talked her into giving up the baby, then talked my father into marrying her so they could adopt me."

"And Lily-Mae agreed to that?"

Lily shook her head. "She didn't find out until years later, when it was too late. She saw my father and me at the park one day and got suspicious. Apparently, Caroline was only too happy to confirm what Lily-Mae already knew, that her own sister had schemed to steal her husband and her child."

"Jesus. Where is she now, your—I mean, Caroline—sorry."

Lily waved away his apology. "Don't be. I don't know what to call her, either. She's back in New York. Or will be as soon as her plane lands."

"How did the two of you leave it?"

"I told her I didn't want to see her for a while. Or maybe ever. I don't know if I can forgive the things she did, the lies she told, and the lives she ruined. Everything her sister ever loved or wanted, she took, because she was jealous—and because she claims to have loved my father."

"You don't believe her?"

Lily shook her head helplessly, not sure what she believed anymore. "I don't know. It doesn't exactly feel the way love should, does it? Scheming to get what you want. Not caring who you trample on to do it."

Dean's face hardened. "Are we still talking about Lily-Mae? I can't tell."

Lily stared at him, her face blank until she realized with a vicious jolt that he must be referring to his plans to get his hands on the cottage. It seemed impossible that she could have forgotten something so egregious, but the truth was she absolutely had. Over the past few days, she'd given little thought to anything but the tangle of lives Caroline St. Claire had knowingly left in her wake. Now, though, the reality of it came crashing down, the weight of it heavy on her chest.

"If you're asking, was that a reference to your plans to sell my cottage, then no, it wasn't. Though, it should have been. Lucky for you, my mind has been"—she paused, waving a hand around the cluttered bedroom—"on other things."

Dean eyed the mess again, as if he were surveying the remnants of a small explosion. "What is all this, by the way?"

"Lily-Mae's trousseau," she told him coolly, unable to tell if he really cared or was just trying to change the subject. "At least I think it is. Things Roland bought for her while they were on their honeymoon."

"But that was decades ago."

"Yes."

"And it's still here?"

"Yes."

"Why?"

Lily narrowed her eyes at him. "Why do you think? She kept it because it meant something to her. Every minute she spent with my father *meant* something. And this was how she held on."

"Held on?" Dean repeated, his voice almost chillingly quiet. "My father tried to hold on. All he did was make himself miserable. Is that what you're trying to do, make yourself miserable?"

"I was just going through her things."

"Really? Because to me, what it looks like you're doing is wallowing. Believe me, Lily, I know it when I see it, and this is exactly how it starts. You rake through the memorabilia, then you rake through it some more, and then before you know it, it starts to consume you."

"She was my mother."

"You never knew her."

"Which is exactly *why* I need to do this. I *want* to know her, how she lived, how she survived so much unhappiness and kept on going. She died here—alone. At the end of her life, she had no one. No lover, no sister, no daughter. No one."

"And how does this little pity party of yours change any of that? The woman is dead, Lily. And nothing is ever going to change that. But you keep dredging it all back up so you can wallow some more."

"That isn't what I'm doing."

"Lily, you were crying your eyes out when I walked in, sitting on the floor in a dead woman's wedding dress like some modern-day Miss Havisham—over a woman you've never laid eyes on. That's what happens when you keep digging through the past. You find out things you don't want to know, things you can't ever *unknow.* I told you when you first came that you should knock this place down, or at least haul all those damn boxes away, but you wouldn't listen. Now look at you."

Lily stole a sidelong glance at the mirror. He was right. She did look ridiculous—a thirty-five-year-old woman dressed up for trick-or-treat—but that was her business. So was Lily-Mae, and Sand Pearl Cottage. Dragging the pillbox from her head, she laid it on the bed, then turned a sickly sweet smile in Dean's direction. "And here we are again, back to knocking down the cottage—your solution for everything. Forgive me if I'm just a little skeptical about your motives."

"You think that's what I've been doing with you all summer, trying to romance this place out from under you?"

"Spare me your righteous indignation, although I must say, you do a fair impression. It would be a lot more convincing, though, if you hadn't announced your intentions to do just that the first day we met. I believe I even called you on it. Guess the joke's on me."

Dean crossed his arms, chin jutting, nostrils flared. "Nothing between us has ever been about this cottage, Lily. Not in the beginning, and not now. But you keep the damn thing. Turn it into a shrine, for all I care. It's not the only piece of beachfront on the Gulf Coast. But just so you know, I said what I did about flattening the place because I think it would be the wisest thing for *you.* Just bulldoze it down and move on."

It was Lily's turn to cross her arms. "Is it really that easy for you? There's something you don't want to deal with—something you don't want to feel—so you just toss it aside and move on?"

"It's worked so far."

The words stung more than she expected. "Has it?"

"Mostly. Yes. And if you're honest with yourself you'll admit that I'm right. Tell me you weren't happier before all this started, that it wasn't easier when you could just pick up and move on without looking back."

Lily scooped a nightgown off the floor, plucking at its satiny folds as she contemplated the question, fairly certain he hadn't been talking about Lily-Mae. "It was easier," she answered finally. "A lot easier, in fact. But I can't turn my emotions on and off like a light switch, or toss the past out onto the curb like it never happened. Feelings aren't always convenient, Dean. In fact, they almost never are. All you can do is live with them until you don't feel them anymore. I don't expect you to understand that, though. You haven't let yourself feel anything for thirty years."

"That isn't true."

"No? You can't even muster enough sentiment to name your dog."

Dean's face clouded. "What the hell does Dog have to do with this?"

"Everything. You just can't see it. You think staying detached will keep you safe, that empty walls and a dog with no name mean you can't get hurt the way your father did. But that isn't how it works. People get hurt. Everybody gets hurt."

"Look, I don't know why we're talking about my walls, but sometimes there are things we're better off not knowing—or feeling. I thought we agreed on that at the start of this thing. It's called self-preservation."

Lily nodded slowly, vaguely numbed by his use of the word *thing*. He was right, though. They had agreed—once. There *were* things you were better off not feeling, but once you *did* feel them, you couldn't go back. "I guess I don't believe that anymore," she said finally. "You do, though, and always will. You act like your father going to pieces over your mother was wrong, like his life, and yours, would have been better somehow if he had just pretended not to care, like you did—like you're *still* doing."

Dean stiffened. "Please leave my parents out of this."

"I'm not the one who brought them up. And you do it all the time; anytime we talk about anything remotely serious, up comes your mother and what she did to your dad. You carry it around with you like a piece of shrapnel. And yet you stand there telling me I should forget about Lily-Mae."

Dean met her gaze, steely-eyed and rigid. "I don't need psychoanalyzing, Lily. I'm not the one sitting on the floor in a wedding dress."

Lily blinked at him, stunned by the ice-cold edge that had crept into his voice. "Can I ask you something? That tough-guy thing you do—like you just did there—is that for show, or do you really believe that nothing can touch you? Not love or guilt or sadness?"

Dean turned away, feigning interest in the jar of shells up on the bureau. He lifted one out, peering at it so long that Lily started to wonder if he'd forgotten she was there. "You're right," he said with a chilling frankness, when he finally dropped the shell and turned back. "It is for show, or used to be. An act I put on to save my skin, but it hasn't been an act for a long time. It's who I am now, an actor who's played a part so long he's forgotten it isn't real. That other me—the one who used to feel all those things—doesn't exist anymore. In fact, he's buried so deep I don't think I could find him if I wanted to."

"And you don't want to," Lily said softly.

The words hung heavily, filling up the silence. Finally, Dean's eyes slid away, the only answer he needed to give.

Lily felt the knot in her throat tighten, but swallowed past it. "What did you want?"

"What?"

"You came over for a reason. What did you want?"

"Just to tell you I was back. So we could . . . talk."

"Talk?" Lily stared at him, wondering what either one of them could say that hadn't been said already. "I think we just did."

"Yeah," Dean said flatly. "I guess we did."

Lily said nothing as she watched him go. She always knew there would be this moment between them—the end of things. She just thought it would be tidier when it came, no emotions left dangling, no hurt feelings or bruised egos. At least that had been the plan.

FORTY-TWO

1995
Hideaway Key, Florida

The beach was a sleepy stretch of muted blues and whites as Lily stepped out onto the cool morning sand. She had come awake with a jolt, stiff and bleary-eyed after a very long and very restless night. She still couldn't say what had awakened her. There had been no wisps of unresolved dreams floating around in her head, no startled echoes of sound or movement, just the abrupt awareness that she was wide-awake and finished with sleep.

The moon was still up as Lily set off down the beach, fat and milky against an opalescent blue-white sky. The sea, too, was quiet at this early hour, shiny-smooth, and nearly silent as it purled lazily around her ankles. It was too late, but she bent down to give her cuffs another turn anyway. As she straightened, her eyes slid reflexively toward Dean's house. The lights in his office were already on, and for a moment she imagined him sitting at his drafting table, sipping from the cold cup of coffee at his elbow, groping about on his desk for the pencil he had absently stuck behind his ear.

Averting both her eyes and her thoughts, she pushed on, turning her attention to the early-morning quiet and brine-scented breeze, the silver-white flash of gull wings out over the water, the sticky-wet give of sand between her toes, carefully etching each sound, and sight, and sensation into her memory.

This was good-bye.

It was what had awakened her, she realized with sudden clarity—the knowing. The eerie, almost jarring stillness that rushed in after decisions were made, when all the humming and whirring finally stopped, and there was just you and the thing you had chosen. A week ago, she had imagined Hideaway as a tiny slice of paradise: sunny, warm, and filled with promise. Now it seemed only a place of sadness, of betrayals and rifts, of inevitable endings—of memories that weren't hers but ached as if they were.

And now she had unhappy memories of her own.

She couldn't stay. Not after having been such a fool. And not when it was so plain that Dean didn't want her here. She had convinced herself they could get past it, that in time they might even be friends—when the weirdness wore off, and her bruises began to fade. And maybe they could have. But not now, after yesterday's bluntly illuminating conversation.

The thought of turning her back on her father's gift broke her heart, but she'd been wrong to ever think she belonged here. Wishful thinking, that's all it was. Not a sign. Not fatherly wisdom. Wishful damn thinking. Like trying to wedge the wrong piece into a jigsaw puzzle; you could force it, but it would never truly fit.

She dreaded having to tell Sheila that her plans had changed again, and sitting through the exasperated but well-meaning lecture that would certainly ensue. She needed to get it over with, though—the sooner, the better. They were meeting later on for a late lunch. She'd break the news then. She felt like the worst kind of heel, but at least she wasn't backing out completely. She'd just be handling her duties long-distance.

She'd be gone next week if all went according to plan, as soon as she could get the cottage packed up and finalize the details of the sale. She had an old flatmate who was working in London and had been nagging her for years to come visit. It was as good a place as any, she supposed. She'd take some time off, bum around the British Isles, somewhere damp and gray and rainy, where everything she looked at didn't remind her of Hideaway Key.

It was one o'clock and the deck at the Sundowner was humming with lunchtime activity, the tables full, the air thick with music and coconut-scented tanning oil. Lily wove her way through beachwear-clad patrons, scanning the crowd for Sheila. Bubba and Drew were at the bar, looking like twins in their ball caps and golf shirts. They were bantering about something over their beers, sharing a basket of fries—a happy couple enjoying the day and each other's company.

Bubba picked her out of the crowd and raised a hand in greeting. Lily returned the wave but kept moving. It was strange, but in her mind her decision to leave Hideaway had recast her as an outsider, a stranger just passing through town. Everywhere she looked was something she would miss.

She was almost relieved when she finally spotted Sheila in the shade of a large striped umbrella, looking sunny and fresh in melon-colored capris and a crisp white blouse. She reached for a smile as she dropped into the opposite chair, glad to see that Sheila had taken the liberty of ordering a round of drinks.

"You look amazing. That's a great color on you."

"Thanks, I feel amazing." Sheila's smile was closemouthed and vaguely conspiratorial. "Which is why I went ahead and ordered you a drink. We're celebrating."

"Celebrating?"

"I heard from my doctor last night. I'm clear."

"Oh, Sheila, that's wonderful!" Lily was surprised by the acute rush of relief she felt on hearing the news. She hadn't wanted to think about the possibility of a negative report, especially when she was about to deliver unwelcome news of her own.

"It was such a relief to get the call," Sheila said. "Now I can concentrate on learning what I need to from you."

Despite her best efforts, Lily felt her smile fade.

Sheila noticed instantly. "What is it? What's wrong?"

"I know I said I was staying, Sheila, but something's come up."

"Oh." Sheila's face registered shock, then disappointment. "Is the something in Milan?"

"Actually, the something's here."

"So it's Dean? You two really can't work it out?"

"No, we can't. And staying isn't going to work. It would be awkward—for him and for me—but that doesn't mean you and I can't be partners. I want to be a part of what we've started here. I just need to do it from somewhere else."

"So you're running again."

Lily pressed her lips together, stifling her first response. She'd been expecting this, and it was a fair assessment from Sheila's point of view. "I'm not running, Sheila. I'm not taking a job anywhere, so that's progress, right? I think I'm going to just travel a little and see what turns up. I actually think it might be fun."

"Who are you trying to convince, me or you?"

Lily shook her head but summoned a smile. "This is what I need to do right now, Sheila. Maybe not what I want, but what I need."

"And your mind's made up?"

Lily nodded, tracing a finger around the rim of her drink, then licked the sugar from her fingertip. "I leave next week."

"Not messing around, are you? Have you told Dean?"

"No, but I will. He'll want the cottage, so I can kill two birds with one stone."

"And if he asks you not to go?"

"He won't."

"But if he did—would you stay?"

Lily was spared having to answer when Salty appeared with a basket of shrimp and a second round of drinks. "On the house, ladies. Drink up."

"On the house?" Lily said, quirking a brow up at him. "What's the occasion?"

"Can't a man be in a good mood without a reason?"

Lily supposed he could at that, though the wink he threw Sheila as he turned to go hinted at something else. As did the flush that had crept into Sheila's cheeks.

"What was that all about?" Lily hissed when she was sure Salty was out of earshot. "And don't say *nothing*. You turned three shades when he winked at you just now. Don't tell me he finally got around to asking you out."

"No," Sheila said, with a Cheshire grin. "I asked him."

"Well, good for you. And about time, too."

"I don't know what got into me. I got that call from the doctor just as I was leaving the shop, and the next thing you know my car was steering its way over here. Thought maybe it was time I took my own advice."

Lily had just raised her glass, about to offer a toast, when Rhona descended in her customarily pungent cloud of patchouli. The salmon-colored hibiscus behind her left ear trembled dizzily as she dropped an arm about Sheila's shoulder. "So happy to hear the news," she chirped less than discreetly. "Yes, yes. I've heard, but then, I always do, don't I? Apparently, your cards didn't lie when they said all would be well."

Cards? Lily barely had time to shoot Sheila a look of astonishment before Rhona's attention shifted in her direction. "Ah, and Ms. St. Claire, how are you enjoying your time in Hideaway?"

Lily managed an uncomfortable smile. "Very well, Rhona, thank you."

"Good. I'm glad to hear it. Come by the shop sometime, and I'll read your cards. I specialize in matters of the heart, you know, and the first reading's free for locals."

Rhona moved off with a breezy wave, descending a moment later on a woman in a large straw hat several tables away. Lily leaned in the second she was gone. "You went to her for a reading? I thought you said she was a crackpot."

Sheila hung her head sheepishly. "I did say that, and she is—a little. But when you're scared to death you'll do anything to feel better. And who knows? She did turn out to be right. Maybe you should pay her a visit. You heard her. She specializes in matters of the heart."

Lily flashed her a dark look. "I thought that was your specialty."

"Yeah, well, I haven't exactly been helping, have I? Or you wouldn't be hightailing it out of here next week."

"We'll work it out, Sheila, I promise," Lily said, finally lifting her glass. "Now let's toast to your good news."

Lily was relieved to have the conversation with Sheila behind her, though it had actually gone more smoothly than she'd expected. There had been no lecture, no condemnation or third degree. Either Sheila had known her words would fall on deaf ears, or she had been distracted by her impending and long-overdue date with Salty.

Now, back at the cottage, it was time to face the thing she'd truly been dreading: looking Dean in the eye and telling him good-bye. No reason to dally or put off the inevitable. She'd swallow her pride and accept his offer to buy the cottage, then pack up Lily-Mae's things and hand over the key. In six months the place would be gone, razed to the ground along with its memories, and she would be somewhere else.

It was for the best, really—a win-win solution for them both—at least that's what she'd been telling herself since lunch, and was still telling herself as she left the cottage. She opted to go to the front door. This wasn't a social call; it was business. She rehearsed her words as she crossed the driveway, then ducked through a space in the hibiscus hedge. She was about to pass through to the other side when she saw Dean step out the front door, an overstuffed duffel over his shoulder, Dog dancing anxiously at his heels.

She watched from the cover of the hedge as he tossed his duffel into the back of his truck, then climbed into the cab after Dog. Off to Chicago again, she supposed, or perhaps some new client. It didn't matter. With any luck she'd be gone before he returned. The sale could be handled long-distance, and there was really nothing more to say. They'd done their good-bye, such as it was.

Standing over Lily-Mae's desk, she penned a brief note apprising Dean of her plans and giving him Stephen Singer's number as a contact since she was likely to be out of the country for some time. She was preparing to seal the envelope when she remembered the key to Dean's house. Wrestling it off her key ring, she dropped it in and sealed the flap. There was a sense of finality as she slid the envelope under his front door and turned away. All that was left now was the packing—and the leaving.

FORTY-THREE

Five days had passed since Dean loaded Dog into the truck and drove away, five days since Lily slid the note under his door, and still no word or sign of his truck. Business must be booming. If her luck held another few days she could make good her escape and spare them both an awkward farewell. She tried not to imagine his relief when he returned to find her packed up and gone. Or his satisfaction when he learned that the cottage was his for the taking if he still wanted it—which, of course, he would.

She had hoped to be gone by now, but packing up and disposing of Lily-Mae's things had proven more complicated than expected. After everything that had happened, everything she had learned, she possessed neither the discipline nor the clarity to make such decisions. She had planned to hire movers and let them handle it all, but found she simply couldn't bring herself to make the phone call.

There were a few things—not many, but a few—that she preferred to pack herself, personal items that held special meaning for her: the journals, of course, and Lily-Mae's jar of shells, Chessie and the things from under the bed, the clothes in Lily-Mae's closet, and her trousseau, certainly. The list seemed to grow every day, as did the collection of sealed and labeled boxes mounting once again in the tiny living room.

And as the list grew, so did her need for boxes. Luckily, they knew her at the liquor store after her first round of decluttering, and they had promised to save her all the boxes she needed. Hopefully, today's trip would be her last. If her calculations were correct, another two days and she'd be ready for the movers. Then there were the little odds and ends to be seen to before she locked up for the last time: utilities to shut off, the refrigerator to empty, the bed to strip, one final load of laundry.

The thought made her want to turn around and head to the Sundowner for a protracted happy hour. Instead, she cut the engine with a sigh and opened the car door, wrestling with an armload of empty liquor boxes as she climbed out. As she stepped up onto the porch and fumbled with her keys, she couldn't help recalling her first trip up those sagging wooden steps. It seemed a lifetime ago now, and perhaps it was. So much had happened since that night, so much had changed.

It was a strange sensation. When she left for Paris she had parents, and a home to return to. Now, as she prepared to leave for London, she had neither—no home, no family to speak of, no ties of any kind. She was untethered, like a ship cut loose and set adrift, not moving toward anything, simply drifting away. Lily-Mae must have felt something similar, the keen but hollow awareness that there was nowhere on earth she could truly call home, no one anywhere she could call her own.

There was another wave of déjà vu as Lily opened the door, the memory of other boxes stacked floor to ceiling, but there was no time to explore it. Something, a sound or some bit of movement out on the deck, caught her attention. Abandoning her cartons, she stepped to the sliding glass doors to peer out.

Her breath caught when she saw him, standing with his back to her, elbows propped along the deck railing, eyes trained out to sea. He turned when he heard the doors slide, and stood looking at her.

"You thought I'd gone," she said quietly.

"Yes."

"So you thought you'd come over and get a jump on your plans."

"I was just . . ." He broke off, reaching into his back pocket.

Lily watched as he produced the envelope she'd slid under his door and held it out to her. She looked at it, then at Dean. "I know what it says. I wrote it. I'll be gone in a few days. You can make all the plans you like then."

"Lily, I'm sorry."

"Don't be," Lily told him with a shake of her head. "This is what was supposed to happen. I just got caught up in everything and forgot. You were right. I was always going to sell you this place when I left. I shouldn't have freaked out."

"I wasn't talking about that. I was talking about the other day, about the things I said. I was insensitive, thoughtless, whatever you want to call it, and I'm sorry."

"Forget it. I said some things, too. Things that were none of my business. I let Lily-Mae's story get to me. You were right. I was wrong."

"No," he said, after what seemed a very long time. "You weren't wrong. The things you said about me—all of it was true. And it does have to do with my mother leaving, and what I watched it do to my father. Then that night when you started talking about jumping off cliffs . . . It spooked me. I went into retreat mode. Although, for the record, I wasn't coming over here to call it quits the day I left for Chicago."

Lily nodded, afraid to trust her voice. In the end she turned away, not sure she could trust her face, either. "We don't need to do this, Dean. Really. It's over. You're going your way and I'm going mine, just like we promised."

"I've been at my father's."

Lily's head came around slowly. "I thought you went back to Chicago."

"My father's," he said quietly. "It was time."

"How'd it go?"

"It was hard. For both of us, I think. There was a lot to say."

"But you said it?"

"We both did. Apparently, I wasn't the only one holding things back. We fought a little, too, about how he was after she left, how he couldn't let go of a single thing that reminded him of her. I didn't understand how he could bear holding on to all those memories when it had ended so badly, how he could go on loving her after what she did to him—to us. And then I realized it didn't matter how. It just mattered that he did. And I made my peace—with all of it. My mother. My father. Myself."

Lily couldn't help but think of Caroline, of the hatred and anger she had allowed to poison her life, and of the anger she herself now bore toward Caroline, and would have to learn to let go of, if she could. "Just like that?" she asked quietly. "After all the years of blame and anger, you're just . . . over it?"

Dean laughed, a brief, brittle snort. "I didn't say I was over it. At least not yet. I said I made my peace with it. They're not the same thing. One is about how I feel. The other is about how someone else feels. I realized it isn't my business—or my job—to decide how my father feels about my mother—then or now. Especially when most of the time I choose not to know what I'm feeling myself. I'm not sure when, but at some point I obviously I decided the best defense was to just stuff everything down, pretend I didn't feel anything at all. That way I could maintain—how did you put it?—that tough-guy thing I do."

Lily winced. "I'm sorry. I was mad. I should never have said that."

"Why? It's true. Everything you said that day was true. All these years I've been seeing my father's grief as a weakness, which is why I decided I wasn't going to be like him, wasn't going to be sniveling and weak. So I shut down. That way there was no possibility of getting hurt. Or so I thought."

She nearly reached out to touch his cheek, shadowed with several days of dark growth, but stopped herself in time. "You look tired."

"It was a rough week, but a good one."

"I'm glad."

"You're the reason I went." The words came out softly, almost breathlessly, as if he'd been holding them in a long time. "Because of the things you said. I was afraid you might be right, and I didn't want you to be. You were, though. I've been an ass. When you showed up in Hideaway, all I could think of was finally getting my hands on this place. Then I got to know you, to like you, and I thought, *Why not? It's only for the summer.* It felt—"

"Safe?"

"Yes. But something happened. I felt things changing between us, and I didn't know how to process that. All I knew was it scared the hell out of me. We had a deal, no complications, and all of a sudden . . ."

"Things were getting complicated."

"Yes," he said quietly. "When you said you were staying, I didn't—"

"Dean, I told you, we don't need to do this. I'm leaving Hideaway, and you can have the cottage. We're back to the original deal."

"I don't think you understand what I'm trying to say, Lily." He looked down at the envelope in his hand, sadly mangled now, and held it out to her. "I don't want this."

Lily eyed the envelope. "This?"

"The cottage. I don't want it anymore."

She stared at him, letting the words settle while the breeze whipped her hair about her face. "You're right," she said finally. "I don't understand. Your clients—"

"I found them another lot, a bigger one."

"Well, then, I guess you're back to your original plan. You can knock it down, along with yours, and build a great big house for yourself."

"I don't want to knock either of them down. Especially not mine."

"Why not yours? I thought—"

"Because it isn't just a house now. Not when you're there."

Lily's heart suddenly wobbled against her ribs. "What are you saying?"

"What I should have said weeks ago, before I wrecked everything: that you don't have to leave . . . that I don't *want* you to leave." He paused, swallowing hard enough to set his Adam's apple bobbing. "I know it's not what we agreed on, but I was a fool to say yes to that stupid deal."

Lily blinked past a sudden blur of tears. "You haven't been the only fool. I was so busy analyzing you that I forgot to take a look at myself. Sheila pointed it out, but it was Lily-Mae who finally made me understand. She was so strong, for Caroline, and for my father, so determined to rescue them from pain and harm. She was willing to face anything, to sacrifice *everything*. But when it came to herself—to looking after her own heart—she ran every time, just like me. She was afraid of the pain, afraid to risk her heart, and she wound up alone, living on memories and regrets. I don't want to end up like she did. I don't want to be alone."

Dean reached for her hand, winding warm fingers tightly through hers. "You don't have to be alone, Lily. Neither of us does."

She tipped her head back, meeting his gaze with an intensity of her own. "I don't want to get it wrong this time, Dean. I need to know what you're saying, straight-out."

He drew her close then, until she could feel the thud of his heart against her ribs, weighty and just a little fast. "I'm saying I'm ready to jump off a cliff, Lily—with you."

Lily blinked once, twice, feeling almost dizzy. "Are you sure? I mean, really sure?"

Dean's arms tightened with a sudden fierceness. "I am. And the reason I know I am is because I'm absolutely terrified, and I'm ready to jump anyway."

A tiny half smile tugged at the corners of Lily's mouth as she went up on tiptoe. "Good," she murmured whisper-soft against his lips. "Now we're getting somewhere."

FORTY-FOUR

Lily lifted the hair off the back of her neck, letting the warm sea breeze caress her damp skin. For what was supposed to be the *end* of summer, it certainly was hot. Not that the heat had stopped the Labor Day weekenders from piling into Hideaway, their SUVs and minivans crammed full of coolers and rafts and barbecue grills.

The whole town was jumping, motels booked to capacity, restaurants staffed to the max, shops stocked to take full advantage of the season's last hurrah. And yet the beach behind Sand Pearl Cottage was deserted, the private stretch of powder-white sand unspoiled by trash barrels overflowing with soda cans and empty potato chip bags. She gazed out over the water, at the smooth swells pushing their way up onto shore, wishing there were time for one more walk before the movers arrived. There wasn't. In fact, they were already late.

Ducking back inside, she was again struck by the sight of so many boxes—nearly as many as there had been that first night—and by the unnerving emptiness of the place, stripped bare now of Lily-Mae's things, of the knickknacks and whatnots that had once made it hers.

Lily was reaching for the phone to call the movers and get a revised ETA when she saw Dean coming up the back steps, his ever-present canine companion eagerly in tow. She barely had time to put down the receiver and brace for impact.

"Chester!" Lily laughed as she staggered backward against sixty pounds of flying fur and lolling tongue. "You'll knock me down!"

"Chester." Dean repeated the name slowly, as if tasting it, then shook his head. "I'm still not used to the new name. He's been Dog since the day I found him. Now all of a sudden he's Chester."

"He likes it," Lily protested. "Look at him. He's smiling."

"He likes *you*. He doesn't care what you call him. Not that I fault him for his taste. Anyway, I'm done moving all the boxes you wanted over to the house."

"Thank you, but are you sure you don't mind me cluttering up your place with all my stuff?"

"Yes, I'm sure. And it's not my place—it's *our* place. I love you, Lily St. Claire. And the reason I know this is because I let you name my dog. Next thing you know, I'll be hanging pictures on the walls."

Lily grinned at their small private joke. "Easy, Romeo. One step at a time."

"Speaking of hammers and nails, my guys should be here bright and early tomorrow morning to start the renovations." He paused, dropping a kiss on the top of her head. "It's a good thing you're doing, Lily, setting up the foundation and turning this place into a retreat for breast cancer survivors. Lily-Mae would be pleased. And proud."

Lily looked around the cottage, stripped to the bare walls now, and tried to imagine it when the renovations were complete. "I hope so," she said almost gloomily. "I'd like to think I made her proud, that I'm doing something worthwhile with what she and my father left me. Sheila said something once that stuck with me. She said when she was diagnosed and going through chemo she wanted to run away, to hide, but that there was nowhere to go. I started wondering how many other women felt that way. And then I remembered a line from one of Lily-Mae's journals. She wrote that the cottage had always been a place of refuge and healing, and I thought maybe it could be that for other women, too. And it's a way to honor her memory. Her life might not have been a happy one, but in the end it will stand for something. I want Sand Pearl Cottage to be a place for hope and healing—everything it wasn't for Lily-Mae. And if it works, I'd like to set up more like it all over the country."

"I think it's a wonderful idea. You always wanted to do something meaningful, and here you are—doing it."

"My North Star," Lily said, smiling past the lump in her throat.

A knock sounded at the front door before Dean could respond. At the same time the phone began to jangle. Dean headed for the door, and presumably, the movers, while Lily grabbed the phone.

"They're here!" It was Sheila, out of breath and nearly squealing on the other end of the line. "The first shipment of samples just came."

"Wow, almost two weeks ahead of schedule. How do they look?"

"I don't know. I didn't want to open the box until you were here. Can you come over?"

Lily mouthed a silent *thank you* to Dean as he took charge of the movers. He'd been so helpful over the past few weeks, and so supportive of her new endeavors, of the Lily-Mae Foundation and her plans for renovating the cottage, volunteering his time and professional skills for any and all future plans.

Sheila was still rambling excitedly on the other end of the phone. Lily waited until she paused to take a breath. "Unfortunately, the movers just showed up, which means I'm stuck here until they're through, but I can come by later. I can't wait to get a look. All I can say is this new line had better be a success. Lord knows I've burned my bridges with Izzani, and probably everyone else."

"Maybe. But look what you're doing instead. I'm so proud of you, Lily. The foundation is going to make a difference in hundreds of women's lives."

"I couldn't have done it without you, Sheila. I had an idea, but it was your experience and connections that really got it off the ground. By the way, in case I forgot to say it, thanks."

"You didn't forget. And you're welcome." There was a pause, followed by what sounded like sipping and swallowing. "So . . . movers. Doesn't sound like fun. Have you decided what you're going to do with Lily-Mae's things?"

"Not all, no. Some I'll bring back after the renovations are finished. It feels right having some of her things in the cottage. The rest will go into storage until I decide what to do with it. It's a lifetime's worth of stuff. I want to get it right."

"Sugar, there isn't a chance in the world of you doing anything but. Your daddy knew exactly what he was doing when he left you that place. Now go crack the whip on those movers, and get over here as quick as you can."

Lily wove in and out of each room, making one final check. It had taken the movers less than two hours to strip the cottage bare, but she wanted to be sure nothing had been overlooked. Her footsteps echoed sharply in the empty quiet, hollow-sounding and vaguely disturbing. Stripped of all signs of inhabitation, the place looked shabby and sad, but Lily-Mae's things—some of them, at least—would be back soon enough. It was comforting to know that Lily-Mae would never quite be gone from Sand Pearl Cottage, that some part of her would always linger. She thought her father might like the idea, too.

"Lily?"

It was Dean, calling from the living room. "I'm coming," she called back, stealing one last glimpse of the sea before pulling the curtains closed. It was time to go.

Dean was waiting by the sliding glass doors when she stepped back into the living room. "Ready?" he asked quietly, as if he, too, felt the weight of the moment.

"Yes."

"Don't be sad, Lily. The next time you see this place it'll knock your socks off."

"I know it will."

Still, she felt forlorn as she retrieved her purse from the kitchen counter, along with the last of Lily-Mae's journals. She'd been carrying it around for weeks, like a prayer book or a talisman. Silly, perhaps, but it gave her a sense of connection, a slender thread tying her to the mother she never knew, and the woman who had inspired her to undertake this new mission. Lily swallowed the sudden ache in her throat. She had promised herself that she wouldn't cry. This wasn't the end of anything. It was a beginning—new, fresh, hopeful. And yet Lily-Mae's presence seemed to linger, her story unfinished somehow.

"Lily?"

She looked up, smiling wistfully. "I know. Time to go."

She stared at the journal another few moments, then dropped it into her purse as she turned toward the sliding glass doors. She was startled when it thumped to the floor, splayed facedown at her feet on the scarred pine boards, not because she had managed to miss her purse entirely, but because she was staring at what appeared to be a sheet of pale blue paper peeking from between its pages. But how? The journal contained only a handful of entries, and she'd gone over each one at least a dozen times. She would have seen a letter, especially one written on Lily-Mae's stationery. Unless . . . Yes, of course.

A little thrill ran through her as she recalled the stained pages near the back of the book, mottled with some unnamed gooey brown substance. She hadn't paid much attention at the time, since the involved pages all appeared to be blank. Could it have been hiding there all the time, pressed between two gummy pages, inadvertently hidden from sight?

Dean scooped up the journal, closing it gently as he placed it in her hands. The bit of blue paper had disappeared again, but it was still there somewhere, tucked between the pages. Laying the journal on the counter, Lily turned to the back, carefully teasing apart the clumped pages. Perhaps it was nothing, an address or a grocery list, tucked away and forgotten, but deep down she knew better. And then she was staring at it—a creased sheet of familiar blue stationery.

Her heart squeezed against her ribs when she saw the writing. Lily-Mae's loopy script and slanting lines were unmistakable but were also difficult to decipher, especially near the bottom, as if penned in haste—or in pain. Lily scanned the first few lines until they began to jumble and blur.

"He was here," she whispered, reaching blindly for Dean's hand. "Listen . . ." Dashing away her tears, she began again at the top, hands trembling as she read aloud.

EPILOGUE

My beloved Roland,

After all my books and all my scribbling, I find there are no words to express what these last few weeks have meant to me, or what my heart felt when I looked up to find you standing there, tears in your eyes for the sight I've become, a shadow of the woman you once loved. I pretended I didn't want you here—didn't want you feeding me, reading to me, holding my hand while I slept—but you would not go, and after a while I stopped asking.

Thank God.

We have had our little time together, our blissful beginning and our bitter end, and now—at the last—our stolen moments of reconciliation, of salving wounds and making amends. I will cling to them when I am gone, to those first days, when we walked hand in hand, hunting shells to mark the days, and to these last precious few, when you carried me, bundled against the November wind, down to the water's edge, to press a small shell into my hand—a bittersweet echo of those early times, when everything was new and unspoiled. But it must all end now, my love, as we both knew it would.

But first, my dear Roland, there are things to say, curtains to draw, and loose ends to tie up—things about our child. You have never told her the truth, though whether that has to do with my wishes, my sister's, or your own, I do not know. I only know I'm glad. She might have wanted to come to me, out of anger or pity or mere curiosity, and I don't think I could have borne it—seeing her after so many years, and knowing all I have missed.

I forget sometimes that she's all grown-up, imagining her still as a tiny flame-haired girl perched on her father's shoulders. Silly, perhaps. Time marches on. But I have only laid eyes on her twice in my life, once when they pulled her red and squalling from my body, and then that terrible day in the park. I have missed her so, and miss her still, but that is as it must be. There is no time for regrets, even if I had them. I haven't much to leave, only this cottage, which you gave me, and the little bits I've collected over the years. Nothing of much consequence, but they're yours when I'm gone, to deal with as you see fit. And to do with as you please when you, too, are gone. I will leave no wishes, but trust you to do what is best.

I have been thinking about time lately, taking the measure of my days, as we all must, or should, when we finally come to the end of our road. And I have come to mine. People will say I took the coward's way out, swallowing a handful of pills rather than letting God have his way. Let them say it. I have not chosen it because I'm afraid of what comes next, of the pain or the dying—I've endured much worse than dying. It's that I have had so few choices in my life. Now, finally, I will choose.

And it has been my way, has it not—to make a hasty exit? I've been making them all my life, after all. When I learned I was pregnant. When I heard you had married Caroline. When

I saw you in the park that day with our daughter. I ran, and I hid. Not because I was afraid, but because I was so very tired. Tired of hurting, of weeping, of losing things I cared about. Life has left its share of marks, deep and bloody ones, but it's the self-inflicted wounds I have suffered from most, the harms I've done to myself, and to you, my darling. I should have trusted you—should have trusted us, and what we had together—instead of always running. And yet here I am, making another exit. My last, as it were. At least this time I have said good-bye.

Do not regret losing me, my love, or be angry with me for the way I have chosen to leave this world. We lost each other years ago. This time, these last few weeks, were merely stolen, a kind of dream to ease my way. And you have eased it, my love, more than you will ever know. I hurt you once, and for that I will always be sorry. But it was done for love, and love is always the right choice.

Love endures.

Love forgives.

I must cross now, my dearest. Come to me when you are ready. I will be waiting for you on that other shore, with my little jar of shells.

—LM

Lily blinked away the tears trembling on her lashes, and they spilled down her cheeks as she raised her eyes to Dean's. "He was here," she whispered. "At the end, he came to her. After all the years, all the lies and betrayals, they found a way back to each other."

Dean took the letter, scanning it briefly before folding it carefully along its creases and laying it on the counter. "He never stopped loving her. Or she him."

Lily shook her head, trying to let it sink in. "All this time, I've been imagining her living out her last days with nothing for company but her memories. But it wasn't like that at all. My father was here, reading to her, feeding her, carrying her down to the beach."

"Making up for lost time."

"Yes," Lily said softly, wiping at her tears with the back of her hand. "But so *much* time, so much sadness and grief. How could they ever get past it?"

Dean laid a hand on the folded letter. "It's right here," he said quietly. "'Love endures. Love forgives.'" He reached for Lily's hand then, folding her fingers warmly within his own. "You asked me once if I thought people stopped loving just because the other person wasn't there anymore. I told you I didn't know. But I know now, because I've seen it. My father never stopped loving my mother. It was the same for Lily-Mae and your father, only with a happier ending. They made mistakes. They had regrets. But they were together at the end. That they still loved each other was all that mattered."

Lily felt the tears welling again as Dean drew her into the circle of his arms, tucking her cheek into the warm hollow of his throat. "Love endures," she breathed softly.

Dean crooked a finger beneath her chin, tipping her head back to touch a kiss to her forehead, then another, featherlight against her lips. "Yes, Lily St. Claire, it does."

CONVERSATION GUIDE

SUMMER AT HIDEAWAY KEY

BARBARA DAVIS

This Conversation Guide is intended to enrich the individual reading experience, as well as encourage us to explore these topics together—because books, and life, are meant for sharing.

QUESTIONS FOR DISCUSSION

1. Mt. Zion Missionary Poor Farm was fictional but depicted conditions prevalent in many poor farms in the United States during the twentieth century. Before reading *Summer at Hideaway Key*, had you ever heard the term *poor farm*? If so, from whom, and in what context?

2. In the first of Lily-Mae's letters, she mentions Catherine Earnshaw, the tragic heroine of Emily Brontë's *Wuthering Heights*, comparing her life with Catherine's. If you have read *Wuthering Heights*, in what ways do you see Lily-Mae's life mirroring Catherine's?

3. When Lily and Dean first meet they appear to be polar opposites and rather ill suited, but as their individual stories unfold, parallels begin to appear. How do their differences and similarities work together to help each become more self-aware, and ultimately embrace change?

4. On the bureau in Lily-Mae's bedroom stands a jar containing forty-nine shells. What did the shells symbolize for Lily-Mae, and how did that symbolism ultimately come full circle by the end of the book?

5. Throughout the novel we see Lily pondering the question of finding her North Star, a seed planted early in her life by her father. What do you think Roland meant when he encouraged Lily to seek it, and why do you feel her finding it was so important to him?

6. Sometimes we need a friend to help us see where we've gone off course. Discuss the ways Sheila helps Lily see herself more clearly and eventually face the fact that it's time to make some changes in her life. Discuss how Lily does the same for Sheila.

7. The theme of forgiveness recurs heavily throughout the book. Discuss the role forgiveness plays in each of the main characters' stories, and how it ultimately allows them to finally move toward happiness.

8. It is said that one cannot forgive others without first learning to forgive oneself. In your experience, is this true, and why? Discuss the various ways each of the main characters were holding themselves back because of an inability to forgive and move on.

9. Another predominant theme in the book is the self-inflicted damage we do when we continually run away from the things that scare us. By the end of the book we see Lily-Mae admit that many of her woes stem from her tendency to run rather than stand and fight. What do you see as the defining moments for both Lily and Dean in learning to stand and fight?

10. In the novel, Lily-Mae willingly sacrifices herself to spare the people she loves. In your opinion, when does sacrifice cross the line from nobility into martyrdom? Are there people in your life for whom you would make such sacrifices in spite of their ingratitude?

11. In what ways do Lily's and Lily-Mae's stories mirror each other? What insights do you feel Lily-Mae's journals provide in helping foster Lily's emotional growth over the course of the novel?

12. In your opinion, what would have to happen for Lily to forgive Caroline for all the years of lies and deception? Do you believe forgiveness of such grievous deeds is even possible?

13. Discuss the ways Lily has grown as a person by the end of the novel. What factors do you feel contributed to this growth?

AUTHOR'S NOTE

While working on *Summer at Hideaway Key* I have been very surprised by the number of people who had no idea poor farms actually existed. I assumed that at some point everyone had heard their mother or grandmother say, *You're going to drive us to the poorhouse,* or that they might recall Ebenezer Scrooge's callous lament, *Are there no workhouses?* I also assumed most people knew what those phrases meant, but I soon realized this wasn't at all the case.

The concept of caring for the poor in America began back in the seventeenth century and can trace its roots to the workhouses and almshouses of Europe. In the US, poorhouses were usually publicly funded institutions set up to provide housing for those who couldn't support themselves. In addition to state- or county-run institutions, private entities like churches and other charity groups operated such facilities, providing refuge to the indigent, elderly, abandoned, and infirm. The number of inmates could range from a mere dozen to more than a hundred, based on population and economic conditions of the time.

In rural areas, poorhouses often took the form of poor *farms,* where able-bodied *inmates,* as they were called, worked the fields and barns for their keep, and often benefitted the establishment by helping to produce surplus foodstuffs, which could then be sold at a profit. Poor farms varied greatly in size, but generally consisted of crop fields, as well as small numbers of cattle, pigs, and chickens. Healthy male inmates were expected to work the farm itself, while females cooked, cleaned, or worked in the laundry.

A common misconception about poor farms is that they were a form of *debtors' prison*, where inmates were forcibly housed and made to work against their will. Residence in US poor farms was actually voluntary, though a place of last resort. In most cases inmates who came to the poor farm did so because economic circumstances left them no other choice. Conditions at the farms were stringent, and rules were strict. Populations were often put to hard manual labor, and in some instances were subjected to physical punishment.

Births and deaths were daily occurrences. Deaths were usually recorded in ledgers, but little effort was made to mark individual graves in the poor farm cemeteries. Often, graves were merely marked with a wooden stake and a number that corresponded to a name and date recorded in an infirmary ledger. Sadly, many of these records have been lost over time, though in recent years there has been a resurgence of interest in America's poor farms, and in particular about inmates who died while in residence. Many counties and historical societies are now making stringent efforts to research and locate burial sites and to provide families with death and burial records.

By 1960 the need for poor farms had begun to decline, thanks to the passage of the Social Security Act of the 1950s. Ten years later, poor farms had become largely extinct, with the majority of the buildings abandoned or demolished, though a handful lingered well into the '70s. Many facilities became county-run homes for the elderly and chronically infirm, and a few became correctional facilities, but in most cases the land was sold to private owners, often blotting the existence of the poor farm from even local memory.

Poor farms were a sad part of our history, though I in no way mean to suggest with Lily-Mae's story that all poor farms were nefarious entities. Many were truly caring and charitable institutions, but in certain cases abuse and graft created conditions that were less than humane, and at times bordered on criminal. Mt. Zion Missionary Poor Farm is purely fictional, a composite based on research gleaned about poor farms all over the United States. The fire that took the lives of Ruth and Harwood Zell was based on a fire that occurred at the Wood County Poor Farm infirmary in Parkersburg, West Virginia, in 1950. The fire is thought to have destroyed twenty-five years' worth of death and burial records, and was the imaginative seed of poor Cindy Price's lost grave in *Summer at Hideaway Key.* The cemetery affiliated with Wood County Poor Farm is still open today, and is located near West Virginia University.

Photo by Lisa Aube

After spending more than a decade in the jewelry business, **Barbara Davis** decided to leave the corporate world to pursue her lifelong passion for writing. She currently lives in Dover, New Hampshire, with the love of her life, Tom, and their beloved ginger cat, Simon. *Summer at Hideaway Key* is her third novel. She is currently working on her fourth book, anticipated in 2016.